Deadman

J.H. SMITHSON

Deadman
Copyright © 2022 by J.H. Smithson

All rights reserved. No part of this publication may be reproduced, distributed, or transmitted in any form or by any means, including photocopying, recording, or other electronic or mechanical methods, without the prior written permission of the author, except in the case of brief quotations embodied in critical reviews and certain other non-commercial uses permitted by copyright law.

Tellwell Talent
www.tellwell.ca

ISBN
978-0-2288-6633-6 (Hardcover)
978-0-2288-6631-2 (Paperback)
978-0-2288-6632-9 (eBook)

For my family,
who helped and supported me
through the long process
of bringing Deadman to life.
A huge thanks to all of you.

This could be Rabbit Season
And for no reason I could blow off your head
Because maybe I'm the devil
Or maybe I'm your friend
Or maybe I am God
I am with you to spend
Your life in the end.
-Heavy Mellow

Before We Begin...

...A Brief History Lesson

Of all the people over so many years that have been lucky enough to stand on the sandy shoreline of the lake and gaze across its crystal blue waters, breathing the evergreen fresh air as it drifts in over snowcapped mountain tops, most end up with the same question poised behind their lips: how is it possible that such a beautiful spot, utterly untouched by the concrete and iron grip of mankind, could be christened with a name so dismally morose?

Deadman.

It was a name more befitting a dehydrated and cracked lakebed in the barren deserts of Nevada than a naturally pristine body of water in the Cariboo Mountains of northern British Columbia.

As well, a majority of those who choose to ask the question already assume, even before a single word of this story has been spoken, that the answer will involve a man. Logical, and in some ways correct because the beginning of this tale is about a man. But the ending is about a fish. A fish named Oscar.

To start, a short lesson in folklore. The name Oscar is not particular to any one fish in any one lake. It is in fact, the name of a mystical creature that exists in almost every lake in BC that has drawn man and fishing pole to its waters. An elusive and cunning animal, capable of biting through all gauges of fishing line, straightening any manner of hook, and even snapping the fishing rods of those not familiar enough with tension and drag. It flips just the right way to avoid the net and jumps at the exact moment to escape the boat. It is ten, twenty, thirty years old, dwelling in the deepest, darkest sections of the lake. It weighs fifty pounds, though it has never been weighed, and is two, possibly three feet long depending on the boldness of the one claiming to have seen it. It has been the thing of countless stories, told over endless six packs of beer.

Oscar is the one that got away.

But, as was said, the beginning of this story is not about Oscar. It is about a man named Old Dan Slowfoot and his quest to capture a myth.

Old Dan was descended from the Squamish Indian band on his father's side. His mother was believed to have been a farmer's daughter from Saskatchewan, but she died bringing him into the world, so he was primarily raised by half a dozen different aunts. His father had very little involvement in his upbringing. His name was Timitao Slowfoot, and he was one of the principal scouts and hunters for their village, which made him a very distinguished and important man. Unfortunately, it also made him a very busy man. The only real memories Old Dan had of him were the times he had spent sitting up in the evenings, huddled around the central fire, listening as Timitao recalled the tales of his many hunting adventures. Tracking through the dense BC forests in pursuit of deer, elk, moose, and at times even bear. His every trip into the wild filled with unknown dangers. Close calls so numerous and frightening that the young, wide-eyed boy would often shiver despite the warmth of the fire.

Strangely, of all the accounts of excitement and danger his father shared, it was one of the tamer stories that stuck with Old Dan through his many hard years. It was the tale of Oscar. The one that got away.

Every spring his father would travel to a remote lake in northern BC. If the boy could turn into an eagle, he had told his son, and fly over the lake, he would see it was shaped just like an old flintlock pistol. It was located forty kilometers west of a small white man settlement called Terravale. In this lake, his father claimed, existed a rainbow trout so large and strong it could bite through any net. So smart it could steal bate right off the hook without tensing the fishing line and then it would jump high into the air and splash water into his canoe. At times, it would suddenly swim up and knock against the bottom of the canoe, taunting him, possibly even attempting to roll him into the water. Year after year his father returned to the lake, each time promising this would be the last. This time he would finally catch the fish and then christen the lake with a name. But after each trip he would return home empty-handed and still the lake would have no name.

Shortly before Dan's thirteenth birthday, Timitao's fishing days ended forever when he slipped while retrieving a snare trap and tumbled over the edge of a twenty-foot cliff. The fall itself may not have killed him, but unfortunately he landed on a splintered old tree stump and was torn in half at the waist.

After his father's tragic death, Dan's ties to the village quickly diminished and he left as soon as he was of age. He spent the next forty-five years rambling around the province, doing odd jobs here, panhandling there, existing as best he could. He also became quite skilled with his pocketknife; using simple pieces of wood he found in his travels, he was able to carve almost anything. Small figurines, miniature totem poles, walking sticks, even smoking pipes. All of which were very popular with tourists and most other folks he came across. With the sale of these trinkets, and his few minor endeavors, he always had enough to keep boots on his feet and a hat on his head.

In the early spring of 1959, he found himself in the white man village of Terravale. Here he was again reminded of the story of the pistol-shaped lake and the uncatchable fish. The return of these fond memories gave him a wonderful idea. One that excited him more than anything had in a long time. What if he could catch the fish that had bested his father all those years ago? Then he would cement his name in history by naming the lake after himself. To accomplish such a momentous deed as this, Old Dan thought he could finally find the meaning and worth that his life had always lacked.

Most of the locals knew of the lake and it was not difficult for him to find out exactly where it was. So he bought some meager provisions and headed into the woods.

Four months later, Old Dan returned to Terravale. He told any who would listen that not only had the big fish survived these many decades, but it was just as brazen and cunning as ever, thwarting his every attempt at catching it. Time and time again, bested by Oscar.

Old Dan stayed in the village through the winter, spending most of his time, and what little money he had, in the local tavern. Roddy McTaggart, the owner of said tavern and a kind man at heart, even went so far as to set up a cot in the storeroom so the old man had a place to sleep off his stupors. But as soon as spring smiled its golden face in the sky, the half-blood native was back up there, sitting in his handmade boat on that lake.

This is how it was for a long time. Summers spent on the lake, winters spent in the tavern. Each fall he would regale all with the latest high-jinx of the monster fish called Oscar. It was a battle of the fittest that had only two eventual outcomes. Either Old Dan would kill Oscar, or Oscar would kill Old Dan. And year after year that lake remained unnamed.

Until, in the fall of 1966, Old Dan Slowfoot failed to return to Terravale. Roddy, who had become accustomed to having the old man around during the winter months, was mildly concerned. After the first dump of snow, which brought two feet in just over twenty-four hours, Roddy became more concerned. When the temperature dropped below -15 degrees Celsius, he decided it was time to head up to the lake and see if he couldn't find out what happened to Old Dan. The next morning he hopped on his snow tracker and ventured into the forest. The powerful machine cut an easy path through the snow-packed hills, the skilled rider weaving around the dense growth of evergreen trees with effortless grace. He made the forty-kilometer distance in a lightning-fast fifty minutes.

The frozen surface of the lake was blanketed under a foot of snow. Roddy followed the tree line around, being weary of branches so heavily weighed down by ice that they dipped almost to the ground.

About halfway up the western side of the lake, he stopped in front of a large cone-shaped mound of snow. This was Old Dan's summer dwelling; a teepee styled rustic cabin, about ten feet round at the base, slung together with twine and sealed with moss and mud. Because the snow was fresh, still light and powdery, it took Roddy only moments to dig out the front entrance into the teepee. Pulling a flashlight from his pocket, he stepped inside. He wouldn't have been surprised to find Old Dan lying on top of his cot, dead from the heart attack or stroke that lingered so inevitably. But that was not the case. Save for his few varied possessions, a small table, chair, potbellied stove and his cot, the cabin was empty.

Roddy searched around the area for a while, looking for tracks, or blood, or any visible signs of the old man. All he found was cold, white powder. It quickly became an obvious fact that if Old Dan had expired before the first snow, his body could be buried anywhere. It would be like trying to find a needle in a haystack.

When more snow began to fall from the gray sky, Roddy reluctantly abandoned the quest and returned to Terravale. He promised himself—*and Old Dan*—that he would continue the search after the spring thaw.

And that is exactly what he did. But, that next spring, when he maneuvered his jeep out of the trees and parked by the edge of the lake, what he found was definitely not what he expected. He stood for some time, looking across the smooth water, shielding his eyes from the glare of a new spring sun.

Old Dan was there, sitting in his boat, in his favorite spot three-quarters of the way across the lake. Roddy called to him, waving his arms. Not surprisingly, the old man did not respond. He rarely acknowledged anyone when he was hunting Oscar. Regardless, Roddy continued to call out, over and over again, waving his arms. Finally, as his throat began to feel raw and sore, he stopped. Feeling there was nothing else he could do, he reluctantly left the lake once again.

Early the next morning, just as the sun was peeking over the mountains, shimmering golden through the mist that floated off the surface of the lake, Roddy was back. This time he had his own boat in the bed of his truck. Gazing across the water, he saw that Old Dan was still out there. The position of his boat had not moved.

Roddy paddled slowly, not sure what he expected to find. Perhaps the old man would just look at him with his squinty, dull eyes. "What the fancy fuck are you doing out here?" he'd squawk. "You's scarin' off Oscar!" That would be nice. Roddy would happily leave him to his fishing and head back to town, probably feeling a little bit silly.

When he was fifteen feet from the boat, he called out. "Dan, you old dog! Where you been hidin' all year?"

No response. The old man didn't move.

Sighing, he rowed closer. "Dan, you sleepin' or what?" Coming up behind the boat, he reached out and grabbed it. He walked his hand along the edge, drawing the small vessel up the side of his boat. Now he was right next to Old Dan, looking at the profile of his head. He immediately noticed his ear was black. Another foot and Roddy could see his face.

He drew in a quick, gasping breath. Old Dan's entire face was also black, the skin sunken in, squeezing against his skull like dried leather. His lips were peeled back from his brown, rotting teeth, the corners of his mouth twisted into a snarled grin. His eyes balls, now the sandy color of soured milk, had fallen deep into their sockets, reminding Roddy of the finger holes in a bowling ball. He was sitting perfectly straight up in the boat with his hands resting on the knobs of his knees. Three of the fingers on his left hand were gone.

Because the sun had not yet reached this far into the lake, Old Dan's entire body was still frost-covered and a thin layer of unmelted snow carpeted the bottom of the boat. Roddy saw something else there as well. Something that dragged a second gasp out of his throat.

The largest trout Roddy had ever seen was in the boat with Dan. It was at least two feet long and eight inches thick through the middle. Like the old man, the fish's body was in a badly mummified state; skin pitted and peeling, eyes milky. The smell of spoiled meat drifted up from the carcass.

One of Old Dan's missing fingers lay just in front of the fish's head. The severed stump of another peeked out from its mouth. The third, which Roddy did not see, was probably in the giant fish's stomach.

Not able to deal with the stink of the dead any longer, Roddy pushed himself away from the boat and started back towards the shore. As he paddled, a scenario of what must have happened ticked through his mind like an old silent movie. It would be nearing the end of the season and Dan went out for one final showdown with Oscar the fish. He anchored in his favorite spot and cast out his line. Of course, it was impossible to know how long he'd sat out there, but at some point, he got a strike. The strike he had been waiting for. He would have fought gallantly, struggling with the huge animal. After what could have been hours, the brave half-breed finally did what his father could not. He got the big son of a bitch into the boat. But that was when things went wrong. Somehow the fish got ahold of Old Dan's hand and bit off three of his fingers. The pain and shock and blood loss would have been very hard on a man whose primary meals came from a whiskey bottle. He had himself a big fatty heart attack and died right there, perched in his boat with his prize.

The cold came shortly after, freezing both man and fish as solid as chickens in a deep freeze. Then the snow fell, burying them along with the rest of the forest. There would have been a hump in the otherwise flawlessly smooth lake of snow, but Roddy had not noticed it in his earlier search. So Old Dan sat out on that frozen, snow cover lake for the entire winter, unnoticed and untouched by man, animal, and nature.

Two days after Roddy discover Old Dan's body, a helicopter airlifted the boat and its occupants out of the lake. Eventually Old Dan was returned to what remained of his family for a proper burial. And, what happened to Oscar? Well, as is the fate destined for most mystical creatures, the fish disappeared, never to be seen again.

Roddy remained in Terravale for two more years before relocating to Kelowna. He, himself rarely talked about Old Dan or Oscar. But the story lived on anyways, growing in power as the years passed, until it became as mystical as Oscar the fish. Some say now, if they were asked, that there never was a giant fish. Old Dan died in that boat, drunk and alone, having accidentally cut off three of his fingers with his own carving knife. The fish was only added to the tale as an attempt by Roddy, a truly kind man at heart, to fulfill his good friend's last wish.

The pistol-shaped lake was finally christened with its name in 1968. In honor of a determined old man and the winter he spent sitting in his boat. With or without Oscar, that's for you to decide…

DEADMAN

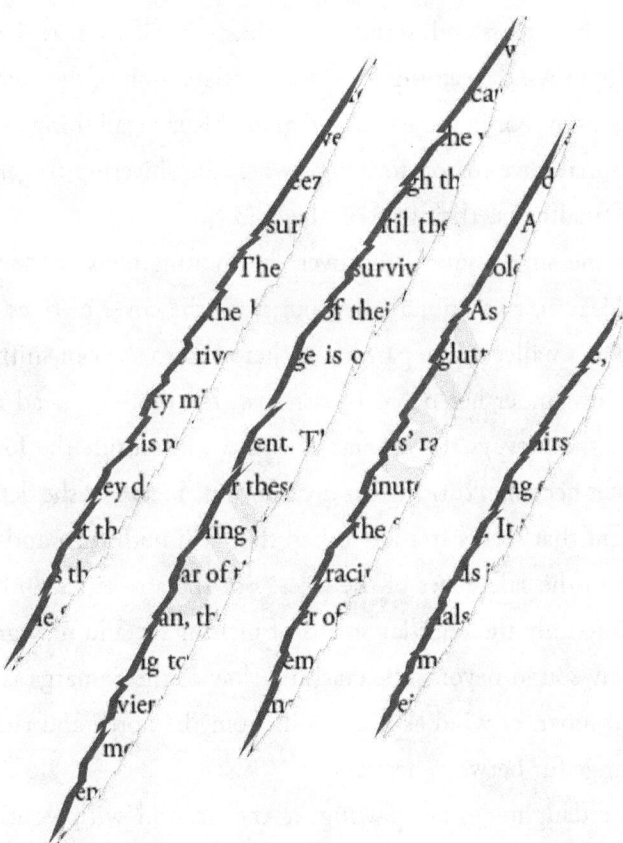

1

A frosty push of early spring air moves over the white hills of Primorsky Krai, kicking up a fog of dry snow in its wake. In the east, behind the twisting flow of the Samarga River, huge rises of rock and ice punch into the blue sky, sculpting the frozen peaks of the Sikhote Alin mountain range. The grass along the edge of the river is just beginning to peek out from under the aging crust of snow, anxious to drink in the healing rays of the new sun. West, beyond these grassland, stands of birch and coniferous trees sway in the light wind, seeming to dance in celebration of the coming warm season. For in the Far East region of Russia, all things earth and animal have reason to rejoice when the shivering fingers of winter finally ease their grip on the land.

As the sun is just rising over the mountainous shadow of Tordoki Yani, two animals step out from the cover of trees and stop. The smaller of the pair lowers her head so she can sniff the hard snow under her paws. In contrast, her mother's head rises high as she surveys the aromas of this world outside the forest. She takes her time, turning her nose into the breeze. If she detects any scent that seems strange to her, they will both turn and flee back into the safe cover of the trees. But the air brings nothing alarming, only the familiar smells of melting ice and new grass. The only sound beyond the crashing flow of the Samarga is the musical moan of wind as it drifts in from the north and ruffles the orange fur between her ears.

Her daughter, now pawing at the ground with youthful impatience, watches her closely. She is yearning to gallop across the snow to the river's edge and lap up the sweet, crisp water that awaits her. It has been some time since either of the animals has had a good drink and the sick feeling of dehydration is becoming quite real. But until her mother signals everything is safe, she will not move.

After one last deep breath in, she finally lowers her head. A small grunt low in her throat is all that is needed to release her daughter. Like black and orange paint splashes on a blank white canvas, the two Amur tigers start across the frozen landscape.

The surface of Samarga River spends the winter season's four or five months in a state of freeze. Though the water does continue to flow beneath the iced surface, until the early April thaw it is virtually unattainable. The tigers survive this cold time by eating snow and drinking the blood of their prey. As a result, the first spring visit to the river's edge is often a gluttonous one, lasting fifteen or twenty minutes.

This year is no different. The tigers' ravenous thirst consumes them as they drink. For these few minutes, nothing else matters to them but the quenching waters of the Samarga. It is this reason, as well as the loud roar of the river racing towards its final destination in the Sea of Japan, that neither of the animals sense the third tiger that is creeping towards them. A large male, easily one hundred pounds heavier than the mother and eight inches taller than her daughter, moves cautiously, with an uncanny silence that should have been all but impossible for an animal his size. He closes the distance between them quickly, drawing within ten feet. *Pouncing range.* He stops, his legs instinctively tensing beneath him. His long tail twitches back and forth across the snow, puffing up tiny white clouds behind him. Although he is still a juvenile, incredibly large for the age of sixteen months, his hunting skills have improved greatly over the long winter. His mother has taught him and his sister well.

Just as the muscles in his legs pop, propelling his huge body forwards, the younger female's head jerks up suddenly. With amazing speed, she snaps around, leaping towards him with her front paws raised. They collide in the air. The male, though two hundred pounds heavier, has been surprised by her unexpected counterattack and is driven backward, away from the river. They crash down into the snow, a hissing, twisting ball of orange and black power. Billows of white powder burst up around them as they roll about, snapping and pawing at each other with harmless enthusiasm.

The older female continues to drink as her offspring wrestle playfully. She has not reacted to the surprise attack because to her, *there was no surprise.* Despite her preoccupation, she had caught her son's distinct smell the moment he stepped out from the trees. He is indeed becoming a good hunter, but there are still many things that he and his sister need to learn before they are ready to go off on their own. They will continue to stay with their mother over the summer months, possibly through the fall and into winter as well. In this time, she will carry on teaching them, helping them to hone their hunting skills. It is these skills especially that will keep them alive in such a harsh and unforgiving environment.

Even now, in play, they are learning. How to stalk prey, how to attack, how to defend themselves. Everything is a lesson, and each lesson is imperative.

The young female leaps away from her brother suddenly and darts off. He immediately gives chase, growling softly in his throat as he pounds across the snow after her. At the top of a mild rise in the land, she stops. Just on the other side of this peak is a twenty-foot drop off into a small valley. She crouches down, watching as her brother bounds toward her. When he is within ten feet, he leaps, just as instincts told her he would. She moves quickly, jumping to one side. Her brother flies past, missing her by mere inches, and then over the peak. Suddenly he is flipping and skidding down the steep incline. His feline agility keeps him upright most of the way down and he lands at the bottom on his paws. He shakes himself off, splashing a puff of snow into the air. He looks up and sees his sister's face peering over the peek. If she possessed the ability to smile, she surely would have been doing it. Instead, she cuffs at him, producing a small sound similar to a bark. A tiger's way of taunting, *'I'm better than you!'*

Abruptly the sound of their mother's roar cuts through the quiet spring air. Both tigers' heads come up, their ears twisting towards the call. At once their instincts tell them this is not just a normal *'let's get moving'* roar. Something is wrong. *Their mother is in danger.*

Then a short explosion, loud and crisp, cracks across the sky. It is followed immediately by a second, and a third. After a brief moment of eerie silence, a different noise. This one neither of the tigers recognize; it is high pitched and squealing. The sound of a dangerous animal they have never before had the misfortune of hearing, but one many others of their kind would have known all too well. And if they survive hearing it, they will also know to fear it.

It is the laughter of man.

The female looks down at her brother, fear sparkling in her amber eyes. Then she turns and disappears from his view. He roars, trying to call her back. Calling her away from the terrible cackling sound that makes the skin under his fur quiver. But she does not listen. She is gone.

He jumps, digging his two-inch claws into the icy slope, holding himself up while his back legs kick frantically, trying to find purchase. His paws slip and scrape, finding nothing but stony ice, until his four hundred and fifty pounds of weight tear out his hold and he falls back into the valley. He backs away, roars, and jumps again…

2

Vlad Trovoski has been hunting in the mountains of Sikhote Alin for as long as he'd been able to hold a gun. First with his grandfather and father, then with just his father. Now, ten years after the old man was laid to rest in the Cemetery Complex of Khabarovsk, Vlad is hunting with his own two sons, and he could not have been prouder of them both as he is at this moment. The most he had hoped for was perhaps a buck deer or an elk, but now they are kneeling beside a three-hundred-and-fifty-pound female Amur tiger, the largest cat in the world. They had stumbled across the tiger as it drank from the river and, though Vlad knew very well the animal was an endangered and protected species, and he was by no means a poacher, this opportunity was just too great to pass up. Each of them had fired a single shot and all three of these shots found their target, putting the animal down after only a single mystified roar.

"Derzhat' golovu," *Hold its head up,* he shouts at them in Russian. "Ya khochu sfotografirovat'," *I want to take a picture.*

Each of the laughing boys grab hold under the cat's jowls and pull its head up. They both grin into the camera and give a victorious thumbs up.

"Great, great," Vlad says, snapping the picture. "Just one more and then…"

Suddenly the smiles evaporate from below the boy's wide eyes. They drop the animal and scramble backward, pushing themselves away from Vlad with the heels of their boots, their young faces painted with expressions of fear.

Still holding the camera up, Vlad stares at his boys. "What…"

"Za toboy!" *Behind you,* one of them screams.

Then they are both shouting, "Pozadi tebya yeshche odin tigr!" *There's another tiger behind you!*

Vlad throws down the camera and spins around, grabbing for his rifle that is slung over his shoulder. But it isn't there. *Of course, it isn't,* he remembers dismally. It is lying in the snow beside the dead tiger, along with his boys' guns and their backpacks.

The second tiger has stopped about twenty yards from where Vlad stands. It is crouched down, ears folded back and hissing wildly, batting at the snow with its front paw.

Vlad smiles. To the frightened boys he says in Russian, "Don't worry my sons. It's only a baby. Just like the two of you." On his hip hangs a two-foot-long military sword that he uses for clearing brush. It is old but well cared for and very sharp. He pulls it free now and holds it out, letting the sun glint off the polished blade.

The small tiger remains where it was, screaming at him. Its piercing amber eyes shift from Vlad to the blood-soaked animal lying motionless behind him. The hissing stops for just a moment, then it glares back at him again, teeth bared as its lips peel back into a snarl.

"Brave little thing," Vlad says, taking a step towards the animal. "Let's see just how brave you are." He takes another step, and another, closing the gap between them.

Still, the cat holds its ground.

"Father," one of the boys calls out. "I have my gun. Shall I shoot it?"

"Christ no," His father shouts back, holding up his free hand. His attention remains riveted on the angry animal in front of him. "You would probably hit me instead of it. Just stay where you are. This won't take a minute."

He keeps advancing. Ten yards…eight yards…five yards. "You really are a brave thing, aren't you," he says, moving the sword to his right hand. "Come on. Let's see if you can…"

The tiger pounces, roaring. It hurtles towards him, teeth and claws bared and visions of death darkening its young eyes.

With the smooth speed of an experienced hunter, Vlad steps to one side, brings the sword around in a tight arc and cuts the animal's head off in mid-air.

3

The male tiger stops fifty yards from the river, watching as the scene unfolds further down the slope. His sister is confronting a strange beast that is like nothing he has ever seen before. It balances on two legs so it can use one of its front paws to hold a long, glistening object. Behind this strange creature lies his mother, a crimson stain growing in the snow around her. Two more of these two-legged animals stand by the fallen female, silently watching the confrontation. They are also hold something—like long, oddly shaped sticks—and are pointing them towards his sister.

Suddenly she lunges at the creature, propelling herself forward with all the strength of her back legs.

The two-legged beast moves quickly, raising the shiny object and…

His sister's head is rolling across the snow. Her once elegant body flops down onto the ground, legs still twitching and kicking as though she were trying to flee *The Death* that has come for her. But it is too late. Not even the power of an Amur tiger can defeat *The Death*.

The other two rush over, still pointing their sticks at his sister's body. Then they are all standing over her, staring, making those same strange, cackling sounds.

The tiger is filled with rage. It consumes him, dissolving all of his other instincts in an ocean of boiling fury. His ears flatten against his head as he starts his advance towards the river, keeping his body close to the ground. He makes not a sound, just as his mother has taught him, moving across the snow with speedy agility. His prey does not see him. They are busy poking at his sister's corpse with their sticks. They have no idea that death now stalks them, moving closer and closer. The tiger yearns for their blood. He will spill it and splash it everywhere, painting all the snow red with his anger.

Twenty feet away, he prepares himself for the final attack. Powerful muscles in his legs tighten, coiling under him like overwound springs, ready...

4

Whatever triggers Vlad's senses at that last vital moment will always remain a mystery to him. Perhaps it is a small sound, or a smell, or even a mild change in the temperature? Something subconscious, or maybe something mystical? He will never know. But right then, an icy sense of danger shivers up his spine and pops into his mind like a burrowing worm. His reaction is honed and instant

He spins around, raising the sword. The speedy suddenness of his movement startles the young tiger in the last seconds before it pounces. Now, instead of lunging, the animal hisses and shrinks back against the ground. The fur on its shoulders stands straight up.

Vlad scrambles backward, shouting at his sons to stay behind him. Both boys now have their rifles, yet neither of them seems to remember what they are for; they are clutching them in their hands like useless pop guns.

Vlad stares at the crouching animal with shocked amazement showing in his eyes. He is quite sure this has never happened before. Three tigers, all in the same area, one seemingly trying to protect the next. It is unheard of. While it *is* true that a mother will protect her young, in this case, it is very apparent this kind of family dynamic is not what's happening. It seems to be the opposite. The mother being the animal they shot first by the river. The female he had beheaded was small, definitely a sub-adult, and most likely the daughter. Now this big boy. Could it be the son? The way it had been easily startled, and its hesitance to attack now definitely screams juvenile.

God, it's so big! He thinks, all of these thoughts having flashed through his mind in a split second. *It's the same size as any adult male I have seen before. Maybe even bigger. But males are loners. They only pair with females when it's time to mate. An adult male does not stick around to help raise the young. It just doesn't...*

The cat lunges suddenly, lashing out at Vlad with its huge paw. A claw catches his coat and tears a gash in it, spilling cotton batting into the snow. Vlad grunts and brings the sword around. Unfortunately, he has a poor grip on the handle and when it hits the tiger in the shoulder, it has twisted sideways and does not penetrate its thick fur.

Hissing, the animal strikes out again. Two-inch, dagger-sharp claws rake across Vlad's lower leg, slicing through his wool pants and into his flesh just below the knee. Vlad screams, stumbling back. He almost loses his footing but is saved a tumble into the snow by his sons. They are behind him now, pushing against his back, keeping him on his feet. Blood pours out of three deep gashes in his leg, painting the white powder around his boots red.

"Sukin syn!" *Son of a bitch*, Vlad bellows, reaching up to grip the sword with both hands.

The cat backs away a few feet, then charges forward. This time Vlad is ready. He slashes the sword downwards, dragging the blade across the tiger's nose and jowls. The tender flesh of its face splits open with a burst of blood. Once again with the precision and speed of a master swordsman, he pulls the blade back up, slicing into the tiger's neck just below the jawline. More blood splatters across the white ground.

The animal wails in pain and jumps back, pawing desperately at its injured nose.

This is the moment Vlad needs. He drops the sword and grabs the rifle out of his son's hand. He fires at the tiger without aiming.

The bullet pops into the snow about a foot to the animal's left. Startled by the gunshot, as well as hurt and sensing defeat, the cat turns suddenly and runs for the cover of the forest.

"Shit!" Vlad shouts, pulling back the bolt and jamming another bullet into the chamber. He aims and fires.

This bullet hits the ground just behind the fleeing tiger's rear paws.

"Shit, shit, shit!" He yells again. He throws down the weapon and turns to his other boy. "Give me your gun!"

He passes it to his father with trembling hands.

Vlad raises the rifle to his cheek just in time to watch the animal disappear into the trees. "Fuck!!" he screams and fires the gun anyway. The bullet whistles over the snow and lodges in a tree, sending a burst of bark into the cool air.

Vlad lets the rifle fall and drops slowly onto his butt. His leg throbs and is oozing blood in thick ribbons. Immediately his sons are kneeling beside him. "Father, father. Are you okay?" They are both crying.

He looks at the boys, and then, strangely, starts to laugh.

They stare at him with stunned expressions.

"Nikto nikogda ne poverit v eto," *No one is ever going to believe this,* he says and keeps right on laughing.

5

*The Tiger runs. As fast as he can. Trying to outrun the strange two-legged beasts that have killed his mother and sister. He runs away from the image of his sister's headless body, twitching and kicking in the snow. His mothe*r, never to finish teaching him the skills of survival, *lying in a growing pool of blood. And he runs to escape his pain. The pain of his torn nose and his injured throat...and the pain in his thumping heart.*

When, at last, exhaustion leaves him no other choice, The Tiger finally stops. He lays down under a large birch tree. His nose has stopped bleeding, though it still hurts him badly. The scar it leaves will be with him for the rest of his life. As will the one left by the cut to his throat. This scar, however, will not be visible to the eye. His thick fur has protected him enough that the sword did not cause serious damage. But the tip of the blade has grazed his hyoid bone, just below his larynx. As this tiny sliver of bone heals itself, the scaring will cause it to become rigid and brittle. Soon this change will give the animal a new ability. It is one many of the smaller of his species already possess, but never his kind. It will become the sound of his unending rage.

His anger at the two-legged beasts will never abide. It is as much a part of him now as the instincts that make him a tiger. Revenge will become as sought out as food or water or a mate. All the cackling, two-legged creatures will die.

After he sleeps, The Tiger continues deeper into the forest. When he comes to a mountain, he climbs it. Higher and higher until there are no mountains left to climb. It is here that he will stay, growing larger and stronger each day. Teaching himself as his mother should have. To stalk, to ambush, to kill. To devour and destroy.

Only then, after many years have passed, and the gnawing, scratching need for revenge forces itself back into the front of his instinctively driven mind, will he descend the mountain again.

The Tiger will come for them all.

6

Six years later.

Yuri Pintovich has always prided himself on being a funny guy. The funniest guy in the room you might say. Definitely the funniest soldier in the Russian Army, *though when it comes to whimsy, the army offers little competition.* Humor is something that has always come naturally to him; reading the mood of a gathering or party and instantly knowing the right joke at just the right time to get the biggest laugh. To Yuri, a good joke or one-liner is as much an art form as painting a beautiful landscape

At this very moment however, as he glances at his wife's pale face, Yuri finds himself hard-pressed to come up with anything, joke or word, that can improve the current situation. He knows Danika is uncomfortable, and getting more so with each passing minute, but he doesn't have any idea what to do about it. This day was supposed to be one for the memory books. Planned and executed with flawless excellence. Every detail realized. The perfect weather. The perfect spot—*which he spent hours scouting out on his one and only day off the previous week*—the perfect food, and of course, the most perfectly beautiful wife. Unfortunately, the one thing he had not considered was this far from perfect—*bumpy ass, shitty, pothole infested*—road and the effect it is now having on said perfect wife and her very pregnant body. The *close to non-existent* suspension of the army Jeep they are riding in is not help matters either. All in all, his lack of foresight here has been… well…*just perfect!*

Of course, Yuri also knows that the anger he feels with himself is not shared by Danika. Uncomfortable or not, she is far too laid back to let something as simple as a bumpy road upset her. *Her stomach maybe, but not her.* But this fact does not make his frustrations any less. Nothing will do that until they get to the clearing, and he can start making it up to her.

Danika sits beside her husband, watching him from the corner of her eye. He is gripping the steering wheel of the Jeep so tightly that his knuckles have gone white. The collar of his pale-green army shirt is darkening with anxious perspiration. Every time the truck bounces through a pothole or bangs off a large stone, he glances at her, a glint of sorrow in his eyes. And each time he looks at her, she wants to tell him to stop being silly. It is all right. Everything is fine. Yes, the ride is a wee bit uncomfortable—*meaning that for the last half hour or so it has felt as though the tiny person inside her belly is doing a Russian folk dance on her kidneys*—but it is just a little jostling, no damage being done. He has worked so hard to make this a wonderful day out together. It is the last

Saturday of the summer season. The sun is shining in the sky. The scenery around Bikin River is stunning, and a picnic basket full of goodies waits in the back of the truck.

If it hasn't bounced out. This thought brings a tiny smile to her face.

Danika will not let a lack of road maintenance ruin this day for either of them.

But trying to tell this to Yuri is a pointless endeavor. He was raised in a military family and, though his parents were not unkind, they were strict and orderly. At eighteen he joined the Russian Ground Forces, where his sense of organized precision was chiseled so deeply into his psyche that it had become the most dominant trait of his personality. Even his humor—*the second most dominating trait*—is ruled by his unwavering need for perfection.

So, no matter what she might say to him now, there is nothing that will make him ease up on himself until *he* decides it is time to ease up on himself. Before that, she will just have to stay quiet and let him take his bumps, *like she is.*

"Ty dumayesh', eto namnogo dal'she, lyubov' moya?" *Do you think it is much farther, my love,* she asks after the truck pounds over another rock, reminding her that now, to help make matters a little bit more uncomfortable, *she has to pee.*

"Just over this rise," Yuri promises her, also speaking in the mother tongue of Russia. "One minute more and we will be there."

Danika smiles sheepishly at him. "I have to tinkle quite badly."

"I'm sure it is…hold on…I think…*Yes, this is it,*" he announces, twisting the steering wheel. He drives the Jeep into a natural clearing just off the bank of the river and stops. "We have arrived."

Yuri says, the relief not hidden in his voice. He jumps out of the truck and rushes around to her side.

"It is a lovely spot," she says as Yuri takes her hand and helps her down from the seat.

"Worth the drive, yes?" he asks, looking at her hopefully.

"Of course. It is simply beautiful." She says, and it is. They are looking out over a fairy tale spot of lush green grass, sloping gently down to the bank of the river. On two sides, spruce trees stand straight and tall like soldiers sworn to protect them. Flowering bottlebrush bushes growing nearer to the water fill the air with the sweet aroma of citrus.

"A beautiful spot for a beautiful woman." Yuri adds.

She smiles at him. Behind her, late summer sunshine crackles off the flowing water of the Bikin River with golden brilliance. "I thank you, my love. But before we continue this romantic moment, you must show me to the bathroom."

"Bathroom?" he echoes, his tone slightly surprised. *Something else I did not consider.* "Um, darling, we are in the Bikin Natural Reserve. It would be at least a half-hour drive to the nearest bathroom."

Danika giggles. "Then please get me a napkin while I pick a bush to pee behind."

7

Yuri has packed a wonderful lunch for their picnic. Fresh bread and cheese, cucumber and tomato salad, pirojki with mushroom filling, and sour cabbage slaw from his family's own recipe. They eat on a blanket under the shade of a spruce tree, enjoying the sound of the river and the scores of songbirds chattering from the branches above them. Crickets chirp in the grass and frogs croak as they chase flies along the riverbank. A warm breath of wind rustles through the leaves, the whisperings of a summer season that will soon be no more than a memory.

After lunch, Yuri sits against the tree with Danika's head resting in his lap. He runs his fingers through her dark curls, breathing in the sweet lavender and honey scent of her hair.

"Thank you, Yuri," she says, gazing up at him with her magnificent amber eyes. "It has been a perfect day."

He smiles. "Try to keep that in your mind as we are bumping our way back home."

"It wasn't that bad. It was like one of those coaster rides at the fair in Khabarovsk."

"A pregnant woman would not be allowed on any of those rides."

"That's true," she agrees, rubbing the swell of her belly. "But I'll survive."

"Maybe we can—"

A squirrel darts out of the trees and stops at the edge of the blanket. It rises onto its hind legs, looks first at the two surprised bystanders, then at the remaining food that is still laid out beside them. An instant later, the animal vanishes back into the forest with a large crust of bread in its mouth.

Danika covers her mouth in amazement. "Yuri, did you see that?" she says, giggling into her hand.

He nods. "Gutsy little critter. A red squirrel."

"It did not look red."

"No, but you can tell by its white belly. There are lots of squirrels in this forest. Chipmunks and rabbits too. I should probably get this food packed up before we have a stampede."

"Oh, not yet—" Danika sits up. She grabs a new bread loaf from the basket and tears off a piece. "Let's see if we can get it to come back. It is so cute." She tosses the crumb closer to the tree line.

Yuri chuckles. "It will be back, and with a bunch of his friends, I'm sure."

True to his word, within only moments there are half a dozen squirrels and two chipmunks sniffing around their blanket. Danika is overjoyed, cooing and fussing over the tiny animals as if they were all her own children. She pulls off piece after piece of bread, at first just throwing it to them, but then, as she begins to feel braver, she is feeding them right out of her fingers. As soon as the loaf is gone, she is reaching for a new one, a pink glow of delight in her cheeks.

Yuri touches her hand gently. "Maybe we should not feed them anymore. I don't think bread is very good for them."

Danika frowns, disappointed, but she does agree with her husband. "You're right, Yuri. But they are so darling, I want to take them all home with us."

"In about two months our house will be quite full."

She lays her head back down, watching as the small animals continue to scurry around in search of any remaining goodies. "Full of love."

Yuri kisses her forehead. "Overflowing."

"What other kinds of animals live in this forest?" Danika asks.

"Every kind I guess."

"Are there..." she pauses, props herself on her elbow, and in very rough English says, "Car-nee-voor?"

"Khishchnik," Yuri says, echoing the word in Russian. "It's a forest, so I suppose there are."

As she looks at him, Yuri can see a sudden hint of fear cast its shadow over her pretty face. "We...are safe?" she asks.

"I would never bring my Love to a place that is not safe," Yuri says.

"I know that, but...if there are big animals around here..."

Yuri puts his arm around her shoulders and pulls her to him. "I said they are in this forest, but nowhere near here."

"How do you know?"

"We are on the outskirts of the Bikin Reserve. Barely within its borders. Any big predators are much deeper into the interior. They would never venture this close to the edge."

Danika begins nibbling at her lower lip, which Yuri sees as a sure sign she is not totally convinced, so he presses on. "Animals like tigers and bears do not want to be around people any more than people want to be around them. They fear man, and every instinct in their body tells them to stay away. They won't come near roads or villages. Nowhere that humans might be." He knows that he isn't being completely honest with his wife, but he is not really lying to her either. Generally, the big animals do stay within the interior of the reserve. There have, however, been sightings closer to the road and the surrounding villages. There have even been one or two tiger sightings near the town of Bikin itself. But they are very rare, and there is no point in mentioning any of it to Danika. Sometimes part truth is better than the whole truth.

At this she does seem to relax a little. But a sparkle of uncertainty remains in her eyes. "Okay. But Yuri, I think I am ready to go now."

"You are still frightened?"

"No," she tells him. "But my bottom is getting a little sore from sitting on the ground. And we still have the long ride back, and…"

Yuri kisses her mouth. "Of course, we can go, my sweet. We came here to have a picnic and that is exactly what we've done. Just let me pack up and we'll be on our way."

Yuri stands up and turns to help his wife to her feet.

"It was a lovely time, Yuri." She says as she takes his hand.

"Very lovely," he agrees.

"And now my bladder calls again. I'm off to my bush."

"I will start getting things cleaned…" Yuri's words fade off. His wife, on the way to her bush, has stopped in the middle of the clearing, her head tilting to one side.

"What is it, my sweet?" he asks.

Danika frowns. "Do you hear that?"

Yuri listens, turning his ear towards the forest. Other than the flow of the river there is only silence. "No. I hear nothing."

She looks at him. "That's what I mean. Nothing. It is so quiet."

Now he cocks his head as well. No birds singing from the trees. In the grass, no crickets chirp. The bouncing croak of frogs has ceased. Even the wind has stopped its whisper.

Yuri contemplates the noiselessness for a moment, and then shrugs. "The forest can be a strange place. It moves in cycles. One minute, everything is awake and rustling and calling. The next minute, all things sleep. Five minutes from now, it will all start back up again. Cycles. It can be a little creepy, but it is only nature doing what it does."

"Well, I think it is very creepy," Danika says. "Which means now you have to sing to me. Sing so I know all the world has not disappeared around me."

"A song to pee by," Yuri muses as his wife continues towards the edge of the river. "What shall it be? There are so many good tinkling tunes that it's hard to choose. But…Ah, I have thought of just the one." His voice rises into an operatic howl. *"Those evening bells! Those evening bells! How many a tale their music tells! Of youth and home and that sweet time, when last I heard their soothing chime!"*

"I love this hymn," Danika says, ducking behind a bush. "But you must sing louder. Now that I am by the river I can barely hear you."

Yuri clears his throat, raises his arms high in the air and bellows, *"Those joyous hours are passed away, and many a heart that then was gay."*

Danika joins him, their voices dancing together in the treetops. *"Within the tomb now darkly dwells, and hears no more these evening bells…"*

She continues into the third verse, calling out the song in a loud, yet musically sweet voice. *"And so 'twill be when I am gone; that tuneful peal will still ring on…"* Then into the fourth verse… until, about halfway through this final section, she suddenly realizes that Yuri is no longer singing with her.

"Yuri," she calls, using the napkin and standing up. "Yuri? Did the beauty of my voice shame you into silence?"

No response.

She comes around the bush, brushing her skirts down flat with the palms of her hands. The blanket and food basket is still laid out on the ground. Behind this, the Jeep sits like a silent steel dinosaur. Yuri is nowhere to be seen.

"Yuri?" She moves into the middle of the clearing and stops. "Yuri, where are you?"

Still, there is no answer.

She looks at the food. All is as it had been. Nothing touched by man...*or squirrel*. She looks towards the river. Water swishes and swirls past, crisp and cold. No Yuri.

She gazes again at the truck. It is where...

Then she sees something. Something that is not as it should be. A spot in the clearing, halfway between the truck and the river; the grass here is flattened down and gouged. Chunks have been torn out in places. It looks like some kind of a—*life or death!*—struggle has taken place. The sunshine is glistening off the grass in a way that is not right. Shiny and slick as though it is covered with...

Danika's heart suddenly squeezes painfully inside her chest as a black storm cloud of horror folds over her mind. Her trembling hands rise to her mouth, barely holding back a scream that balances on the edge of her lips.

It is blood. Not just a little, like from a cut or scrape, but lots. So much that there is no doubt how this—*life or death!*—struggle must have ended. No creature on earth can lose this much blood and survive.

Her eyes focus on something else then. Something that at first her brain refuses to recognize. She stares at it, pushing her mind to accept what she is seeing. When it finally does, the scream that she had managed to hold back now echoes through the trees.

In all that blood, an ear lies there.

With every ounce of her will, Danika forces herself to look past this spot, towards the trees. There are more flattened areas, grooves in the grass. It looks as if something—*Yuri!*—has been dragged away. There is also more blood. *So much blood.*

At this moment, Danika's mind and heart are at odds. Her mind screams for her to stay. Wait. It promises her that this whole business is a joke and when Yuri comes back, *which is going to be any minute now,* then they will go home, and it will all be over. But her heart tells her to follow. Even if the blood—*and the ear?*—is not Yuri's, he is still out there. He has to be. He might be hurt. Maybe even...*Dying!* He could need her help. She cannot just stand here and let him *die!* She must be brave. Brave for Yuri, the way he would be brave for her.

Not indulging the matter with any more thought, Danika makes her way around the bloody patch in the grass and follows the grooves into the forest.

"Yuri!" she calls out, watching her steps carefully. The grass ends just inside the tree line. Now the ground is littered with large stones and zig-zagging tree roots. But, because this area of the reserve is not densely treed, a good amount of sunshine is still able to sneak past the treetops, giving the uneven forest floor a golden glow. Against this hue, the splashes of blood stand out in stark contrast and remain easy to follow.

"Yuri, are you there?" Her calls echo back to her, answered only by the groan of trees as they sway in a light wind. Her fear is growing more and more with each step. Tears, darkened by the makeup around her eyes—she had wanted to look pretty for their picnic—leave bluey-black smudges down her pale cheeks. "Please my love! Where are you?"

Danika walks for ten minutes, weaving through trees and shrubs, all the time fighting against a growing terror that screams for her to *turn and run back to the clearing!* The forest is now beginning to tighten in around her, blocking out more and more of the sunlight. In the thickening shadows it is quickly becoming harder to keep track of the trail. She slows, curling her arms around her belly protectively.

A few more steps and her foot suddenly tangles in a root. She grabs feebly at branches jutting out around her but still goes down hard onto her knees, crying out in surprised pain. A wave of frustration and fear falls over her, threatening to drown out any will she has left. But she fights it, pushing it back. She needs to go on. Without Yuri, there is nothing for her to return to. She has to find him.

With a determined grunt, she struggles back to her feet and glances around, trying to locate the trail again. This is when she sees Yuri.

He is on the ground, rolled onto his left side, only forty feet from where she stands. The way he is laying hides his face from her, but she has no doubt it is him. Even in the deepening gloom, she can easily recognize his green army fatigues. "Yuri," she cries and runs towards him as fast as her pregnancy and twisted ankle will allow. "Yuri, my love, I'm here."

As she draws nearer and more details come into view, her run slows. Five feet away she stops. She can now see that the back of his shirt is streaked with blood. She takes a hesitant step forward.

His hair is wet, plastered to his head. Another step. "Yuri." No more than a whisper. "Are...are you alright?"

One last step and she is standing above him. She kneels beside her husband. With a trembling hand, she reaches and touches his shoulder. "Yuri?" She pinches his damp shirt with her fingertips and rolls him onto his back.

Yuri Pintovich, who has always considered himself the funniest guy in the room, had no face. His eye sockets, nose and jaw have all been torn away, leaving a skull that is now little more than a gruesome, empty crater. The throat and chest are also gone, the ribs smashed in, all the organs devoured. His spinal column, the only thing left connecting his legs to the hollowed skull, is stark against the inside of his blood-soaked shirt. Each vertebra has been cleaned to a grisly white.

Danika does not scream. She does not cry. She does not even move. She just kneels there on the rocky forest floor, her hands resting on the top of her belly, staring at the grotesque thing that had only a short time before been the father of the child growing inside her. A man that had been her lover, her best friend, her companion, and her husband was now...*meat to some wild beast.*

How long she sat like this, staring at Yuri's body, Danika does not know. Minutes? Or had it been hours? In her shock, time had become irrelevant. It is the sound of snapping branches behind her that finally drags her out of this horrified trance.

As she turns her head towards the noise, her shock-rattled mind has a disturbingly humorous thought. *Maybe it's our little squirrely friends from the picnic, come back to eat what's left of my husband.*

But the huge animal that creeps out of the trees, so close to her now its blood-soaked breath feels hot against her face, is definitely not a squirrel.

Strangely, the first thing Danika notices as she gazes into the tiger's striped face is the dark scar that runs across its nose. For just a moment, she has an odd urge to reach up and touch it. Drag her fingers over the crevasse of what must have been a very serious wound—*though, not compared to what it has done to my husband.* So strong is this urge that her hand even starts to rise off the swell of her baby.

But then the tiger begins to purr. It is a low, rumbling sound from deep down in the animal's massive chest. It is a sound like nothing Danika has heard before. It drags her back from wherever she has been hiding, and for the first time since she had found her husband's corpse, her eyes open fully to reality.

The terror she had felt before floods back in. She has never seen a tiger this big. Not on TV or in books or anywhere. It is standing directly in front of her, its head hanging down, so its yellow eyes are level with her amber ones. Looking up its neck, its massive striped body must be almost five feet tall to the shoulder. Shadows hide most of its rear, but she can hear its tail thumping against the ground as it swishes back and forth.

The tiger's lips peel back, revealing gore-covered fangs as long as Danika's index finger. Her husband's blood still drips off its jowls.

It continues to purr and moves closer, its scarred face now mere inches from her own.

Danika begins to cry softly. Not for herself. Without Yuri she is not even sure she wants to continue living. She is crying for her baby—for their baby. Now, the child growing inside her is the only part of her husband that remains. She wants it to live. Needs it to live—to grow up happy and thrive and become as good a person as he had been. Living each day to the fullest. Keeping Yuri's memory alive.

She cries because she knows this is not to be. This beast that has stolen her husband will now take her and their child. Their tiny family will be gone from this world.

"Da prebudet s nami gospod' v nashem puteshestvii," she whispers through her tears.

May The Lord be with us on our journey.

9

The Tiger stops purring. His curled lip slips back down over his teeth. Then he is just looking at this one; this… female. His yellow eyes blaze from inside his fiery face. He stares into the pale amber of its eyes and for the briefest moment, in the very deepest reaches of his subconscious, something seems familiar. For just that instant, the rage that has burned so hot, dictating his every action, is cooled. And floating in the gray haze of his mind, the ghost of a memory…

10

"Eto sdelat'!" *Do it!* Danika cries suddenly and bows her head, hugging her belly. She cannot stand to look at the beast any longer.

The tiger raises its head and roars into the summer sky. The sound vibrates through the treetops, sending up an eruption of birds in a blurred frenzy. It turns its attention back to Danika one last time, sniffing the top of her head. Then, seeming satisfied, it steps over the sobbing woman and grabs Yuri's remains in its mouth.

Sometime later, time again having little meaning, when Danika finally raises her head up and gazes slowly around, the tiger and her husband are gone.

11

Seattle- One Month Later

Benjamin Treager Jr. wonders, *if I were to stand up right now and slap this asshole in the mouth, would that be enough to get him to leave my office?*

The asshole in question is Walter Waterson, a man as old as Noah's Ark and as thin as an anorexic crack addict. He is currently seated across from Ben—three feet of the finest quilted oak desktop separating them—hunched over several open files that lie scattered about in front of him. Behind Ben, unseasonably warm sunshine passes through a large picture window and glistens against the tight skin of Waterson's bald head like neon off wet concrete. The old man has been the senior financial advisor at Treager Enterprises since Ben himself was still in pre-school. A wise, loyal, and trusted employee of the company, he was always the first man that Benjamin Sr. consulted when in need of direction or advice.

At the moment however, as Ben listens to him mutter through pages and pages of financial schematics, this fact does not make Walter any less of an asshole. Benjamin Sr., the founding patriarch of Treager Enterprises and Ben's father, was three years in the ground thanks to a two pack a day cigarette habit. Benjamin Jr. is now the reigning CEO and if he had his way, Waterson would have been sent packing the moment Big Daddy Treager gasped his last cancerous breath. But Senior had also been wise and must have suspected this would be the case. He had a clause added to his will that promised Walter a job until the old man either retires of his own accord or croaks of God's accord.

As of this sunny October afternoon, neither has happened.

Waterson's dull, chalky voice drones on, every word blending into the next to create a mind-numbing verbal mishmash. If, by chance, the information being relayed does have any actual relevance, it is being all but destroyed by a system of delivery that is offensively monotonic.

Or in simpler words: *it's impossible to give a shit what is said when the voice saying it is like fingernails dragging over a blackboard.*

Again, Ben's mind turns back to the idea of slapping Walter in the mouth. So vivid is the thought. His hand lying quietly on the desk blotter jumps up suddenly, lashing out with a speed that could surprise even a young man. Waterson will have no chance. Ben can almost feel the slight sting as the back of his hand slams into the old man's mouth, exploding his ancient lips like overripe cherry tomatoes.

And then, God helps us all, Walter will wipe away the blood and just keep on talking.

This image brings a humored smile to Ben's face. He raises his hand to conceal it, but alas, is not quick enough to elude the old man's *anti-fun radar*.

Waterson's words hiccup in his throat and then stop. He turns his head up, dragging his attention away from the files. For a moment, Ben is sure he can hear the bones of his impossibly thin neck creaking like unoiled hinges. Then the old man is staring at him—his rheumy, brown eyes looking inhumanly large behind thick bifocal lenses.

"Something, sir?" he asks tonelessly.

Ben almost laughs right then but, with great effort, is able to wrestle the feeling into submission. "No," he replies. "Nothing."

"Shall I continue?" His stick fingers tap the pages on the desk.

"Actually," Ben says, leaning back in his leather office chair. "I do have a question."

Walter's expression twitches with mild annoyance. "I think we should finish this first."

Ben's brow creases as his urge to laugh is instantly drowned by a wave of anger. The way the *bald artifact* spoke just then—*slow and with a hint of gentle impatience*—as though he is talking to a child rather than his superior. It doesn't matter how long the old fuck has been drawing a paycheque from the company or what Big Daddy Sr. may have thought of him; *no one speaks to Ben Treager like a child!*

Once again requiring the greatest effort, Ben keeps his tone calm and says, "Last time I checked, I was the CEO of Treager Enterprise. The title may be short, but it means I'm the boss. So, if I want to ask a question or sing a song or tell a joke or say anything else that might pop into my head, there is no one in this building that will tell me otherwise. That includes you."

Walter shrinks back, pulling his hands into his chest. Those huge alien eyes flutter nervously behind their optical prison. "Sir…I didn't mean to insult. I was simply expressing the importance of—"

"I know what's important," Ben interrupts him. "That's why I have a financial team of over thirty personnel. I pay them to deal with this kind of crap…" he waves his hand over the files. "I've told you this before. Unless the company is about to go bankrupt, I don't want to know about it. I have things that are my job to deal with, and then there are the things I pay others to deal with. This shit is the latter. And yet every couple of months, here you sit."

"These the fiscal quarterly reports, sir," Walter says. He begins closing the files and gathering them into a pile. "Your father thought they were important."

"I didn't say they weren't important," Ben barks. "I said I have people that are paid to deal with them." He leans forward then, fire burning behind his hard, gray eyes. "And if you ever mention my father again, I will personally throw your skinny ass out of this building."

The old man stands, cradling the precious fiscal reports in his arms. "Perhaps we should reconvene at another time," he says, turning to leave the office.

But Ben stops him, "Waterson."

"Sir?" He replies, turning back slowly.

Ben takes a deep breath and folds his hands on the blotter. "Are you a hunter, Walter?"

"Sir?"

"A hunter," he repeats, pointing a finger at Waterson and cocking his thumb. "You know; *bang, bang!*" The question is more or less rhetorical. Ben is quite sure the only time Walter takes off his suit at all is to shower, *and even this may be questionable.*

Sure enough, his head rolls side to side like a squash on a bean pole. "No. I've never found much enjoyment in the outdoors."

"Well, I am. I love it. I think I've probably killed something in every state in this beautiful country. A lot of other places too. Africa, Asia, Australia, the three big A's. You name the species and chances are I've shot it."

"Sir, what does that—"

"You need to let me finish, Walter," Ben snaps, cutting the old man off a second time. He waits for a moment—watching humorlessly as Walter fumbles with the chaos of files clutched in his arms—before continuing. "As I was saying, I love to hunt. But do you know what it is I love the most?" Ben holds up his hand, pushing past the question before Waterson can open his mouth. "It's not the majesty of the great outdoors. It's not bonding with my fellow man. Hell, it's not even the thrill of the kill. What I love the most is the power. When I'm looking through that scope, targeting some beast in the cross hairs, this surge of power comes over me. In that moment, I am God. I can take life or give it. I can pull the trigger and end another living thing's existence. Or I can stay my hand. Let the creature live to see another day. It is the power of life and death. He giveth or he taketh away. Nothing else can compare."

Walter is staring at him with wide, confused eyes. He has stopped fumbling and is now pressing the files to his chest like they are his only protection against a sinister entity that has somehow crept into the office.

Ben grins. "Now, you're wondering why I'm telling you this. What's my point?" He raises his arms, gesturing around the large office. "This company gives me that same feeling. I decide who stays and who goes. Who prospers and who fails. I am God. It doesn't matter how hard you work or how smart you are. If I make the decision, stay or go, live or die…well, there is no power above me. Keep that in mind the next time you talk to me with any less respect than I am warranted. You do not want to be that beast in my cross hairs because, Walter…*I never stay my hand.*"

Just then, as if to emphasize these final words, the phone on Ben's desk suddenly begins to buzz and flash.

Walter—stunned and eyeing the younger man as though he has no idea who he is— jumps at the sound. One of the folders slips out from under his arm and hits the floor in a small explosion of white paper.

"You see," Ben exclaims, the grin stretching even wider across his face. "This phone is my job. If I don't answer it, then who the hell will?"

He scoops up the receiver. "Yes Margaret?"

"Sir, there's someone on your private line," the receptionist tells him. "It's quite a poor connection, but I think it might be Bronson Collique."

Ben glances up and sees that Walter is still standing there, gazing at him nervously. He puts his hand over the mouthpiece. "I think we're done here Walter. You can go. Try to remember what we talk about."

"Sir," Waterson chirps and bends to scrape the fallen papers off the carpet.

Into the phone, Ben says, "Who did you say?"

"I think it's Bronson Collique," Margaret repeats. "As I said, it is a bad—"

"I'll take the call," Ben tells her and thumbs the flashing button for his personal line. "Barney you French son of a whore!"

He is met with a barking snarl of static. "Barney," he says. "You there?"

A voice floats out of the crackling turmoil, so faint Ben has to plug his other ear to hear it. "Monsieur Treager? Is that you, mon ami?"

"Yeah, it's me Barney. But I can barely hear you..."

Another belch of static, and then the line suddenly clears. French words burst out of the phone like a mini bomb being set off in Ben's ear. "Peux tu m'entendre maintenant?" *Can you hear me now?*

"Christ," he mutters, jerking the receiver away from his head. "You trying to blow out my eardrum you croissant eating bastard."

Behind the last few hisses of static, Collique chuckles. "When France invades your puny country and hangs all the militant assholes from their heels in time square, you shall regret those words, yes." A slight pause, then, "And stop calling me Barney."

"Frenchmen can't hold their dicks, never mind a gun. I'm not worried."

"Ah, mon ami, I do not have to hold my own dick. I have ta mere...*Your mother*. She holds it for me, uh."

Now Ben laughs. "You can have the old bitch. She's a dead lay anyway. So, where are you?" he asks, his tone becoming serious. "Obviously not here in Seattle, the connection is horrible."

"No, I am far from Seattle. À travers une terre et un ocean."

Ben's French is rusty, but these words he understands. *"Across a land and an ocean*? What's with the cryptic French babble? I'm paying you very well to travel around this planet, which means I should know where you are at all times. So, where the hell are you?"

"Mother Russia, mon ami. The home of fine vodka and hairy women."

"Russia? How the hell did you end up in Russia? The last time we spoke you were in Louisiana chasing alligators."

"I came out here to confirm some information for myself before I called you. I am in a small place called Bikin, about five hundred kilometers from Vladivostok. Primorsky Krai, the Far East, yes. Cold and miserable place, even now, before it is wintertime. But I am happy to say, Monsieur Treager, that the trip was worth it. I have finally found the thing you have been seeking for so long."

Ben's heart rate leaps in his chest. "What...are you sure? You have proof?"

"It left three bodies in a small village called Agzu. Two women and a child. One of them was, uh…complètement mange, *completely consumed*. Only bones remained. All three were attacked within two days. I am told the militia became involved then. They tracked the animal for almost one-hundred kilometers before they finally got close enough to hit it with a tranquilizer dart. It is a male. *Tres grande*. Over eight- hundred pounds."

"Eight-Hundred?" Ben echoes. "That's impossible. There hasn't been one that big since…"

"The fifties," Collique finishes for him. "That one was said to be Eight-hundred and forty-seven pounds. But it was not confirmed. Could be connerie…*bull shit*, uh. This one is not. I have seen the beast with my own eyes."

"Where is it now?" Ben asks. His mind is already churning with plans, even before he is sure he believes what he is hearing. "Is it safe?"

"Qui, for now. It was brought down here by the military, but then immediately confiscated by some big-shot Russian scientist types. Bikin is just outside the borders of a protected national reserve. They released it in the interior of the park, hoping to study it in its natural surroundings. Find out…Ce qui le fait taper, um…*what makes it tick* as they say in your country. But, well you know the fucking Russians, uh. Guess whoever was supposed to be doing the studying must have nodded off at the wheel. Lost track of the thing somehow. It managed to kill an off-duty military man named Yuri Pintovich. The unlucky *fils de pute* was having a little picnic with his pregnant wife by the Bikin River. Didn't know what hit him. It was a completely unprovoked attack. This thing is un vrai man mangeur."

A true man-eater. To Ben, there are no words more beautiful in any language.

"Jesus, Barney," Ben says. "If this is true, do you understand what you're saying? This is huge. Shit, it's huger than huge. It's… unbelievable. But…fuck…can you get it? I mean, you have to get it! Anything you need. Any amount."

"I've already made some arrangements," Collique says. His voice, unlike Ben's, remains level and calm. "The animal has been recaptured. But many of the people I am forced to deal with are… how would you say it… très désagréables.…*very unsavory*. I will not finalize anything on my own. You are going to be needed here in person. Can you get away?"

Ben chuckles. "I own a billion-dollar company, a yacht, a jet and a helicopter. Two helicopters actually. I don't think getting away is going to be a problem. How long can you hold things down there? I'll need about a week."

"A week I can do. The animal is safe for now. I have people in place, protecting it. But some of the locals, they are very upset about Yuri. I understand he was a well-liked man. And others, they are saying that this beast is not natural. Many are frightened. They are calling it zhnets cheloveka. *Reaper of man.* I fear as more find out that the animal still lives…the worst it gets, yes. Do not delay longer than you must."

"I'll be there in a week, no more," Ben says. "You need to keep things mellow, Barney. Don't let me down."

Collique grunts indifferently. "As soon as I am able, I will send you all the necessary info. Travel safe." Then he adds, "And stop calling me Barney, you militant asshole," and hangs up.

After the call is disconnected, Ben quickly buzzes his receptionist. His mind, *mercifully clear of any visions of Walter Waterson or fiscal quarterly reports*, swirls with thoughts of what needs to be done. Plans to make. If everything works out—and Ben would make sure everything did—then many great things were coming. Yes, it is true this game he was about to put into motion was a risky one, with no guarantees of how it would turn out. But *good God*, isn't it risk that makes life truly worth living. *Hell yeah it is!*

When Margaret picks up the line, Ben says, "Find me Morgan Malo. I know she's somewhere in the building. Let her know that she is required in my office asap. I'll also need you to contact several people for me. We will be having a conference call. I'll have the list ready for you in fifteen minutes."

He hangs up as she is asking if there is anything else she can do for him.

"No," Ben says to the empty room. He leans back in his chair and swivels it around. The sky beyond the window is a pale shade of blue, dulled by the smog that is a part of every big city. One of the many costs that must to be paid so human beings can have it all and have it right now.

It is a cost Benjamin Treager Jr. is happy to pay.

12

Russia- 6 Days Later

The darkness that surrounds Yosef Zemin is total. Deep enough that if he was to bring his hand up and hold it an inch from his eyes, he would not even see an outline. Chernyy kak smol'. *Pitch black.*

Within this blind void, however, his other senses still verify the presence of *the thing*. The smell of *it* floats through the confines of the bunker. A stench of wet dog and rotting grass—*and blood*—sting Yosef's sinuses like a whiff of strong vinegar. But even more offensive than *its* stink is *its* sound. A thick, rumbling purr, as mechanical as an idling chainsaw, yet unnerving in its sheer power. It forces a memory in Yosef, dragging it out of his subconscious. When he had been a young boy, maybe five or six, his parents had taken himself and his older sister on a trip to Moscow. From their home in Perm, it was a fourteen-hundred-kilometer drive. Two long, dreadfully dull days spent sitting in the back seat of his father's old 1968 GAZ. About halfway through the trip, a rock had hopped up from the road and punched a hole through the car's muffler. For the remaining seven hundred kilometers of the journey, he and his sister were forced to listen to the mind-numbingly monotonous roar of the car's engine. It was an unwavering sound that vibrated the back seat to the point of making both children nauseous. It had been one of the most unpleasant days of his childhood.

The noise that is coming out of *it* is exactly the same as that 1968 GAZ.

"Molchi," *Shut up,* Yosef whispers. In the darkness, he raises his arm and touches the cattle prod he is holding in his hand to one of the iron bars. A crackling explosion of white sparks burst from the end of the Hotrod, filling the small bunker with a surge of bright light. For a brief moment, everything comes into view. The prison cell. The damp, mildew-covered concrete walls. Yosef, in his black militia uniform, sitting on a wooden stool just outside the cell. And behind the iron bars, lying against the back wall of the cell is the tiger. With each breath, the nightmarish purring sound rumbles up from deep inside its chest. Its yellow eyes are locked on the soldier, unmoving even in the sudden bursts of electricity.

"Do you like that, fucking cat?" Yosef says in Russian. He taps the Hotrod to the bar again. Sparks erupt into the air.

Still the tiger does not move. It does not flinch. It just lays there, purring. Its eyes boring into Yosef, even after the blast of light has winked out.

Yosef touches the bar again and again, each time exploding with a borage of sparks. The complete darkness in the cell makes it seem like a fireworks display worthy of Red Square on Victory Day.

In each blast of light, the cat is there, staring at him, purring.

"You dumb fucking beast," Yosef says. "You're even too stupid to know when to be afraid. Maybe if I touched this thing to that torn up nose. Would you be afraid then, *cat?* If I fried your fucking face?"

The steel door behind Yosef comes open suddenly and hits the concrete wall with a loud *boom*! Startled, the soldier jumps in his seat. The Hotrod slips out of his hand and clunks against the concrete floor.

Before he can turn around, the bunker is filled with brilliant fluorescent light. Yosef throws up his arm, shielding his widened pupils from the burning glare.

A large man stands in the doorway, his hand still hovering near the light switch. "What the hell is going on in here, private?" he bellows in Russian. Like Yosef, he is also wearing a militia uniform, but with one significant difference. Four yellow stars on the right shoulder.

"Nothing, Captain," Yosef says, leaping off the stool and facing his superior. "I was just monitoring the prisoner…tiger, as instructed."

"With the goddamn lights off?"

"I…I…" He glances around the small room, as if by some miracle the answer is hidden somewhere in the damp gray walls. "I was conducting an experiment," he says reluctantly.

Captain Nikolai Vlastov's brow creases above his dark brown eyes. He looks at the cattle prod lying on the ground, then at the enormous animal in the prison cell. Finally, he looks back at the soldier. "An experiment? Do you take me for an imbecile?"

"No sir."

"Well, I have you know my mama did not squeeze me out of her twat just yesterday, Private. It's obvious what is going on here." He takes a step farther into the bunker. "You were torturing this animal."

"No sir!" Yosef says, shaking his head.

"If you lie to me, private, you *will* find yourself in the stockade. Now you *were* torturing this animal!"

"Captain, I…" He looks at his superior, his face solemn. "It killed Yuri. He was my friend. And now his wife is a widow. The horror and grief she has endured pushed her into labor two months early, and even now the doctors don't know if his baby son will survive. I pray he does, but what then? He will grow up never knowing his father. So much tragedy, and yet this beast still lives. Why, sir? Why have we not killed it?"

Captain Vlastov's brow smooths. He puts his hand on Yosef's shoulder. "I understand how you are feeling. I knew Yuri as well. He was a formidable soldier, and a good man. Dealt an unfair hand. No one had expected the animal to travel so far in such a short time. What happened was a very unfortunate accident."

"Accident," Yosef echoes, spitting the word out as though it were poisonous. "The thing ate him. Left nothing but his arms and a hollowed-out skull. How in God's name is that an accident?"

"Careful, private," The captain remarks. "Do not forget who you are talking to. A tone like that is guaranteed to get your ass thrown into the stockade."

"I'm sorry, Captain," Yosef says, staring down at the ground. "I just don't understand why it still lives."

Behind Yosef, the tiger purrs on. Even with the soldier's back to it now, its eyes remain riveted on the young man, a cold patience glimmering behind their yellow sheen.

"It is not ours to kill," Vlastov tells him. "Someone is paying a lot of money for it. So, until that someone arrives to take it away, I am bound to protect it, which means that you are also bound to protect it. I am sorry for what has happened, but we must not forget that business is business. Do you understand, private?"

Yosef nods slowly. Then he looks back up, meeting the captain's eyes with his own. There is a shadow of unease showing in them. "It is not natural. How big it is, and how healthy. Man-eaters are always sick or hurt. There is always a reason for what they do. But not that thing. It looks better fed than most dogs I have seen. You must see this as well as I do, Captain. So why does it kill men?"

"Because it's an animal, and animals kill," Vlastov says impatiently. "No other reason."

"It has no fear," Yosef continues. "All tigers are afraid of fire. Fire and lightning. But that…" he flicks his head towards the prison cell. "It doesn't even bat an eye. Just lies there, staring at me. Like its waiting for something. It's not normal."

"It's just a stupid animal," The captain repeats. "I don't need you going all squirrelly on me, private. I've already got enough people around here acting squirrelly. Tomorrow, God willing, the cat will be gone. Until then, I need you to stay on point. Can you do that? Hold it together?"

"Of course," Yosef says.

Vlastov walks around the soldier and picks up the Hotrod. "And this…" But his words die in his throat. As he straightens up, he suddenly finds himself face to face with the tiger. Somehow, without being noticed, it has stood and moved to the front of the cell. Its scarred nose is now a mere foot away from Vlastov's face, with only the iron bars between them. For a moment, the two starred at each other, locked together by an invisible bond. In that instant, the captain realizes just how wrong he had been. This is not a stupid animal. Hiding behind those burning yellow eyes is much more than just instinct. It is not intelligence, at least not in the human sense of the word, but something far more disturbing. *It is cunning.* A bloodthirsty cunning that has only one sole purpose. *The bringing of death.*

"Dammit," Vlastov says, taking a shaky step back. "Fucking thing snuck up on me."

Yosef is watching him closely. "You saw it, didn't you? Just then, you saw what I was talking about?"

The tiger turns and saunters slowly away from the bars, its long tail brushing back and forth across the concrete like a clock pendulum. In the back of the prison cell, it flops its huge body onto the ground.

The captain watches it for a second more, then turns his attention back to Yosef. "All I saw was a stupid fucking animal," he says, holding out the cattle prod. "Now take this thing."

Yosef takes it.

"If you are caught using it for anything more than protection, well…you know where you'll be going."

"Yes sir."

"The cat is gone tomorrow." Vlastov walks past him and out the doorway. "Until then, keep it together," he adds and slams the door shut.

Yosef goes back to his stool and sits down. From the gloom of the cell, the tiger is staring at him again.

"Captain can say what he wants," Yosef murmurs. "But I'm going to make you afraid, you fucking beast." He begins hitting the Hotrod against the palm of his hand. "For Yuri, I promise, before they take you away, I'm going to make you afraid."

The tiger's rumbling purr is his only response.

13

If a good businessman's word is his promise, and a great businessman's word is his bond, then Ben Treager's word is his life. And his life means everything to him.

So true to his word, exactly seven days after he hung up the phone with his global scout of the French persuasion, Ben is stepping off the Teager Enterprises' Embraer E2 jetliner in the cold, rain-soaked city of Vladivostok. Behind him, a stunningly beautiful woman also exits the aircraft. She stops for a moment on the landing and glances up miserably at the charcoal-colored sky. From inside her trench coat, she produces a compact umbrella and pops it open above her curls of auburn hair. Then she follows Ben down the stairs and into the icy rain.

Bronson Collique, a short man with a long, graying ponytail, is already rushing across the runway before they have stepped off the last stair onto the tarmac. He is shouting greetings to them in French, though the pounding rain makes his words almost impossible to hear until he is directly in front of them. He grips Ben's hand in both of his and pumps it up and down vigorously. "Bonjour, mon ami, bonjour! I am praying the trip for you and your adorable amie was très bon! A good one, yes?"

"It was very long," Treager says, lifting the collar of his trench coat. "And now it's very wet. What do you say you get me, and my five-thousand dollar suit out of this miserable rain?"

"Of course, of course." He replies, glancing appraisingly at the exquisite woman standing beside Ben. "Let me get you both out of this horrible weather. Right this way please. Your chariot awaits."

By this point, a great deal of money has already exchanged hands for many different reasons. One of those reasons was to null the usually unavoidable and grueling trip through Customs into an unnecessary ordeal. Now, because the right wheels have gotten just the right amount of grease, instead of leading the pair into the airport terminal to endure the viciousness of Russian Custom practices, he hurries them directly to a Sikorsky Blackhawk helicopter that waits, its engines already warm and running. They are back in the air within fifteen minutes of Ben's arrival.

Inside the insulated cabin it is warm, and the three passengers are able to talk without wearing the clunky headsets that seem to be part of every helicopter flight in every movie ever made. Bronson informs them that the flight time from Vladivostok to the town of Bikin is two and a half hours.

"Barney," Treager says, peeling off his trench coat. "You remember my assistant, Morgan Malo?" He hangs the dripping garment from a hook at the back of the cabin.

Collique smiles at the young woman, flashing two front incisors that are capped with gold. "Of course," he says, taking her hand. "Il m'est impossible d'oublier une telle beauté." He kisses her soft skin. "Mon chéri."

Even in the gloom of the dimly lit helicopter, Morgan's pale green eyes shimmer above her lightly freckled nose. "Thank you," she replies. "But I'm afraid I don't speak French."

Collique reaches around Morgan's shoulders to help her out of her wet trench coat. "It matters not." He whispers in her ear. "Everything in the French language means love."

"And bullshit," Treager adds. "Don't forget bullshit, Barney."

Morgan giggles behind her hand.

Collique sighs as he places her coat beside Ben's. "You see, mon cheri. The English language is so…how would you say it…*coarse*. Like a rough stone. And it becomes even worse when spoken in the tongue of American militant asshole."

"Dickless frog," Treager grumbles apathetically.

"Mr. Treager!" Morgan gasps, the tone in her voice matching the embarrassed glow in her cheeks.

"Oh, that is alright, Mademoiselle," Collique tells her, taking a seat across from them. "Monsieur Treager and I go back many years. I know him well. I understand that his coarse, hurtful words come from a place he keeps buried deep inside. A painful place where he hides his most shameful desires. Like his unrelenting need to make a sexually explicit movie with *sa mère*."

Morgan's eyes widen. "Sexually explicit I understand, but what is a *sa mere*?"

"Well," Collique says, grinning his golden toothed grin. "Quite simply it is his…"

"Never mind," Treager groans, running fingers through his wet hair. "I am way too jet-lagged for your sense of humor, Barney. Let's move past the comedy act and call this one a draw."

"Qui monsieur. To be resumed another day. But until then, you militant asshole, stop calling me Barney, huh."

Waving his hand dismissively, Ben slumps back against the seat. "Fine…Monsieur Bronson. Just keep that French tongue flapping and bring me up to speed. How are things proceeding here in the lovely land of Russia?"

"Très bien," Collique begins.

He speaks for well over an hour, explaining all the actions that have already taken place, as well as the plans and events that will be taking place over the next thirty-six hours. All scenarios have been investigated and everything that is to proceed from here on has been planned down to the finest of details. It would be virtually impossible for anything to go wrong.

Once Collique has finished his point-by-point of the coming days, Treager asks him, "And what about the prize?"

Morgan, who has seemed to be in a semi-doze for most of the flight, pops awake suddenly. "Does it really weigh eight-hundred pounds?" She asks with a slight apprehension edging her tone.

"Indeed, Mademoiselle," he says, patting her thigh suspiciously close to the hem of her skirt. "I have been able to get it weighed with the finest equipment. Eight hundred and thirty-eight pounds as of three days ago. I believe that would be a world record for one from the wild, non?"

"A world record that will never make it to Guinness," Treager says. "How about health? How's it holding up?"

"No problems, mon ami. As long as we can keep the locals from cutting its head off."

"Any locals touch that animal, and heads will roll alright," Treager comments. "That's a promise."

"I can understand why they're upset," Morgan says. "I mean, what if it had hurt your family?"

"My family?" Ben shoots back. "Shit, most of them are money grubbing imbeciles. I'd buy the goddamn thing a steak dinner."

Morgan gasps. "You don't mean that, Mr. Treager."

"The hell I don't." But then he contemplates for a moment before adding, "Except for my Aunt Mavis. She makes the best damn beef wellington I've ever eaten."

"Well, it is not too worrisome now," Collique says. "For the time being the cat is protected. And after tonight, it will be on its way to Canada. Aussi sûr qu'un bébé dans le ventre de sa mère."

As safe as a baby in the mother's womb.

14

An hour later, the helicopter touches down on a cracked and broken concrete pad centered in what appears to be an abandoned army base camp. Several decrepit wooden buildings are scattered here and there around the property. Some look to be only moments away from falling down completely, while the best of them have obviously not been in use for many years. And dropped in the middle of this building graveyard, right next to the slowing rotors of the Blackhawk, is a concrete barracks that looks like an escapee from the island of Alcatraz. The husks of dead vines snake up its walls, crisscrossing over the blackened concrete like cracks in the skin of a mummified corpse. Iron bars feign a sense of security over the many dark and glassless window openings. A tall man in army fatigues stands outside the main entrance to this concrete artifact, waiting as the three new arrivals exit the aircraft.

"Dobro pozhalovat'!" He calls out as they approach. He raises his hand in greeting. "Welcome, welcome!" he adds, now in heavily accented English. "Come inside, out of this damn cold. Always the weather is shitty here. What can you do?"

He ushers them through the doorway into a small office area, then pulls the door closed behind them. "The weather around here," he comments again. "Wet and shitty in the summer, cold and shitty in the winter, and just plain shitty the rest of the time. I long for California."

He turns and holds his hand out to Ben. "Bronson I have already met. You are Mister Treager?"

The soldier has a strong handshake. Ben likes this. Leave the limp handshakes to politicians and queers. "Ben Treager," he says.

"I am Captain Nikolai Vlastov. It…is…" his eyes drift to Morgan. She is standing just behind Ben, pulling her wet hair back into a ponytail. "*A pleasure*," he finishes, now moving past Treager as though he has suddenly vanished from the room. He offers her his hand. "A most unexpected pleasure."

Morgan smiles uncomfortably as she accepts the handshake. He lays his other hand on hers. "I was not expecting such a… *Amerikanskaya krasota.*"

She looks towards Ben, but his attentions have momentarily shifted to the task of hanging his coat. Seeing zero assistance there, she reluctantly turns back to the leers of the Russian soldier. "I…"

Collique steps up beside them. Under his breath, he tells Morgan, "He called you an *American beauty*," Then to Vlastov he says, "May I introduce Morgan Malo. She is Monsieur Treager's assistant."

"Hello," she says, throwing Collique a grateful glance. Her small hand is still sandwiched between Vlastov's callused fingers. "Thank you for your kind words, but actually I'm Canadian."

"Huh! Even better." Vlastov exclaims. "I love Canada. Go hockey!" Then he releases her from his grip and pumps his fists in the air "Our hero Gretzky!" One pump for each word.

Finally freed, Morgan quickly shoves her hands into the pockets of her coat.

"I don't believe Gretzky is Russian," Collique comments. He takes Morgan by the elbow casually and guides her away from the captain. "Captain Vlastov has been overseeing the operations here." He smiles at the Russian before adding, "And doing a fine job of it, I'd say."

Vlastov's eyes search the Frenchman's face for hints of sarcasm, then he grunts out laughter. "Operations? Is that what we are calling it? More like nyanya, huh. *Babysitting*."

Having found no acceptable place to hang his coat, Treager finally relinquishes it to the back of a chair. "You can call it what you like," he says, rejoining the group. "But it's still costing me a shit load of money."

Vlastov grins at him. "To you a shit load, to me a load of shit. A mere drop in the spit bucket to a man that has it all, I think, Huh?"

"Well, drop or not, I guess it was enough to buy you...Huh?" Treager remarks. Firm handshake aside, he isn't sure he likes this *Captain Vlastov*.

The soldier's smile fades. He looks at the other man with contempt hardening his face.

Collique notices this and steps towards Ben, watching Vlastov closely. He readies himself to defuse any possible situation before it can develop. It is a task he has become quite accustomed to since entering Treager's employ. Sometimes the man's tact is almost nonexistent.

But this time, it is an unnecessary maneuver. Only a moment later, the solder's expression smooths, and his grin returns larger than ever. "That is true," he says and claps Treager on the shoulder. "But I am Russian, and we come cheap." Then speaking in his mother tongue, he adds, "I'll bet you paid at least two shit loads for the green-eyed cupcake, huh?" He winks in Morgan's direction.

Treager brushes Vlastov's hand off his shoulder. "I've had a very long day, so if we can dispense with the pleasantries and move our business towards a speedy conclusion."

Vlastov's brow creases. "I have some knowledge of the English language, my friend, but truthfully...I have no fucking idea what you just said."

"The tiger," Morgan answers from beside Ben. She has unbuttoned her coat now, but her hands are once again buried deep in the pockets, just in case Vlastov is not quite done with them. "He's saying he wants you to take him to the tiger."

"Ahh, of course," the captain says. "From the mouth of an angel come words I understand. The animal is here, safe and sound. Just as promised."

"If you could show us the way," Treager says. "I'd love to get this wrapped up so I can get to the hotel. This jet lag is kicking my ass."

"Yes, yes. Of course, I understand. Not another moment shall be wasted, my friends. This way."

He leads them through a door at the back of the office and into a long corridor. The air in here reeks of mildew and rotting cabbage. Naked bulbs hang down from the ceiling, shedding a shadowy light that seems to shift and move of its own accord. Doorways line the walls on either side of this hallway, many of which yawn open to the dark and long abandoned rooms behind. In one of these rooms Morgan sees an old hospital gurney turned over on its side. For some reason the image of it sends an eerie chill up her spine.

"Has the rest of my team arrived?" Ben asks

"You three are the first," Vlastov says, speaking to Treager over his shoulder.

"I'm expecting four more men and a supply truck."

"They will be greeted with kindness." The soldier is silent for a moment, considering his words. Finally, he adds, "As we are at this time business partners, I would like to offer you some advice."

"If it is at all relevant to the current status of our ongoing endeavor, then by all means proceed." Ben replies, and smiles at Morgan. *You're so mean,* she mouths back at him.

"Once again, Mister Treager, I do not understand your fancy words," the soldier says, not noticing as Morgan puts her hand over her mouth to stifle a wave of giggles. "But as your business partner, I'm going to give the advice anyway."

Through another door and they enter a descending stairwell. It is damp and cold and somehow manages to smell even worse than the corridor they have just exited.

"Please watch your step," Vlastov warns. "The stairs can be slick."

"Is that the advice?" Ben asks.

Vlastov chuckles. "No, no. That was mainly for the lovely young woman. I noticed she is wearing tall shoes, and I would hate to see her fall."

"Thank-you," Morgan says. "I'll be careful"

"That would be wise. Now for you, Mister Treager, the advice. I start by saying I do not know how much you have paid for this animal. It is, of course, not my business. I only know what you have paid me…what was it you said?"

"A shit load," Treager reminds him.

"Yes, a shit load. I will not try to guess the total of your costs, and again I say, a man with everything feels little loss. But in this case, I am afraid you have made a grave error. This animal is not right."

"Not right?" Ben repeats, irritation in his tone. *This Vlastov is becoming more annoying by the second.* "Okay, now *I* don't understand *you*. How can a tiger be *not right?* Is it missing its tail? A leg? What?"

At the bottom of the stairs, they come into a large empty barracks. Above them, a pair of long fluorescent tubes cast dirty yellow light onto the concrete floor. In each of the three adjacent cinder block walls are two evenly spaced steel doors. Beside the door they have just come through, a soldier sits on a wooden stool, playing cards on a very rickety looking table. He barely glances at them as they enter.

Vlastov stops just inside the room and turns to the soldier. "Private, go upstairs and wait," he tells him in Russian. "We are expecting three more visitors…"

"Four," Treager corrects him. Counting to ten is one of the few things he remembers from his two years of Russian Language during high school.

Vlastov throws him a dry look. "Four then…four more visitors. Watch for them and bring them down when they arrive."

"Da," the soldier grunts, gathering his cards into a pile.

"Also call Powroznik in from patrol. We may require his assistance."

The Private nods. "Da." He stands, and after an uncomfortably long assessment of Morgan Malo's inventory, he disappears up the stairs.

"Nice to be so popular, huh?" Vlastov says to her and winks again.

"Let's stay on topic, Vlastov." Ben says. "You were saying…?"

"*Captain Vlastov,*" the Russian snaps. "I may come cheap, but the title did not. It took me twenty years and two wives to earn."

"I'm sorry…Captain Vlastov." He bends very slightly at the waist. "You were regaling us with your advice. Please continue."

Vlastov shrugs, shaking his head. "I know you will not listen to what I say. Your American ears cannot hear anything but what they want to hear. But I will give you the advice because it is the right thing to do. There are many stories of tigers becoming man-eaters. Some of these stories are false, some are true. Of the true ones, meaning the cases that have been proven and documented, all but two were in India and the animals were Bengal tigers. Until now, Russia has had only two incidences of man-eaters. One in 1997, many people killed. One of them was a poacher that had shot and wounded the animal before it killed him. The second incident was also a badly injured tiger. Starved and dying. It killed one man." Vlastov taps his chest reflectively. "I was involved in the hunt that brought it down. Before the bullet killed it, this cat was only days away from death. You may think these tigers were not right. But for man-eaters, they were exactly as they should be. Injuries, sickness, and starvation. These are the reasons tigers become man-eaters. In all cases. Bengals in India and Amur here." He stares at Treager and repeats the three words again. "Injuries, sickness, starvation."

"But I thought our tiger was healthy," Morgan says, directing her comment to Treager.

"It is," Ben agrees. "And I'm pretty sure that's the point he's going to make."

"I have told you monsieur," Collique says, speaking to Vlastov. "We are well aware of the type of animal we are dealing with."

"No, I do not believe you are," the soldier counters. "This cat does not kill man for food, or because it's sick. It kills man because it wants to. Needs to. When you look into its eyes, you can see the desire. No…" he shakes his head. "Not desire…stronger…. It has man killing *instinct*."

"Goddamit Vlastov," Ben snaps. "Will you get to the advice part of this story so we can move on."

"This animal should be put down," he says quickly, this time ignoring the lack of rank in Treager's address. "Eliminated. That is my advice. It should not leave this compound alive. It is evil. *Zhnets cheloveka*."

Ben sighs. "I've heard that name before." He wipes his forehead with the back of his hand and finds he is sweating, despite the murky chill of the barracks. "Look, I appreciate your concern, if that's what this is. And if it will make you feel any better, I promise you that this cat's days are number. I have every intention of killing the fucking thing. But as for it not leaving the compound alive? Well, I'm afraid that's impossible. Like you said, I have invested far too much of my money and time to abandon this project now. That is something that simply cannot happen."

"We are very educated and prepared for managing this animal," Collique adds. "Highly skilled handlers and state-of-the-art equipment. You needn't worry."

"You misunderstand me," Vlastov tells them. "I am not worried. In two hours, the cat will be gone from here. No longer my concern. But I believe this beast's killing time is far from over. I tell you this not because it is my worry, but because it *should be yours.*"

"Your advice has been received, considered and rejected," Treager says. "Now can we please return to our regular scheduled program?"

"You fucking Americans and your poisonous tongues. My honor and your money are all that stop me from pulling it out of your mouth like a diseased slug."

"Everything's as it should be then," Treager says, a grin appearing above his chin. "Now if you please, lead the way."

Vlastov turns to Morgan, his angry expression becoming solemn. "Run away from this man. What he is doing will bring only pain." He gives her a quick sympathetic smile, then spins and walks away. "You all follow me."

Still grinning, Ben flashes his two companions a thumbs up. They follow the captain across the barracks to one of the doors in the back wall. He pounds his fist against it, calling out in Russian, "Open up, private. The Americans have arrived."

They wait. Other than the *plop, plop, plop* sound of water dripping from the concrete ceiling, it is dead silent.

Another volley of whacks, these hard enough to dent the steel. "Goddamit Private! Open this door!"

"Maybe he had to pee," Morgan offers.

"Russian soldiers do not *pee* unless they are told they can *pee*," Vlastov says and pounds again.

After another moment with no response, the soldier finally pulls a ring of keys off his belt. Cursing in Russian, he finds the proper key, unlocks the door, and pushes it open.

They are met with darkness. "Son of a bitch," Vlastov growls, reaching through the doorway. "Private, I warned you what would happen if I caught you torturing that animal again."

He finds the switch and the room instantly fills with light. Vlastov storms inside, shouting, "Now you will find what the—"

Treager goes through the door after him, but Vlastov has stopped only a few feet inside the room, and he almost runs into the captain's back.

"Shit," Treager chirps. "What the hell…"

Then he sees what has halted the man in his tracks. The room they have entered is about twelve feet wide from the door to a wall of iron bars that enclose the prison cell behind. Lying on the floor directly in front of this cell is a young man in Russian army fatigues. He is on his back, his right shoulder jammed between two iron bars. On the other side of the bars, where his arm should have been, there is only blood and tiny bits of flesh. Ben can see the white gnarled tip of clavicle bone jutting out from the ragged sleeve of his shirt. His face is also in ruins, shredded to the point of being unrecognizable as a man, and he has also been torn open just below the sternum. But these wounds, though horrific and bloody, seemed secondary in nature. The image that flashes through Treager's mind at that instant is the tiger snatching the unlucky soldier through the bars, then using its heavy claws to hold him immobile while it eats his arm. There is blood splashed on the walls, the bars, even up to the ceiling.

The tiger is at the back of the cell, sprawled out across its length. It is licking its blood-soaked paws with such a gentle calmness, they could have been watching a house cat as it fussily goes about grooming itself. But this house cat weighs eight hundred pounds.

It had not even glanced up when the door burst open and the lights came on. The animal seemed quite content. For now.

When Morgan suddenly screams from behind Vlastov and Treager, things start moving very quickly. Vlastov is still staring at the dead man on the floor and now begins bellowing in Russian. He takes several steps farther into the room, grabbing at his belt. He is fumbling with the latch on his gun holster as his eyes finally come up and lock on the tiger.

Knowing what is about to happen, Treager turns. Collique is there, his arm around Morgan's shoulders. "Control this," Treager says to him.

With no hesitation, and speed that should have been impossible for a man of his stature and age, the Frenchman produces a gun from inside his jacket and is across the room. He brings the weapon up with a rock-steady hand and presses the muzzle against the Russian's temple.

In contrast, Vlastov's hands are shaking badly as shock and dismay course through his body. He has only managed to get his holster unlatched when he feels the sudden chill of steel just above his ear. His fingers freeze around the butt of his gun.

Ben points at Morgan. "You, stay here."

She nods, clasping her arms around her trembling body.

"Captain Vlastov," Ben says, walking over to the two men. He spares a quick look towards the tiger, but it is still cleaning its paws and seems quite uninterested in whatever is going on outside its prison.

Collique's eyelids have closed to mere slits, and a strange half smile has crept across his round face. It is an odd expression, almost sleepy, like a terminal patient who has self-medicated with about three doses of morphine too many. Ben knows the look. He has seen it several times over the years, and until he can get this unexpected development dealt with, the little Frenchman has become a very dangerous man.

Treager comes around the soldier so he can see his face. Vlastov's entire body is vibrating, but the hand that is gripping the gun remains unmoving. "As we are business partners," Treager continues. "And remember, those are your words, not mine—I would like to offer *you* some advice. Shall I go on?"

Vlastov glares at him with blazing eyes. "I am a captain in the Russian..."

Collique shoves the gun harder against his head and leans in slightly. "Shall... he ...go on?" he whispers.

The soldier grimaces, his face twisting with shocked rage, his eyes darting frantically around the small barracks, looking for a way out. But of course, there is nothing. Finally he lets his gaze drift back to Yosef's ravaged body and nods his head slowly.

Ben smiles. "I like you, Vlastov. You have integrity, and a good firm handshake. Those are excellent traits in a man. I'm also presuming you are relatively smart, I mean...you are a captain in the Russian army. So, here's the thing; what you feel pressed against your head is the business end of a Beretta M9 handgun. It's not the most powerful pistol ever made, not even close actually, but it is still a very decent weapon. Reliable. And my French friend here is very good at using it. Even if five of your army buddies rushed in here right now, guns drawn and ready, my money would still be on Barney. And your brains will be on the floor next to your comrade. But that's only a *what if*. Not gonna happen. What is going to happen is you're going to take that toy you're packing and hand it very slowly to Monsieur Collique. Then he'll take his gun away from your head, and we'll all get back to business. Because really Vlastov—" Treager pauses and taps his own forehead. "Sorry, I forgot—*Captain Vlastov*—really nothing has changed. I'm sorry about your comrade, and I guess this does proves you were right. That is one badass kitty cat. Man-hater to the bone. But it is my bad kitty and I'm taking it out of here no matter what. So, what do you say? The quicker we get back to business, the quicker we'll be gone, never to return. Of course, there will also be an extra bonus provided. To help with…clean up."

Vlastov looks at the tiger. It has finished with its paws and is now watching them with mild interest. The rumbling sound from its chest has started again.

Then he notices something else in the cell. Lying on the ground beside the cat, partially hidden by shadows. It is Yosef's cattle prod, scratched up and splattered with blood. The very one he had been using to torment the animal.

"What do I care," Vlastov says, pulling his gun from the holster very slowly. He hands it to Collique. "Yosef was a shitty soldier anyway. If he had been a good soldier, I guess he would still be alive."

"Excellent," Ben declares. "That's the attitude."

Collique waits until he gets a nod from his boss, then he lowers his gun and backs away from Vlastov. He stuffs the second weapon into the waistband of his jeans, but keeps the Beretta in his hand, just in case the captain is not being completely sincere.

But this is another unnecessary precaution. Vlastov is done. He wants nothing more to do with any of it. "You and your people are here now," he tells them. "You do not need me or my men any longer. If I allow one of them in here and they see... this soldier... like that," he nods towards the body but does not look at it. "I will not be able to protect the beast. Then, I suppose we will be forced to find out if you are right about Mister Collique's skills. So, I will take my men and go. This base has stood empty for many years. The body will remain here until I can have it dealt with safely. For now, just drag it out of your way."

"But what about your bonus?" Ben asks. "You should be compensated for the loss of your man."

"Keep your money, Mister Treager. Just get that fucking beast out of my country. It is...merzost'." Vlastov turns and starts for the door.

"Captain Vlastov," Ben says.

The Russian stops.

"There is one small consolation I can offer you."

Vlastov looks at him over his shoulder.

Treager takes a small black case from his pocket and flips it open. Inside is a silver cylinder tipped with a hypodermic needle. "This is a tranquilizer dart. It contains three milligrams of Etorphine. Do you know what that is?"

"It is an opioid drug," Vlastov says. "Used for immobilizing large animals."

"Wow, you really are smart. That's exactly right. So, you know then that this little dart packs one helluva wallop. Enough to put our kitty cat friend down for the count." Now Treager reaches inside his jacket and removes an air pistol from the holster strapped to his side. He holds it out to Vlastov. "Would you like to do the honors?"

The captain turns around to face Treager. But, before replying he looks into the cell again. Even through the thick shadows that shroud the dismal space, he can see the tiger easily. It is lying against the back wall, tail flicking across the cold concrete. Its paws are still dark with Yosef's blood. And those yellow eyes… they are staring out of the gloom, locked on him. Daring him.

"Mister Treager," he says. "I do not know what your want is with this animal, and I do not care to know. But whatever it is, it will end badly. For you, for Mister Collique, and for the lovely young Ms. Malo. I will pray that she takes her leave of you before the end, but I fear that won't be the case. I think there will be others who pay as well. So, if you want to do me a ….*consolation* was it? If that is what you want, put a bullet in that thing instead of a dart. End it now."

Vlastov turns and leaves the room, wishing Morgan well as he passes.

After he is gone, Morgan goes over to where the two remaining men stand, careful to keep her head turned away from the dead man on the floor. She puts her hand on Ben's shoulder.

"Mr. Treager, he's gone."

"I am very aware, Morgan." Treager replies.

"But…don't we need him?"

"Barney," Ben says, pushing her hand away as he turns his attention to the Frenchman. "Go up top and find a spot that has cell reception or use a landline or the radio in the helicopter or a fucking cup on a string, get ahold of someone and find out where the fuck the rest of our people are. We needed to get out of here ASAP."

"Oui Monsieur," Collique says, finally returning his Beretta to its shoulder holster. "Perhaps Mademoiselle Malo should accompany me. A woman should not be forced to endure all this... mess. She would be more comfortable in the helicopter, non?"

"No," he says. "She can stay here. I think it's time we had a little chat."

Collique looks at Morgan. She smiles at him, just a hint of apprehension showing in her green eyes.

"As you say, Monsieur," he replies reluctantly. "I shall return très vite." He hurries towards the door.

"Mr. Collique," Morgan says, stopping him just before he exits.

He turns. "Bronson, mon chéri. Please call me Bronson."

She smiles. "Okay, Bronson. What is merzost'?"

Collique looks at Treager. He is staring in at the tiger and again appears to be paying them no attention.

"I fear it is not a pleasant word," he tells her. "In English it means *abomination*."

Once Collique has left, Morgan stands beside Ben silently, both of them looking at the tiger. It stares back, the rumbling drone from deep in its chest being all that disrupts the moment of quiet calm. That, and the bloody corpse on the floor.

"I could have told you what merzost means," Treager says at last.

"I already knew what it meant," Morgan tells him, slipping her arm around his waist.

"Then why did you ask?"

She thinks about this before replying. "I like him. I guess I was just trying to make him feel good. Knowledgeable and helpful, you know?"

Treager chuckles. "Don't let his romantic little Frenchman demeanor fool you. You saw the way he handled that Beretta. He's helpful alright. When he needs to, he can be as much an animal as our friend in the cage."

Morgan shrugs. "I still like him."

Ben turns and pulls her body against his. "As much as you like me?"

"Why, Mr. Treager," she says, pushing back lightly in a feigned attempt to escape. "I believe interoffice romances are frowned upon at Treager Enterprises."

"We're not in the office. So how about we do it right now? Right here so the fucking cat can watch."

"Not a chance," Morgan says in disgust. This time she does pull away from him. "It's a vile, disease-ridden prison cell. Who knows what viruses are creeping around here. And..." She grimaces. "There's a dead body right there."

Ben looks at the one-armed corpse and sighs. "Okay, I guess that does take some of the romantic feel out of the moment."

"You think," Morgan quips, wrapping her arms protectively over her breast. "I can't believe you even thought about it."

"Come on," he says, pinching her chin playfully. "I was only joking. Where's your sense of humor?"

"It's waiting for me at the hotel in Vladivostok. How long until we can go get it?"

Now Ben shrugs. "As soon as the team gets here. We'll get our kitty cat packed away into its new home and be on our way." Then he takes the air pistol out of his jacket again. "Until then, we have a job to do. Would you like the honor?"

Morgan turns back to the tiger. The animal is no longer looking at them. It is staring directly at *her*. Their eyes meet, and for a moment she is drawn into its glassy stare. There are flames there, yellow and hot. A blazing, jagged fury that bites and claws. Devouring everything in its path. Now Morgan can feel its hate. It is burning into her. A fiery rage so obvious she cannot believe she hadn't felt it before. This animal does not just want to kill her. It wants to destroy her. Shred and tear until it reaches her soul, and then it will devour that as well. It will eat and eat and eat until she is completely erased. Not even a memory of her will remain. She will be nothing…

When Ben lays his hand on her shoulder, Morgan screams and spins around, her eyes as wide and round as silver dollars.

Startled, Ben jerks backward and almost drops the air pistol. "Holy shit," he says. "What's up with you all of a sudden?"

"Sorry," she says. Her voice is shaky and frightened. "I…I guess Vlastov's story got to me more than I thought. I got kinda weirded out there for a second."

"Come on." He brings her into him, hugging her. "Don't let some Russian's paranoia get to you," he says softly and kisses her. "It's just an animal. Not some man-hating demon incarnate. It is an Amur tiger, nothing more."

"I know." She wraps her trembling arms around him. "I do. I think I just need to get out of here."

"Then I'll take you back to the helicopter," he says. "But first…" He steps away from her suddenly and turns, a grin erupting across his face. He raises the pistol. "Night, night kitty cat." And pulls the trigger.

The tiger does not even flinch.

15

Kamloops, BC- 3 Days Later

Ben sits in an overstuffed leather chair, staring into a roaring fire housed within an enormous stone fireplace. Open in his lap is a Fortune 500 magazine that he has barely glanced at. On the table beside him, an untouched cinnamon latte. The lobby of the Executive Hotel and Convention Center hustles and bustles around him, but he takes no notice. Like the reflection of flickering flames that dance in his gray eyes, a swirling mass of thoughts dance through his mind.

He would never have admitted it to anyone, but he is actually feeling the beginning twinges of stage fright. This is an alien feeling to him, especially given that the deal they are about to present is by no means the biggest he has ever tried to sell. Hell, it isn't even close in fact, at least from a monetary standpoint. He has orchestrated land deals worth close to a quarter of a billion dollars without breaking a sweat. This situation, if all things go as planned, would net him maybe five million after expenses. A drop in the bucket by comparison. Yet, he cannot shake this feeling of unease. The only reasonable cause he can come up with is that *what* they are attempting to sell today is foreign to him. Property and financial investment, these are his type of deals. Something like this however, where money is not the leading factor, definitely put the whole thing far out of his wheelhouse. Maybe as far as the deck of another ship.

But wheelhouse or not, it is still fucking exciting. A tickle to the nervous system is a small price to pay for an opportunity like this. A once in a lifetime chance that will never come around again, for him or anyone smart enough to join him.

"Fancy meeting you here, tiger."

The words float into Ben's ear on a cool, minty breath against his neck. He turns his head and now the coolness becomes warmth, pressing against his lips, pushing inside his mouth. It twirls around his tongue, grazing his inner cheek lightly, and then it is gone.

Morgan draws away. Her wet lips glistened in the flickering light. "You might want to wipe that lipstick off before the big meeting...*tiger*."

"Yeah, thanks for that," Ben says. He takes a handkerchief from his breast pocket and drags it across his lips. "Didn't we agree a long time ago to keep that part of our lives behind closed doors?"

Morgan comes around the chair and stands in front of him with her hands on her hips. She is wearing a green Yigal Azrouel dress. It hugs every perfect valley and rise of her figure and is hemmed a generous four inches above her knees. With black Louis Vuitton shoes wrapping her feet, this outfit is perfect for the job at hand. It screams, *I've got something to sell...and like it or not, you're buying!* She is looking at Ben with a stern expression, but the sparkle of mischief in her green eyes is quite apparent. "Look around," she says. "We're in Kamloops, British Columbia. This is about as Canadian hick-town as you can get. And there's not a soul around here that gives a shit who we are. So, what does it matter?"

"With you dressed like that," Ben says. "I guarantee you that every man in here is wondering who you are, and what the hell we're doing here. There's also Collique, and the rest of the group. That's at least six people that know exactly who we are."

"They're off tending to the striped prince. I haven't seen anyone I know since we got here."

"I don't care, rules are rules."

"Rules are rules," she echoes, her tone high and mocking. *"No inner office shenanigans please."*

"Don't be a child, Morgan."

"A child?" Morgan turns sideways, arching her back and pushing out her ample bosom. "How many children do you know that look like this?" she purrs, running her fingers through the loose curls of her auburn hair.

"Jesus, Morgan." Ben glances quickly around the lobby. A group of grinning Japanese businessmen all raise their cell phones at the same time and start snapping pictures of her. "Can we please be professional?" he groans, knowing the internet is soon be blessed with multiple images of his assistant.

Morgan frowns and plops into the chair beside Ben. "Why are you being such a stick in the mud?"

"Let's just get this done," he says. "Then I'll stick it wherever you want."

"Promises, promises," she muses. "So how much longer till we start? This sitting around thing is getting old."

Ben closes the Fortune magazine and places it on the table beside his cold latte. He looks at his watch. "Just about time," he says. "Everything should be assembled."

"Good." She is quiet for a moment, watching the flames as they swirl and lick through logs in the fireplace. Finally she adds, "It's weird, but I'm feeling a little bit nervous."

Not as weird as you might think, Ben thinks, but to her he says, "Shove that shit down. You can't let your nerves affect your mind."

"Of course not. I was just saying."

"You should also never let anyone know how you feel, Morgan. Not even me."

"What if I feel horny," she says roguishly. "Should I let you know about that?"

Ben stands. "You're in some kind of mood today," he says, smoothing creases from his suit jacket. "How about we try to focus on the sell. Let's close this thing."

"It's gonna close," she says and stands up beside him. "Who in their right mind would pass up an opportunity like this?"

"No one, *if we stay focused.*"

"Worry not, Mr. Treager. I'm focused. So, are we going into this thing bunny or bear?" she asks.

"Neither," Ben says, a small grin pulling at his lips. "We're going in *tiger.*"

16

It's silly, and Morgan *knows it's silly,* but it doesn't matter how many meetings of this type she is involved in, she can never quite shake the feeling that she is in a room filled with severed heads. *Talking, severed heads.*

Of course now, as she stands gazing around the hotel's brightly lit conference room, she has to admit to herself that—*along with the absolute silliness of the whole feeling in general*—the boardroom in the Seattle office is much worse than what they have set up here. The Executive Hotel has accommodated Ben's needs by arranging two tables end to end with four viewing monitors per table, making eight screens in a single row. For some reason this seems much easier to take than the perfect square of fours stacks of four back in Seattle. A few times, when all of those monitors were fired up at the same time and all sixteen of those heads were squabbling and squawking like some ghoulish church choir, it took every ounce of Morgan's strength to stop herself from running out of the room screaming.

She always did manage to stop herself, though because they weren't really severed heads at all. They were the video images of real living, breathing people who had not been able to attend this or that particular meeting in person. It is the power and convenience of technology. She can sit on her phone video chatting all day long with no problem, but just look at one stack of TV screens with grinning ghoul heads in them, and she wigs right out. *Weird. Right?*

But again, what is set up in this conference room is not quite as daunting. The monitors have been positioned directly in front of the table where Morgan and Ben now stand. Beside them, Bronson Collique waits patiently for his cue. Four curtains hang down from the ceiling behind him, hiding a twelve-foot square area.

The eight monitors are filled with the faces of men, mostly middle-aged, some graying slightly, while others are showing signs of balding. All looked perfectly normal, no different than any other forty-something males living on this side of the planet.

These eight men, however, hold a combined net worth greater than the economic value of many medium sized countries on the other side of the planet.

"Gentlemen," Ben begins, a smile stretching wide across his face. "I am very glad you all could join us here in the lovely Canadian city of Kamloops, *in mind if not in body*. I know that up until now I have kept the details of this meeting quite cryptic, and I do apologize for that. But I guarantee, what I will be offering you today is an opportunity that will come along only this one time in *all* of our lives."

The monitor heads all begin talking at the same time, *as they generally do*, and Morgan feels the mild sting of unease. She forces it down, shoving it back where it came from. She will not allow anything to jeopardize this deal, least of all some childishly silly video phobia that is ridiculous beyond belief.

Without knowing it, Ben also helps her in this regard by holding up his hands and saying, "Gentlemen, please. If you will let me have the floor, all your questions will be answered a lot quicker."

After a few more random grunts and cuss words, the heads do as they are asked and fall silent.

"Thank-you," Ben continues. "To begin, I believe most of you know my assistant Morgan Malo."

Smiling uncomfortably, Morgan raises her hand to the heads. "I'm happy you all could make it," she says. *If being a creepy monitor head can be considered* making it.

"And my business associate Bronson Collique, whom I'm sure all of you have gone hunting with at one time or another. He is one of the best guides for large game in the world."

"Bienvenue messieurs," Collique says.

"Now, whether I am associated with you through business or pleasure, each of you has been chosen to participate today for the same reasons. First, you all have more money than you could possibly spend in ten lifetimes. Second, you are, in my opinion, the top eight hunters on this continent. Possibly even the world. For these reasons, I now give each of you the chance to bid on the most unique and thrilling adventure of your lives. A large game hunt that will make hunting black rhinos in Africa seem like rabbit season."

"A hunt?" one of the heads mutter. He is a middle-aged man with deep-set eyes. His graying hair has been combed carefully across his head in a failing effort to cover a rather large bald spot. "All this fuss is about a hunt?"

"This sort of thing is generally arranged through my assistant," another monitor voice says. He is also in his mid-fifties. A brown skinned man with a single bushy, black brow planted above his eyes. "I'm a goddamn busy man, Treager."

Others begin to comment as well, but Morgan quickly interrupts them. "Sirs! I believe Mr. Treager has more than earned each of your respect. He has never steered any of you wrong. If I remember correctly, Mr. Lemmings," she nods towards bad comb-over. "Did Mr. Treager not include you in a company merger project that netted full seven figures above original estimated returns? And Mr. Salverez," looking at uni-brow now. "Is there not an eleven-foot-tall silver back grizzly standing in your den because of a hunt Mr. Treager and Monsieur Collique organized?"

Some minor grumblings from the ghoul choir, but then blessed silence.

Morgan looks slowly from one head to the next. "Please, hear what Mr. Treager is offering before you make your judgments. He deserves at least that much."

"Thank you, Ms. Malo," Ben says after a few moments of quiet. "I will get right to the point as quickly as possible because, as little Stevie Salverez has pointed out, we are all busy men."

"You're an ass, Treager," Salverez's monitor head snaps.

"Keep that in mind at the end," Ben replies. "Now, in Northern British Columbia, about two hundred miles southeast of Fort Ware, there is a plot of crown land approximately one-hundred and fifty square miles in size. It is squashed right between the Akie River on its south side and the Truncate Mountains on its northern. Absolutely beautiful land, evergreen forests, small lakes, and glacier rises to twelve hundred feet. Cold as a nun's hoop on black Sunday, but really quite stunning." Some chuckles from his television audience before Treager can continue. "Most recently it was used by the government as an agricultural testing area. In an effort to prevent external contamination at the time, the area was surrounded by a twelve-foot-high chain-link barricade with electrical protection capability. This fencing alone has cost several million dollars. But, unfortunately for the Canadian Government, last year's financial crisis in the States forced them to scrap the project and the land was put up for long term lease. I am very pleased to say that quite recently, the entire plot was secured by Treager Enterprises.

"This will be our hunting ground. It is secure and isolated. Anything put inside will stay inside. Anything outside will stay outside. Think of it as one very large prison yard. Also, because it is privately owned land, no hunting laws apply within its borders. If it's alive and inside the fence, it can be killed. To be sure there is plenty of wildlife to...*enjoy,* I have had several specific species introduced to the area. Mountain lions, timbers wolves, deer, elk and moose. Of course waterfowl come and go as they please. I wanted to have bear as well, but this time of year they're asleep so, not too challenging. Maybe come spring."

"I don't understand this, Ben," Lemmings says. "Why? Anyone with a hunting license can hunt any of those species pretty much all year long. What makes this so special?"

"I'm glad you asked, Bill. It just so happens there *is* one additional species that I have not mentioned yet. *Panthera tigris altaica.*" Ben glances at Collique. "If you please, Monsieur Collique."

The Frenchman pulls down on a ripcord, releasing the square of curtains. They crumple to the ground, revealing a large, clear acrylic cube. The tiger is inside, supported by a harness system around its mid-section. Its legs dangled straight down from its body. The head, cradle by a separate harness, is held high and proud, despite the animal being caged and unconscious. Tubes run from almost every opening in the creature's body. Multitudes of wires slither across its fur, winding down to the floor of the crate where they disappear into a cavity below. Unseen machines pump and ping from this hidden space.

"The Amur tiger," Ben announces proudly. "Also known as Siberian tiger. The largest cat that walks our planet today, and one of the most fearsome beasts of all time."

There is some excited chatter from the monitors. Questions, opinions, comments, all mixing together into a verbal diarrhea that hurts Morgan's mind.

It takes Ben several minutes to calm down the group. Again and again promising their questions will be answered if he is allowed to continue. Finally the voices begin to mellow, and then quiet. Ben takes advantage and speaks quickly. "As you all should know, there are only four hundred or so of these magnificent creatures left in the wild, and this one, gentlemen, is very special. It is a male. In its prime, probably six or seven years old. It is thirteen and a half feet long from the tip of its nose to the end of its tail. Sixty-one inches tall to the shoulders. That's only three inches shorter than lovely Morgan here. And it weighs in at a staggering eight-hundred and forty pounds. No tiger this large has ever existed in the wild before. At least not in modern times. It really is an amazing creature.

"Now, you're all probably wondering what this fancy glass box is all about." Ben walks over and, with a gentleness that verges on loving, he runs his fingers across the acrylic surface of the crate. "Well, we call it *'Mother's Womb'*. It is essentially a life support and enhancement system. To begin with, the inside atmosphere of the crate is precisely monitored, exact oxygen levels, humidity, temperature, all maintained at optimal levels for any specific species. The harness system keeps its body erect, which helps substantially with blood flow. As the animal slumbers in medically induce hibernation, vitamins and proteins are being administered through IV, as well as down the throat and into the stomach. The stuff every healthy, growing tiger needs.

"Then, there is the multitudes of wire and tubes. Some are, of course, for monitoring all the aspects of the creature's life support. But the real exciting part is the other wires. They are introducing low-level electrical pulses into the tiger's muscles, simultaneously promoting growth, strength, and longevity. In other words, gentlemen, when this animal wakes up and leaves the *womb*, it will be up to five percent larger and stronger than it was when it went in. It will be a super tiger."

More noise from the group, but Ben keeps speaking, pushing through the squalor. "Please my friends, I haven't even told you what makes this animal truly special. Different from any other Amur tiger in existence. In Far Eastern Russia, the locals were calling this tiger zhnets cheloveka. Translated it means *reaper of man*. It is a man-eater like no other; driven purely by its hatred of mankind. Not motivated by starvation or sickness, it kills only for the joy of tearing apart human flesh."

Ben speaks for another ten minutes, giving the group a brief history of the tiger's run of bloody terror through Far Eastern Russia. When he finishes with the death of the Russian soldier by the caged animal, he pauses, mostly for dramatic effect, but also anticipating a barrage of questions. Instead he is greeted only by stunned silence. *Now I gotcha,* he thinks. *In my crosshairs, ready for the kill.*

"So, gentlemen," he continues. "This is an animal that is not going to cower behind a tree, or flee into the mountains to hide. No, this beast will be hunting you as you hunt it. This will be a game with no guaranteed ending. The survival of the fittest. Or should I say, *the deadliest*. And that is why each of you has been chosen for this opportunity. Anyone of lesser skill would probably end up in this thing's stomach.

"Now, to wrap up. Because of the extreme rareness of this hunt, there will be no calibers larger than 303 British, and no scopes rated higher than 3- 9x36. Besides those occupied by myself and Mr. Collique, there are only four other seats in the helicopter that will fly us into the compound. Which means four of you will be joining us and four of you won't. As well, just to keep things interesting, whichever of you, if indeed any of you, land the kill shot, not only will you keep the prize, but your entire payment will be returned as well.

"This will be run as a closed auction, with all bids being emailed directly to Ms. Malo. Bidding starts at two point five million per seat and lasts for twenty-four hours. I will be back in Seattle in approximately one week and will personally contact the winning four bidders then. We will have three days in the compound with Collique as our guide. If the animal is not dispatched within those three days, it goes back up on the block.

"Lastly, and this is probably an unnecessary warning, but I'm going to say it anyway. What we are doing here is obviously extremely illegal. Secrecy is of the utmost importance. For this reason, no one can know where we are or what we are doing. You each will be responsible to detail your own stories. I don't care about the specifics of your lies, but make them good. Also, make all necessary final arrangements. I'm quite certain that a group of skilled huntsmen such as yourselves have little to concern about, but if the animal should manage to get the better of any of you, your body will be disposed of, and you will be listed as a missing person. Remember, *the greatest spoils go to those who take the greatest risk*. Gentlemen, thank you for your time and I look forward to seeing half of you very soon. Mr. Collique will remain for fifteen minutes to answer any further questions."

The eruption is immediate, but Ben and Morgan pay no attention. They exit the conference room through heavy double doors, leaving the bellowing monitor heads in the care of Monsieur Collique.

17

"I am so fucking horny right now," Morgan growls, her tone low and husky. She pushes Ben through the doorway of his hotel room. "I feel like I'm on fire."

She slams the door shut and lunges across the room, barely giving him time enough to turn and face her. Again she shoves him, sending him stumbling back. He collapses in a chair that is beside the bed. "Morgan…what…"

"The way you handled that meeting," she says, coming towards him, pulling her dress slowly up to her waist. "You were like an animal yourself. So…fucking…hot." She straddles him, folding her thighs around his hips, grinding herself against him. He groans and grabs her, thrusting upwards. Even through his pants, the smoldering heat of her desire finds him.

"There you are," she breaths, and then her mouth is over his, her tongue exploring his taste. She plunges her hand down between them. For a moment, she finds herself, brushing her fingers gently across a silky warmth that yearns just below the thin lace of her panties. Then she goes to him, pulling his zipper down. She takes him into her hand. "You're my tiger," She whispers into his ear, breathing hot minty breath against his cheek. She squeezes. "And I'm on the hunt…"

Ben's cell phone begins to vibrate and buzz in his pocket. Startled by the sudden intrusive noise, Morgan's hand jerks and she inadvertently pulls much harder than she has meant to.

"Oww, fuck!" Ben bellows. He bucks, grabbing at his injured member. Morgan tumbles off his lap and lands flat on her back at his feet.

"Shit, fuck, goddamit!" Ben rants. He is leaning forward now, holding himself in both hands. "Christ, I think you yanked the fucking thing off!"

Morgan sits up, then scrambles to her knees. "I'm sorry, Benny. The phone rang…it scared me."

"Yeah, I get that," Ben says. "Just gimme a minute to take inventory, make sure everything is still where it should be."

From his pocket, the cell phone continues to rumble and buzz unrelentingly. After another moment, satisfied that all is as it should be, he lifts one of his hands and drives it angrily into his jacket.

Flipping the phone open, he barks, "This better be important, or heads are gonna roll." *Kinda like mine almost did.*

"Mr. Treager," a male voice says. "It's Pete. Pete Collingwood."

With the pain in his crotch beginning to ease, and knowing all is lost for the time being, Ben gently recoups himself and pulls up his zipper. "Pete…" His slightly rattled brain is having a hard time processing. "Pete?"

"Pete the pilot," the phone voice reminds him.

Morgan has gotten to her feet now and is pulling her dress back down over her hips. She is looking at Ben with an unsatisfied tension showing clearly in her face.

"Yeah, sure," Ben says. "Pete the pilot. Your timing sucks, Pete old buddy, but what can I do for you?"

"Have you been watching the weather reports," Pete asks.

"Well, no. I've been just a little busy the last couple hours. Afraid to say I haven't had much TV time, Pete."

"It looks like there's a big storm coming in from Alaska, heading south across the interior. Gonna bring wind, and a lot of snow. They're warning it could develop into a blizzard."

"That's interesting news. Everyone likes a good blizzard," Ben says with disinterest. "What's your point?"

"It's supposed to hit tomorrow night, Mr. Treager. Directly over our flight path to Fort St. John."

Ben feels a knot tighten in his stomach. But he refuses to give it any worth. "Again, what's your point?"

There is a brief silence, and then Pete says, "I think we may have to delay the flight till the weather warning is lifted."

And there it is! Those three words that seem just so damn simple. Delay the flight. Sure, why not. No problem. We'll just hang here in Canada Town, living in the hotel. Hopefully they allow pets because we'll have an eight-hundred-pound tiger in our room. No fucking problem at all!

"I'm sorry, Pete," Ben says, fighting to keep his tone level. "Did you say *delay the flight?*"

"Well...yes sir. I'm afraid we may not have much of a choice."

"Ah, you see. That's where you're wrong. There's always a choice. Every single day we make choices. Some are small, some are big. Do I wear the red tie or the blue? Do I have my eggs scrambled or over easy. Do I keep my job or *delay the fucking flight.* Choices, right Pete?"

"Mr. Treager," Pete says, his voice low and stunned. "I…"

"Let me explain something to you, Pete. We're not talking about some pleasure trip to Niagara Falls with the wife and kiddies. What we are talking about is moving an endangered and extremely illegal species from one end of British Columbia to the other. Even without having to cross an international border, there is still a multitude of facts that need to be dealt with. Customs, flight paths, air space coordinates, air traffic control, radar. Fucking airports. You think we're just going to load the kitty cat into our plane and fly out of here without having to explain ourselves to somebody. The only way this works is if we are invisible. And being invisible does not come free. It costs a boat load. It cost *me* a boat load. So we are going to stick to the schedule, because if we don't, we may as well put a fucking bullet in the animal right now and be done with it." He pauses long enough to switch the cell phone to his other ear. "The window of opportunity I have purchased is a very tight one. It absolutely cannot be dicked with. If you are unable to fly my plane out of here tomorrow, then I'll find someone who can. Or I'll fly it out myself. But I promise, if you let me down now, you won't be able to get a job flying fucking crop dusters in Utah. Do we understand each other, Pete?"

There is a long pause. Ben can hear him drawing nervous breath, weighing the pros and cons. Pete undoubtedly knows as well as anyone that Treager's word means everything. If he says he will ruin the pilot's career, then that's exactly what he will do. No compromises.

"I understand, Mr. Treager," Pete says at last. "Not to worry. I'll get us out of here."

"I knew you would," Ben says, sounding as though they were suddenly the best of friends. "And you know what else? Weathermen are a bunch of fucking clowns anyways. There's never snow this early in the season. First week of November at the earliest. Goddamn forecasters are walking around with their heads up their asses. So you got nothing to worry about, Pete. I guarantee it."

"Sure, Mr. Treager. I'll have everything ready, on schedule."

"Good man. We'll see you tomorrow." Ben disconnects the call and tosses the phone onto the table.

"Problem averted?" Morgan asks. She has been sitting on the edge of the bed listening.

"Of course," Ben says. "Nothing is a problem when you have the strength to fix it." He looks at her. "But I'm thinking maybe we should arrange for you to go back to Seattle instead of…"

Morgan is already shaking her head before Ben can finish. "No," she says. "This deal is a much mine as it is yours. I'm coming with you."

Morgan stares at Ben, her pale green eyes gleaming fiercely. He knows the look all too well. There would be no talking her out of this. "Okay," he says, touching her thigh. "Whatever you want."

A playful smile touches Morgan's lips. Reaching under her dress, she slips off her panties and kicks them aside. Then she lays back on the bed, her knees gliding apart invitingly. "Well, if you feel up to it, even after such a traumatic episode, why don't you get over here and I'll show you exactly what I want."

Ben definitely felt up to it.

18

Deadman Lake, BC- The Next Day

Eli Foley pushes open the screen door with his shoulder and steps out of his house onto the front deck. In the distance, the sun is a brilliant yellow half-circle peering over the white peak of Mount Baldwin. The sky is flawless, pale blue, not a single cloud to mar its splendor. The thinly iced water of Deadman Lake reflects golden shards of light against the vast evergreens that line its shore.

Eli loves this time of day; early morning, just as the sun is coming up. It is so peaceful and quiet, with only the songs of birds moving through the air, pushed here and there by the slightest breeze whispering over the treetops. Looking out at the lake, as sunshine dances across its mirrored surface, is like staring into the lens of a kaleidoscope. Even after ten years, Eli is still taken aback by the beauty of the morning.

He stands there for a moment, steam spiraling up from the mugs of coffee he holds in each hand, and pulls in several deep breaths of cool fall air. To the right side of the door he has just come through, there is a thermometer attached to the house. It had been a housewarming gift from his younger sister and depicts a cartoon man in a thick parka, holding up his fishing pole proudly.

Written below the picture is, *'Only real men go ice fishing'*. The dial is sitting at minus two degrees Celsius.

Though this is a perfectly average temperature for mid-October, the snowstorm that is being forecast for this evening is not average. In the years Eli has lived on Deadman, he has never known the initial big dump of snow to come before the first week of November. Sometimes as late as the second week. If the weatherman proves to be correct, this year will be an anomaly.

Eli walks to the edge of the deck and looks down into the yard. As he suspected, his wife is there, sitting thirty feet back from the shoreline, a small fire crackling in the stone fire pit in front of her. She is in one of the wooden deck chairs with a woolen blanket over her legs and a book in her hands. She does not appear to be reading, however, just gazing into the distance.

Sighing, he descends the porch stairs into the yard. As he approaches her from behind, his wife's head turns slightly, acknowledging his presence.

"Good morning, my love," Barbara Foley says to her husband as he sits down beside her.

"A warm brew for my Baboo," Eli says, holding the steaming mug out.

She takes it happily, wrapping both hands around the warm cup. "Thank you. I was just thinking it was time for a coffee."

"You see, I knew that. That's why my nickname is Eli the all-knowing."

Barb smiles. Even at sixty-eight, she is still a beautiful woman. Silver hair, bright hazel eyes, almond skin. The few lines that do show give her face the appearance of distinction rather than age. Eli has always thought himself a lucky man. "All knowing indeed," she says, then turns her head and looks back out at the lake. "Gorgeous morning."

"Yes it is," Eli agrees. He glances at her legs. They are trembling ever so slightly under the blanket. "How long have you been up?"

Barb shrugs. "Not long."

"How long is not long?"

She blows into the hot coffee before taking a sip. "Couple of hours maybe. Not too long."

Couple of hours? That usually means at least four. She has most likely been sitting out here since 3am. "It's cold," he says. "You could end up catching something."

"I built a fire, and I've got my blanket. It's fine. I love the crisp air."

Eli is trying to read her expression, figure out how bad it really is. But her *I'm okay* look has slid over her face like a veil. "Was it legs, or pain?" he asks cautiously.

She is quiet for a moment, blowing into her coffee. Finally she looks at him. "Little of both, I guess. I took a pill, so that helped. The legs were...not too bad." But her eyes say more. They tell him it had been very bad.

Three years early, she had slipped on ice while coming down the porch steps and hurt her back. The injury itself had not been especially serious, but the pain was severe. As months went by, instead of getting better as it should, the pain only got worse. It started spreading out from her back. Her shoulders and neck. Her arms. Her entire body ached. Times with no pain quickly became fewer and fewer. Her life was a constant battle, each minute of each day a fight against pain. Terrified he was losing the love of his life, Eli shuttled her from one doctor to the next, specialist after specialist. Some said arthritis, others tissue damage. A few thought Fibromyalgia, an untreatable form of chronic pain. But the symptoms seemed wrong, so it was ruled out. One doctor had even tried to tell him it was all in her head. That particular physician had come extremely close to feeling a bit of chronic pain himself.

She was given pills and creams and tonics, none of which did anything but make her constantly drowsy or incredibly nauseous. They tried home remedies and secret recipes, handed down from generation to generation. Those also, in addition to tasting God awful, did nothing.

She was told to start swimming more. Within a week, the pain went from bad to excruciating. Well, of course, they were told then, she shouldn't be swimming at all. Walk more, unless the pain persists, then walk less. Get lots of sleep, but she was in too much pain to sleep, so she was sleeping less and less. Get plenty of rest, but stay active, though avoid activities that are too strenuous.

In the end, after two years of failed diagnosis and ineffective medication, Barb had done the only thing that was left for her to do; she learned to live with it.

Then, as though the All-Mighty Maker had not smiled down upon his sweet wife quite enough, the jumping legs began. Restless Leg Syndrome. The overpowering sensation, especially when laying down or trying to rest, that the legs need to be moving. In other words, now she was not only in pain, but most nights she couldn't even lay down for longer than a few minutes without feeling like she needed to leap out of bed and two-step across the carpet.

His wife is a strong woman, however, and will seldom fuss. She keeps quiet about how she feels, even when Eli pushes her. *It's fine, I'm okay, not so bad.* The words he hears most often. Her constant refusal to be a burden. Years earlier, before they moved to Deadman, Eli had been the sheriff down in Terravale. Ten years spent keeping the peace in that town certainly had not been a difficult job, and in all that time he never carried a gun. But, the job did train him in expressions. In fact, he became an expression specialist. Reading faces, eyes, the tone of one's voice. Body language. Even mood. This ability helped him to defuse a situation before it became one. Now, it is this skill alone, rather than Barb's words, that reveal the ultimate truths.

Her eyes are telling him, without any doubt, that it had been a bad night. Possibly one of the worst. "You should have woken me," he says to her. "I could have started the fire, kept you company."

"You need your sleep," she says. "If the weather turns the way they're saying, there's going to be plenty to be done around here."

Eli looks up at the cloudless sky. "Weathermen," he muses. "I don't think there's one good brain in the lot of them. Does this look like a sky that's ready to blizzard?"

"No," she agrees. "But we've seen the weather change quickly before. It happens. And…" Her words fade away.

"And?" Eli echoes, his eyes locked on her face.

She smiles weakly. "And, I just have a feeling they might be right."

Because you had a bad night. It's always worse when the weather is about to change. But saying this to her is pointless. So instead he says, "Well, I guess we'll find out. They're saying two, maybe two and a half feet by tomorrow morning."

"That's enough to cut us off," Barb says, more fact in her tone than any real concern.

"Maybe for a couple days. Dwayne and the Terravale guys will have us dug out in no time."

"Will the electricity survive?"

"Hard to say," Eli says, and takes a warming sip from his coffee. "Only the Lodge has hard electricity, so it won't affect us one way or the other. We got the generators."

"I know that Eli," Barb says, throwing her husband an annoyed glance. "I only ask because the funeral is set for today. If they'd waited even one more day, it may not have happened at all."

"Oh, shit," Eli says. "I forgot that was today. You feeling up to it?"

"Are you kidding me," she replies, her voice high and amused. "Big Dwayne would be carting me over there in a wheelbarrow if I tried to back out."

Eli knows this is the truth. Dwayne Trapper loves the Deadman funeral, and he won't stand for any 'rounders to not be in attendance. Especially now, with only a hand full of them left.

The Deadman funeral—a rather morbid name that has been around far too long to change now—is a yearly celebration with a dual purpose. Saying goodbye to the summer season and hello to the winter season. It is usually held sometime in October, around the second or third week. This is the quietest time of the year on the lake. The summer residents have closed up their cabins and headed back to the city. And with the snow still two weeks or more away, unless the weatherman's prediction proves correct, the winter tourists would not start arriving until mid-November. The Lodge, as well as the two year-round Bed & Breakfasts—one of which is run by Eli and Barb—are all empty. In the past, there have been eight, sometimes ten residences occupied through all four of the seasons. This year, however, has been an especially rough one. Horace Benson, whose log cabin is one of the largest on the lake, was diagnosed with stomach cancer last May. The chemo treatments have forced Horace and his wife to move back to the Vancouver area. Then, in July, Charlie and Margaret Wagner, a lovely older couple running a B&B near the south-west end of Deadman, had lost their only son in a motorcycle accident. The trauma was extremely hard on them, and they left the lake to be closer to their daughter. It is still unclear if they will be back or not, though Eli has heard Margaret is having a very difficult time coping with her grief, so it seems quite doubtful.

That leaves only six year-round residences this year, making up a grand total of fourteen people—affectionately known as *'rounders* to most. This includes brothers Dwayne and Wayne Trapper, who own and operate the Lodge and Deadman Rentals. There is also Saul Jenkins, a newbie, embarking on his first winter. Back in June he had purchased the old Chamber's place; about a third of a kilometer away from Eli and Barb's B&B and the last residence at the northeast tip of the lake. It is just himself and his seventeen-year-old—*or is she eighteen, Eli cannot remember for sure*—daughter, Sidney. The poor man's wife had passed away the previous year after a two-year battle with brain cancer.

As Eli sits in front of the fire pit, a hot coffee in his hand and his wife at his side, he begins to realize just how much tragedy has tarnished the serene beauty of their lake this year. Pain and suffering, sickness and death. It is all around them. For the first time since Eli began calling Deadman his home, the name of today's gathering seems fitting. It really is a *funeral*.

"You're probably right," he says. "I suppose Dwayne knows as well as any of us that we need all the friendly faces we can get this year. Start the winter off right."

Barb doesn't respond. She just sits, sipping her coffee, looking over the water. Her silence is enough to tell Eli she understands exactly what he means.

They remain quiet for a few minutes, contemplating the day ahead. Finally Barb says, "Well, I guess I better go in. Have a bath. Make us a bite to eat. We should be heading over to the Lodge for around one o'clock I imagine."

Eli stands and takes his wife's hand, helping her to her feet. He can see her grimacing with the pain of it, even though she is trying her best to hide it. "Are you okay to go up alone," he asks. "I was thinking about walking over to the old Chamber's place, say morning to Saul."

"You should start calling it the Jenkins' place," Barb reminds him. "But, yes, that's a good idea. He is such a nice man. He has a kind heart. And his daughter is just lovely. But…sometimes he seems…so…"

"Sad," Eli finishes for her.

She nods. "I was going to say lost, but sad works too." She leans in and kisses him on the cheek. "I'll be just fine. Go over and have a little visit. No more than an hour, though. I'll have eggs on the table."

"If you need anything, give a shout and I'll come runnin'."

"I am perfectly capable of taking care of myself, *Eli the all-knowing*. I won't need anything." She turns and starts towards the house. "No more than an hour or you'll be eating cold eggs."

"No more," he says, watching her cross the yard. He waits as she climbs the stairs, ready to run to her if she shows any signs of difficulty. But she reaches the porch without pause and disappears inside the house.

Eli stays where he is for a few moments; sitting, enjoying his coffee. The air is still cold, but the sun, which is now a full glowing orb in the clear sky, feels surprisingly warm on his face.

When his mug is empty, he puts it on the small wooden table set between the two chairs, telling himself he'd better not forget to bring it in when he returns or there'd be hell to pay. The fire is almost out, so he kicks a bit of sand on it just to be sure, then walks off towards the Old Chamber's place. *Sorry Barb—the Jenkins' place. Gotta remember it's the Jenkins' place now.*

19

Like Eli, Saul Jenkins is also indulging in a cup of morning java, though with two substantial differences. First, he is sitting at the table in his kitchen, next to him a warm fire pops within the heart of a wood stove, and second, there is a sizable shot of rum in his coffee. Instead of looking out the window, appreciating the scenic beauty that blooms behind the glass, he is staring down at the mug of spiked beverage, his eyes glazed and distant. Inside his mind, her face is there. The image is becoming hazy now, unfocused, like a badly developed picture. Yet the pain that comes with it was still just as sharp as the day he had held her hand for the last time.

The mornings are always the worst. Waking up alone, her side of the bed cold and undisturbed. Then the dismal shroud of truth is there waiting for him. Anxious. Eager to welcome him to another day. Whether a good day or a bad day, it really doesn't matter, because all it will ever amount to is just another day without her. She will still be gone, buried under the ground in Mt. Pleasant Cemetery. Every morning, when he opens his eyes, this was his only greeting.

But the coffee will help. And what's in the coffee will help even more. A fundamental mixture of caffeine and alcohol to numb the senses. Nothing better to help a man pick himself up and slog through the next twelve hours of his life. Good or bad, with rum it makes little difference.

Saul raises his cup in a silent toast to nothing in particular, then takes a long, satisfying gulp. The tightness in his heart loosened just a bit. Most mornings, by the time he finishes the entire mug, the pain will have diminished to a reasonable level, unless it is a particularly bad day (like their anniversary or her birthday), then he might require an extra couple of pulls right from the bottle. But today isn't one of those, and he is already feeling okay.

He stands up and goes over to the stove, then uses an oven-mitt to pull open the firebox. As he bends to pick up a log, his daughter comes into the kitchen. She stays quiet for a moment, standing behind him as he digs through the pile in search of that just right, perfect for the job piece of wood. Apparently it is an exact science, requiring a skilled eye for detail.

"There you are sucker," he mutters at last, yanking free a log that looks suspiciously similar to all the rest.

"Are you sure that's the right one, dad?" Sidney says.

Saul jumps, almost dropping the stove length log he has searched so hard to find.

Sidney snickers into her hand. "Sorry 'bout that, didn't realize you were so wound up."

He looks at her, trying to feign an annoyed glare, but it is no good. He isn't even capable of pretending to be angry at her. "Sneaking up on an old man is a good way to give him him a heart attack," he says and shoves the log into the stove.

"You're forty-seven, dad," she says, walking past him to the refrigerator. "Not ninety."

"Sometimes I feel ninety."

"That's 'cause you're wound too tight. You gotta loosen up." She removes a carton of orange juice and swings the door closed again. "Maybe you should try Pilates."

Saul gets his daughter a glass from the cupboard and then joins her at the table.

"I'd sooner do pole dancing," he says. "More my style."

Sidney cringes. "Now there's an image that will haunt me at night. Thanks a lot."

He grins at her. "Why? You don't think I'd look good spinning around a pole in an orange speedo?"

"Stop," Sidney cries, clamping her hands over her ears. "No more!"

"I think I'd dance to the song 'Relax' by Frankie Goes to Hollywood. It's got a real good groove."

"That's it, I'm calling child services and reporting you. This is definitely child abuse."

Saul begins singing in a high voice, *"Relax, don't do it, when you want to go to it."*

"Please," Sidney pleads, laughing now and covering her face. "Stop."

But Saul's voice only gets louder. *"Relax, don't do it, when you want to--"*

"Don't you dare say it," she shouts, laughing so hard now she can barely get the words out. "I'll be scarred for life."

"Uhhhggg," he grunts in a triumphant finale, and then the laughter takes him as well, and he is happy to go.

It feels wonderful. The simplicity of it. To be able to joke around and have fun. Giggling, being silly. Finding joy in these small moments. For so long after Penny died, Saul didn't know if either of them, Sidney or himself, would ever laugh again. The pain for them both had been so overwhelming. It consumed their lives, sucking them deeper and deeper into a hole of despair.

But it was Sidney who first started the long climb back out. Just two months before her graduation from high school, she confronted her father, convincing him that their need for a change was quickly becoming desperate. She put her own plans of college on hold, opting instead to stay with Saul, each of them guiding the other through the darkness of grief. She reminded him of the good times. Summer vacations at the campsite on Deadman Lake. Fishing and swimming and hiking. Her mother especially loved these trips. She looked forward to them all year long, even to the point of becoming giddy like a child at Christmas. It was the life Penny would have wanted for them. Not just for and week or two in August, but always. So Sidney planned everything. Renting out their house in Burnaby. Contacting real estate agents and investigating properties. When the Old Chambers cabin popped onto the market, they were ready to jump at it immediately, purchasing the place outright with some of the insurance money (Saul and Penny had both taken out life policies shortly after their daughter was born). And finally, it was Sidney who drafted a heartfelt letter to the Vancouver School Board, securing her father's leave of absence from Charles Tupper Secondary.

As one of the finest math teachers working in the district, Super Intendent Doyle Grady had responded. *Mr. Jenkins is entitled to as much time as he requires to recover from this tragic event. We all pray he will one day return, but also understand if he feels he cannot.*

It is because of Sidney that they are here now, laughing in the kitchen with the sweet smell of hickory smoke floating up from the stove. She had gotten them through the worst of it. To the point where recovery finally seemed like a possibility. It is true that Saul still uses a shot of rum in his coffee to get through the morning, but it is his daughter that gets him through life.

Once Sidney has regained some of her composure again, she says, "You seem to be in a fine mood this morning."

"Well, the sun's shining and the coffee's hot," he says. "All the reasons I need to be in a fine mood."

"I guess," she says, eyeing him suspiciously as she pours herself a glass of juice. "The shot of booze in your hot coffee doesn't have anything to do with it?"

Saul frowns. "What makes you think there's booze in my coffee?"

"Please dad, I may be only eighteen, but I still know what rum smells like. Plus you left the bottle sitting on the counter."

"No I…" He turns his head and sees it, sitting beside the sink, right where he had left it. "Oh. So I did."

"It's not a big deal. I know it helps you, and that's fine. I just… worry a bit, that's all."

Saul meets his daughter's blue eyes with his own. "You don't have to worry. I Promise. One shot is a wake-up…helps me forget my dreams."

"I get that," she says. "But I still worry. With mom gone, it's like…my job now."

Saul shakes his head. "Your only job is to be a teenager and enjoy your life. Worrying about me is not part of that." He stands up, goes to the sink, and empties to rest of his coffee down the sink. "And besides, there's nothing to worry about."

"I know," she says, and then a smile brightens her face. "Except the pole dancing. That's a serious worry."

He chuckles. "Well, maybe I'll try the Pilates instead. I think I'd look great in a pair of Lulu Lemon yoga pants."

"Oh, God," Sidney groans.

Saul sits down again. "So what about breakfast. Pancakes or scrambled eggs?"

"Pancakes sound good. Can Chloe have breakfast with us?"

"No problem," he says. "Are her parents not back yet?"

Sidney drains the last of her juice and sets the glass down. "Nope. She says they'll be back tomorrow."

Saul's brow raises. "Tomorrow? It's supposed to dump snow tonight. Maybe two feet. That could make getting in here a real problem."

"Really?" She says, sounding suddenly excited. "We'll be *snowed in*? Like that creepy hotel in *The Shining?*"

He nods. "Yeah, but hopefully without all the blood and *Heeere's Johnny*. Could be two or three days before they can dig us out."

"That's so cool. I've never been snowed in before."

"No," he says, his tone laced with unease. "It'll be a first for the both of us."

"If it does snow, can Chloe stay with us till her parents get back? She'll probably be afraid by herself."

"I doubt that. Her family has lived up here for quite a few years I think. It's definitely not going to be her first snow in."

Sidney shrugs and stands up. "Still, it would be fun."

"Sure. She can stay with us as long as she likes."

"Okay good," she says, grabbing her parka from the coat rack by the back door. "I'm going to take the truck and run over to her place. Should be back in an hour or so."

"Well have fun," Saul says. "If this storm does come tonight, it could be a while before we can even get the truck out of the driveway."

"I know. So exciting."

"I guess," he agrees, though still sounding hesitant. "You want blueberries in the pancakes?"

"Sounds good. But if you hold off a bit we can help with the flippin'."

"I will. Think I'll have another coffee and meditate."

Sidney stops, her coat halfway on, and glances back at him.

"With cream and sugar," he says, holding one hand up and laying the other on his heart. "Scouts honor. The rum is going back in the cupboard."

She smiles. "I love you, dad."

"You too. See you in a while."

Sidney turns and pulls open the door.

An old man in a dirty baseball cap is standing on the other side of the door, his raised hand fisted and poised to knock.

Startled by his unexpected presence, Sidney yelps and jumps back, though she does recognize him immediately.

"Mr. Foley," she says, letting out a long, relieved breath. "You scared me."

"So it would seem," Eli says. He pulls off his hat, revealing a smooth, bald head hidden beneath. "Thought for a sec there was a mountain lion standing behind me."

"No, no," Sidney assures him. "I just wasn't expecting you."

Eli grins. His teeth are amazingly white and straight. "I was about to announce myself, but you beat me to the punch. Or should I say knock." He raises his fist again and rocks it back and forth, knocking into the air.

With the red in her cheeks betraying her embarrassment, Sidney giggles softly as she sneaks past him. "Yeah, right. Well, be seeing you. I was just on my way out."

"Course, young lady," he says. "Take care, though. Watch out for them mountain lions."

"Sure, and bears too, right?"

"Naw, you got no worry there. Bears are hibernating…"

But he is only speaking to the squirrels now. Sidney has already disappeared down the stairs.

He stands there for a moment, looking where she had been. Then he turns and slips his hat back over his chilled head. "Sweet girl," he says, chuckling, and goes into the house.

20

They sit at the kitchen table, Saul with a cup of coffee, Eli with orange juice—*one cup 'o' joe's my limit,* he'd told Saul some months ago. *Anymore and the bone rattles kick into high gear.* The old man's hat sits beside his glass on the table. Warm sunlight shining through the window glows a brilliant yellow against his bald head.

"So, do you believe the weatherman?" Saul asks, spooning a heap of sugar into his mug. "Sure doesn't look like snow right now."

"Weather can change darn fast up here in the mountains," Eli says. "I was a tad doubtful, but the wife seems to think it could storm. She's got a better feel for these things than me, so I guess it could. Hard to say for sure."

Saul frowns, wondering if this answer is a *yes,* a *no,* or a *maybe.* It is tough to tell. "Okay, let's say it does snow. Big dump, two or three feet. What happens then?"

"Not much. You'll be digging yourself out of this cabin I suppose. No ice fishing, though. Lake won't be frozen through for a bit yet, I'm afraid."

"I mean as far as the roads go," Saul says, sighing softly to himself. "That kind of thing."

"No roads," Eli says, his tone passive. "Not for a couple days at least. Maybe a week. By that time, big Dwayne should be able to get us dug out. Not even four-wheel drive vehicles get you out before then. But it ain't no worry. Same thing every year, so we're pretty much good to go. The Lodge could lose power, but we all run off generators and solar anyway so won't affect us none. Plenty of dry firewood. Lots of food, water…should be no issues. Never are."

"So we sit here until someone digs us out?"

Now it is Eli's brow that creased. "You planning a trip or something? I'd advise against it if you are. Not a good time of year for traveling."

"No, of course not. It's just that I've never been trapped by weather before. What if there's a medical emergency? Someone gets hurt or sick. What then?"

Eli studies Saul's face, as though trying to figure out if he is being serious or not. "Never took you for bein' the nervous type," he says frankly. "Odds of an emergency coming about in the one week of the year with no road access is darn slim I'd say. Suppose if something did happen, Dwayne's got the Sno-Cat. Not too roomy, but he could drive someone out in a pinch. Dozen or so snowmobiles as well. Get you to Terravale, then ambulance you out from there. Chopper if it's really bad. Whirlybird could get a person out to the Kamloops hospital in about two hours I guess. It ain't a worry though. Doc Copper's been a 'rounder for a couple years now, so he can handle most medical emergencies on his own. Granted, he's still not back from the city yet." Eli ponders this for a moment, then shrugs. "Still no worry, though. In my ten years we've never had an emergency that couldn't wait till the roads get plowed. Billy Bellow's wife cut one of her fingers pretty bad with a kitchen knife. She'd been making supper. Cutting up cabbage or celery or something and darn near hacked her index finger right off. Bled a lot. She was a tough old girl though. She waited two days till Dwayne got the road open. Bud Fleming, he runs the grocer in Terravale, had been a doctor in his old life. Sewed her digit up just as neat as you please. Guess she was a little more careful with kitchen knives after that. Odd, though, can't recall her name. Just another part of getting old I suppose."

"So, someone could get out in the Sno-Cat?" Saul says, again feeling unclear if his question has been answered. "If it was an emergency?"

"Could do. As I said, it's not too roomy. Cab's pretty tiny, then you squeeze Dwayne in there. Don't leave a whole lotta room for nobody else. You'd be spending the entire trip pushed up against the side door. Probably be better to run someone down on a snowmobile. Not as warm, but a helluv a lot more accommodating. Couldn't imagine bein' cooped up with Big Dwayne that long. Packing around all that pudge, and he's definitely not a fella too concerned when it comes to personal hygiene."

"Okay, so we aren't totally cut off?"

Eli takes a long, slow sip of his orange juice, staring at Saul over the rim of his glass. "I Don't understand the concern," he says, using his sleeve to wipe juice off his upper lip. "You're healthy, your daughter's healthy, and you seem intelligent enough to avoid poor choices, like juggling chainsaws or making toast in the bathtub. I'd say you got no worries, Saul."

Saul nods. "I know I must seem paranoid, but this is a real change for me. *For us.* I was raised a city boy, and I've raised Sidney a city girl. All this," he waves his hands around the kitchen. "It's so different. It'll take me a bit to get used to, that's all."

"I don't doubt it," Eli agrees. "Now that I think about it, Barb and I might have been a wee bit jumpy our first winter. But once you get past it, you'll see it's really not anything to be concerned about."

With this, the knot of unease in Saul's stomach loosens slightly. He knows he is being irrational. Even childish. Everything Eli is saying makes perfect sense. But, unlike his daughter, the thought of being snowed in, completely cut off from civilization, does not excite him at all. It makes him feel trapped and, strangely, *claustrophobic.*

"You be sure to chat with Dwayne this afternoon," Eli goes on. "He'll tell you the same thing."

This afternoon? Saul thinks. *Why would I be seeing Dwayne...*

Then he remembers. The party...or gathering...celebration, whatever it is. It is happening today. He had completely forgotten about it. "That's right," he says. "The party... thingy. It totally slipped my mind."

"To be honest, it slipped mine as well," Eli admits. "But nonetheless, today is the day."

"What's it called again? *The awakening...the bar mitzvah?*"

Eli chuckles. "The funeral."

"That's right, the *funeral*. Kind of a morbid name for a party, don't you think?"

"I guess we're a morbid bunch. Been calling it the same thing from long before my time. Suppose no one's ever had the sense enough to change it."

"So who can we expect," Saul asks. "Aren't most people gone for the winter?"

"Yup. Not a lot of us 'rounders left, that's for certain. There's Dwayne and Wayne and their boys…"

Dwayne and Wayne Trapper. The strangest set of twins Saul has ever come across. Anyone who doesn't know them personally would never guess them as brothers, let alone twin brothers. Other than their height, both standing just over six foot, they look absolutely nothing alike. Wayne is a walking skeleton, weighing not an ounce more than one-fifty. He is bald as a baby's belly, but wears a long black beard. And he lives off cigarettes and coffee. Saul is quite sure that nothing ever passes into the man's mouth that isn't either poured from his beat-up Tim Horton's travel cup, or sucked through the filter of an Export A green.

Dwayne Trapper on the other hand, tips the scales at not an ounce under three-hundred and fifty pounds, and this is being extremely kind. But do not be fooled by his weight, Dwayne is no soft and squishy fat man. His stomach is the size of a medicine ball and as hard as a metal trash can. His feet are so large he is unable to find shoes that fit him properly, forcing him to wear sandals all the time, including the winter months. Shaking his hand is like greeting a baseball player who has forgotten to take off his catcher's glove. A full head of thick, curly black hair sits above his huge, whiskerless face. Also, as Eli had pointed out, personal hygiene is not one of his strong suits. The single benefit of this fact: he is rarely bothered by mosquitos.

There is one thing the Trapper brothers do have in common, however. Saul has been given both stories by Eli and each is as different as the brothers themselves, yet end with the same result:

they are both single fathers. Dwayne's wife left him for another man—who had a villa in France instead of a lodge in British Columbia—when their boy Danny was only a year old and Matty, Dwayne's son from a previous marriage, was six. On each of their birthdays since then she sends them a fifty-dollar bill, but that has been the extent of her motherly input. On the opposite side of the spectrum, Wayne's wife had been struck down and killed in a Walmart parking lot. The driver of the SUV that hit her was drunk and had received a four-year sentence for driving under the influence and involuntary manslaughter. He was out in sixteen months, and driving again in eighteen. Wayne was left to raise their seven-year-old son Greg alone.

"Of course," Eli continues. "It's the Trapper brothers that put this little shindig on every year, so their attendance is kind of a given I suppose. Let's see, there's also the Coopers."

"Burt and Colleen still haven't gotten back from the city," Saul reminds him. "So there's only Chloe."

"Oh," Eli says, his eyebrows raised. "Just mentioned that myself didn't I. The old mind sure ain't what it used to be. Thank God I got Barb. She's better at keeping track of stuff than I am. Your daughter and the Cooper girl, they seem close. Like two peas in a pod."

"They've become good friends. It was really nice to find someone her own age up here that she could bond with. Helps with the…circumstances."

"Yes," Eli says. He lapses into silence then, staring down at the glass still clutched in one of his knobby hands. When he finally looks up at Saul, he smiles weakly. "I suppose it would help."

"So is that it," Saul asks, anxious to move away from this potentially awkward moment. "Just the Trappers and Chloe?"

"Well, no. There's myself and Barb, and you and Sidney. And of course Betty Abernathy and that fella that's been shackin' up with her. Can't recall his name, though. Barb would know."

"Betty Abernathy? I've heard the name, but I don't think I've met her."

"No, you probably haven't. She keeps to herself most of the time. Lives in the big old cabin halfway up the west side of the lake. First real cabin ever built here. Less you count Old Dan, but that wasn't really a cabin at all. More of a tent is what I'd say."

"Old Dan?" Saul says. "From the story? The dead guy in his boat?"

"One in the same," Eli says. "Lake got its name because of Old Dan Slowfoot dying and sitting out in that boat all winter. Apparently Betty's cabin is built in the exact same spot Old Dan's hut had sat. She has some way back relation to him. Great niece, or distant cousin, something like that. She's a bit of an odd duck, though. Has these…spells I guess you'd call them. Visions of the future, if you believe in that sort of thing. I myself do not. I think she's just a flat-out nut job. Barb would give me the evil eye for saying so, but the truth's the truth."

"She can see the future," Saul asks, suddenly fascinated with Betty Abernathy. He'd always had an interest in ESP or sixth sense. Mind control. Anything of that nature. "Has she predicted anything that's come true?"

"Naw," Eli says, shaking his head. But then he pauses, rubbing the gray stubble that is just beginning to show on his chin. "Well, there was this one thing. Kinda odd. It was a few years back, can't say for sure how many. Betty had come out of her cabin in a real fuss. She had a fella she was with, a different guy than she's with now mind you. Most of her men only last a couple of years or so, then she trades them in for a newer model." He chuckles. "That's what Barb calls them, the newer model. Like they were cars rather than people. Anyways, she jumped on the back of her beat-up old quad bike and had this fella run her up to Kenny Ferguson's place. Now, you gotta understand, Betty ain't the visiting type. She shows up at the funeral every year, but beyond that, she mostly stays to herself. So when Kenny opens his door and sees her standing there on his porch, all outta breath and sweaty, he's darn surprised to say the least. She doesn't bother with any pleasantries. Just right to the point. *You going hunting today, Kenny?* she asks him. Well, this was Thursday, and everyone knows that on Thursdays Kenny would head out to this blind he's got rigged up high in a tree. He'd sit up there with his rifle and a couple of beers, waiting for a deer to come along. Sometimes he'd get one, sometimes he wouldn't, but every dam Thursday you bet he'd be up there. He tells her, *yeah, I'm goin' hunting. What of it?*

"Don't go today, she says. *It's okay to go tomorrow, but don't go today. Somethin' bad is gonna happen today. You gotta stay out of that blind.*

"I guess Kenny could smell the booze on her breath, and this was still a fair bit before noon. So to get her off his porch, he agrees. Says he won't go. Course it's a lie as I said, just to get the crazy bird off his porch. He has no real intentions of missing his Thursday in the blind. His wife, though, she was scared out of her wits. She'd heard what the woman said, and for some reason it really upset her. She wouldn't let Kenny go for nothing. No amount of talk would change her mind. I guess she wore the pants in that house, cause he didn't go sitting in his blind that day. He doesn't go until Friday. And what do you suppose he found when he got there to his tree? Well, it must have had some kinda root rot that Kenny didn't know about. The darn thing had fallen over. His blind was smashed to beejesus under this huge tree. If he'd been in it when it fell, well, that would have been it for Old Kenny Ferguson.

"Course, Kenny's a sensible man, like myself. He don't believe in no premonition bologna. That tree could have fallen over anytime in the week since he was there last. Just cause she said it, doesn't mean it had fallen right at the time he'd be sitting in his blind."

Eli picks his hat off the table and begins fumbling with the sizing clasp absently. "A day or so later, he gets together with his buddy Trent, who was down from Terravale to do some fishin'. Trent listens to the story, and near the end his eyes are wide like saucers. So Kenny asks him what's the matter? Trent tells him that as it happens, he'd been out hunting that Thursday morning. He comes across Kenny's blind, the tree was still standing. He remembers this distinctively because he even called up, thinking Kenny might be up there, it being Thursday and all."

Saul is looking at Eli, and like Kenny's buddy Trent, his eyes are also wide like saucers. "So that means he would have been in the tree when it fell?"

But Eli is shaking his head again. "Or it could have fallen that night. Or the next morning, before Kenny got there. It doesn't mean anything in my books, except it was a coincidence. That's about all I'm willing to give."

"That's one hell of a coincidence. Betty warns him, then the tree falls within twenty-four hours."

"I just told you the story cause you asked me. Being polite and all. Doesn't mean I give it any credit as being truthful. As a somewhat intelligent, sensible man, I won't do that."

"Well, it was an interesting story all the same," Saul says. "I look forward to meeting her at the funeral."

Eli shrugs. "That's all fine and dandy. But do yourself, and everyone else, a favor. Once the Old bird has been into the cups, you'll want to avoid her. She's harmless, but often what she has to say is not. Remember that."

Just then the door comes open and Sidney and Chloe burst into the kitchen. They are both laughing as though they have heard the funniest joke ever told.

Any seriousness that may have lingered in the room disappears with the girls' arrival.

21

As far as parties go—*or funerals for that matter*—the Deadman funeral celebration turns out to be not a bad one. The festivities are held on the large, covered deck area of the Lodge. Half a dozen propane patio heaters sit in strategically chosen spots around the space to help keep the bite of the cold afternoon at bay. In the sky above the lake, several puffy white clouds have rolled in now. Although they do block out most of the pale blue splendor of that morning, there is still little to indicate a storm on the horizon.

At the head of the deck, nearest to the Lodge itself, the massive barbeque station is in full swing, with big Dwayne Trapper ruling over it like an army general. Steaks, hamburgers, hotdogs, and chicken are all on the menu, plus potato salad, baked beans, pickled beets, Caesar salad and coleslaw. There is easily enough food to feed three, even four times the amount of people who are actually present. It can be said that Dwayne Trapper has his fair share of negative attributes, but being stingy with food has never been one.

Tables fan out around the barbeque, two under each heater. Towards the back, and coldest area of the patio, a couple of these tables stand empty. Otherwise, all the others are occupied with people eating and drinking and generally having a pretty good time. As it turns out, there are quite a number more patrons than Eli and Saul had figured. It seems that with the amount of 'rounders at an all-time low, Big Dwayne had taken it upon himself to invite several of his Terravale buddies and their families, and given the promise of free food and drink, most of those invited had not let the hour drive into the forest stop them. So, besides the dozen official year round residents, there are easily another twenty persons in attendance. Everyone enjoying the momentous merriments of the funeral.

At one table Eli, Barb and Saul sit chatting. The two men each have a bottle of beer in front of them, while Barb is sipping a glass of ice-tea. She had considered having a beer herself, but decided against it. With the numerous medications she is on, even a single beer can have a negative effect. At the moment she is feeling okay, and she doesn't want to do anything that might jeopardize that. So ice-tea it is.

Sidney and Chloe are also sharing the table with them, but they have just wandered off to do a little—as Sidney put it—*mingling among the local stock.*

Barb is entertaining herself, and her two companions, by recounting the many strange, yet oddly interesting habits of those same *local stock*. Listening to her speak, with such vividly entertaining narrative, Saul was not surprised to find out she had dabbled in journalism before a giant life change brought them first to Terravale, and then to Deadman.

"Now," she is saying and leans in a little closer to Saul. "Do you believe in magic, Saul?"

He smiles. "I'm not sure. I guess it would depend on how impressive the trick is."

"Well, do you see Wayne over there?" she asks, gesturing with her head.

Saul turns, looking around the deck area. Wayne Trapper is at a table on the far side of the deck. He is sitting with his son—*Saul thinks his name is Greg…or is that one of Dwayne's boys, he wasn't sure*—and another man he doesn't recognize. Wayne is wearing a black knit cap over his bald head and a denim jacket that does little to bulk up his stick-man frame. There is a coffee in one hand, and a curl of smoke drifts up from the cigarette in the corner of his mouth.

"Sure," Saul says. "I see him."

"What a lot of people don't know," Barb continues. "Is that Wayne is a magician."

"Really," Saul muses. He glances at Eli, who was already chuckling softly behind his hand.

"Oh definitely," she says. "But you have to watch him. Only for a couple of seconds. It usually doesn't take long."

"His trick?"

"Yes, his trick. Now watch." She nudges him. "Or you'll miss it."

Saul turns his attention back to Wayne.

Nothing at the table has changed. Wayne is not doing anything very interesting at all. He is not even involved in the conversation that is going on between his boy and the unknown man. He appears to be just sort of staring off, possibly watching his brother as he flips burgers with the speed and grace of a line cook.

After a few seconds, as Saul is about to ask if there is anything in particular he should be watching for, Wayne's right hand comes up and plucks the cigarette from its perch in the corner of his mouth. Then he centers it in his lips and takes a drag. A very deep, long drag. The cherry at its end blazes a brilliant orange, sending tiny pops of sparks into the air. One second, two… three seconds pass and the brightness of the cherry never falters.

At last, after longer than some people can hold their breath, he pulls the cigarette away from his mouth. Now the coffee comes up and at the same time he is tapping ash onto a tin pie plate, he drains the full cup in two swallows and sets it back down. The cigarette finds its home again in the corner of his mouth.

Saul waits, knowing something else should happen. But nothing does. The moment is over. He turns back to Barb, his eyes wide and astonished. "Where'd it go? The smoke? Where the hell did it go?"

Barb is grinning happily. "That's his trick. It goes in but it doesn't come out. His body absorbs it somehow, like a sponge sucking up water."

"Or he farts it out later," Eli adds and laughs. "That's my theory."

"Eli," Barb snips. "No one needs your profanity, or your theories."

"Sorry Baboo," he says, though it is some time before he is able to stop laughing.

"So, he's just going to spontaneously combust one day," Saul offers. "Burst into a huge ball of coffee and cigarette smoke."

Now Barb is also giggling. "Poof!" she announces, throwing her hands in the air.

"Better him than his brother," Eli says, finally beginning to compose himself again. "Lot less mess to clean up."

"Now I think we're just being mean," Barb says. "Dwayne can't help he was born with big bones."

"Big bones?" Saul echoes. He looks towards the barbeque area just in time to see Dwayne stuff down half a bratwurst hotdog in a single bite. "Indeed."

"The Trappers are both good men," Barb says. "They've done more for this community than anyone else. You can rest assured that either of them would give the shirts off their backs if they were asked."

"If it was for a shelter, I'd sooner have Dwayne's," Eli comments, his white teeth gleaming behind a grin.

"Eli! You just stop it, now. You're being cruel."

"I was just saying matter of factly," Eli replies. "Funny though, you'd never guess to look at him, but Dwayne is easily the richest man between here and Kamloops."

"I'd say between here and Vancouver," Barb adds.

Eli nods. "Owned some big construction company in his old life. Lot of those high-rise buildings in the Vancouver downtown got built with him at the helm."

"Really," Saul states, though he isn't that surprised. Despite his size, Dwayne carried himself like a man who has earned respect. "How'd he end up here?"

"When the Lodge and rental shop came up for sale, he sold his company and bought both properties. And while he was at it, he also bought all the land on the east side of the lake. That's why there ain't no cabins. He don't like neighbors. Campground and the Lodge is all that's on this side."

"That's a big chunk of land."

"You bet it is. Your place is the last cabin at the northern tip. Nothing else between there and the Lodge. A stretch of about six kilometers. Then the campsite starts and runs to the southern tip. All the residences are on the western side of the lake. Dwayne owns the rest."

"Wow," Saul breaths.

Eli nods again. He drains the last of his beer and taps the empty bottle on the table. "Guess I'll see if I can't rummage up another cold one. Saul, *pour vous a vous monsieur?*"

Saul's brow creases. "What was that?"

"It's supposed to be French," Barb sighs. "The more bottles he empties, the more of it you'll hear."

"*Correct'e'vous.* Didn't realize an old small-town boy could be so refined, did'ja now?" Eli says as he stands up. "So what about it? 'Nother of Canada's finest for you…monsieur?"

"Sure, I could do one more. Thanks."

"Good man." Eli smiles at his wife. "And you mademoiselle? Do you require *vous too*?"

Barb raises her half full glass. "I'm fine, my love. Be careful. Don't trip and break a hip."

"Fear not," he proclaims gallantly. "My hips are made of iron and my will is made of stone. I shall *return'e'vous.*" Then he turns and struts off in the direction of the bar.

"That," Barb says, shaking her head slowly. "Is my husband. You just gotta love him."

22

Masked by thickening cloud cover, the setting sun has become no more than a pale-yellow glow that slips through the sky, marching ever closer to its demise behind the peak of Mt. John Oliver in the west. The first delicate snowflakes of the season, virtually invisible in the failing daylight, have begun to float down from the gray heavens. This new dawning of winter, however, remains unnoticed by any of the patrons enjoying themselves on the deck of Deadman Lodge.

With the afternoon quickly changing into evening, Big Dwayne Trapper has at last relinquished his apron and spatula to his oldest son, Matty, with his other boy Danny as second in command, though in reality the eight-year-old is managing little more than annoying his older brother. This allows Dwayne himself the opportunity to start his slow mingle around the patio. And being a firm believer that the funeral is a gathering of the 'rounders, regardless of the number of non-rounders in attendance, he makes a point of choosing Eli and Barb's table as the first stop in his tour. By this time, Sidney and Chloe have also rejoined the little group.

Hauling a chair up to the table, Dwayne drops his massive body onto it without a care. The chair legs groan under the strain, and for a moment everyone cringes, each of them sure the big man is bound for the floor. But somehow, whether a bona fide miracle or simply the magic of quality construction, the chair holds.

They make small talk for a few minutes; *how is everyone? How was the food? Have you gotten enough drink?* And any other surfacey- type banter that seems necessary to begin a conversation.

Once this is out of the way, Big Dwayne says to Saul, "So, how does it feel to be embarking on your first winter as a 'rounder?"

"Good," Saul replies. "I think we're both looking forward to it."

"That's great. I've seen a lot of city folk come up here looking for a lifestyle change. Some are running away from something, others are running towards it. It don't make much difference really. The first winter usually surprises them a bit. So, I like to offer a summary of what to expect over the next six months."

"That would be helpful," Saul says. He glances at his daughter. "Don't you think, Sidney?"

"Sure," she agrees. "A wintery summary. Kinda like a *springy fall*"

A grin curls between Dwayne's round cheeks. "*Winter*-y *summer*-y. I get it. Good one. I'll have to remember that." He smiles at her another moment, presumably locking the phrase away in some mind vault, then finally turns back to Saul. "Anyways, I know you've spent time here in the summer, this year and previous, so you know it can get mighty busy when the sun's shining. The winter has its moments as well. Terravale gets most of the cold traffic. A bulk of their economy happens during the winter months. Snowmobile jocks mostly, but a whole lot of cross-country skiers, climbers, and hunters as well. They all flock to that little town. We get the overflow. By mid-November the Lodge will be to capacity, and both Foley and Cooper B&B's will generally have no problem staying occupied. But the ones staying on the lake are just a tip of the ice burg. The traffic through here can get a little hairy at times. Not that I'm saying winter people are uncourteous, but it's always a good idea to stay alert when you're out and about. Snowmobiles are fast and heavy. If you find yourself in a showdown with one, you will lose."

Saul frowns. "So they just blast around wherever they like? Aren't there trails they should be sticking to?"

"Oh, there's plenty of designated trails," Dwayne says. "Shit, I help groom most of them. But like any activity that involves people, there'll always be those who think they're above the law. Don't have to follow the rules and whatnot. So all I'm saying is to stay alert. It's a helluva lot easier for you to see them than for them to see you."

Everyone nods in agreement.

"Can anyone ride a snowmobile," Sidney asks. "Or do you need a special license?"

Eli says, "That's one of the problems. Anyone who has a machine or can get their hands on one, can ride. No experience necessary. Stick a few novices out there in the snow, bombing around like a bunch of no-minds, then you can have some real trouble."

"That's true," Dwayne agrees. "But I think what you're asking is if *you* can ride one. Am I right?"

Sidney smiles. "I think it would be really cool."

"It is very cool," he says. "Both my boys have been riding since before they could peddle a bike. And Ms. Chloe here, she is also an excellent rider. Safe and confident. Isn't that so, young lady?"

Chloe shrugs shyly. "I guess," she says, her cheeks darkening. "I'm okay."

"Bah, she's just being modest," Eli says. "She's one of the best riders on the lake."

"Yes she is," Dwayne agrees. "And I bet she'd be happy to give you a few pointers. Her family has two Skidoos of their own. Or Wayne would be glad to let you try out one of the rentals. You and your dad should both give it a go."

"I'd love that," Sidney says, her face suddenly glowing. "Wouldn't that be cool, dad?"

"It would. In my younger days I rode my share of dirt bikes. Snowmobiles only once or twice, but it's been years for either. Sounds like a blast, though."

"It's a hoot alright," Dwayne says. "Them machines pack a *shit* load of power. *Pardon my French*, ladies."

"How soon after the first snow would we be able to go riding?" Sidney asks.

"Well, an experienced rider could head out the moment there's padding on the ground. If it's a big dump though, two or three feet, you'd want to wait till some grooming gets done. Checking for drop pockets and avalanche potential, that kind of thing. Of course my priority is getting the roads open, but between me and Wayne and our boys, we usually got things cleaned up within a week. I guess, though, if we're talking about a little harmless ride around this immediate area, that'd be fine within a day or so. Just give the powder enough time to pack down a bit."

"That's awesome," Sidney beams. "So if it starts snowing tonight like they—"

From behind them, a woman's angry voice erupts through the evening air, cutting Sidney's words in mid-sentence. "Are you calling me a liar Wayne Trapper?"

Everyone at Eli's table turns towards this unexpected shout. Across the deck, Wayne is now seated at a different table than earlier, though the ever-present coffee in his hand and cigarette clipped in the corner of his mouth has not changed. A heavy-set woman with gray specks peppering her short black hair is standing over him, her finger raised and waggling only inches from his nose. Rage twitches the muscles of her wrinkled face like an uncontrollable tick.

Saul does not recognize her, though he has a very good idea who she is.

"What's Betty up to now?" Eli wonders aloud, confirming Saul's assumption.

"You think you're just so darn smart!" Betty Abernathy continues, her voice thickened by anger and alcohol. "But you don't know half as much as you think you do!"

Another man, presumably Betty's latest fella, has come up beside her now. He says something and puts his hand on her shoulder. But she immediately shoves him away and growls, "Shut up, Earl!"

"I didn't call you a liar," Wayne says calmly, smirking around his cigarette. "I just said..."

"You said I was full of shit," Betty shot back. "That's as good as callin' me a liar and you know it!"

At Eli's table, Dwayne stands up and says, "Excuse me for just a minute. I'll see if I can't defuse this. Wayne's never been very good at holding his damn tongue."

"Would you like me to talk to her?" Barb asks.

He shakes his head. "Naw. This ain't the first time these two been at each other. I'll put an end to it easy enough. You just stay here. All of you, enjoy your drinks and I'll be right back."

In the fifteen seconds it takes Dwayne to walk across the deck, Betty's voice continues to get progressively louder. Her eyes are bulging and bloodshot behind her horn-rimmed glass as each angry word seems to vibrate through her entire body. "Just because you don't have the brains enough to see what's right in front of your darn face, you turn your nose up and call it shit!"

"I didn't call it shit," Wayne says. "I said you were full..."

"Dammit, Wayne," his brother snaps as he comes up on the quarreling pair. "You need to learn when to just smile and nod, I swear to God."

Dwayne's massive presence has always demanded attention, and it was a rare situation when any was taken away from him. This particular situation is definitely not one of those, as even Betty becomes silent, turning her angry eyes to him. "The funeral is a time for people to enjoy themselves," He continues. "And right now neither of you are helping anyone do that. What's the issue here, Betty? What's upsetting you?"

"He come up to me," Betty says, pointing a shaky finger at Wayne. "I didn't ask him to, but he did. Start askin' me questions and whatnot."

"I was making my rounds," Wayne says to Dwayne. "Just like you. Came over to see how the old duck has been holding up, that's all. Made the mistake of asking how she was, you know, just friendly like. Well she goes off, spouting all this doom and gloom crap. End of the world nonsense that nobody wants to hear. So I'm just trying to quiet her down, that's it."

"He said I was full of shit," Betty cries, her voice beginning to rise again. "Cause he's too darn ignorant to see what I'm sayin' is the truth, he says it's shit! Well it ain't shit you damn skinny runt…"

"Now let's cut out the name callin', Betty," Dwayne says. He puts his hand on her shoulder. Unlike her fella's attempt, she allows it to stay for the moment. "We're just gonna sit back down here and you can tell me what you were trying to tell Wayne. Everyone knows I ain't ignorant. So I'll decide what's shit and what ain't. What do you say?" As he talks, he is guiding her back to her chair.

"Don't care if people think what I say is shit," Betty goes on. "I know what's the truth. The spirits talk to me. They tell me stuff, and ain't none of it shit."

"Everything you say…" Wayne begins, but stops suddenly. His brother is staring at him with an expression he knows very well. It is one he had seen all too often when they'd been kids. Back then he had learned to fear it because usually it was followed by a good beat down. Of course, they weren't kids anymore and Dwayne had stopped giving his brother beat downs many years ago, but it is still a look that Wayne understands. It means, in no uncertain terms, *don't fuck with me right now.* So, instead of continuing to speak, he turns his eyes to the ground and takes a long pull off his cigarette.

Dwayne gets Betty seated again, then pulls up a chair and sits himself down beside her. Her fella—Dwayne knows his name is Earl Hodgson because he insists on knowing *everyone* who is making Deadman their home, regardless of how temporary it may be—wanders around the table and plops into a chair across from her. He tries to take her hand, but for the second time she shakes him away.

All around the deck, most conversations have dropped to mere whispers, and many interested eyes are now locked on this new and potentially fascinating development.

"Okay, Betty," Dwayne says, lacing his sausage-sized fingers together over his enormous gut. "What have the spirits been saying?"

After a supercilious glance at Wayne, she says, "There's something coming, Dwayne. From the sky."

"Sure," Dwayne agrees. "You don't need spirits to tell you that. Weatherman's been saying all week that tonight could bring the first snowstorm. Little early this year, but nothing to get in a tizzy over?"

"I ain't talkin' about the darn snow," She snaps at him. "It's what's comin' with the snow, that's what I'm talkin' about."

"And what might that be, Betty?"

"A judgment. The spirits will cast down from the sky a judgment on every one of us. It will be a stark presence against the white snow. Seeking each of us out so it can peer into the deepest parts of our soul. If it finds sin there, harbored inside your heart, then you will be judged as unworthy of this paradise and banished to the black world of the damned. Trapped there forever, where only pain and sorrow dwell."

Dwayne's brow creases. He looks at his brother again, but this time his expression is rueful. "Told yah," Wayne says and drops his cigarette butt into an random beer can.

"Yes, well that is an interesting story, Betty," Dwayne says. "But if what I remember is correct, and I will give you it's been some time since bible class in the basement of St. Jude the Baptist, don't we all live with sin? Wasn't that the point of the Holy Son and all that what not?"

"Then we're all in danger," Betty says. "For no sin will go unpunished. Each of us is bound for the blackness."

"Well jeez louweez, that's not very uplifting is it? And it sure ain't the kind of talk we need at the funeral, despite what the name may imply. It's the sort of talk that should be kept behind closed doors, don't you think?"

"Everyone needs to be warned," Betty says, her voice rising. She twists around in her chair so she can gaze at each group of people, from one to the next. "It has been shown to me by the spirits so I can warn each of you. This judgment is coming. It comes from the sky, floating down on top of us with the snow. No one can run from it or hide from it. Your only hope is to cleanse yourselves before the spirits. Wash away your—"

"Okay, that's enough," Dwayne says. He stands up and points at Betty's fella. "It's time for old Earl here to take you home. You two can feel free to continue this discussion inside your cabin, but there'll be no more talk of it here. I'm sure we've all heard plenty."

"I'm telling the truth," Betty cries again. *"The spirits showed me…"*

"I'm sure they did," Dwayne says, taking her by the arm. "But as I said, there's a time and a place for talk like that, but this is not it. Maybe we can revisit the topic once you see that nothing is falling from the sky but snow. Now here, let me help you up."

She jerks her arm away. "I don't need your darn help. I am perfectly capable of standing without your fat hands pawing all over me."

Dwayne steps back. "Then be my guest. Up and at'em. Earl's just itchin' to get you home."

Earl is beside Betty as she gets to her feet. This time however, he doesn't bother trying to take her arm. "Come on Betty. The quad's parked just over there."

"I know where the quad is parked you darn oaf." Then she turns back to Dwayne again. "You'll be seein'. Every darn one of yah. The spirits never lie. And when you're cryin' and beggin' for forgiveness, you won't be findin' any from me. No sir. You're all headin' for the dark, mark my words."

"Earl," Dwayne says, struggling now to keep his voice calm. "You need to get her home. My patience is runnin' as thin as a thread."

"Come on, Betty," Earl pleads with her. "Let's go home."

"I'm comin'," she barks. "I ain't one to stay someplace I ain't welcome." Then she plucks a half full beer can off the table. It just happens to be the same one Wayne pitched his butt into. "And I'm taking this with me. There ain't a darn thing you can do about it."

"Good night, Betty," Dwayne says.

Betty grunts something inaudible before finally wandering off, with Earl nipping at her heels.

"She's full-on nuts," Wayne says as they watch the pair climb onto Betty's quad. "That's what I think."

"And you always seem to be the one that's pointing it out to her," Dwayne says. "I'd think by now you'd have brains enough to stay the hell away from her."

"She started in on me," he counters defensively.

"This ain't a goddamn schoolyard and we ain't kids. Last time I checked you were forty-nine years old. Let's try to act it from now on."

"Well, last time I checked you weren't my goddamn daddy," Wayne shouts. "So stop actin' like you are." Then he also stands up and storms away, leaving a curl of cigarette smoke in his wake.

23

"That was interesting," Barb says as Dwayne returns to their table. "Quite the fanciful yarn she was weaving."

"Yeah, well you know how she can be once she gets into her cups. And Wayne's a fine enough fella, but for some reason he enjoys getting her all fired up. The two shouldn't be allowed in the same goddamn room. 'Scuse my French ladies."

"So is that a normal occurrence," Saul asks.

"Wouldn't say normal," Dwayne says. "But they've been at each other before."

"Actually, I mean the things she was saying," Saul says. "Her premonitions?"

"Oh. I guess she's had them before. Thankfully she don't socialize a whole lot, so generally she keeps them pretty much to herself. When she is out and about, though, there's usually something leaking past her lips. Not many pay her any mind though."

"What about Kenny Ferguson?" Saul asks.

Dwayne shoots a look at Eli before answering. "He don't pay her any more mind than the next person I guess. The things she told him was her just speculating. Pure coincidental situation, that's it. And Kenny'd tell you the same exact thing."

"Yeah, that's what Eli said. Does seem a pretty big coincidence though. The tree falling like that. Crushing his blind."

"S'pose," Dwayne admits reluctantly. "But that's usually what coincidences are. *They're big*. Otherwise they wouldn't catch your attention enough to be called anything at all."

Saul shrugs. "Tough to argue with that."

"What's this about, Saul," Barb asks him. "Do you believe her? That something is going to come out of the sky other than snow? Something that will send us all to hell?"

Saul can see Sidney watching him. Her blue eyes are wide and apprehensive. He says, "No, of course not. I'm just curious about her. Where these premonitions come from."

"I think she had a few too many pulls off the old peace pipe in her younger years," Eli says. "That's what I think. Done some kind of damage to her brain."

"That's what you would think, Eli," Barb snaps, suddenly furious with him. "Just because she has some indigenous heritage, then surely she must be smoking drugs through a peace pipe. How typical."

"I was just sayin,'" Eli says, his tone lower and embarrassed. "Didn't mean nothing by it."

"Betty is an oddity," Dwayne says, allowing Barb a moment to continue glaring at her husband. "Pure and simple. She has dreams, just like any of us, except for one reason or another, she takes hers as being messages from the Gods, or spirits, or whatever the heck it is she calls them. Most of the time she keeps these messages to herself. But occasionally, usually when she's been into her cups, she shares them with others. Does that make it any more of a premonition than the dream I had last night? No it don't. If I told you a leprechaun was going to slide down your chimney tonight and leave a basket of chocolate-covered dog turds on your kitchen table, would you take it as the truth just because it's something I dreamt? No, I certainly hope you wouldn't. So, let's not make this anything more than it is. The old bird is an oddity."

"Well said, Dwayne," Barb agrees.

Saul is also nodding. "Okay, I get that. And I agree. Unless I wake up in the morning and find a basket of turd treats in my kitchen, then it becomes a whole different thing."

"But you won't," Dwayne says. "Any more than some great judge is going to rain fire and brimstone down on us all."

"Speaking of things from above," Eli says, pointing towards the trees beyond the covered deck.

They all look in the direction of his finger. Large, puffy flakes of snow are drifting out of the darkening sky. At this point, they are few and will disappear the moment they touched the ground, but it is the beginning.

"It's snowing," Sidney says, her voice high and cheery.

"Yes it is," Dwayne grunts as he lumbers to his feet. "Guess I best get on with my socializing before people start taking to the road." He extends his hand to Saul. "If there's anything you need, or have any other questions, don't hesitate to drop by. The door is never locked."

"Thank you," Saul says, watching with some amazement as his normal sized hand is practically engulfed by Dwayne's huge one. The man's grip, however, is surprisingly gentle. "I'm sure we'll be seeing plenty of each other then."

"Good. And you, young lady," He continues, smiling at Sidney. "You take it easy on the hills now. And never ride alone."

"I won't," Sidney promises. "Thanks for all your advice."

"Advice and cholesterol," he says. "I got plenty of both." Then he says his goodbyes to the rest of the group and wanders off to the next table.

"Well," Saul says, picking up his beer. He gazes out at the trees that are now no more than shadows in the dimming twilight. "Looks like there's one premonition that's going to come true."

From the deep gray sky, the snow is falling faster.

24

Northbound- Early the Next Morning

Pete Collingwood glances down at his watch. It is 1:57am. Which means they have been in flight for fifty-seven minutes. If all things go as planned, they would be touching down at North Peace Regional Airport in Fort St. John in approximately one and three-quarter hours. But, as he struggles with the controls of Treager Enterprises' Embraer jetliner, Pete has the sickening feeling that things are not going to continue as planned.

At just thirty years old, Pete is at the youngest end of the jetliner pilot spectrum. His father's career as a pilot with TWA had spanned over thirty-five years, and in all that time he'd never had a single in-flight incident. Pete had grown up in awe of his dad. Since he was old enough to understand what airplanes were, he'd dreamt of flying. The freedom it gave, to go anywhere. Nothing capable of standing in your way. Not water or mountains or valleys. At the controls of an aircraft, there was nowhere out of reach. So he had worked hard, single-mindedly following his dream. At eighteen he'd gotten his first private pilot certificate. Then his multi-engine rating at twenty. And just a week after his twenty-second birthday, he passed his CPT, which awarded his Commercial Pilots license. He spent one year getting his CFI and another two as a flight instructor. Oddly, many of the people he taught during that time had more flight experience than he did. Then, just three years ago, he finally achieved the fifteen-hundred hours of flight time requirements and was granted his Airline Transport Pilot Certificate. Pete can still recall, so vividly it may have happened yesterday, the look of unwavering pride in his father's face when his only son walked through the front door wearing his own Air Canada pilot uniform. That day had been one of the happiest of Pete Collingwood's life

Now, staring through the Embraer's windshield into the spiraling white snow, and with a young punk kid sitting to his right who is, so far, failing miserably at pretending he knows what the fuck was going on, Pete wonders how everything could have gone so wrong so quickly. It seems impossible that in only three years his life has taken such a massive nosedive. From a commercial pilot with one of the largest, most prestigious airlines in the world, to working for an asshole who insists on flying through what is rapidly becoming one of the worst snowstorms Pete has ever seen.

Unfortunately, the answer to this question is, in fact, quite a simple one. He'd made several bad decisions in a very short period of time.

The first had been leaving Roosters Bar in Vancouver one night and deciding he was alright to drive himself home, despite the five beers and two shots of tequila that had found their way down his throat. That bad decision had resulted in a three-month driving suspension, and the first red flag against his pilot's license. The next was about a month later. Running late for a flight to Calgary out of YVR, he'd decided it would be better to risk driving than missing the job. Really, what were the odds he would get pulled over the one time in three months he chanced getting behind the wheel.

Apparently, they were very good. This bad decision lost him his driver's license for an additional three years, and another, much larger, red flag with the CFPA.

Finally, there was Lloyd Gustovson. A sixty-year-old paper and office supply salesman from Richmond BC. Heading home after a weekend sales seminar in Portland, Oregon, he boarded flight 377 from PDX Portland non-stop to YVR in Vancouver. The co-pilot working this particular flight was none other than Pete—*two strikes*—Collingwood.

About twenty minutes into the sixty-five-minute flight time, Mr. Gustovson began acting peculiar. He ask the attendant for a glass of water, but when she brought it he told her that he didn't want it. Then another five minutes later he asked for water again. Being a patient and professional attendant, she brought it to him. But once more he said he did not require it. So she took it away. When, a few minutes later, he asked a third time, she said no. She told him as politely as possible that she didn't know what game he was playing, but she would no longer play along.

Mr. Gustovson instantly became enraged. He began shouting profanities at the young lady. Hoping to defuse the situation, the stewardess chose to ignore him and returned to the hostess station. But he immediately left his seat and followed her, continuing to yell and threaten her. Several passengers confirmed that he said more than once, *I will get the damn water myself so I can throw it in your bitchy face.*

It was at this point that Co-pilot Pete Collingwood exited the flight cabin in response to raised voices. After checking the cabin door was locked and secure, he went straight to the hostess station where he encountered a very angry Mr. Gustovson and the frightened attendant. Collingwood placed a hand on the man's shoulder in an effort to calm him and begin moving him back to his seat. But instead, Gustovson spun around and lunged towards the co-pilot, continuing to shout irrationally. Surprised by the sudden attack, Collingwood shoved him backward, possibly using more strength than he had intended. Sixty-year-old Gustovson stumbled out of the station and into the aisle where he fell, striking his head on the lower bracket of passenger seat 43B. He was immediately rendered unconscious, and blood began to pour out of his torn scalp.

This was exactly how it had been laid out during the hearing, and how it continued to play in Pete's mind. Point by point, over and over again. The same old story.

The old man had been okay, of course. There'd been a doctor on board—*ironically, sitting in the exact seat that had split Gustovson's head open*—and he was able to get the bleeding stopped and Lloyd stabilized. The plane was diverted to Seattle International where it made an emergency landing. The flight attendant, whose name was Mary-Ann Jackson, had thanked Pete numerous times. She even went so far as to call him her hero. This had made him feel pretty good at the time.

But only for a while. Mr. Lloyd Gustovson, as it turned out, was an important member of his community, running numerous charities and fundraisers through his parish at St. Gregory Ukraine Apostolic Church. He was also a regular volunteer at the New World Homeless shelter in New Westminster.

But this was post 9/11 and none of these things would have mattered. Even if it had been the Holy Pope himself that had freaked out on that airplane, he would have found himself up a creek of blessed water without his fancy hat.

Once again however, the evil, unfair fate known as *chance* ripped a nasty hole in what should have been a cut and dry situation.

While in the hospital being treated for his head injury, doctors discover that Gustovson was suffering from the early stages of Alzheimer's disease. Though the beginning symptoms of the disease were generally minor, they could be further agitated by mental stresses such as anxiety or claustrophobia. These symptoms can include temporary memory loss, and erratic, sometimes aggressive behavior.

Mr. Gustovson's lawyers fell on this new information like a school of frenzied piranhas.

They filed a class-action lawsuit against Air Canada, citing unfair treatment of a senior resulting in bodily harm. They claimed that if the correct procedure had been followed, which would have allowed the passenger time to calm down, then the entire situation could have been defused without the need for physical contact. Only a few moments of investigative conversation on the part of Mary-Ann and Pete could have quickly shown them that Gustovson was suffering from mental distress due to undiagnosed difficulties. As employees of the airline, they were obligated to help the passengers remain calm, using physical contact as only the final step in the most extreme altercations.

It was all bullshit, and everyone knew it, but then to make an already bad situation even worse, Air Canada back-peddled in an attempt to cover their own asses. They unmercifully threw Pete to the snapping piranhas by stating that when he left the cock pit during what had been a potential security breach, he was in violation of strict in-flight protocol. This claim, along with the two red flags already hanging over his head, got him not only fired from Air Canada, but also thrown out of the CFPA pilots union. So now, despite the fact that he had not lost his pilot's certificate, there is not a single airline outside of Guatemala that will hire him. Or in other words, *his career is over.*

Well, maybe not quite over yet. Good old Ben Treager has seen to that. He'd made Pete an offer he couldn't refuse. Personal Pilot of Treager Enterprises. Sounded impressive enough at the time and the money is great, but Pete should have been leery when Treager told him that some flights might require a little stealth, flying under the radar type stuff.

But Hey, Treager had said as he handed Pete a thick envelope of cash. *By the looks of your record, this kind of thing should be right up your flight path.*

If Pete had known this *flight path* would involve transporting an illegal endangered species across the mountainous terrain of northern British Columbia in the middle of a snowstorm, he would have told Treager exactly where he could stick that envelope.

"I can't see a goddamn thing," Pete's co-pilot says, leaning forward and squinting his eyes. Beyond the windshield, snow twists and swirls, churning in a wind that howls loud enough to be heard even in the cockpit.

Pete glances at him. His name is Gavin...*someone or another,* and with the squinty expression he has on his face at this moment, Pete cannot believe he had just thought of him as *co-pilot.* The better term would have been, *the guy with the stupid looking face that is currently stealing my oxygen.*

"There's nothing to see," he tells him. "Just keep your eyes on the gauges. We're getting blown around pretty bad and I want to know if we veer off course."

"Yeah, sure," Gavin says. "Gotcha." He stares down at the console as if it is something very new to him. Surprisingly, however, after only a second or two he begins relaying the required information. "Looks like 53.584001 by -121.852630, traveling 357 degrees northeast, with flight speed…" he taps a gauge with his finger. "Four hundred seventy-seven knots."

"Shit," Pete murmurs. They are already off course. About fifty kilometers east, give or take. But at this point there is very little he can do about it. Trying to make any strong corrections right now would be suicide. The heavy snow and wind were already putting a massive amount of strain on the wings. If he was to start cracking the ailerons to correct their eastern slide, the starboard wing could, quite literally, snap right off. Then they would have a hell of a lot more problems than a paltry fifty kms off course.

A massive gust of wind suddenly slams against the plane. It lurches sideways, then drops with the gut-wrenching force of a roller coaster. "Son of a bitch," Pete bellows, thumbing off the auto pilot. He yanks back on the yoke, attempting to level off the plane. But just as the nose is coming up, another gust pounds into their side, rocking the plane like it was made of balsa wood. The wheel jerks to the right, folding one of Pete's fingers back painfully as it tears free of his grip. "Ow, shit!" he cries out. Grappling with the yoke, he shouts at Gavin, who is sitting slack-jawed, still staring at the control panel. "Grab your goddamn wheel and help me control this pig."

Gavin glances at him, his eyes bulging. "Yeah, yeah," he says and grabs the control with both hands. "Okay, I got it, what… what now?"

Great! Pete thinks miserably. *The very question every pilot wants to hear from his co-pilot.* "Don't jerk it," he tells Gavin. "Smoothly, and with me, we're going to port the wheel."

"Port the…?" Gavin echoes. His voice is high-pitched and scared.

"Turn it counterclockwise, to the left. We've got to straighten out. And as we turn, pull back gently so the nose stays up. Only slightly though. Too much and we'll flounder."

"Okay, sure."

Slowly they start the turn. The yokes vibrate in their grip as turbulence continues to pummel the exterior of the aircraft. At first, even with the assistance of hydraulics, the wheel will not move. "Come on, come on," Pete whispers, gripping the handles of the yoke so tightly his knuckles are whitening noticeably. Finally it begins to move, stiff and sluggish. With his heart galloping in his chest, Pete's eyes lock onto the turn coordinator, watching for any movement. The gauge twitches. Once. Twice. Then another. At last it starts a continuous, though glacially slow, creep towards the left. Gradually the path begins to straighten out.

"Okay, that's looking good," he says, exhaling a deep, relieved breath. "Now I want the nose up a bit more. Pull back, gently. Good, that's got it. Level off now."

"Holy shit," Gavin groans. "I've never felt turbulence like that before."

I'm sure the only turbulence you've ever felt, Pete thinks as he reengages the autopilot, *is the vibrating bed at Hon's Hotel of Hot Love.* But to Gavin he says, "Well, don't get too comfortable." In front of him, beyond the wrap of three-inch-thick safety glass, the storm that has bounced them around like a bird in a wind tunnel is just getting started. "I guarantee you we're not out of the woods yet."

25

"Shouldn't you go up and make sure everything is okay?" Morgan says, clutching Ben Treager's arm tight enough to cut off the blood circulation.

Ben looks at her. The terror on her face is as pure and obvious as a Halloween mask. Her green eyes are glazed, and she is blinking too much. He wants to say something reassuring to her, like *everything will be fine* or *it's just a little wind,* but at the moment he can't seem to do it. So instead he says, "What good would that do? I'm not a pilot. Even if there was something wrong, what am I going to do about it?"

They are sitting side by side, belted into leather seats in the forward compartment of Treager's jet. Behind them, the rear passenger cabin of the plane and the luggage compartment have been partitioned off and retro-fitted to receive the *Mother's Womb,* where the tiger continues its slumber. Bronson Collique and the veterinarian are also stationed in this specially constructed hold, which is now equipped with safe but far less comfortable bumper seats. They are keeping watch over the prize with the same vigil attentiveness as the Royal Guard at Buckingham Palace.

In the front of the plane, behind the closed door of the cockpit, Pete Collingwood has just turned the autopilot back on after a very close call.

This leaves Ben and Morgan alone in the main cabin. Morgan is seated next to a portal window, though she has slid the blind down with the complaint that looking out into the swirling snow was making her feel nauseous.

Compared to what they had just gone through a few moments earlier, the turbulence they are feeling now is minor. Some bumping and knocking, as though they were driving down a gravel road in a car lacking any form of suspension. But Ben knows without a doubt this is only a brief calm before the real storm begins. He can hear the wind howling around them, and he'd seen how heavily the snow was coming down before Morgan closed the shade.

Ben, however, is not afraid. He had learned a long time ago to keep such childish emotions at bay, relying instead on more sensible attributes such as common sense and rational thought. They will make it through to Fort St. John because the odds dictated it to be true. Of some 36 million flights that take off around the world every year, all but eighty make it to their destination without incident. This means that the odds of a plane crashing are less than one in 2.5 million.

Factoring in the rather precarious circumstances of this particular flight, such as the lack of external radar and trajectory assistance, crew experience and current weather conditions, their odds may plummet to half that. Still substantially better than the chance of being hit by lightning in any given year. Ben wasn't always a play the odds type of guy, but in this situation, those odds just couldn't be disputed.

Not that he is denying it has been, and would continue to be a rough flight. The weather change was like nothing he'd ever seen before. Take-off conditions in Kamloops had been overcast with a mild easterly wind. Yet within half an hour, they found themselves battling through a full-scale blizzard.

Typical. The one time you want the weatherman to be wrong.

Another blast of wind jostles the aircraft, and Morgan's death grip on Ben's arm tightens painfully. She isn't just afraid, she is terrified. He can feel the fear radiating off of her in waves of heat. Her eyes are locked onto the door leading to the main cockpit, as though she expects at any moment it will burst open, and the pilot will run out screaming *the plane is going down and everyone is doomed*—something that will never happen of course. *Any experienced pilot will simply announce it over the intercom.*

Ben had thought it was a bad idea for her to come along on this part of the journey. He had tried several times to convince her to fly back to Seattle instead. Her refusal had been single-minded and stubborn. She was coming and there was nothing he could do to stop her. So, against better judgment, he finally gave in. Now here she is, terrified and strangling the life out of his arm. He'd been silently hoping she would find a way to overcome her fear, as he had. But he has quickly realized that this is not going to happen. So again going against his better judgment, he says to her, "This is a good plane, Morgan. And we've got an excellent pilot. One of the best. You've got nothing to worry about."

She looks at him, trying to smile, but her fear makes it look more like a scowl, so she gives up. "Is he? Is he really a good pilot?"

"Really," Ben nods. "He's one of the youngest commercial jet pilots to ever work for Air Canada." And this is the truth. Except that Ben holds back the fact that he'd only flown for them one year before being fired and drummed out of the pilot's union. "He's a natural."

"The way you talked to him on the phone," Morgan says. "I got the feeling you didn't like him much."

"I like him fine. That was just business, you know."

"How long till we can land?" she asks hopefully. "It feels like we've been in the air for hours."

If by *hours* she means *one* then she is bang on. "We're about halfway," he says. "Maybe another hour. Then we land in Fort St. John, and we've got twenty-four hours to relax before the helicopter takes us to the compound. And then the excitement really starts."

"Is it okay back there?" she asks, glancing over her shoulder towards the rear of the plane. "The tiger I mean. It must be getting bounced around pretty bad."

"Not at all. That is one comfy kitty. In the harness system, its body is more or less suspended in mid-air, totally protected from bumps and bruises. I promise you, old Barney is a hell of a lot more uncomfortable than our prize."

"Do you think he—"

Without any warning the aircraft lurches into a steep upwards climb, cutting off Morgan's words and pulling them both back into their seats with savage force. Around them, the plane begins to rattle violently, its cylindrical body groaning under the unexpected strain. Ben feels an enormous pressure shoving down on his chest, making each pull of breath a painful labor. For a split second he is able to imagine this must be similar to the feeling astronauts experience at the moment the rockets fire and they are blasted into space.

He tries to turn his head but is unable. Even over the noise as everything inside the cabin crashes and thumps, he can hear Morgan's breath. It sounds rapid and haggard, as though she were hyperventilating. She is still clutching his arm, digging her fingernails into his flesh. Outside the window next to her, the jet engine mounted below the wing is screaming. It is a sound he recognizes from countless action movies. The high-pitched wails of full throttle.

Oxygen masks are released from above them and one drops down, dangling in front of his face like a spider dancing at the end of its web. It is a stark and grisly symbol of how perilous the situation has suddenly become.

Are they still climbing? It is impossible to tell. The intense turbulence that is pummeling the aircraft has not eased at all and they are being knocked around like a couple of boxers, but the pressure on his chest has let up slightly. "M…M…Mor…gan!" he shouts, his voice vibrating as though someone had him by the throat and was rattling the hell out of his vocal cords. "Are…Y…You…Okay?"

With great strain, he is finally able to turn his head. Morgan is there, her upper body sunk into the seat back. Her eyes are squeezed shut and her lips have peeled away from her clenched teeth. Her skin is extremely pale, almost white, giving her face a skull-like resemblance. "Mor…gan!" he shouts again, but she shows no signs of hearing him.

The jet engine is getting increasingly louder and louder. Screeching. Just as Ben had told Morgan only moments ago, he is not a pilot, yet he knows without any doubt this whaling noise he is hearing now is very bad. Even at the best of times, the engines should never to be worked this hard. And in this weather…*Christ!* Ben has no idea what Pete is up to in that cockpit, but if he doesn't throttle back soon, it is going to…

As if confirming Ben's thoughts, there is a huge WHUMP! sound outside the window beside Morgan. Then, barely a second later, an even louder explosion. In that instant, it is like a vengeful giant has reached into the sky and smacked the plane, knocking it sideways with mind-scrambling force. Despite the safety restraints, they are both thrown to the left, Ben slams into Morgan, and Morgan slams into the inside wall of the plane. Her head impacts with the steel edge of the portal, splitting the thin skin just above her temple. A burst of blood splashes across the white window shade. Immediately her entire body goes limp. She slumps over, her head bouncing freely on top of her neck, knocking against the wall again and again.

With her unconsciousness, Ben's arm is released from her grip. He reaches for her, his hand vibrating so badly it takes him several tries before he can get a good hold on the sleeve of her blouse. First he pulls her towards him, then pushes her upper body into her lap as he folds himself over as well. In his mind, three words flash in bright neon; *BRACE FOR IMPACT.*

He turns his head, laying his cheek against his knees. Blood is running from Morgan's wounded head, dripping off her brow, painting the tan carpet floor a bright crimson. *When this is over,*

Ben thinks, trying to keep her body as steady as he can, *she is going to have one whopper of a headache.* When this is over—

"Hang on," he whispers to her and closes his eyes. "It'll all be over soon."

26

Through a haze of churning snow, the shadow of the mountain is just beginning to materialize in front of Pete Collingwood's eyes. Figuring in their current airspeed and rate of drop, he expects the belly of the plane will be skimming across treetops in approximately thirty seconds. This means that in forty-five seconds, they will most likely be dead. It is a fate he has no problem accepting, as he's always assumed he would die at the controls of an airplane. But in his mind's version, the circumstances leading to the crash would be the fault of someone else, not his own. A mechanic who fails to tighten a critical bolt to the proper torque, or the on-position air traffic controller giving him bad coordinates as he glides a fully loaded 727 in for a landing at LAX. Seized ailerons, a flock of geese, a group of hijackers armed with box cutters. Or simply an unexplainable act of God. *Anything but his own goddamn stupidity.*

Moments after they had won their first battle against the pounding storm, and Pete had reengaged the autopilot, he'd asked Gavin the co-pilot to continue his assessment of the flight controls.

Gavin begins calling out the information in a voice that was still rattled and nervous. Position, flight speed, fuel levels, cabin pressure, altitude…

"Wait," Pete says, his mouth suddenly becoming very dry. "Read off that altitude again."

Gavin repeats the number.

"That can't be right," Pete says, looking at the panel himself. But, to his horror, the altimeter confirms his co-pilots reading. *8100 feet.*

Even traveling under the radar, as they are, they should be flying at no lower than 22000 feet. 24000 to be on the safe side. And they had been. He is sure of it. He had seen the numbers with his own eyes. But then the turbulence had rocked them, and he'd become preoccupied with controlling the aircraft. He was aware they had gone down some, but that much, so quickly? It isn't possible.

He glances at the attitude indicator. It shows them level, perhaps up a few degrees. He looks again at the altimeter. 8089 feet. *They are still dropping.*

"What the fuck," Pete says. He reaches out and taps the glass face of the AI. The line of horizon drops suddenly to thirty degrees below level, then it jumps back up to thirty degrees above for a second before leveling off again. "Oh shit," he groans. Somehow, during the severe pounding the airplane was taking, the attitude indicator must have been badly jarred, causing the vacuum pump to fail. If this had been a normal flight, with a decent co-pilot and control tower assistances, the malfunctioning gauge would have never gone unnoticed. Adjustments would have been made, the dropping altitude corrected. But this is no ordinary flight. It has been…

On the console, a proximity warning light begins to flash, strobing bright red in the dimly lit cabin. It is accompanied by a high-pitched buzzing, similar to the terrified scream of a woman.

"What's happening?" Gavin asks, his eyes locked on Pete. They are the size of silver dollars, glazed with fear. "Wh...what's that light mean?"

"Shut the fuck up," Pete screams, his heart hammering painfully in his chest. Panic races through his blood stream like a galloping stallion, slamming into his brain with force enough to eject any rational thought.

Then he does the only thing he can think of. He flicks off the auto-pilot and pulls back on the yoke as hard as he can, dragging the nose of the jet upwards into a sudden, steep climb. The entire body of the plane immediately begins to rumble under the strain, the yoke shaking in his hands with the power of a concrete vibrator. "Push forward on the throttle," he shouts at Gavin. "We need more power!"

But for a moment, Gavin doesn't move. His eyes are still fixed on Pete, his jaw slack, bouncing open and closed in perfect rhythm with the rattling aircraft.

"Grab the fucking throttle," Pete yells again.

Gavin blinks several times as though he is trying to adjust his eyes to a bright light, then he nods. He closes his hand around the throttle and starts pushing. "How far?"

"All the way," Pete tells him. "We need to get this bird up!"

"But won't that put too much strain on the engines?"

So now you're a fucking expert! Pete thinks. *Where were you when the goddamn plane was falling out of the sky?* "Just do it for

Christ's sake or we're gonna slam into the side of a mountain! Full throttle!"

Gavin shoves the controls all the way forward. The engines roar in protest as the plane hurtles through the air, driving Pete's head back hard enough to strain his neck. Through the windshield, past the back-and-forth clunk of the wipers, there is nothing to see but a blur of white. So instead of looking there, Pete watches the altimeter.

8300 feet. Then 8400. 8450. Steadily climbing. 8600 feet. Higher and higher. But is it fast enough? The red proximity light continues to flash. 8700 feet. The engines scream behind them, shaking the aircraft even harder than the turbulence. 8900. *Shit*, Pete's frantic thoughts bellow inside his head, *why is that damn light still flashing!* 9000 feet. They won't be able to hold this rate of climb much longer. The engines just aren't going to take it…9100 feet…

The proximity light stops flashing, mercifully taking the mind-numbing buzz with it.

Thank God, thank God. Easing off the yoke just a bit, Pete says to Gavin, "Okay, start bringing the throttle back…"

That is when the port-side jet engine explodes.

27

It is impossible to know exactly why the engine blew up. It could have been the strain of full-throttle or the pressure of the steep climb. It could also have been the heavy snow or the ice from the thick cloud cover being sucked into the intake, freezing up the turbine. Or any other foreign debris such as an unfortunate lone goose that had lost its flock in the storm. It may have been a combination of factors.

But now, as Pete stares through the windshield, watching the jagged outline of trees beginning to take shape, he supposes it really doesn't matter. The end result will still be the same, regardless of the technical reasoning. They are going to crash, and it is his fault. As the lead pilot of the aircraft, it is his sole responsibility to keep the plane and its passengers safe. He should have noticed the dropping altitude, the malfunctioning attitude indicator. He should have known how much pressure the engines could take. And most importantly, he should never have allowed the take off in the first place. He let himself be manipulated by Ben Treager, bullied into flying when every nerve ending in his body warned him against it. He had feared the damage Treager could do to his career, when in fact there wasn't much left to damage thanks to Pete's own actions. Now they are all going to pay the ultimate price.

After the engine exploded, Pete had immediately locked it off and cut the fuel. The plane had reached an altitude of just under ninety-two hundred feet when the engine went. The powerful burst knocked them to the right and up another fifty feet. With turbulence continuing to pound the aircraft, Pete begins making the necessary control adjustments for single engine flight. Then the starboard engine stalls. On the console, orange lights flash warning of the failure, as if the pilot wouldn't have known otherwise. Pete tried repeatedly to restart the engine, but to no avail. The longer it goes without running, generating the heat necessary to prevent ice buildup, the more likely it becomes the turbines will freeze solid inside the manifold, permanently incapacitating the engine.

After several more minutes of trying to get the engine running ends in failure, their altitude begins to drop again. Feeling frustrated and alone (Gavin is attempting to assist, but his fear and discernable lack of knowledge are rendering him next to useless), Pete at last resigns himself to the fact he is going to have to attempt a landing. Luckily—*a strange word given the circumstances*—the port side wing has not been badly damaged by the explosion, so Pete is afforded some glide control. But visibility is less than two hundred meters, meaning even though he can control the plane, he won't know the best place to try and land it until they are only seconds from impact.

With both engines down, all mechanics of the aircraft are now running off of battery power. Console functions are minimalized to only the now useless attitude indicator, air and vertical speed indicators, altitude, and a few other vital gauges. To lower the landing gear—*which will be more in effort to slow their descent than actually imagining they would be landing on the wheels*—he has to do it manually. With the assistance of his co-pilot they are able to accomplish this, and Pete also trims the flaps to twenty degrees which should cause even further drag.

But as the ground slowly becomes visible through the snow, emerging from the gloom like a specter stepping out of a foggy night, Pete quickly realizes the impossibility of what he is about to attempt. Below them, for as far as the limited visibility will allow, all Pete can see is the tops of snow-covered trees. No fields, or lakes or even rock faces. Only dense, white forest.

Beside him, Gavin groans. "We're going to die," he says. Oddly, his tone is no longer frightened. The words come out as though he is merely commenting on a news article he'd read in the morning paper. "Now who's going to feed my cat?"

Again Pete feels the weight of what is happening. It is his fault, and there is nothing he can do to change that. But at least he can try to make his co-pilot feel better in their last seconds of life. "Don't give up on me, Gavin," he says. "We can still pull this off. If you help me, we can keep her traveling perfectly straight, we could aim for any break in the trees. Shoot into the forest like a torpedo. Probably lose the wings, but as long as we avoid hitting a tree dead on, we'll skid to a stop on the forest floor. We *can* survive this."

Gavin looks at him. In the strobe of orange emergency lights, his face resembles a strange, unsmiling jack-o-lantern. "You're crazy," he says simply.

"That may be, but just grab the yoke anyway. Let's try to land this beast. What have we got to lose? Like you said, we're dead anyway."

His co-pilot stares at him for another moment, then nods. He reaches out and grabs the Yoke. "Let's do it," he says.

Grinning triumphantly, Pete turns his eyes back to the storm. "What's our altitude?" he asks.

"Twelve hundred seventy. Air speed, one hundred thirty-nine knots."

"Okay, we're coming in hotter than I would like, but we should still be able to glide her for another thirty seconds. Scan the forest. Try to find any kind of an opening in the trees. A space we can aim for."

"Everything looks the same," Gavin says. "All blurry and white."

How right he is. Trying to find any kind of an opening as they pass over the forest at better than two hundred and fifty kilometers per hour, is like looking for a lone rowboat in the vastness of the Pacific Ocean. And they are very quickly running out of time. They are low enough now that the airplane's running lights are glistening yellow against the white treetops. They resemble the jagged teeth of some snarling beast.

"Anything at all," Pete says, "The slightest shadow could be a gap."

"There," Gavin shouts suddenly, pointing towards the left. "See that shadowy spot, not as crisp white as the rest."

Pete sees it. Almost directly ahead of them, port about thirty degrees. Definitely something is causing a shadow in the sea of white. It has to be a gap in the trees. "Port the wheel," Pete says, and cracks the ailerons up to forty degrees. "We're going in…" At this moment Pete realizes he has not sent any word back to the passengers, warning them of the situation. But it is far too late now, and if Ben Treager isn't smart enough to figure out they are in trouble, then he deserves the surprise. After all, as he had pointed out to Pete the night before, *it is his plane.*

"This is it," Pete shouts as the forest looms ahead. He can see the gap in the trees now and it is very small. At least one of the wings is going to hit. Pete chooses the left wing, and pivots the aircraft that way. "Brace for Impact!"

As they enter the tree line, the running gear drags over the tops of old growth trees, then snags in some thicker branches and is shredded off the bottom of the plane, a deformed ball of metal and rubber smashing into the forest floor. The left wing collides with a tree at mid-length and is sheared off as neat as a dandelion head. A second later, another tree pounds into the wing only feet from the aircraft's body. This section of metal is thicker, and not so easily torn away, causing the plane to jack knife to the left. The tail section, just behind the main cabin, impacts a tree trunk and is ripped away from the rest of the body in a grotesque scream of ravaged, twisting metal. As the rear half of the fuselage disappears into the trees, the main section is jerked forward again, affording the pilots a last view of what is to come.

A snow-laden tree branch, the thickness of a brawny man's thigh, juts out directly across the torpedo's path. Spotting it a split second before they hit, Pete folds his body sideways as far as the restraints will allow. The branch tears through the safety glass like it is tissue paper. Gavin *someone or another*, whose only other job as co-pilot had been with his father in a 1968 Cessna 172 crop-duster, is instantly obliterated from the shoulders up. The bottom of the branch drags across Pete's face, peeling away his left ear and most of his cheek, so quickly he feels only the slightest tug and nothing more. The entire upper section of the cockpit is gone, crashing through the forest like a giant Frisbee.

When the right wing connects with another tree, the plane's forward motion has diminished considerably, so instead of breaking off, the wing catapults the aircraft around ninety degrees. The nose cone slams into a huge stump, flattening it like a paper cup. Inside the cock pit, the lower section of the console explodes inward, pulverizing both of Pete's legs.

The sudden stopping force of the impact drives the rear of the wreckage into the air, where it hangs for the briefest moment, as if held by invisible hands, before crashing back to the forest floor. And then it is still. A dead, misshapen carcass, with only the flurry of wind worried snow moving around it.

28

Deadman- 2:30am

On the night of the first big storm of the season, there are twelve winter residents on Deadman Lake. Of these twelve, only three witness the strange lights falling out of the snow-choked sky at just after two AM in the morning. And of these three, none have any real idea of what they are actually seeing.

Barb Foley is sitting in her rocking chair, looking through the large parlor room window into the chaotic beauty of the storm. Her hands rest in her lap, the fingers laced together loosely. Her face, slightly paler than it had been at the funeral, is clear of expression. If anyone had stood in the room with her or spied her through the window, they may have thought her to be a woman deep in thought, perhaps thinking of pleasant moments past, like the last real holiday she and Eli had taken to the Grand Canyon almost five years ago. Or maybe she is simply enjoying the current moment, quiet and calm in the face of winter's madness. Only her husband's watchful eye would have seen beyond this practiced mask of quietude. He would have recognized the small indicators of his wife's suffering. Her laced fingers clenching tighter every few minutes as pulses of pain claw up her spine, grappling her neck and spreading out into her shoulders. Her eyelids dropping gently against the tears that want to flow, but never will because she refuses to allow it. And her feet, wrapper in fuzzy pink slippers, trembling uncontrollably, tapping out a silent distress signal on the hardwood floor.

This night, for reasons she has not pin-pointed yet, has been very bad. The pain in her back and shoulders is excruciating. Like the tide of the ocean, it would roll out, dragging the agony with it until the pain is almost bearable. But then, minutes later, it would return, crashing into her, pounding with the fury of waves against the beach. It hurts to lay down, it hurts to stand up. Sitting hurts as well, but generally proves to be the mildest aggravator of the three. Remaining perfectly still helps to keep the tide out, until the pins and needles in her legs become so unbearable that it is either move or face complete insanity. It is a vicious circle of torment.

Thankfully there are also the pills. Before coming into the parlor room, Barb had taken four ten-milligram Oxycodone tablets. This doubles her recommended dosage, but she knows from past experience that when the pain is this bad, taking only two pills will have the same beneficial quality as putting a Spiderman Band-Aid on the stump of a severed arm. Tonight, in fact, has brought such unrelenting torture that she had briefly considered pouring the entire bottle of pills into her mouth and washing them down with a good long pull off a gin bottle. No more pain. Ever.

It isn't fear that stops her, this time or any of the other bad days when her mind turns to suicide. The idea of death brings no feelings of anxiety or dread. Just the opposite, she longs for the day when the pain will finally be gone. When she can at last lay her head down and rest, giving herself over to the greatest mystery of life and whatever it may bring.

What stops her is Eli. She worries about him. In many ways he is like a child, with so much life left in him still, years of happiness and fulfillment. He loves their life together on Deadman Lake, running the little bed and breakfast. It had been his dream for ten years before they were actually able to do it, many times seeming to be the only thing that got him through day after miserable day in the city. The thought of them together, living in this wooded paradise. But what if she is suddenly gone? The woman that has shared his bed for the better part of forty years, has been his wife for thirty-five, his best friend, companion, the one person he has come to rely on for so many things? Could he keep going without her? Continue to live, seeking out the happiness beyond what they have built together? Or will he close in on himself? Give up? Possibly even seek to join her? As well as she knows her husband, she still cannot be sure.

It is this thought that frightens her. Leaving Eli alone. The sorrow it brings to her heart is worse than any amount of pain she can imagine. She is afraid (no, terrified is a better word) that he isn't ready for her to be gone. Just like a kitten's personality can be damaged if it is taken away from its mother too early, what if Eli is also not prepared to be alone. It is something he has never experienced. So it is her responsibility to be here for him until he is ready. For however long it takes, she has to stay until the time is right. Will she know when that time is? Possibly not, but God will know. She will leave this final decision up to him. No matter how bad things get, she must believe that God will not test her beyond what she can bare. Not her God—

Another bolt of pain claws mercilessly up Barb's spine. Her hands clench, digging her fingernails into her palms. Her eyelids begin to drop, a futile effort to close out the agony. But, just before her eyes have completely close, she catches a glimpse of something through the window that causes them to pop open again. She squints, straining to see past the panicked swirls of snow.

In the distance, the dark bulge of Mount John Oliver blackens the horizon like the twisted body of an ancient specter. Above its massive shadow, looking no larger than a quarter at this distance, a dim white light shoots across the muddled sky. It comes in high up, traveling at a sharp angle towards the mountain. Passing the shadowy peak, it continues its downward path for another few seconds before finally disappearing into the opaque cloak of the forest.

Barb blinks, her attention momentarily, *and oh so mercifully*, focuses on this odd light instead of her pain. In total, it had existed for four or five seconds at most, yet there is no doubt in her mind that she had seen it. Even through the pulsing shroud of storm-ravaged snow, the light had been bright enough, and real enough, that there was no mistaking it for some strange game the oxycodone was beginning to play with her eyes. She *had* seen it.

But what was it? A bolt of lightning? During a snowstorm that seems unlikely. Plus it had been far too slow, lasting too long. She'd heard of ball lightning, floating spheres of electrically charged air. But never around this area, and she also doesn't think it works that way. Not large enough to be seen at such distance, or strong enough to survive the driving force of a blizzard.

Perhaps a meteorite? A falling space rock, glowing from the intense heat generated as it passed through the earth's atmosphere?

This idea seems possible. Or even a shooting star. The swirling snow may have played tricks with her eyes, making the light seem to be falling to earth when really it was only passing by. That is very possible. In fact, that is most likely what it was. It makes the most sense.

Then her pain flares again, a returning fire that burns through her body as if she were a straw-filled scarecrow. As she closes her eyes, praying the oxycodone will begin numbing her body soon, she forgets about the strange light, having never considered that it could be an airplane.

29

A kilometer and a half farther south from Eli and Barb's cabin, the Cooper cottage trembles in the billowing wind as it pounds against the cedar siding like fists in the night. Behind these shuddering walls, Chloe Cooper lies wide awake in her bed, her head turned so her cheek rests on the patterned yellow pillowcase. And though her brown eyes stare towards the bedroom window, she is not seeing the storm that funnels furiously beyond the glass. Her mind is occupied with the warm vision of something far more beautiful than winter's angry tirade. Something that carries feelings of unexplored excitement, tantalizing passion, yet at the same time a subtle pain in her heart where the fear of the unknown and a childish dread of rejection sit like a heavy stone.

She is thinking about Sidney Jenkins. Her flow of blonde hair and sparkling blue eyes. The unblemished skin of her face, her quirky smile, the sound of her laugh. The smell of her, spring flowers blooming in a golden field, as they embraced in greeting. Hugging each morning as friends. Only friends. Because as of now, that's all there is. Nothing more.

Chloe has known she is drawn to other girls from the time she was old enough to understand the feelings of attraction, though as of now she still has not officially *come out*. Not because she is embarrassed or ashamed. Despite the numerous cliques and a naturally inbred feeling of what is considered right, she has always felt pride in herself and her individuality. Nothing would change that, no matter what anyone thinks or says, and nothing is more important to her. Until this point in her life however, she has not met a person who moves her in that special way, igniting the fire that resides deep inside her body. She has also never been a big talker even at the best of times, so the thought of discussing something as personal *as love* before there actually is someone *to love* seemed moot and pointless.

But now there is Sidney. They had met not long ago, when Sidney and her father moved into the Chambers' place. Less than five months, yet almost immediately that cool place inside Chloe had roared into fiery life, flicking heated flames across her heart. It is the first time she has ever felt such a strong attraction to another person. A strange and wondrous thing because in all her years living in the city, surrounded by people of all types, she met no one that interested her, but move into the *middle of nowhere* and find the love of her life.

But she isn't the love of your life is she, Chloe's thoughts remind her. *Or doesn't know she is at least because you haven't told her.* A *real piece of work you are. Is the big proud gay girl too afraid to tell Sidney the truth?*

No. That isn't it. She isn't afraid. She is just being cautious. She doesn't want to come on too strong until she is sure that Sidney is...well...ready for that. Moving too quickly could scare her away, even as a friend. Her friendship means too much to Chloe. She will not risk losing it.

So she will wait until the time was right. There is no panic after all. Neither of them is going anywhere, especially now with a foot and a half of snow piled up outside and more falling from the sky in buckets. Better still—*and this may seem rude, but she doesn't care*—her parents had not gotten back before the storm, so now Chloe is invited to go over and stay with Sidney and her father until the roads are cleared. When she is spending every day and all night with her, the right time will have to come. That perfect moment, when the stars will come to a line and the planets will float into formation as a giant glowing heart in the sky...

Chloe closes her eyes and giggles into her pillowcase. *Okay, maybe a moment that perfect will never happen, but it is a fun thought.*

When she opens her eyes again and gazes through her bedroom window into the storm, she noticed something else beyond the flurries of snow. A light, high in the sky, moving across the horizon towards the mountain. Frowning, Chloe raises her head, propping herself up with one arm. Because the Copper cottage is farther south on the lake, she is afforded a slightly better view of Mount John Oliver than Barb has in the Foley's sitting room. Possibly because of this, the first thought that pops into Chloe's mind is the very thing Barb had not considered at all. *It's an airplane.*

But this made no sense. Who in their right mind would be flying an airplane on a night like this? The wind screaming across the sky, scrambling the snow into a frenzied, opaque sheet. Visibility would be near zero. It would be impossible for anyone, no matter how good a pilot, to navigate an aircraft over the mountains in weather this bad. *Impossible.*

Then it must not be a plane, Chloe now thinks as she watches the light dive past the mountain peak. A moment later it is gone, swallowed up by the thick shadows of the forest. She continues to watch, hoping to catch sight of it again. But there is nothing else to see except the swirling masses of snow.

Finally, she sighs and lies her head back down. Whatever she has just seen, she is quite sure now that it could not have been an airplane. No airport would allow a plane to even take off in this kind of weather, much less attempt a flight over Northern BC. It must have been something else.

But what? Maybe…a meteorite? Is that possible?

Sure it is, and it makes a lot more sense. A meteorite that has possibly traveled millions of light-years through space has just crash-landed into the forest behind her family's cabin.

Chloe smiles. What an exciting thought. A piece of space rock, lying out there in the trees. Waiting for some explorer to come along and find it. An explorer who is, most likely, the only person to have witnessed its landing. Now, this would be a momentous adventure indeed.

In the morning she can head out on one of the snowmobiles. It would be no problem at all. She is a good rider with lots of experience, and fresh powder is her favorite terrain. Laying heavy on the throttle, a huge rooster tail of shimmering snow erupting into the air as the powerful machine speeds across an untouched blanket of perfect white. She also feels confident that a space stone wouldn't be hard to find. First, she has a very good idea where it came down and second, the intense heat of the rock would melt a massive hole in the snow. It should be simple to spot.

Of course, she would invite Sidney to come alone. This idea was even more exciting. Maybe even…*perfect*.

With these new and exhilarating thoughts dancing through her mind, Chloe closes her eyes and at last drifts off to sleep.

30

Wayne Trapper and his fifteen-year-old son Greg live in the apartment that is connected to the back of the rental shop. Across the gravel road from the shop looms the bulky shadow of the Lodge, its huge girth quite effectively blocking any view of the lake that may have once been afforded to the apartment. But Wayne doesn't mind. From the small, covered deck, he can sit and look at the mountains, which he thinks are much more impressive than the lake anyway.

At 2:35am on the morning of the big snowstorm, that's exactly what he is doing. Sitting in his chair, a cigarette pinched in the corner of his mouth, staring into the snow-choked sky. Only seconds before he had seen a strange light shoot across the jagged black silhouette of the mountain peak and then vanish out of sight. From where his apartment is barely a half kilometer from the southern tip of Deadman, Wayne is protected from the hardest hits of wind, but his sightline is also blocked by the forests to his west, allowing him only a quick view of the anomaly. It had appeared, passed in front of the mountain, then disappeared mere seconds later. It was enough, however, to leave no doubt in Wayne's mind that he has seen something special.

It was a coughing fit that had woken him about an hour earlier. He had jerked up in bed gasping, fighting to get even the tiniest breath between the burst of retched hacks. These fits were becoming more common over the last couple of months, but this one was especially bad. It had taken him close to five minutes to get himself under control (*the whole time trying to stifle the noise so as not to wake Greg*) and when it did finally begin to subside, he was shocked to find blood coating his lips, and several more drops on his pillow. There had never been blood before, and he could feel a rasping pain in his chest that was also new. Fear had crept in then, wrapping around him like the arms of an estranged lover. In his mind, one word flashed over and over again in brilliant red neon: CANCER.

So in an effort to clear this horrifying word out of his brain, he had gotten up, dressed, and come out onto the deck to watch the snow. After only the briefest hesitation, he lit a cigarette and took a long pull. The flashing neon immediately began to diminish, as did his feelings of fear. After the second drag, the pain in his chest abated. Once the smoke had burned halfway to the filter, he was feeling like his old self again. So he finished it and lit another. And then a third.

It was as he was reaching into his breast pocket for the fourth time that the white light had appeared through the falling snow, darting its way across the sky.

Instead of instantly trying to figure what the light could have been, as was the mindset of the other two wakeful observers, Wayne's thoughts turned to Betty Abernathy.

What the hell was it she had said? Something about judgment. *A judgment will come from the sky and peer into our souls. Then, if sin is found in our hearts, we will be banished to some black place.*

It is total fucking hog-wash of course. The rantings of a crazy woman who should probably be locked up in a mental ward.

Yet, as much as Wayne wants to, it is hard to deny the coincidence. Something, God knows what, just fell out of the sky. He is sure of it. His vision is 20/20, and the strongest thing he'd drank in the past five years is coffee. His mind is as clear as a Hawaiian surf. He feels total certainty that there was something in the forest now that hadn't been there a minute ago.

Still watching the skyline closely, hoping to spy another glimpse of light, Wayne finishes the job of pulling his cigarette pack from his pocket. He pinches one out with his teeth and lights it.

He thinks of his brother Dwayne, who will be heading out in the Sno-Cat as soon as the snowfall lets up. This will probably be shortly after first light or mid-morning at the latest. As always, Danny, his younger boy, will be riding shot gun while Matty follows on a snowmobile. In the last few years, it had become somewhat of a tradition for Dwayne and his sons, the initial trek out into the newly fallen snow. The plow will not be mounted on the front of the Sno-Cat because road clearing will not begin for a couple of days, after the snow has a chance to settle. No, this first trip out is strictly a sightseeing tour. A chance for them to take in the beauty of the smooth, unblemished cover of snow. Dwayne has always said he loves this time most because it is the *cleanest* the forest will ever be. Perfect, untouched by man or animal. But Wayne knows this is not the entire truth. For some reason he has never quite understood, it is very important to his brother that it be himself who lay the first tracks through this fresh snow cover. As if this meaningless gesture (though calling it *meaningless* within Dwayne's earshot would not be wise) somehow garnered him rule over every other living creature in the forest. *All hail Big Dwayne, The King of Deadman.*

More hog-wash in Wayne's opinion. Of course, he would never think of his brother as crazy, not like that nutty Abernathy broad, but this fact didn't make it any less hog-wash.

Wayne puffs his cigarette, the coils of smoke instantly swept away in whips of frigid wind, thinking again about what he has seen in the sky. He supposes that in the morning he could mention it to Dwayne. Not make a big deal about it as some, less stable people might. Just bring it up as Big Dwayne is getting ready to head out. Let him know to keep his eyes open, that's all. Watch for anything different. Out of the ordinary.

Like a phantom bringer of death? "Hog-wash," Wayne says out loud, flicking his spent cigarette into the storm and reaching for a new one.

31

Icebound- First Light
"…Collique…"

The word floats in, as though it has traveled from a great distance through a storm of brilliant white. No shadows here, only white. So bright it makes his head ache.

"Mister...Collique..."

Again the words, breathed to him across an expanse of time. He begins to search for the source, squinting, trying to see through the intensity of white. But still nothing. The shroud is too thick, hiding all things.

"Open your eyes..." the voice, getting closer now. The faintest shadow darkens the brilliance, swimming into view like a shark emerging from the murky depths. *"You have to wake up...Mister Collique..."*

Mister Collique? Bronson Collique? He is Bronson Collique. This voice—owned by the shadowy figure slowly materializing through the storm—it is calling...to him. Beckoning him back from the chaos of white. Trying to lead him out. Again and again the words come, and now he follows them, letting them drag him back. The shadows continue to deepen, becoming features. Swirling and twisting until they draw together, forming a face. It is a face that he knows.

Veterinarian. This man is a veterinarian. His name is...is...

But Bronson cannot remember. His mind is whirling with jumble thoughts. He blinks his eyes, and more of the white melts away. Around the face of the veterinarian, things come into view. Metal and plastic, broken glass, wires and cables hanging everywhere. Everything smashed and twisted like the corpse of some ravaged animal. His neck creaks as he turns his head, looking around, trying to remember what this is...where he is.

To his right the battered metal carcass surrounding him ends in a gaping hole. He is looking into the white again. But this white is different. A colorless veil of ice-cold, pierced here and there by trees as they stretch towards the dismally gray sky. More torn bits of debris are scattered all around, tarnishing the freshness of the newly fallen...snow... *snow-covered forest?*

Just as the chaotic gray features had come together to form the face of the veterinarian, suddenly the spiraling thoughts in Bronson's mind begin to fit together like the pieces of a jigsaw puzzle. Pictures form. Memories flow back to him in waves.

An airplane. He is in an airplane. He works for Ben Treager, and this is Treager's airplane. They had been flying at night and... had flown into a storm and...and...

He looks at the veterinarian again, whose name is Dave Saunders. Bronson remembers now. "Wha..." but all that comes out is a painful croak. His throat is so dry it feels as though he has swallowed a hand full of cactus burrs.

Saunders leans over him, looking down at him with wide, frightened eyes. The vet is bleeding from a cut on his cheek and both of his lips are swollen. It makes him look like a platypus. "Wait," he says through his platypus lips, and brings a water bottle to Bronson mouth. "Don't try to speak yet. Drink first."

Bronson's does, sucking the cool water down in hungry gulps.

"Thank God you're awake," Saunders continues as he feeds Collique more water. "I thought you were never going to wake up."

"What..." Bronson starts again, liquid dribbling through the wispy hairs of his beard. "What happened?"

"The plane crashed." Saunders spits the words out like they taste foul against his tongue. "Crashed right into the middle of the goddamn forest."

Bronson looks at the ragged hole to his right again. "Where's the rest of it?"

Saunders shakes his head. "Don't know. Things happened so fast. We were flying, hit some big turbulence, something exploded, then we were here."

"Merde," Bronson curses, and shifts his body, readying himself to stand up. Instant bolts of white-hot pain tear up his legs and slammed into his knees. Gripping both of his thighs, an agonized squeal shoots past his clamped teeth. It is a pain more savage than any he's felt before. Like someone is smashing his kneecaps apart with a ball-peen hammer.

Saunders grimaces. "Yeah," he says, his tone taking on the calmness of a doctor who has been well versed in the dos and don'ts of bedside manner. "It's probably best if you don't try to move around a whole lot. Your legs have taken a bit of a knock."

Still clenching his jaw against the pain, Collique slowly looks down at his legs. "Fils de pute," *Son of a bitch,* he mutters.

Both of his legs have been crushed from the knees down. His feet are twisted in odd upward angles and have swollen so thick that the laces of his boots are stretched tight enough to snap. Lumps and bulges push against his pants, the jagged tips of snapped tibia tearing through the material in a few places, resembling the jagged fingers of some alien being trying to rip itself out of his body—through his legs rather than his chest. His knees are two huge, deformed masses the size of volleyballs.

"A knock?" Collique groans, echoing platypus mouth's choice of words in disbelief. He looks away, a rolling nausea bubbling up inside his guts.

"During the turbulence," Saunders goes on, "just as we started to go down, Mother's Womb broke free of its restraints. It slid across the hold and...hit you. You were strapped into your seat, and it just hit you. A couple of times I think."

"Mother's..." Bronson says, his eyes widening as the memory of why they were flying through a storm at night punches into his brain. He glances quickly around the destroyed cargo hold, temporarily forcing the pain into the background of his mind.

Nothing. No sign of the box anywhere. *Jésus nous aide!* He thinks. *Jesus Help us!*

"Where is it?" Collique shouts, still ignoring the bolt of lightning that burns up his legs. "Where is the box?"

"The box?" Saunders says, suddenly sounding like a confused schoolboy.

"Mother's Womb," Collique tells him. "The tiger! Where the fuck is the tiger?"

Again the vet shakes his head. "I don't know. It must have fallen out after we broke away from the rest of the plane. I...I didn't see. I had my eyes closed. We were crashing for Christ's sake!"

"Jesus..." the Frenchman moans, passing a hand over his face. His fingers are ice cold against his skin.

"You don't think it survived?" The vet asks. "It couldn't have survived."

"We did," Bronson says. "Look at you, barely a scratch," *Beside those damn platypus lips.* "And that animal was protected inside the box. It most certainly could have survived."

"Then it would still be trapped, unconscious."

"Maybe," Collique says. His legs blazed like two burning stumps. "But if it broke open…"

"Don't you think we've got bigger problems right now than worrying about some drugged, half dead cat," Saunders wails, suddenly edging into hysteria. "We're separated from everyone else, lost in the woods. There's two feet of snow on the ground and it's freezing cold. We have no food, and both of your legs are broken. Doesn't that seem to be our main problem at this moment! What the hell are we going to do?"

Bronson looks at him stunned, the throb in his legs pulsing in rhythm with his pounding heart. When he speaks he forces his voice to remain neutral because if he yells, Saunders might go into total meltdown. And right now he needs the vet more than he has needed anyone else in his life. "We're not going to be doing anything if that animal is still alive out there. You're the doctor, you should know even better than me what it's capable of. How can you not be concerned?"

"I'm just a fucking anesthesiologist," the vet tells him. "All I was supposed to do was keep it asleep. The real doctors are already at the compound, readying for its arrival. Guess they're in for a long wait." A maniacal cackle barks past his puffy lips. His eyes are wide and wild.

Collique frowns. Saunders is even closer to complete panic than he thought. He had to do something quickly. Get him moving. Give him tasks so his mind will be occupied with constructive actions rather than dwelling on the bleakness of their current situation.

He begins to look around again. Right away he notices that it isn't just Mother's Womb that has vacated this section of aircraft. Anything that had not been attached in some way is gone. Luggage, equipment, supplies, all sucked out by the force of the crash. Everything will now be scattered all over the forest floor, buried under a foot of snow. All that remains are the three other bumper seats, and several cabinets and storage bins, most of which lay open and empty.

In the back of the cargo hold, a section of the tail has been torn away, leaving another jagged hole, though not as large as the one where the rest of the aircraft had once been. Basically, they are inside a giant funnel; snow-covered forest visible at each end. Beyond these ragged openings, in the glow of brightening new morning light, the snow has stopped falling. The devastating wind that had helped bring the plane down has all but ceased, and thankfully the mild breeze that remains is blowing around the wreckage rather than through it, so for the most part they are protected from its chilled bite. As well, and again thankfully, the cargo hold had been kept at a cool temperature even before the plane crash, requiring both of the occupants to wear parkas. The cold at this point is one of their lesser problems. Bronson, who has always tried to be *a glass is half full* kind of guy, thinks this is good.

Moving as carefully as he can manage, he unbuckles the seatbelt that is still pinning him into his seat. Then he pushes his hand inside the hip pocket of his pants, gritting his teeth against jags of pain, and feels for his keys, finds them, and pulls them out. *More good news.*

"Take these," he says, holding the keys out to Saunders. "There's a gun cabinet. A tall thin case near the back. Inside are two air guns and half a dozen tranquilizer darts. Get them."

"What good are air guns going to do us?" Saunders asks without reaching for the keys. "We need food, water…a fucking cell phone."

"Even if we had a cell phone," Collique tells him calmly. "It wouldn't work out here. And all the food and water…and *medical supplies* are either lying out there in the snow or in the front section of the plane. You need to go find it."

Now it is Saunders who looks stunned, his already wide eyes bulging above his gigantic lips. "I…me—you want me to go out there? By myself?"

"Of course. I can't go with two broken legs. You need to find the rest of the plane and bring back supplies. Bandages. Something we can use to splint my legs. Otherwise, we're both going to die out here. So take the goddamn keys."

Saunders is shaking his head. "No way. I…I think we should stay here…together. Help could come. Maybe Ben Treager or the pilots. Or a search party."

"If Ben is alive, he's with the front section. He won't leave it. And there's not going to be any search party. No one knows we're here. This was an unscheduled flight, under the radar. Even when Treager is missed, which could take a week or more, no one will know where to look. We're on our own. You have to go. There's no other choice." He jingles the keys.

"Shit," Saunders groans, scrubbing his hands through his hair. "This is so fucked up." Then he reaches out reluctantly and takes them. "What about the tiger? It could be out there somewhere."

"I thought that was the least of our worries?" Collique says.

"In here maybe. But out there," he says pointing into the windswept whiteness. "It becomes a big fucking worry to me."

"If the animal *is* out there somewhere, being inside this wreck isn't going to protect us. Besides, that's what the gun is for."

"A lousy trank gun? Isn't there any real fire power?"

Bronson can feel the budge of his Beretta 9M under his parka, but for the moment that is right where it's going to stay. To the vet he says, "There's enough Etorphine in one of those darts to kill a two-hundred-and-fifty-pound man. It will knock any large animal down as fast as a bullet, I guarantee it."

"I know what Etorphine is," Saunders snaps. "I'd still feel better with a twelve gauge."

Bronson tries to chuckle, but is only able to groan. "A shotgun would barely part its hair. Just get the guns, will you."

Saunders stands up hesitantly. "I still say we should stick it out here," he says, but with much less conviction.

"Get the guns," the Frenchman says again, meeting Saunder's nervous eyes with his rock-steady stare. "*C'est la seule manière,* you know. It is the only way."

"*Fuck,*" the doctor grumbles and moves off towards the back of the hold.

Collique lays his hands on his thighs and closes his eyes. The pain from his shattered legs pounds with unrelenting savagery. It feels as if his lower legs have been rolled in shards of broken glass and then, just for good measure, hit several times with an aluminum baseball bat. If Saunders is unsuccessful in his quest… if he can't find the plane and get back with the medical supplies— *drugs…surely an anal retentive like Treager kept some sort of pain killers on hand at all times*—then Bronson supposes he will be pulling the Beretta out after all.

To use on himself.

32

As Ben Treager backs slowly out of what is left of the pilots' cabin, his expression drawn and stunned, a memory suddenly rises up in his mind. A long-ago experience that he had not thought about in years. It had been not long after his sixteen birthday and he was out cruising his birthday present, a 1965 Corvette Stingray, down Jackson Street in central Seattle. It was around two in the afternoon, and traffic for the area was relatively light, but he was still only doing about twenty-five miles an hour; mainly because he'd already gotten two speeding tickets and some serious shit would hit the fan if he got a third. He was reaching out to change the station on the radio when some skinny ass chick in a very short skirt and very high heels darted off the curb directly in front of him. He jammed on the brake pedal with both feet and skidded to a stop with barely two feet to spare. The crazed chick, definitely tripping on some wild drugs, continued her bolt across the street without even noticing him. She made it halfway through the inside lane and was hit dead-on by a Ford pickup truck that was traveling at well over the inner-city speed limit of twenty-five. Ben would never forget the wet, yet oddly crunchy thump sound her body made as it connected with the truck's massive grill. Somehow, instead of rolling over the truck, or being knocked away from it, she flew thirty feet straight up into the air and came down on her head not ten feet from the front of Ben's car. A thick spurt of blood splashed across the windshield, bits of bone tinkling musically against the glass. The girl lay in the street, her skinny legs splayed out in a V, her feet bare—*they would find one of her high heel shoes in a flowerpot on the third-floor balcony of a nearby apartment*. From the neck up she resembled a watermelon that had been pitched off a five-story building. This, being a time before the internet allowed non-stop access to multitudes of grotesque images to any and all who care to search, was Ben's first brush with death, and he had done what any other strong, masculine youth would do. He threw up right there in the street beside his shiny corvette.

The experience, so vivid in his mind it might have been thirty minutes ago rather than thirty years, now seems somehow diminished. Compared to the horrifying carnage he has just witnessed inside the pilot's cabin *(Blood...so much blood everywhere)*, that long-ago drama carries about the same shock value as a paper cut.

Ben reaches out his hand and pulls the cabin door closed. The hinges are twisted, squealing in protest, and the latch is no longer lined up, but the door does stay closed. *This is good,* Ben thinks as he stares at the bent door. *Keep all that death in there. Away from me...*

"Ben..."

Us...not just me...us.

Ben turns around. Morgan is staring at him with huge green eyes. *God, her face seems like it is all eyes. Giant, terrified eyes. Looking at him to make the fear go away.*

For the first time in his life, Ben doesn't know if he can.

She is sitting in the seat that had been Ben's before the crash. A wrap of cloth he had torn from the tail of his shirt runs across her forehead, wrapping around her head. On the left side, a penny-sized spot of blood is bright against the pale blue material, a crimson-colored reminder of the deep gash that is hidden underneath. Her left cheek is also badly swollen, darkened to the angry purple hue of spoiled plums. Old, tear drawn mascara tracks and caked blood paint her face, turning her from beautiful into the crazed, murderous clown inside every kids' nightmare. She has Ben's wind-breaker drawn tightly around her shoulders, but she is clutching herself and shivering noticeably.

With thousands of dollars'-worth of Gore-Tex winter gear packed away in the cargo hold, and here they are, freezing to death.

"Well..." Morgan says, her eyes cutting him with their ridiculous expectancy.

Ben shakes his head.

"Are...are you sure?"

He thinks again of the blood. All that blood. The entire cabin painted the crimson color of death.

"I'm sure," he tells her, dragging his right hand through his hair. His other arm is tied against his body in a make-shift sling. Upon an earlier inspection, he is quite sure the wrist is broken, and the gravelly pain in his shoulder tells him with little doubt that it is dislocated. It also hurts to breathe, which makes him suspect he has at least one broken rib. *Not bad when compared to those poor fucking pilots.* "Everything is destroyed," he adds dismally.

"God," Morgan moans. Not surprisingly, she is starting to cry again. She has been crying almost non-stop since regaining consciousness. Ben supposes it is understandable. They are seriously up shit creek without a paddle. But this knowledge does not stop the constant sobbing from quickly beginning to get on his nerves. Right now he needs to think. That is the most important thing. Figure this shit out. If there is going to be any chance of them getting out of this alive, they have to keep a level head. So far, they have been relatively lucky. They survived a plane crash into the Canadian wilderness with seemingly minor injuries. They can both move, walk, talk, and think. They have a little food and a couple bottles of water. Sure, they hadn't foresight enough to keep any warm jackets in the passenger cabin, but they could light a fire. Maybe make some half-assed jackets out of the seat material. Or…

"What about the satellite phone? Or at least coats," Morgan says, as if she'd been reading Ben's thoughts. "Something to keep us warm?"

Ben shakes his head again. "It's all destroyed up front. There's nothing we can use, trust me."

Christ, I threatened to ruin Pete Collingwood's career the last time we spoke. Guess I managed to do that alright…

But Ben pushes this thought away. This is not his fault. None of it. If Pete had been a better pilot, they wouldn't have crashed. Storm or no storm, a good pilot would have gotten them through. That's all there is to it. The only part of this situation that is Ben's fault is hiring a guy that didn't know a plane from his asshole. Collingwood got what he deserved.

"I'm so cold," Morgan cries, tears streaming down her swollen cheek.

"So am I," Ben says. He steps through the scatters of debris on the cabin floor and sits down beside her. He puts his good arm around her shoulders. Behind them, an icy breeze blows in through the yawning hole that used to be the cargo hold. "But as cold as we are, you know we can't let ourselves get down. We need to stay focused."

She looks at him, her wet eyes blinking. "Focused? On what? How cold I am? Or that my head hurts? Or that we're lost in the woods and totally screwed?" Her voice sounds old and pathetic through her sobs.

"That's exactly what I'm talking about," Ben says, wanting to yell but not giving in to the need. It won't help at this point. She is bottoming out in self-pity, and he needs to talk her back, just like he would a client who'd lost a hundred grand in an investment gone bad. "We can't let ourselves get down. We need to keep it together and think ourselves out of this."

"Think...ourselves..." Morgan echoes, her tone dumbfounded. "What...?"

"Think first, then act. I mean, it's obvious what we need to do. We need to find the tail section, or at least our luggage. There's a good chance it all flew out when the plane tore apart. It's probably scattered around in the snow. Thermal jackets, gloves, wool sockets. There's even a second satellite phone. Everything we need. We just have to find it. And Collique. He's out there somewhere."

"What if he's..." Morgan's eyes flick to the twisted door of the pilots' cabin, horror showing in their pale green depths. "Like them?" she finishes softly.

Ben shakes his head. "Collique is a survivor. If we made it, so did he. I guarantee it. When we can find him, he'll be able to get us out of here. This is his kind of place…forest, wilderness. The snow. It's all like a second home to him. He thrives in it."

"But couldn't we freeze to death trying to find him?" She says it more as a question than a statement, wiping the tears gingerly off her bruised face.

"We'll definitely freeze to death if we stay here," Ben says. "Moving will help keep us warm, and we can pull the covering off these seats. Leather and foam; wrap it around ourselves. It'll keep us warm enough until when can find the luggage."

"But…couldn't we light a fire? That would keep us warm."

"I thought about that, but there's nothing to burn. And this plane was…*is* full of jet fuel. Maybe it's all gone, leaked away into the snow, but I don't think so. I can still smell it. If we try to light a fire, it might be like lighting the fuse on a stick of dynamite."

Morgan looks at him and he can see she knows he's right, even if she doesn't want to believe it. The odor cannot be ignored. It is a vinegary, chemical smell like a mix of turpentine and diesel fuel. Almost strong enough to make his eyes water.

"Okay," she agrees finally, a deep shiver racking her body. "I guess…but can you walk? The snow is deep and your arm…"

"I'll manage," Ben says. "Any other options are grim. If we move, we live. If we stay here…" He shrugs. "I don't know. If we can find the gear, and Collique, we could come back for the food. Then, walk ourselves right out of here."

Morgan has stopped crying now, but her eyes are red and shimmering. "God, I wish I had listened to you," she moans. "Gone back to Seattle. So stupid."

So do I, Ben thinks. *I care about you…hell, even love you I guess, but right now you are the anchor that could drag this whole ship to the depths.*

He hugs her tighter. "We'll get out. If we keep our heads and keep moving, we'll get out."

"Do you really think Bronson is still alive?"

"Yes I do," he says honestly.

"Then…" she hesitated for a moment, looking into his face. "Does that mean the tiger could still be alive too?"

And there it is. The tiger. Shit. He had been hoping seriously that her mind was far too preoccupied with their current situation to remember anything about the striped fifth passenger. Apparently, however, this isn't the case. So now he is forced to do the only thing that makes sense. "No," he lies to her. "No chance. Even if it survived the crash, it would have suffocated inside Mother's Womb. The box is airtight, and with no oxygen being pumped in, there's no air to breathe. Bye-bye kitty."

"What if it fell out, broke open?"

"Couldn't happen. It was secured inside the hold. And even if it did, that thing was made out of one-inch polyplexolyn. One of the strongest clear materials on earth. No way it would break."

There is, of course, no material on earth called *polyplexolyn*. The Mother's Womb is made out of ordinary half-inch Plexiglas, and though it is airtight, it had definitely not been constructed with an airplane crash in mind. Even a minor impact would have the potential to break it open.

But there is no reason to tell Morgan this. Right now he needs her. He is in a lot of pain, and it will only continue to get worse without the medical supplies. He has to find them and Collique if there is going to be any chance of getting out of this alive. And with the pain in his chest, there is a very good chance he will not be able to dig his way through the deep snow without her help. So, what is the point of adding to her apprehension about leaving the imagined safety this corpse of an aircraft can provide?

"Also," he continues. "There are guns in the cargo hold. I'm sure Collique has already put half a dozen bullets into it, just to be sure."

"Really?" Morgan says, staring into his eyes.

He holds her gaze with unwavering confidence. "Yes."

She looks at him a moment longer, then nods. "Okay. I'm so cold I'll do anything to warm up."

"That's my girl," Ben says and kisses her good cheek. "Let's start by ripping these seats apart."

Reluctantly, Morgan wipes away the last of her tears and stands up.

33

Deadman- 8:30am

Dwayne Trapper, a man two months shy of his fiftieth birthday, had begun visiting Deadman Lake with his parents when he was eight years old. These visits had continued all through his childhood and into his adult life. Deadman became his home away from home. Then, when he was thirty-seven, the opportunity arose for him to purchase the Lodge and rental shop, the campground and most of the vacant land on the eastern side of the lake. He had spent a month thinking it over, turning the idea around every-which way in his mind, looking at it from all angles, discussing it at length with his brother and the woman who was destined to become his second ex-wife. It was a risky endeavor, but in the end, there was really only one thing to do. He sold his construction business—for a sum so enormous it had even surprised Dwayne—and purchased the properties. That summer he had uprooted his family and moved to Deadman. Six years later, his brother's wife is killed by a drunk driver, leaving Wayne to raise their eight-year-old son Greg by himself. Dwayne, who by this time is divorced and raising his two boys with no mother, offers him the job of running Deadman rentals. Wayne accepts the position, and they have both been full-time members of the community ever since.

In all those years, this is the first time a heavy snowfall has come before November. So, now Dwayne pauses for a moment in the rear doorway of the Lodge, looking out at the piles of white powder with a hint of amazement showing in his abundant face. "Damn peculiar," he grunts under his breath, then drives his considerable girth forward, plunging his thick legs through two feet of lightly packed snow. On his red, swollen feet he wears only leather-strap sandals, as it is virtually impossible to find any sort of shoes or boots that fit him. This doesn't matter to Dwayne however, his feet are numb most of the time anyway and he won't be in the snow long enough for anything vital to freeze too badly. From the Lodge to the Sno-Cat, thirty-feet and no more.

The Cat will already be running, warming up with the heater pumping. Danny, his younger boy at eight years old had started it ten minutes earlier and will now be waiting in the cab for his father. His fourteen-year-old son, Matt—an inheritance from his first marriage and Danny's half-brother—is on a snowmobile just in front of the Cat, zooming around and around in a rough figure-eight, snow blasting up from its rear track in a sparkling rooster tail. This fresh powder swirls around in a light wind, pushed and pulled this way and that and eventually cascading down around Dwayne's head as he draws closer to the Cat.

"Cut that shit!" he bellows, his deep voice so loud it easily overpowers even the mechanical wail of the snowmobile's two-stroke engine.

Matty's head snaps around. He jams on the brakes hard, coming to a stop so sudden that it is only the quick tightening of his knees against the machine's seat that saves him from being tossed over the handlebars. He pulls his goggles off his eyes and smiles sheepishly.

"Sorry, dad," he says.

"Christ, you're gonna burn through a tank of fuel before we get off the friggin' property," Dwayne says.

"Naw, Uncle Wayne topped her right up," Matt says. "Good to go."

"Well, quit your clowning around or you won't be going nowhere. You'll be staying here and shoveling out the damn parking lot."

"Sorry," Matt repeats, lacing his gloved fingers together in front of himself.

Dwayne reaches the Cat and climbs laboriously onto its track. He pulls open the door and hands in a red and white cooler to his other son. It contains a six-pack of beer for consumption a little later, *though not too much later.*

"Take this," he says to Danny.

The boy, skinny and blonde with skin almost as pale as the snow—*Dwayne loves him plenty, but will sometimes find himself wondering how a man his size could end up with such a scrawny kid*—reaches over and takes the cooler. He puts it on the floor at his feet.

Dwayne grabs ahold of the steering wheel and is just beginning to haul himself into the cab when a voice comes up from behind him.

"Mornin' there, Dwayne."

Startled and jerking his head around, Dwayne's hand slips off the steering wheel. He stumbles back, teetering on the edge of the track, thinking for sure he is going to do a backward swan dive into the snow. Then there are hands against his ass, shoving him back up. Grunting, he grabs the edge of the door and spins around. "Keee-rist..." he roars, his brow bunching together above his angry eyes.

Wayne stands below him in the snow, smiling. The cigarette pinched in the corner of his mouth feeds curls of smoke into the mild wind murmuring around them. "Well, shit," he says. "That was a close one. Not for my quick hands, you'd be doing the back stroke in the snow right now."

Dwayne is glaring at his brother. "You're a light-footed son of a bitch. I should split your lip for yah, sneaking up on me like that."

"Didn't sneak," Wayne says, plucking the butt from his mouth and tapping ash into the clean, white snow. "Just walked. No different than any other time."

"Any other time?" Dwayne echoes, his tone dumbfounded. "I don't remember you ever leaving your shop this time of the morning. 'Specially in two feet of snow."

From behind his father, Danny's blond head pops out of the Cat. "Hey, Uncle Wayne," he chortles, waving his hand. "What'cha doin' out here?"

Wayne shrugs. "Nothin' special. Just came out to say so long, that's all."

"Well shit," Dwayne says. "I guess there can be a first time for everything, but I know you far too well to believe it. There's no goddamn way you trudged through all this slop to say *so long*. What's on your mind, Wayne? Spill it so we can be on our way."

Wayne shrugs again. "Nothing much really." He pauses, puffing his cigarette. "Guess you'll be heading out Granger Trail, towards Terravale?"

"We go the same route every year. You know that. So, I'll ask one more time, what's on your mind, Wayne?"

"Well, I was thinking maybe…instead you could take a jaunt west, towards John Oliver."

Dwayne looks at him with a pinched expression. "Why?"

"Something different," Wayne says through a cloud of swirling smoke. "That's all."

"Dammit, I'm freezing my balls off out here. If you don't get to the point soon, I'm gonna climb down and jam your bald frickin' head into the snow."

Of course, both of them know this is an empty threat. The days of Indian burns and underwear wedgies are gone along with their youth. But Dwayne's patience is still short, and his puffy cheeks are growing redder by the second, so at last Wayne comes clean. "Thought I saw something," he admits. "I was out last night, having a smoke on the deck. Saw a light shooting through the storm, coming down from the sky and it disappeared into the forest below Oliver."

"Like a meteorite?" Danny says excitedly from inside the cab. "For real, you seen a meteorite?"

"Mind your business," Dwayne says to his son without looking around. His doubtful gaze is locked on Wayne. "So you saw a light? Probably just a shooting star or something similar."

Wayne shakes his head. "I ain't no idiot. I know what a shooting star looks like. And the storm was too thick for that. What I saw was bright enough to break through all that snow. Like your boy says, *a meteorite*. Or maybe an airplane."

"We heading out, dad, or what?" Matt calls, still waiting on his snowmobile. "Starting to get cold over here."

"Just wait," Dwayne snaps. "We go when we go."

Matt groans and smacks his hand against the handlebars.

"You think it could have been a plane?" Dwayne asks his brother, his interest suddenly sparked.

Wayne flicks his cigarette away and reaches for a new one. "Don't know what else it could be. As I said, maybe a meteor come down, but that don't seem too realistic."

"Who in their right mind would fly through a storm like we had last night?"

"Someone with not a whole lot of brains would be my guess."

Dwayne is quiet for a moment, gazing up at the gray sky, pondering the idea in his mind.

"Meteor or plane," Wayne continues. "Either way, it'd be one helluva find, don't you think? And, if it turns out a plane, could even be people alive, needing help. We'd be like…you know, heroes."

"Doubt anyone would survive a crash like that," Dwayne says, still looking into the brooding sky. "And if they did, cold would get 'em pretty quick. Another wave of storms coming too. Be dumping snow again in six hours, I'd say."

"That's why I think you should head that way first, instead of Granger Trail, though I know it's against tradition and all."

"Fuck tradition. I just don't like wasting my darn time." Now he turns his face back down to his brother, his eyes narrow. "You sure what you saw, Wayne? You ain't wasting my time?"

Wayne cups his hand around a new cigarette as he lights it. "I ain't sure what I saw," he says, stuffing his Zippo lighter into his pocket. "But I am sure I saw *something* come down from the sky into those woods. Ain't no doubt in my mind."

Dwayne stares at him a second or two longer, searching his face. Then, satisfied, he shouts over his shoulder to his older son. "Change of plans. We'll be heading west along Loggers Pass towards John Oliver."

Matty stands on the pegs of his machine. "Really," he says, sounding more than just a little surprised. "Up'ta Oliver?"

"Yup. So stay close, don't want you getting turned around up there."

"I know the way no problem," Matt says. "But why? We never gone that way before."

"Never mind why right now," Dwayne bellows. "Just do as I say and stay close."

Matt drops back to the seat of the snowmobile. "Sure, okay," he says, still sounding confused, but now excitement has also made its way into his tone. Grinning, he pulls his goggles over his eyes.

As the snowmobile's engine howls back to life again, Dwayne finishes his climb into the cab of the Cat, squeezing his giant belly behind the steering wheel. He glances at Danny. "Good to go?"

Danny nods. "Good to go, daddy."

Dwayne reaches out and grips the door, but before he can pull it closed, Wayne steps up to the Cat and calls over the rumble of the diesel engine, "One more thing, Dwayne."

The large man sighs. "What?"

Wayne looks up at him, and if Dwayne had been just a bit closer, he would have seen the mild shimmer of fear showing in his brother's gaze. Betty Abernathy's strange prophecy from the night before has found its way into Wayne's brain again this morning, and no matter how repeatedly, or how forcefully he tells himself it is hog-wash, he just cannot squash the crazy bitch's words from his mind.

The spirits will cast down from the sky a judgment.

"Be careful," Wayne says, holding his cigarette in a hand that is trembling noticeably. "You know…just be careful."

Dwayne stares at him, trying to figure out if he is being put on. When he realizes there is no joke, his brow creases above a small, tentative smile. "You don't need to worry about me, brother. I'm the Sheriff in these here woods." Then he pulls the door closed.

34

As Wayne is watching the Sno-Cat disappear into the snow laden trees, at the other end of Deadman Lake Sidney is walking slowly into the kitchen of the Jenkins cabin, rubbing her eyes sleepily. Her blonde hair is pulled into a ponytail that lay across her left shoulder and her pink Teri-towel robe hangs open just enough to expose the white camisole and cotton panties she is wearing beneath. The crisp, wintry cold of the room hits her immediately, and shivering she pulls the robe closed, tying the draw cord around her slim waist. Her breath plumes out from her lips, drifting up like thin smoke in the chilled air.

Although both bedrooms and the bathroom are kept adequately warm by solar powered baseboard heaters, the kitchen and living-room rely on fire to heat them to a livable temperature. In the living-room there is a large stone fireplace, and in the kitchen a rustic looking wood stove holds a dual purpose, cooking the meals and heating the room.

This was, in Sidney's opinion, one of the only drawbacks of living in a cabin on a lake; until the stove is lit, the kitchen remains only a few degrees warmer than the outside temperature. No problem in the spring and summer, but in the winter it is damn cold, almost like walking into a meat cooler.

Clutching her arms across her chest, Sidney goes to the stove. Beside this cast-iron beast are two boxes sitting on the floor, one filled with stove length logs her father has split (a favorite of his chores Saul has admitted to her more than once) and another containing newspaper and kindling. She stands there for a moment, looking down at them thoughtfully.

Normally, her father would have already had the fire roaring before Sidney found her way into the kitchen, but this morning the rumbling sound of his snores are still vibrating the bedroom door. There is a definite possibility that he had participated in a bit more *funeral* cheer—*of the barley, hops and bend your elbow variety*—than he is used to. Even though she knows he has taken to sneaking a shot of rum in his morning coffee lately, he generally isn't much of a drinker. On the few occasions he does partake in an evening of alcoholic festivities, head splitting hangovers the next morning are usually a part of the deal. So for now, being the caring daughter she is, she has decided to let him sleep.

After a few more seconds of shivering, she finally pulls open the fire-box door, wrinkling her nose as the iron hinges squeal sharply, and begins shoving balls of newspaper into the soot-covered cavity. She follows the paper with several pieces of kindling wood. Then she bends down and gazes inside, contemplating. Feeling uncertain, she sighs and jams in three more bunches of paper.

In the cupboard is an old MGB coffee can filled with easy-strike matches. She uses a match from the can to light a twisted-up piece of newspaper, then uses this to ignite the paper and wood inside the firebox.

The fire catches very quickly, much quicker than Sidney has expected, and within only a few seconds flames are jumping out of the firebox, licking jagged orange forks of heat into the air. Sidney yelps, jumping backward away from the scorching flames. She skirts sideways, grabs a split log from the box and uses it to slam the iron trap closed.

At the exact same moment this small door snaps shut with a clank, there is a thudding knock against the kitchen door behind Sidney. With her nerves already as tight as piano wire, the noise startles Sidney much more than it should, and she cries out again. The length of wood slips out of her hand and thumps to the kitchen floor barely an inch from her toe.

"Shit," Sidney sighs, pushing a wayward strand of hair off her face. She listens briefly. Her father's snores continue, unheeded by this sudden moment of chaos. Then she turns to open the door, wondering sharply who would be out wandering around in two feet of snow at this time off the morning.

She half expected it to be Eli, coming to have morning coffee with her dad, but when she rakes the door open, it is Chloe standing in the snow, a red and white woolen hat pulled down over her ears and a deeply concerned look on her face. "Are you okay?" she asks, her brown eyes wide and worried.

"Am I…?" Sidney starts, not sure what her friend is talking about. Then she realizes that Chloe, unlike her slumbering father, must have heard the fire lighting racket through the door. "Oh… yeah sure. I'm fine. I dropped a piece of wood on the floor, that's all."

"I saw a flash of orange through the curtain," Chloe says, looking around her into the kitchen. "I thought something was on fire."

Sidney smiles. "I might have been a bit too liberal with the newspaper when I was lighting the stove," she says, her tone slightly embarrassed. "Almost singed off my eyebrows. No damage done though, see…" She rubs her finger across her brow. "Still there."

"Thank God," Chloe breathes. "For a second I really thought your cabin was on fire."

"My dad usually lights the stove, but he's still sleeping off last night, so I gave it a shot. Next time, *less paper*."

Chloe giggles behind her mitten-clad hand. "Still a city girl at heart, I guess."

"I guess," Sidney agrees. "And speaking of being a city girl, come inside so I can close the door before I freeze to death."

Chloe nods, stamps the snow off her boots and steps inside the kitchen.

Sidney quickly shuts the door and moves in front of the stove, holding her chilled hands over the black iron cooktop. "I can't believe all this snow came in one night," she says through teeth that chattered lightly.

"For this time of year, it is a lot. Last year we didn't get our first snowfall until mid-November. But that was over three feet. This one's not over though. Probably another foot or so will come down by tonight."

"Wow," Sidney sighs, amazed. "In Vancouver, we're lucky if we see more than six inches in the whole year,"

"I know. That's why city people are so wimpy."

"Ow," Sidney pouts, feigning hurt feelings. "You're from the city too."

"Kamloops isn't the same," Chloe says, pulling off her mittens and hat. She fluffs her brown hair with her fingertips and grins into Sidney's blue eyes. "It gets almost as much snow as here. Kamloopian's are tough."

"Kamloopians? That's not even a word."

"Sure it is," Chloe insists. "And we're tough, so you got that wimp thing all to yourself, sister."

Both girls start laughing at this. Sidney turns away from the stove. "You're so weird," she says and hugs her friend.

As Chloe hugs her, Sidney can feel her warm breath against her cheek. Then her head drops slightly, and cool lips graze the inside of Sidney's neck. But a split second later, Chloe is gone, pulling away from her with a sudden jerk.

"Sorry," Chloe murmurs, her cheeks flushing to a deep rose. She starts fumbling absently with the zipper of her parka. "My... my coat is cold and wet. I don't want to...you know...make you... all...cold and wet too."

Sidney smiles at her curiously. "That's okay," she says. "It's actually starting to warm up in here now. I guess I lit a pretty mean fire after all, even if I did almost burn off my eyebrows."

They both begin giggling again as Chloe shucks off her parka and hangs it on the back of a chair.

"Would you like a tea or something?" Sidney asks, taking a kettle from the cupboard and going to the sink.

"If you're having one, then sure," she says and sits down at the table.

They are quiet for a moment as Sidney fills the copper kettle with water. Even with her back to the other girl, she can sense Chloe watching her, running her eyes up and down her body. It isn't a bad feeling. Not really. It doesn't make her feel uncomfortable or weirded out, nothing like that. In some ways, it actually makes her feel good. She really likes Chloe. She is a good friend, always there for her. She had helped make the move to Deadman an easy, enjoyable experience—and not just for Sidney herself, but her father as well. She is fun, and funny, and intelligent. And Sidney thought maybe...*well maybe she even loves her.*

What she doesn't know, however, is if she is capable of loving Chloe in the same way she suspects Chloe loves her. In a way that is so much deeper than just friendship.

In high school Sidney had had two boyfriends. One when she was in grade nine; a boy named Trevor MacIntryre who had been in grade ten. They dated for eight months and never got any farther than necking on the couch in the Jenkin's basement rec-room while Weekend at Bernie's or some other unremarkable movie played on the TV. They had broken up shortly after Trevor discovered there were many girls willing to do much more than just making-out on a couch with broken springs poking you in the back. Her second boyfriend was in grade twelve, while she was in grade ten. She had loved this boy for a time—or thought she had. At the time, her minimal life experience had provided her no better word to describe how she felt. His name was Scott Miller and with him—because she *thought* she loved him—she'd allowed things to go a bit farther. Fingers under the edge of her bra, brushing lightly against her nipples. His other hand in her lap, exploring, trying to sense what wonders lay just under the stitched barrier of her Levis. But never inside her jeans, she hadn't been ready for that, even with someone she *loved*. She *would* take him in her hand because he had practically begged her to, but only for moments at a time. It felt…odd…alien maybe. Like gripping an eel that had been dead just long enough for rigor to set in. No, she had never really liked that part of it.

But, before things could go any farther—*which she supposed they would have eventually because wasn't that what happened when you were in love?*—her mother had gotten sick and Sidney ended the relationship so she could spend more time at home.

That was it. The grand total of her experience in the strange world of love and relationships. So, in truth she doesn't have enough knowledge—even at the ripe old age of eighteen, when most girls have shared their beds with numerous different lovers—to disqualify Chloe's affections simply because she is a girl. If anything, the fact that she doesn't have a stiff eel hiding inside her pants can be counted as a benefit.

Right now, all Sidney can do is keep an open mind. Allow everything to flow in at its own pace. If it works—feeling right in all the ways she thinks it should—then she will let it happen. If it doesn't feel right, then hopefully they can move past it and still keep their friendship intact.

With the kettle filled with water, Sidney turns and sets it on the stove. "So, what brings you around this early?" she asks, going to the cupboard for cups.

"I've got a surprise for you," Chloe says with an excited sparkle in her eyes. "And I think you're really going to like it."

Sidney looks at her friend, intrigued. "Well, I love surprises, so you're halfway there already." She claps her hands in humorous, childlike excitement. "Tell, tell!"

"An adventure," Chloe tells her, grinning large.

"Adventure?" Sidney's brow creases slightly. "What kind of adventure?"

"Actually, it's even better than an adventure," Chloe goes on. "It's a treasure hunt. There's a great treasure out there just waiting to be found. And I think it should be us who finds it."

"A treasure," Sidney echoes. She goes to the table and sits down beside her. "What are you talking about? What kind of treasure?"

"I think I saw a meteorite fall out of the sky last night. In fact, I'm sure I did. Or…well I'm sure I saw something. It landed not far from here, whatever it was. In the forest. And I'm pretty sure I know where. We could find it. You know, whatever it is. If it *is* a meteor, it could be worth something. Maybe a lot. And we could be the ones to find it."

Sidney is staring at her with a mildly doubtful expression. "A meteor? You mean like a space rock? You saw a space rock fall out of the sky? Out of...*space?*"

Chloe nods. "And I know where it landed," she repeats with even more confidence.

"How do you know it was a meteor?"

"What else could it be? It was so bright, it had to be a meteor. Nothing else could be so bright."

"Maybe it was lightning or something."

Now it is Chloe who frowns. "You mean thundersnow? We don't get thundersnow here. That's only back east, in the prairies and stuff. And even if we did get it here, I know what lightning looks like, and it wasn't this. It was a meteor. I'm sure of it."

"Okay," Sidney says hesitantly. "But how would we find it? It could be anywhere?"

"I saw it come down. I know where to look. And meteors are hot. It would have melted all the snow around it. It'll be easy to spot."

"Really," Sidney says, now a hint of excitement edging into her tone. "You really think we could find it? A real meteorite? From space?"

"I know we can find it," Chloe says, and takes Sidney's hand in both of hers. "You and me, Sidney, I think we can do anything. Anything we set our minds to."

Sidney looks down at their hands for a moment, hers folded inside Chloe's. Her touch is soft and warm despite the chill that still lingers in the kitchen. Finally, she puts her other hand on top of her friend's. "Okay," she says, smiling. "Let's do it."

"Excellent," Chloe bursts and gives Sidney's hand an extra squeeze. "Totally excellent."

Sidney is a little surprised by the overwhelming joy she is seeing in her friend's face. It seems too much for the occasion, and suddenly she finds herself wondering if maybe this is more than just a hunt for a meteor in Chloe's mind. After all these months of stolen glances from the corner of her eye and lingering hugs that were just a little too tight to be mere friendship, perhaps this was the day she will finally come clean about her feelings.

Despite her uncertainty about her own feelings, the idea does fill Sidney's abdomen with warm excitement.

"When should we go?" She asks.

"I think we should go right now," Chloe says. "While the snow is still fresh. No markings yet, makes it easier to see anything weird."

"Right now? I'm in my bathrobe."

Chloe smirks at her. "Okay, maybe not right this second. I had a feeling your dad would still be sleeping, so I left my snowmobile at the top of your driveway. I'll go get it while you get dressed. Pick you up in say...fifteen minutes?"

"But I was making tea."

"We'll only be a couple of hours," Chloe says, standing up to pull her parka back on. "We can't stay out too long 'cause more snow is coming. Don't want to get caught out there in another blizzard. We'll have the tea when we get back."

"You...you've doubled someone before?" she asks, her excitement remaining, but now a nervous tint sharpening her voice. "On the snowmobile, I mean."

"I've been riding snowmobiles since I was eight. You've got nothing to worry about."

"I wasn't worried," Sidney states, though her expression is still mildly unsure. "What about my dad?"

Chloe has her gloves and hat back on now. "We won't be long. We'll probably be back before he's even awake. Leave him a note if you want to." She gives Sidney another quick hug. "I'll be back in twenty. Dress warm." Then she turns and opens the door, letting a cold rush of air into the kitchen.

"Okay," Sidney says, but the door has already closed behind Chloe.

She stands there for a moment, her arms folded across her chest. She isn't sure why, but suddenly she feels as if she's been shanghaied. Shanghaied into something she hasn't fully decided she even wants to do. This is her first winter at Deadman. Her first blizzard. And now she is heading out on a snowmobile into the snow—with the possibility of another blizzard only hours away—on some kind of a crazed adventure to find a meteorite that may or may not even exist. The whole thing is crazy.

Sidney sighs. Then she turns and heads for her bedroom to get dressed.

35

Icebound- 9am

When we get out of this mess, Dave Saunders—aka, the veterinarian—thinks miserably, *I am definitely hitting that son of a bitch Treager up for more money. I am not being paid near enough to go through this bullshit.*

This bullshit at present involves being knee deep in the snow, freezing his nuts off, and basically having absolutely no idea where the fuck he is going.

All around him snow-covered trees loom, birches and evergreens reaching high into the gray sky, swaying just slightly in an icy breeze like shivering white soldiers. Behind him, his tracks trailed away, resembling elongated question marks in the deep powder. He has walked far enough now that when he looks back, he can barely make out the tail section of the plane, where Bronson Collique sits, waiting with his demolished legs. It seems very far indeed, as every exhausting step is a battle against Mother Nature's wintry wrath, and yet he has not come across a single sign of wreckage. Not a broken piece of plane, or a suitcase, or seat, or chunk of plastic. Hell, not even a lousy bag of airline peanuts. Nothing. Just trees and snow as far as the eye can see.

"Shit," Saunders groans, his teeth chattering around the word. Although the Gore-Tex jacket he has on is doing an adequate job keeping his upper body warm, his feet, clad only in a pair of Doc Martin leather boots, are already soaked through and freezing cold. It feels like he is wearing a couple of buckets of ice-water for shoes.

He is also beginning to wonder if he has chosen the wrong direction. It really had been a crapshoot when he stepped out of the tail-section—with broken up bits of plane scattered all around in the fresh snow, it was impossible to tell which way they had come in. Collique probably could have figured it out, but he has been rendered all but useless now.

So, Saunders had guessed and just started walking, hoping for a little luck on his side. God knows he feels entitled to some right about now. But it seems that God—*the merciless son of a bitch*—doesn't agree. He is not handing out any *Get Out of Jail Free* cards in this twisted game of life.

So now he has stopped, standing with his frozen feet buried in the snow. He looks around, desperately trying to spot anything that might give him a sense of direction. But everything looks the same. There is nothing that stands out or grabs his attention. *Nothing.* Reluctantly, he begins to consider his options. At this point, there are three; keep going straight and hope to stumble across something hopeful, or veer off in some random direction and hope to stumble across something hopeful, or give up and go back the way he has come. Return to the tail-section where Collique waits with his smashed legs, expecting that Saunders will be coming back with some miracle that will save them both. Shit…if he only knew the truth.

When you're in need of a miracle, Saunders thinks, *I am definitely the wrong guy to count on.*

But he has to do something, make some kind of a decision. Standing here like a deer caught in headlights while slowly freezing to death is certainly not one of his three options.

He looks to the left, sees only trees and snow. He looks to the right and sees a lot more of the same. Finally, with a frustrated sigh, he trudges on in his original direction.

Hoping for the best.

Five minutes go by. Then ten. In some spots, the more densely treed areas, the snow is less, and walking is much easier. But in other spots there is upwards of two feet of snow, forcing

Saunders to practically lunge forward with each step. His feet are now beginning to go numb inside his boots, which is very bad. Numbness comes first, then frostbite…then no more toes.

Fifteen minutes, and he feels sure now that he has chosen the wrong direction. He is almost half an hour away from the tail section and has nothing to show for his pains but frozen feet. Continuing this way is futile. It is time to head back. At the wreckage he can regroup, warm up his feet a little, and then head out again in a new direction. That is…

He spots something. About twenty feet ahead, an odd shape poked up from the snow. Too perfectly square to be anything created by nature. Only man-made things are so flat and mundane.

With a small shout of excitement, Saunders runs. The snow drags heavily against his legs, and once he even trips, doing a full spread eagle into the deep powder. But he is up an instant later, spitting snow from his mouth, and on he runs.

He stops in front of the object and brushes off the snow with his forearm. It is a piece of medical equipment from the plane. An EEG machine. Not exactly what he has been hoping for, but at least it proved he was heading in the right direction.

He straightens up and looks around. There is something else to his left. A larger object jutting out of the ground like a strange, white anthill.

He gets to it. Brushing off the snow, he sees a wooden crate, stamped with the words *Gore-Tex, A Product of W.L. Gore & Associates.*

Winter clothing. Coats, boots, gloves. Who knows what else? Still not exactly what he wanted to find, but better. They will need warm clothes if they are going to try to walk out of here.

Walk out of here? Maybe himself, but it is doubtful Collique will be walking anywhere.

But don't think about that now, Saunders tells himself. *Those problems are for later.*

He glances around excitedly. Immediately he sees more. They are scattered all around him now. Square lumps on the frozen forest floor. Five of them. Ten. They are everywhere. He has found the *plane crash jackpot.*

He hurries over to another one. More medical equipment; smashed up pretty good. The next one is also a crate. It is stamped with a logo that looks like a mountain. Mountaineer Manufacturing Inc. Some kind of outdoor equipment. Tents, snowshoes, sleeping bags. Handy things to have in the woods, but again, not what he is looking for.

He moves on to the next hump in the snow and digs it out. Here is a white tote marked with a large red cross. First-aid supplies. "There you are sucker," Saunders says out loud. He unclips the lid and pulls it open. This is the real jackpot; bandages, ointments, peroxides and sterilizers, even stitching kits and quikplaster for making temporary casts. And, most importantly, *painkillers.* Ibuprofen, Codeine, Morphine, and the ruler of the roost, *OxyContin.* Apparently, Ben Treager is not one to spare any expense when it comes to pharmaceuticals. Everything Saunders needs to get Collique back into some kind of half-assed shape. He'll still be far from perfect, but at least he should be able to move and not be completely useless.

At least, this is what Saunders hopes.

He closes the lid again and gets to his feet. *Gotta get this back to the wreckage,* he thinks. *Fix Collique up, then come back for the rest of the supplies. Might even find the satellite phone. Finally, a little luck on my side. It's about goddamn…*

But then his eyes lay on something that bring his thoughts of luck to a chilling halt. He stares at it for a long time, the hairs on his arm crawling under the Gore-Tex jacket. A bead of cold sweat runs down his forehead and into his right eye. Saunders mops it away absently.

About ten yards from where he stands with the first-aid tote at his feet, there is another hump in the snow. This one is much larger than any of the others. And, though it is also square, it had somehow landed on its edge, burying one of its eight corners into the ground. It now resembles a miniaturized version of an Egyptian pyramid, seeming as out of place rising from the snow-covered forest floor as a snowman would be perched in the desert sands of Egypt. Saunders' eyes squint as he raises a trembling hand to cup his mouth. His stomach suddenly feels like it is full of squirming, coiling snakes, each one trying to slither its way up his dry throat.

That's not it, his mind shouts frantically. *It's something else… some other chunk of the plane. A broken wing, or a bent engine cowl… it could be anything…please…just not…*

But it isn't *anything*. Not *something else*. And despite his mind's senseless tirade of denial, Saunders knows it. This size and this shape, there is only one thing it can be.

Mother's Womb.

At this point, Saunders does the only smart thing he can do. *He grabs the first-aid kit, turns, and runs back to the wreckage as fast as the snow will allow. He splints Collique's legs with precise and speedy skill, then the two of them hike out of the forest, find a road and are quickly picked up by a passing snowplow. And, wouldn't you know it, the driver of the plow just happens to have a thermos full of hot chicken soup and a pastrami on rye sandwich that Saunders gobbles down in three hungry bites. They are all saved. The End.*

Unfortunately, the smart thing to do, and the thing that the stubborn curiosity of the human mind will *allow* a person to do are often as different as night and day. Which is why all this happened in mere seconds, and only in Saunders mind. Instead of running back to the wreckage and bandaging Collique, he pulls the tranquilizer gun out of his jacket and starts through the snow towards Mother's Womb.

The box had come to rest in a small clearing, with very few trees shielding the forest floor. Therefore, the snow is at its deepest within twenty-five feet of the box and any forward movement that Saunders makes is with laborious jumping strides.

As he comes within ten feet away, he stops. Looking at it now, Saunders sees it is only the deepness of the snow that is keeping Mother's Womb teetering on edge. From the angle it sits, he is able to see the two front sides of the strange pyramid, each covered in a thin layer of powder. But no matter how much he cranes his neck, he is unable to see the back.

"Here Kitty, kitty," he mutters, clutching the grip of the gun tightly enough to pale his knuckles.

Slowly, he begins forcing himself sideways, cutting across the front of the box, but only moving a foot or so closer. Again, he stops, stretching his neck, trying to see around the other side. Still it is hidden from view.

"Fuck a goddamn duck," Saunders groans.

For a moment he stands there, not moving, contemplating how he should proceed—or *if* he should proceed for that matter. He is close enough to Mother's Womb now that if the tiger *is* there, and conscious, then Saunders would not be thinking about this at all. He would be dead. So, this means, quite simply, that the animal is either not there or it is unconscious, or best of all, dead.

In his mind, Clint Eastwood's voice rises up with all its grit and bad guy killing power; *do you feel lucky, punk?*

"Fuck it," Saunders bellows suddenly and takes two long, bounding leaps forward. He skids to a stop facing the back of the box, snow billowing into the air in white puffs. His arms are locked, holding the pistol straight out in his best double-handed cop pose.

Around him, everything is quiet, the only sound is a light whisper of wind pushing through the laden branches. Where the back panel of acrylic had once been, there is nothing, and as Saunders had suspected, Mother's Womb is empty. Gazing inside the box, he sees the tattered remains of the harness that had suspended the tiger in its slumber. Wire and tubes dangle down like sprigs of straggly witch hair, but otherwise there is nothing else. The tiger is gone.

He looks around, and leading away from the box is a large, misshapen trench cut into the snow. It continues back thirty yards before disappearing into the thicker brush.

"Son of a bitch," Saunders says, letting the gun drop to his side.

The fucking thing survived the crash. No, wait, it didn't *just* survive. It is completely unhurt. There is not a single drop of blood anywhere.

Well, it's not my problem, Saunders tells himself. *Not my problem at all. This is that bastard Treager's problem. If he's still alive out there, let him deal with it. If he's not, fuck him and the goddamn tiger.*

Right now, Saunders only priority is getting the first-aid kit back to the wreckage. Then he can fix up Collique, and Collique will get them the fuck out of here. Beyond that, nothing...

Behind Saunders, something strikes the snow with a heavy '*whump*' sound. He screams and spins around, jerking the gun up. Without any conscious thought, his finger pulls back on the trigger. There is a muffled 'pop' and a curl of smoke rises from the barrel of the gun. The dart buries itself into the snow twenty feet from Saunders. There is nothing else there. *Not a fucking thing.* What he had heard was a harmless lump of snow dropping from a branch. *'Whump'.*

"Shit," Saunders growls. Because of his stupidity, all he has left in his hand now is an empty air gun. *Just great.* If the tiger comes after him, he can throw the useless fucking thing at it. Maybe take out its eye. *Yeah Right!*

With this thought driving him, Saunders pounds back to where the first-aid kit lay in the snow and grabs it. His options have suddenly become only one. He is getting the fuck out of here.

36

At the same time Saunders is firing his only tranquilizer dart into the snow, Bronson Collique is drifting the outer edges of a semi-conscious state, the wrecked cargo hold a silent corpse of steel around him. His own air pistol is resting on the bumper seat beside him, and the weight of the Beretta still pushes against his side. He is not really unconscious, nor is the doze he is in deep enough to be called sleep, yet his mind is churning with subconscious thoughts that could only be described as dreams. Dark images shrouded in shadow, but still completely recognizable. These pictures in his mind are animals. All the animals he has stalked and killed over his long career as a hunter. Fierce beasts that could have easily finished him if not for his rifle, or bow, or leg trap. So many creatures, all murdered for no other reason than the bragging rights of an angry little Frenchman. But somehow they have escaped from their animal purgatory and are now stalking him. Marching in an organized pack, all unified in their purpose. And leading them, a dark guide towards their deathly goal, is a beast so huge it dwarfs all these other vengeful souls within its monstrous presence. The hatred in its glowing yellow eyes cut into the deep shadows of Bronson's mind like a scalpel through diseased flesh. As it draws slowly closer, and the sound of its fury begins rumbling out of the darkness, a fist of dread tightens around his heart, chilling his skin even under the warmth of his parka. He is overcome by a fear more powerful than any he has felt before. It is coming for him. They are all coming for him. And he cannot run because…because his legs…are…

Collique jerks suddenly, snapping fully awake. He blinks, rubs his eyes, and looks around. For just a moment, as the dream fades away like a mist, leaving his mind foggy with the residue of sleep, he struggles to remember where he is. Then the jagged pain in his legs comes awake and screams, frightening away any last remnants of dream. Reality is slammed back into his brain in a single, savage thrust. His teeth clamp together with skull-jarring force, transforming the scream that is worming up his throat into a muffled sob. His eyes squeeze shut, and his hands shoot out instinctively towards his destroyed legs, but then freeze just short of touching them—palms hovering half an inch above his knees. Heat, as if from the last remaining embers of a dying fire, emanates up from his swollen, angry flesh.

Until now, Collique would have never believed there could be so much pain. Shearing and white-hot. Cutting up his spine and into his mind like the claws of a—

Like the claws of a...

Of a...what?

A tiger...The tiger... Oh God, the tiger is free and it's coming for us all!

Bronson's eyes spring open, bulging, and frightened. Now, with the memory of their current situation stripping away any other thought, his hand moves towards the seat beside him. There he finds the comforting feel of the tranquilizer gun. He scans his surroundings with the attentive care of a deer stepping into a clearing on a chilly fall morning. Here are the remains of the cargo hold; twisted and empty. To his left, the yawning hole where an airplane used to be; gnarled and ragged like torn flesh. And beyond this, the forest; its pristine blanket of snow marred only by the rough trench left by Saunders as he departed.

Departing trail, but none returning, and no sign of the doctor anywhere in the hold. Which means Saunders is not back yet. This in itself is not a cause for worry, depending on how long ago he had left. Collique wears no watch. He has never required one before.

His internal clock has always been as reliable as the Big Ben in Westminster Palace; his keen senses judging the time of day by the sky, or the feel of the air. But those senses are now buried under a deep shroud of pain. Only five minutes may have passed, or it could have been five hours. Bronson has no idea.

So now the question Bronson is forced to ask himself is, if Saunders has not returned, what is it that had woke him so abruptly? He felt quite certain it had been a sound. Something over and above the moaning wind or the creaking sway of snow burdened branches. A noise he is sure had occurred, though is unable to pinpoint. He searches his groggy memory, trying to draw out the identity of the sound, but can find nothing beyond the last fading scraps of his dream.

What had it been? A clunk? A bang? A rustle? Or could it have been a scream...

Then it comes again. The sound. Not loud, but very distinctive. Tentative and cautious, yet easily recognized. It is the soft crunching of snow under a footfall. Just to the right of where the airplane section lay, but still well outside of Collique's line of sight.

The pain remains, not dulling or easing in any way, but for the moment he forces it into the background, like a puppeteer hiding behind a black curtain. Bronson's grip on the pistol tightens as all his concentration becomes focused on his ears. The wind, the swaying trees, a bird singing somewhere in the far distance.

And the sound of shifting snow as a step is taken, and a moment later, another. Then a third.

"Saunders," Collique calls out, straining sideways as far as his shattered legs will allow, trying to catch a glimpse of whatever is approaching. "Is that you, Saunders?"

The mutterings of the wind are his only reply, though at the sound of his voice, the footfalls do pause. But only briefly. A moment later, they continue, slow and deliberate. Moving closer.

"Dammit Saunders, if that's you, say something or you're going to catch a dart."

Then there is another sound, so faint that at first it is almost inaudible. But as the steps move closer, this new sound also grows steadily louder.

It is not wind, or the sway of branches. It is the quick, shallow movement of air as something alive draws breath. The sound of breathing.

"*Baise cette merde,*" *Fuck this shit,* Collique barks. He shoves his hand inside his parka and pulls out the Beretta. Now, with a weapon gripped each hand, he points them both towards the opening. "Come on you son of a bitch," he says, still speaking in French. "*Montrez-vous.*" *Show yourself.*

Seconds pass, each seeming to last an hour, as the footsteps continue to advance. Despite his pain, the hunter inside Collique is awake now. His attention never falters, his outstretched arms unmoving, the weapons' sightlines steady and precise. His fingers curl loosely around the triggers, with every breath leaving his lungs in perfect unison to those of whatever approaches.

Then, just beyond the limits of Bronson's line of sight, the footsteps paused again. He can still hear its breathing. Each breath being drawn in sharply. Quick and investigative, as though it is smelling the air. Smelling him.

Bronson's fingers tighten. His eyes narrow slightly, working to block some of the brilliant white glare cast from the snow. A small bead of sweat breaks from his hairline and trickles slowly into the hollow of his temple.

Another tentative step forward, crunching against the fresh packed snow. Now Collique's breath stops completely. His nerves tighten, surging with anticipation.

Unlike Saunders—whose inexperience in the field had caused him to fire his only dart into the snow—Bronson's expertise allows him to delay his instinctive response by a mere split second. No longer than the blink of an eye, yet still long enough to stop himself from firing both weapons at the moment the large moose steps into view. It stops just outside the opening of the cargo hold and gazes in at him with nervous curiosity.

Collique lets his breath out in a relieved whoosh. He loosens his pull on the triggers and slowly brings the guns down, resting them in his lap. "Putain de merde," he sighs, returning the moose's stare. Velvety antlers push out from the sides of its massive head, stretching almost as wide as the airplane itself. He smiles at the animal. "You gave me quite the start, big fella."

Its tongue flicks out and rolls across its brown nose. Then it raises its head just enough to sniff the upper edge of the hold. After a moment, and with an unsatisfied grunt from deep in its throat, the moose's head comes down again so it can resume its investigative gaze into the bleakness of the hold. The gray winter sky glints wildly in its black eyes.

"I know," the Frenchman says. "I'm a sorry sight. Seem to have gotten myself busted up pretty good."

The animal licks its nose again and cocks its head.

Now, with the excitement seemingly at an end, the pain in Bronson's legs bursts out from behind the black curtain with a vengeance. He moans and winces but still forces himself to focus on the moose intently, hoping it will be enough to keep his mind occupied. "Say, you didn't happen to see un gars…a guy in a blue parka stumbling around out there, as tu?" he says. "J'espère, carrying medical supplies?"

The moose watches him, blinking its round eyes.

"Or maybe un gars dans un ridiculously expensive suit," he goes on. "With a girl who's beaucoup trop jolie pour lui…ah, much too pretty for him. You see either—"

There is a sudden flash of color in the moose's black eyes, and without warning its head jerks up, ears twitching forward under its long antlers. An instant later it has turned and lopes away, disappearing back into the trees.

For a moment Bronson remains perfectly still, watching as clumps of snow fall from branches in the wake of the animal's retreat. His breath has once again come to an abrupt stop. What he had just seen in the animal's eyes—that flash of color—had not actually been a flash at all. It was a reflection. The yellowy-orange reflection of something inside the cargo hold. It is inside the hold with him. *Christ, what have I done?* His senses have failed him a second time—the last time. He had allowed himself to be distracted by the moose, and the beast had crept in through the hole at the back of the hold. And now it is here, crouching right beside him. All he has to do is turn his head and—

The tiger begins to purr. Heavy and deep, like the sound of an outboard motor. Building and diffusing with each breath the animal takes. The purr of a beast. It fills the hold, echoing through the small space with a sudden, vicious intensity.

Now Bronson can even feel its breath, hot and rank against his neck, floating through his hair. He closes his eyes and sighs deeply. The memory of his dream comes back to him now. The souls of all the animals he has killed have somehow become part of this creature, entombed under its skin, mixed into its flesh, fusing with its bones. Now the tiger—*and all of them*— will kill him…

How ironic is this? Collique thinks, and a tiny smile touches his lips.

The Frenchman turns his head slowly—the creak of his neck sounding much too loud in his ears—and looks into the face of the tiger. It is crouched down in the gloom of the hold, not five feet from where Bronson sits. Its yellow eyes blaze from inside its black and orange face. Below its scarred nose, its lips peel back slightly, the rumbling purr rolling past its fangs and carrying the sour smell of death. Deeper in the shadows, behind its tensing, striped body, a long tail swishes and flicks in the darkness like a sightless snake.

Bronson's first thought, coming even before he remembers the guns resting in his lap, is how incredibly big the animal is. So big in fact, he finds himself amazed that they had been able to fit it, as well as Mother's Womb, inside the airplane's cargo hold at all. The cat seemed to fill the space from side to side and floor to ceiling.

Had it been so large when he first saw it in Russia?

As this pointless question flashes in his mind, the tiger's lips skin back even further, pulling away from its teeth into a sinister grin. It hisses at Collique, dragging the ragged sound from the dark bowels of its throat. Warm spittle flicks off its tongue and splatters against the Frenchmen's face.

At that moment, barely a second after he had turned his head, Bronson's instincts pop awake. Unfortunately, it is these same instincts that tell him it is already too late. "Fuck You!" he screams suddenly, his hand jumping up from his lap with the speed and grace of a gunslinger. He is squeezing the Beretta's trigger before the barrel is even level.

But as fast as he may be, he is still no match for the tiger. At the same instant the gun fires, its front paw, easily the size of a bat catcher's glove, shoots out at an arch and tears jagged, three-inch claws into Bronson's arm above the wrist. The deafening roar of the gun explodes through the small space, but the bullet goes low and lodges harmlessly into the metal floor. The Beretta and most of Collique's hand fly across the cargo hold and strike the far wall with a metallic thump!

Bronson glances down at the stump where his hand had been. Blood surges out of the tattered ruin with each beat of his heart and splashes across the front of his parka.

When he looks back up, the tiger is still grinning at him, purring. Their stares meet. Bronson sees himself in the cat's eyes, floating inside the yellow depths. For just a moment, as he gazes at his reflection, he feels as if his soul is being sucked up. Pulled into the animal. Trapped inside the black abyss of the tiger. Imprisoned there forever. It would be a punishment befitting a man whose only real purpose in life was to bring death to this species, and countless others like it.

A befitting punishment for his life.

Then, with the guttural croak of a doomed man, he jerks his other arm around, bringing the barrel of the tranquilizer gun up.

The tiger lunges forward and slams into the Frenchman with the power of a wrecking ball. The massive force of its eight-hundred-pound body tears the bumper seat off the floor of the cargo hold, shearing the carbide steel bolts as though they are made of plastic, then drives the seat and Collique out into the deep snow. Puffs of white billow up around them like a wintry fog. The tiger's jaws come down, seizing Collique, punching long fangs through the muscle and flesh where his neck curves into his shoulder. His carotid artery erupts, jetting streams of blood through the cat's teeth. Then, with one hard, sideways jerk of its head, Bronson's left arm and shoulder tear away from his body and pin wheel across the snow like the severed branch of an old tree, the air pistol still gripped in his dying fingers.

But this would not be enough to satisfy. The Tiger is not even close to finished. He will keep clawing and biting and tearing until it is all destroyed. And when it is finally done, when there is nothing left to devour...He will seek out more.

37

"Did you hear that?" Morgan asks. She is standing in the twisted opening of the fuselage looking out at the winter-dressed trees. Draped over her shoulders are two tattered leather seat covers. They hang down past her hips and are synched at the waist with a length of wire Ben has scrounged from a video monitor. She is shivering badly despite this makeshift jacket.

Ben is behind her, twisting a knot into the wire that he has coiled around his own waist. He knows the jackets are crude and will be little protection against the biting cold, but it is the best he can come up with until they find more supplies. "Of course, I heard it," he says and walks over to stand beside her. "It was a gunshot."

"How do you know?" Morgan says, hugging her arms across her chest.

"I've heard a lot of guns," Ben says. "In fact, I also know that particular shot came from Bronson Collique's Beretta."

Morgan looks at him, her eyes flickering with hope. "Are you sure? That would mean he's alive."

"I never doubted it. He's like me; a survivor."

"What do you think he was shooting at?" she asked, turning her gaze back to the snow bound forest.

"Nothing," Ben replies. "I'd say that shot was to signal rather than defend. He's hoping it will help us pinpoint his location."

"Did it?"

Ben shrugs. "Sure. But it was a wasted shot. All we have to do is follow the crash path of the plane and it will lead us right to the tail section."

"But what if he's not with the tail? What if he was thrown out? Or maybe he left it, trying to find us."

"No," he says, shaking his head. "All the supplies are in the cargo hold. He wouldn't leave it. And if he was belted in, I doubt he could have been thrown. I'm sure he's trying to lead us back to the tail."

Morgan is silent for a moment, staring into the trees. When she finally speaks, Ben hears a distinctive worry in her voice. "The tiger was in the cargo hold. What if that's what he was shooting at? What if its still alive too?"

Now Ben turns his head and looks at her. "That thing is comatose inside Mother's Womb," he says firmly. "It's impossible for it to get out."

"We were in a crash, Ben," Morgan says. "The plane broke in half. I know Mother's Womb is strong, but I'm also not stupid. The force of impact if that thing hit the ground could break it open, and you know it."

Of course, she is right. Occasionally Ben makes the mistake of forgetting there is quite a substantial brain hiding behind that beautiful face. "If the box broke open, then the chances are the cat is dead. And if it's not, I can promise you that's not what Collique was shooting at."

"How can you know that?"

"Because he understands the financial commitment surrounding the animal. *My* financial commitment. I've worked with Bronson Collique for a long time. Unlike most Frenchmen, he is dedicated and intelligent, and I can tell you confidently, that fucking thing could be chewing his arm off and he still wouldn't try to kill it. Tranquilizer darts *only*. No live rounds. Which is the reason he was carrying the only real gun on the plane. He's the only one I trust to do the right thing."

Morgan is frowning at him. "You're saying you think that Bronson would let the tiger live, even if it meant dying himself? You can't be serious?"

"If that's what I told him to do then he would do it."

"Did you?" Morgan asks, dumbfounded. "Did you tell him that?"

"This conversation is irrelevant," Ben says sharply. "Collique was not shooting at the tiger or anything else. It was a signal to help us find him, that's all. The sooner we get moving, the sooner we get to him, and hopefully some goddamn warm jackets. Or we can stand here discussing it and freeze to death. Which would you prefer?"

"You don't need to be an ass, Ben"

"I'm in a lot of pain right now, Morgan," Ben states. "I'm cold and tired and standing in a wrecked airplane in the middle of nowhere, so actually I do need to be an ass. It's the only fucking thing keeping me warm."

Morgan stares at him a moment longer, her eyes blazing with hurt and anger. Then, with only a single word, "Fine," she steps out of the airplane and stomps off through the snow.

Ben watches her depart, just the hint of a smile touching his lips. "Well, at least that got her moving," he says under his breath, and follows her into the forest.

38

As Morgan and Ben are discussing the strength of Bronson Collique's dedication, Dave Saunders is questioning the source of his own as he stands knee deep in the snow with the first-aid tote clutched in his arms. From his position, he is just able to see the cargo hold through the trees, about thirty yards away. Around the wreckage, heavy tree branches sway slowly in a chilled breeze, but beyond that, all seems still and quiet.

This calm, coupled with the fact that Collique had told him there were no guns in the hold other than the two air pistols, confirmed what Saunders already suspected; the gunshot he heard had not come from there. It could have been a hunter, or just some kid with a .22 plinking at squirrels, though neither seems very likely. Who in their right mind would journey this deep into the forest after a raging storm has just blanketed the whole area with two feet of snow?

Someone would have to be nuttier than a jar of Skippy to attempt something that stupid.

So, with these sources effectively ruled out, there is really only one possibility. *Ben Treager.*

This thought immediately raises Saunders' spirits. Perhaps Treager had fired the round to signal the rest of his party. Guide them to his location. If so, he hoped the man had not given up after only one shot. If he would keep shooting, Saunders felt confident he could follow the sound right to his boss.

Yet, in the ten minutes since the gunshot had echoed through the trees, he had heard nothing else but wind and the occational thump of dropping snow. So now, here he stands, his feet popsicles inside his Doc Matins, watching the twisted hulk of wrecked aircraft for even the slightest change. After a few more minutes pass, still without any new movement or sound, Saunders finally pushes on. Like where he had found Mother's Womb, this part of the forest was not thickly treed, making each step a slow and lurching struggle, but now he also has the added bulk of the first-aid tote weighing him down. He is tempted just to toss the box aside so he can make easier progress, though quickly decides against it. He has made it this far with the box and dumping it now that he is so close would be idiotic. Not to mention he needs the supplies to fix Bronson at least to the point of being mobile before they can even start thinking about searching for Treager.

Then he has another thought. Maybe Treager has already found *them*. Maybe he is inside the hold with Collique right now, and the gunshot had been his attempt to call Saunders back. Right now, he is approaching the wreckage from the side and cannot see directly into the hold to confirm this new idea, but the hope is still there. Treager and Collique are both inside, waiting for him to return. Excited by the notion of rescue, he pushes forward even harder.

As he comes to within ten feet of the hold, however, he stops abruptly. He squints his eyes, staring into the snow. There is something strange, near the wreckage. Something that he can not immediately identify. In front of the gaping hole where the plane has torn apart, there is a dark shadow on the ground. At least, that's what Saunders assumes it to be, though looking around he is not able to locate its source. His fear begins to flare again, extinguishing his new—and very short—feelings of hope. He sets the tote down and takes a tentative step forward, studying this darker patch. As he draws closer, it takes him only a moment to see it is definitely not a shadow. It is a large, oblong stain. Deep maroon, almost black towards its center, then fanning out, getting lighter nearer to the edge, fading to a dull pink. Another step closer and now he can smell it as well, sickish and metallic like the rusting corpse of an old car.

Saunders stomach rolls, pushing hot acid into his throat. He swallows hard, barely able to choke it back down. There is something lying in the snow directly in front of him. Almost without thought, he reaches down and picks it up. A boot. Sticky and black. He turns it over in his hands, gaping at it with wide, horrified eyes. A red bone sticks out of the top of the boot. It has been chewed to a round nub, bits of pink flesh and skin still clinging to it in places.

A groan slips past Saunders lips as he lifts his gaze back at the blood-soaked ground. He takes another step closer. Across from him, he sees the remains of a blue jacket lumped in the snow, ravaged and bloody, chunks of white cotton spilling out. Beside this is the other air pistol, partially buried, its barrel poking up towards the gray sky like a long, black finger. The warm blood has melted a shallow impression into the snow and now, staring into it he can see…

His stomach rolls again savagely. Still clutching the boot in his hand, he turns his head and vomits. He retches several times, spitting hot bile onto the chilled white ground. When he finally looks up, with his head still turned away from the sight of Collique's butchered remains, he is looking into the cargo hold. His eyes lock on something lying on the floor just inside the hold. Is it…?

A gun! There is a goddamn gun lying there. And this is not another useless air pistol, but the real deal. Probably the very weapon that he had heard. Where it came from or how it ended up in the hold, he has no idea, but it doesn't matter. With it, he can protect himself from whatever—*the tiger…you know it's the tiger*—has ravaged Collique.

Saunders drops the bloody boot and takes a diving step towards the hold.

From behind him, making barely a sound, the tiger bursts out of a stand of evergreen trees where it has been crouched, watching him with a hunter's patience. It hits Saunders like a locomotive, pounding him face-first into the forest floor. The tremendous force folds his backbone in half, shattering three vertebrae. In the chill of the fresh snow, the tiger's head comes down and its powerful jaws clamped around the back of Saunders' head, shattering his skull with the same ease as an egg in a vise.

39

"We need to go back right now," Morgan sobs through her cupped fingers. Above her trembling hands, her wide green eyes stare with stunned horror at the twisted hulk of airplane in the distance. More specifically, they are locked onto the large, deeply stained patch of snow that pools out in front of the metal carcass like a crimson lake.

Ben is standing just behind her, clutching his injured arm against his body, each labored breath puffing a silver cloud into the icy air. It has been over an hour since they set out from the wrecked fuselage in search of Collique. In that time, he has discovered that battling his way through the deep snow is proving to be a much more difficult and painful task than he had expected. Regardless of how careful he is to keep his arm immobile, each step he takes jars his bad shoulder, sending shock waves of pain into his brain. It's as though someone has clamped jumper cables to his balls and is giving him a good *zap* every time his foot touches the ground.

His breathing is also getting worse. More strained and painful. Ben doesn't need a medical degree to know what this means. One of his broken ribs is beginning to shift, pushing against his lung. If this continues, and the bone moves just the right way, it could pierce his lung. Or worse yet, his heart. He could suffocate on his own blood. Die right here in the shitty, God forsaken snow.

"We need the supplies from the cargo hold," Ben says, pushing a step forward so he is beside her. "We won't make it without them."

Morgan drags her eyes away from the grisly scene to look at him with disbelief. "We...we can't go over there. The tiger... killed...Bron—'"

"There is no reason to believe the tiger is anywhere around here," Ben says to her. This, like almost everything he had told her since the crash, is only a half truth. There is just as much reason to believe the animal *is* around somewhere. Hell, it could be crouching inside the wrecked cargo hold right now...waiting for them. But this is a chance he has to take. Their survival depends on the supplies. And this fact *is* the truth.

"But...the blood..." Morgan says. She is clutching at his right arm now. "There's so much blood. Everywhere..."

"There was a plane crash here, Morgan. A very serious one. We are lucky to be alive. Collique...well..." Ben shrugs. "He wasn't so lucky."

"You...you think all that blood is from the crash?"

"Of course," Ben replies confidently. "The plane was cut in half. It stands to reason that Collique, or the veterinarian that was with him, might have also got cut in half. That would explain this amount of blood."

Morgan grimaces. "God..." Then she is studying his face again with doubt in her expression. "What about the gunshot?

You said it was Collique…signaling us. He couldn't do that if he was…" Her words trail off.

"As I said, the blood is more likely from the veterinarian. Or maybe it's the vet that has the gun now. He could have fired the shot."

"But what if—"

"I don't have all the goddamn answers, Morgan," Ben snaps, jerking his arm out of her grasp. "For all I know the blood could be from the tiger. Being afraid of something that could just as likely be dead is not going to help us here. We need those supplies. Getting them from that cargo hold is the only way we get out of this alive. That's all that matters to me right now."

Morgan stares at him for a few more seconds, then slowly turns her gaze back to the wreckage. The tears on her cheeks are already beginning to freeze. She wipes them away with the back of her hand. "So, what are we going do?"

"You stay here," Ben says. "Keep an eye for any movement. Shout if you see anything. I'll go over there and check it out. Make sure it's safe. Then I'll call you and we'll gather up what we need."

"What if it's not safe?"

Ben looks at her. "Then it really isn't going to matter anymore, is it?" he says flatly, and turns to start his battle through the snow.

40

White. So much white, flashing past like a rolling river that has no end. Crisp and clean, yet also as blank and sterile as a hospital corridor. Even the trees, usually so huge and dominating, seem lost in the wintery shroud of colorlessness.

Someone could almost drown in all this white, Sidney thinks.

She is perched on the seat behind Chloe, gripping the side rails as the snowmobile speeds over the snow. Just as Big Dwayne said, Chloe is indeed a good rider. She handles the heavy machine with the poise of a jockey controlling a thoroughbred. She leans into every turn, using the weight of her small body to navigate the snowmobile through the trees. It seems almost effortless, simple in its elegance. But Sidney knows this isn't true. Her friend just makes it *look* easy.

With the constant rumble of the snowmobile against her thighs, and the blankness of the ongoing forest flickering by, Sidney begins to feel a strange sense of calm; a hypnotic effect that is slowly lulling her into a state of relaxed tranquility.

This is why, when Chloe brings the machine to a sudden stop, Sidney is looking left, staring absently into the frozen forest, and is caught completely off guard. Her bottom slides unheeded over the smooth leather seat, thrusting her body forward. She slams into Chloe, driving the smaller girl's chest into the handlebars. Chloe grunts as all the air is squeezed from her lungs, yet her eyes never leave the object that is protruding from the snow just ahead of where the snowmobile has come to its jarring stop.

Sidney loses her footing on the rails and slips off the seat, landing on her back beside the machine. She lies there for a moment, stunned, gazing up at gray sky beyond the treetops.

When she finally turns her eyes to her friend and sees that Chloe still has not moved, Sidney feels the beginning twinges of worry.

"Chloe," she says, struggling to sit up in the unforgiving snow. "Chloe, are you alright? What is it? Why did you stop like that?"

But Chloe doesn't reply. She just sits, leaning against the handlebars, staring straight ahead.

"Chloe," Sidney calls again, pulling herself to her knees. "Are you okay?"

The other girl remains silent, but at last she does move. Her arm comes up slowly, her mittened hand pointing into the distance.

Sidney turns her head and looks. At first, she isn't sure what she is supposed to be looking for. Other than a lot of trees, all she can see is a large, misshapen hump sticking up in the snow. Maybe a pile of rocks or fallen branches. It really doesn't look like much of anything to her.

But, as she is opening her mouth to say this to Chloe, she notices something else. Another shape pushing towards the sky. And this shape, long and flat and so obviously man-made in this forest of trees, is easy to identify. It is the wing of an airplane.

"Oh my God," Sidney gasps. "Is that…"

"An airplane," Chloe finishes for her, nodding her head slowly.

"Oh my God," Sidney says again. "But how did it get here?"

"I guess it crashed," Chloe replies. "This must be what I saw last night."

"But you said it was a meteorite."

"I was wrong."

Both girls are quiet then, each contemplating, trying to make sense of what they are seeing. Silence hangs between them, filled only by the wind whispering over the white treetops.

"Where's the rest of it?" Sidney asks after some time. "The tail part?"

Chloe shakes her head again. "Don't know. I guess it broke off somewhere else."

Sidney looks stunned. "Broke off? God, how is that even possible?"

"Probably hit a tree. A big tree would be strong enough."

"Okay. I guess you're right. But it's a pretty big plane. I mean, shouldn't there be people? Pilots and passengers? Where are all the people?"

Chloe gazes somberly at her friend. "Dead."

"God," Sidney moans.

"Probably scattered all over the forest. Not many people survive plane crashes."

"Well, what should we do? Should we go look inside? See if there's anyone in there? Someone could still be alive. Maybe hurt."

"Have you ever seen a dead person?" Chloe asks. She has climbed off the snowmobile now and is standing next to Sidney. "Like, for real. Not just in the movies."

Sidney is quiet for a moment, contemplating, then says, "I was with my mom when she died. My dad and me. We were with her in the hospital room."

"Well, I am sorry about that," Chloe says. "But that's nothing like this. These will be bloody. Probably all broken up. Maybe even, you know, guts and stuff. Is that something you want to see, because I sure don't."

"I thought you wanted to be a doctor? What if someone's hurt, or dying?"

"But I'm not a doctor, and neither are you."

"Obviously I know that." Sidney replies, frowning. She is finding her friend's lack of empathy a little annoying. "But that's not the point. We should still try to help."

Chloe huffs, her breath silver in the chilled air. Then she raises her gloved hands and cups them around her mouth. "Is anyone there?" she calls out.

A few disrupted birds flutter out of the trees, squawking their misgivings as they disappear into the cloudy sky. All else is quiet.

"Anybody," Chloe continues. "Anyone alive in there?" Only the wind responds. Chloe looks at Sidney, her eyes showing the slightest shimmer of triumph. "See. No one."

But Sidney is not satisfied. She moves a few steps closer to the wreckage and raises her own hands. "Hello! Is there anyone in there? Hello!" She waits, listening. Still no response, she calls out again, as loud as her chilled throat will allow. "Please, if there's anyone in there, we want to help! Anyone!"

Chloe steps beside her. "Not many people survive plane crashes," she says again. "Especially crashes into the forest. Everything gets...well, all busted up."

Suddenly there is a roar from directly behind them as something very large comes bursting out of the trees. Both girls scream and twist around, their faces drawn with terror. The massive invader screams forward, plowing through the snow towards them, bellowing loud enough to shake loose ice-shards from the branches above.

It jerks around Chloe's snowmobile and slams to an abrupt stop only five feet from the horrified girls, bursting a cloud of powdery snow into the air. It hangs there for a second like a thick fog, before settling back to the forest floor and revealing the invader.

It is another snowmobile. And on this snowmobile, straddled over the handlebars, wearing a grin wide enough to crack his face in half, is Matt Trapper.

With a flick of his right thumb, he cuts the engine. "Ladies," he says as quiet regains its control of the forest. "What are you two doing out here in the big bad woods?"

"Matt, you asshole," Chloe shouts. "You scared the shit out of us."

"Sorry," Matt says, his grin showing no signs of subsiding. "Heard some screaming and thought I better investigate. Make sure everything is okay."

"How could you hear anything over that loud piece of junk."

"It's loud alright, but it's also fast. Faster than that sissy machine you're slugging around…" Matt's words and his grin both die as his eyes suddenly focus on the hulking wreckage beyond where the girls are standing. "What the hell is that?" He breathes, jumping off the snowmobile. "Shit…Is that…Is that a plane?"

"Half a plane," Sidney says. She is looking at Matt with some interest. She has known of him for a while, Big Dwayne's son, but has met him only a couple of times. Never really talked to him more than to say hello or goodbye. Now here he is and she is suddenly feeling as nervous as a lovestruck schoolgirl.

What is wrong with me? She thinks, giving her head a shake. *There are bigger fish to fry right now. Like half an airplane in the middle of the woods for instance.*

Matt is staring at the plane, awe painting his young face. "Have you guys looked inside?"

"No," Chloe says. "Where's your dad, Matt? He's with you, right? In the Cat?"

"Yeah," he replies absently, taking a few steps towards the wreckage. "He's out there somewhere," he adds, waving his left hand at the trees. "Why haven't you looked? I think we should look."

"I think you should go get your dad, Matt," Chloe says. "Go get him and bring him back here."

"There would be a first aid kit in the Sno-Cat, right?" Sidney asks. "If there is anyone hurt, Dwayne could use the first aid kit to help them. Then drive them out before the storm starts up again."

"Hey, did you guys notice those trenches in the snow?" Matt says, pointing towards the back of the plane. "I think they might be tracks, you know. Footprints."

Sidney and Chloe both look. From where they are standing, about twenty yards from the wreckage, they can just make them out. Two thin trenches cut through the snow from the destroyed fuselage and disappearing into the trees. Two trenches mean two people. Or possibly more, following along in the same track.

"Survivors," Sidney says.

"But why leave the plane?" Chloe wonders. "Isn't it safer to stay with the wreckage?"

"Looking for more survivors," Sidney guesses. "Or the other part of the plane."

"Man, I really want to look inside," Matt says. "Could be other people in there. You know, splattered all over the place. That'd be so cool."

"Matt!" Sidney shouts suddenly, any schoolgirl nervousness she may have felt evaporating like a mist in the wind. "You have to go find Dwayne. There are survivors and Dwayne's the only one who can help them before the storm comes back. You have to go now."

"Okay, okay," Matt moans, twisting around in the snow. He starts back to his snowmobile. "I'm going. I was just saying there might be more people in there, you know, that might need help. That's all I was saying."

"Getting Big Dwayne is the best way you can help anyone," Sidney says.

"The faster the better," Chloe adds.

"I'll get him." He climbs onto the machine and pulls his goggles down. But before starting the engine, he asks, "What are you two going to do?"

"We need to get heading back to Deadman," Chloe says. "If the storm catches us out here, those survivors aren't the only ones that are going to need saving. We'll let Eli know what's happening when we get back."

"Okay," Matt nods, though he still looks perturbed about not getting his look inside the wreckage. He thumbs the ignition and is gone in a roar of oily smoke.

41

Ben stands in the yawning mouth of the cargo hold, staring into the gloomy interior with incensed disappointment. It had taken him close to twenty agonizing minutes to struggle his way through the thigh-deep snow, only to find the hold virtually empty. Everything, *including Mother's Womb*, must have tumbled out when the plane impacted the tree. Now it is all scattered somewhere in the forest.

But it may as well be on the moon, he thinks grimly. His ribs are bad enough now that he doesn't think he'll be doing much more traveling until he can get them bound. The big problem is, he has nothing to bind them with.

Behind him, crimson carnage paints the ground. All that remains of his old friend Bronson Collique and some other poor slob—more than likely the unfortunate veterinarian—splayed out in bloody finality. And all around, punched into the gruesome snow, are the huge, unmistakable tracks of his tiger.

Ben understands now. It is impossible to deny. Morgan had been right. The animal is still very much alive. Alive and probably not far away. It has been almost two hours since they heard the gunshot, which meant this violent encounter happened within that time. And, although the tracks do lead away from the area and disappear into the trees, how far could the animal travel in that much time. The snow will most definitely slow it down. It could even be injured, hold up somewhere just inside the tree line. Maybe it is watching him right now.

Ben shudders, tweaking his bad shoulder. A line of pain shoots up his neck.

"Shit," Ben groans from behind a clenched jaw. "Got to calm down. Got to stay focused."

He gazes around the hold, trying to spot anything through the gloom that could be useful. Other than a few pieces of broken machinery and wire, the whole interior is empty. He notices the spot where the bumper seat must have been. The metal is shredded upwards where the bolts had torn out of the floor. The seat itself is now sticking out of the blood-soaked snow. Collique must have been injured. There was no other explanation. On countless occasions, Ben has witnessed his astonishing hunting skills. His speed. His amazing sense of hearing and sight. His almost inhuman instincts. He must have been an injury. Otherwise, the tiger would have never caught Barney off guard. *Never.*

So now what, Ben asks himself. *No Collique. No supplies. And obviously I'm busted up worse than I thought. What's my next move?*

The empty hold is of no help, so Ben begins to turn. Head out, get back to Morgan and regroup. Pain or no pain, they will have to keep moving. Try to find the supplies. It is a big forest but there must be...

Then he spots the gun laying against the wall on the far side of the hold. He shuffles over and picks it up. Grimacing, he wipes away bits of skin and flesh from the grip. Using his thumb, he releases the clip. Eight bullets left. And one in the chamber. One bullet missing.

The shot they had heard. Probably Collique's last-ditch effort to save himself.

Guess the tiger was faster. Sorry about that, Barney.

Feeling his spirits lifting, Ben smiles as he slides the clip back home.

No supplies, but now I've got nine bullets, he thinks, stepping out of the hold into the snow. *Let that cat come now. Try something. I guarantee that I won't be too slow.*

Still smiling despite the pain in his shoulder, Ben starts back to where Morgan is waiting. Twenty feet to his left, the first-aid crate Saunders had dropped lies unnoticed in the snow.

42

No girls are gonna tell me what to do, Matt thinks.

He is sitting on his snowmobile, his goggles pulled up to his forehead, looking into the wrecked fuselage. In exact reflection of Ben Treager's reaction to the cargo hold, Matt is disappointed with what he sees inside the aircraft. No dead bodies, no severed limbs, no blood. Just busted up seats and wires hanging everywhere. Boring.

But it was okay. Getting a look into the wreckage isn't his only mission. He has way bigger plans in mind.

From just far enough inside the tree line so he wouldn't be spotted, Matt had watched the girls mount their snowmobile and head back towards Deadman. Then he had be-lined straight for the wrecked airplane to get the look those bitches had tried to deny him. Even if that Sidney girl is kinda pretty, no one told Matt Trapper what he could or couldn't do.

Well, except maybe dad.

But Big Dwayne isn't here right now, and that's just fine. Matt has no intentions of doing what the girls have asked. No way and hell no. He isn't about to let his dad have any of this glory. Big Dwayne gets all the glory he needs. It's about time Matt got a little attention for himself, and saving the survivors of a plane crash is the perfect way to do it.

Just imagine, riding back to Deadman with the survivors. Getting them out of the forest just in the nick of time. Saving them from the storm. From death. He will be hailed as a hero. Probably the greatest hero in history. Everyone will look at him differently then. They will probably give him presents. Maybe even money. His puke brother Danny will be so jealous he'll probably just lay down and die. But best of all, Big Dwayne will finally have to be nice to him. He might even let him drive the Sno-Cat. How awesome would that be?

Sidney will probably want to go on a date. He can take her for a ride in the Sno-Cat. He'll drive far into the woods so there is no one around for miles. Then they'll kiss. *Making Out* is what they call it on TV. They might even do other stuff. She could put his pecker in her mouth. That would be so cool. As long as she doesn't bite it or anything like that.

Matt winces at this thought. She would never do that, though. Him being be a hero after all.

Sporting his face-cracking grin, and a boner under his snow pants, Matt pulls his goggles back over his eyes. He turns the snowmobile in the direction of the survivors' tracks and roars off through the trees.

43

Morgan is so cold. Colder than she has ever been in her life.

She is sitting, leaned back against the trunk of a large evergreen tree with her knees pulled up to her chest. A canopy of branches fans out above her, leaving this spot with only a dusting of snow. But just beyond the tips of these piney arms, the powder is piled up two feet. And once again, more snow is beginning to drift lazily down from the sky.

From this position, if Morgan cranes her neck, she is just able to peer over the drifts enough to watch Ben's progress. It had been quite easy to tell he was having a difficult time. What normally would have been a two-minute walk had taken Ben much longer. Fighting his way through the freezing snow had been slow enough, but he would also stop every minute or so, his hand pressed to his chest or clutching his bad arm, puffing out silvery clouds of breath.

When he did finally reach the wreckage, navigating a wide berth around the crimson stains in the snow, he had disappeared into the hold. But only a minute or two later he was back out again, empty handed.

Morgan almost started weeping as she watched him begin to battle his way back. He said he would call her over to help gather the supplies, but instead he was returning with nothing. Which meant the hold must have been empty.

But Morgan does not cry. She is too cold, too tired, and too dehydrated to shed any more tears. So instead, she just sits, hugging her shivering body, waiting as Ben makes his slow journey back. In her mind, she now begins to face what is quickly becoming the only inescapable conclusion to their situation.

They are going to die.

Everything is piled against them. It is obvious that Ben is hurt much worse than he will admit. The cargo hold is empty, which means they have no supplies. It is starting to snow again, and Morgan is so cold that her hands and feet are beginning to go numb. In one twenty-four-hour period, everything good in her life has vanished. Hell, she doesn't even have the tears left to mourn her own demise. All she can do now is sit under this tree, watching Ben and waiting to—

There is a noise to Morgan's right, the muffled roar of an engine. She jerks her head around, ignoring the cry of pain from her stiffened neck muscles, and scans the forest. There is nothing to see, but the sound is still there, getting louder. She forces herself up to her knees, keeping her eyes locked in the direction of the noise. Louder and louder, until it is almost a scream, vibrating against the trees.

Finally, it appears over a crest of snow. A snowmobile. Plowing its way across the forest floor, plumes of white exploding around it. The driver spots her under the tree. He leans his body sideways over the handlebars and the machine lurches towards her.

"Thank God," Morgan breathes, struggling to her feet. She steps out from under the branches, pushing her numb legs through the snow. Two steps farther and the snowmobile is already in front of her, rumbling to a halt. A moment later the engine falls mercifully silent.

"Holy shit lady, are you okay?" Matt asks, shoving his goggles up. Though his voice does sound concerned, there is a grin on his face that stretches from ear to ear.

But Morgan barely notices. She is so happy that now the tears do come, rolling down her red cheeks. "Yes…" she stammers. "I mean no…there was a crash. I…we were in a plane that crashed. In the forest…the plane crashed."

"I know," Matt says. "I saw it."

"You saw it? What…"

"The plane. Back there." He gestures over his shoulder. "I was just there. I followed your tracks. That's how I found you. I'm here to save you."

"T-t-t-thank you," Morgan says through chattering teeth. Her entire body has begun to tremble violently. "I…I'm so cold…I can't feel my f-f-feet."

"I'll bet." Matt says, still grinning at her from his seat on the snowmobile. "Jeez, it's gotta be two or three below. And that's not much of a coat you've got on. Mines stuffed with down. That's like duck feathers or something. Shit, it could be minus ten and I'd still be toasty as toast. My gloves too. They cost like a hundred bucks or something. My dad says…" Matt pauses for a second, thinking. Suddenly his cheeks begin to redden noticeably, and he shakes his head. "Ah shit, I'm sorry. You're freezin' to death and here I am yappin' on about my coat. Here, here…" Pulling his gloves off, he jumps off the machine and hurries over to her. He drops the gloves in the snow and unzips his jacket. "You wear this," he says, shucking off the thick garment. He holds it out to Morgan. "It'll warm you up."

"But w-w-won't you be c-cold?" she asks, though she immediately accepts the jacket and is already throwing it around her shivering shoulders.

"Nah. I still got my sweater. Besides, I'm used to the cold. Been livin' out here most of my life."

"Out h-here? In the forest?"

Matt chuckled. "Not like *right* here. I live at Deadman."

Morgan is fumbling with the zipper, her fingers are so stiff and cold she can't get them to grab the little metal tab.

"Do…do you want me to help you?" Matt asks hesitantly. "I mean…I can help if you…if you want."

Morgan drops her arms to her sides and sighs. "Please. I c-c-can't get my fingers t-o work."

"Sure, sure," Matt says. He steps forward, clips the zipper together and pulls it up, his eyes never wandering from the swell of her breasts. "All zipped." He backs away, smiling proudly.

"Thank you. My name is M-morgan"

"Mines Matt. Matt Trapper."

"Thank you, Matt Trapper. Thank you very much."

Matt's cheeks flush with red again. "Sure. No problem."

Morgan looks at the boy's snowmobile. "Are you out here alone, or are there others?"

For the first time since he had ridden up, Matt's grin falters. "Others? What others?"

"Others. Like friends. Or your parents."

Matt shakes his head. "Nope. I don't need nobody else. I can save you perfectly fine all by myself."

"I'm sure you can," Morgan says. "But it's not just me. There's also—"

"Me," Ben calls out.

Morgan and Matt had not heard Ben approaching, so they both jump at the sound of his voice. Morgan's feet slip in the snow, and she almost falls, but Matt grabs her arm just in time, pulling her back up.

"Who have we here?" Ben asks, digging his way through the last couple of yards between them. Tiny icicles have begun to form in his hair, and his cheeks and nose are fiery red. But it's the hand of his bad arm that looks really bad. It is swollen and has turned an odd purplish color like over ripened plumbs. He stumbles two more feet and stops in front of them, breathing heavily and clutching his ribs.

"Ben," she cries, rushing over to him. "Thank God you're back. This is Matt. He's from…." She pauses, struggling to remember.

"Deadman," Matt reminds her.

"Deadman. That's right. Deadman. He found the plane and then followed our tracks here. He gave me his jacket."

"I see that," Ben says, staring past Morgan at the boy. "That was very kind of you. And I'm sorry, but I missed where you were from. Deadpool?"

"Deadman." Matt says again and bends to retrieve his gloves. "Deadman Lake actually. It's kind of a fishing resort type place. Snowmobiling and hunting in the winter. A few people live there all year round. Like my dad and my brother and me. He owns the Lodge, my dad I mean. He's Big Dwayne."

"Big Dwayne?" Ben echoes.

"Yeah. They call him that on accounta he's…you know…*big*."

"And is your dad…Big Dwayne…is he out here too? Looking for us?"

"Nah." Matt pauses, contemplating. After a moment he seems to come to a decision. Looking at the snow cover ground, he says, "I mean yeah. He's out here. Him and my brother are in the Sno-Cat. But they're not looking for you. They're mapping the trail. Only I know about the plane crash. I wanted to save you guys. You know, be a hero an all."

"Alright then, that's fair enough." Ben says, a faint smile touching his chapped lips. "So, what's stopping you? Save us and be a hero."

Matt is still staring downward, pulling at the fingers of his glove. "I…I can't fit you both on the snowmobile. There's barely room for two, never mind three. It was okay until you came along…I mean, you know…when it was just her," he flicks his head in Morgan's direction. "But now, I don't really know how I'm gonna save you both."

Ben looks at the snowmobile parked behind the boy. It is indeed small. Two adults would be hard-pressed to fit on the narrow leather seat. The machine also appears to be quite old and worn out. He glances at Morgan and then back at the boy. "Okay. Then what's the new plan, *now that I've come along?*"

"Well…I guess I could go find my dad. He's probably not too far away. You guys could wait here, and I'll bring him back. There's blankets and a first aid kit in the Cat. He'll get you fixed up and then run you both down to Deadman before the storm really kicks in."

"It's starting to snow harder already," Morgan says. "Can you make it back in time?"

Matt shrugs. "Sure…I guess. If he's not too far away, like I said."

"Okay," Ben says. "That's one idea. But let's put a pin in that for a minute." He walks past the boy and puts his hand on the snowmobile's handlebar. "Is this thing reliable? It looks a little beat up."

"No way," Matt says, his tone defensive. "I keep her tuned myself. She's the fastest snowmobile on Deadman."

Ben smiles. "Okay. I'm sure *she* is. And this Deadman? I'm assuming it's in the general direction you came from?"

"That way," Matt replies, pointing into the distance. "About ten kilometers. But, like I said, the three of us won't fit."

Ben nods. "That's why you're going to stay here. Morgan and I will take the snowmobile and go to Deadman."

"Stay...here?" Matt's questioning eyes flick from Ben to Morgan. "Like...by myself?"

"Big Dwayne will be along any minute," Ben says. "Because, like you said, he shouldn't be too far away. And when we get out of here, we'll let them know where you are. No problem."

Matt is shaking his head. "Nah, I don't think that's a very good idea. I mean, you look all busted up and stuff. Who's gonna drive?"

"Morgan here is an excellent driver. I trust her completely."

Morgan's lips curl affectionally. "That's sweet."

"I still don't think..." Matt begins to disagree again, but clamps his mouth shut when Ben suddenly lurches towards him.

He halts just in front of the startled boy, and takes a deep, painful breath. "Look kid," Ben says, and touches the grip of the Beretta sticking out from the band of his pants. "You're right. I am pretty busted up. I'm in pain, I'm cold, and I've had enough of these fucking woods. So, this right here, what we're doing, it's *not* a discussion. It's me telling you that this is how it's going to be."

Matt's eyes are locked on the gun. His jaw is quivering, but no sounds are coming out. Any complaints he had a few seconds ago have melted away like ice in a furnace.

"Ben," Morgan says, stepping closer to the boy and putting a hand on his shoulder protectively. "You don't need to threaten him. He's just a kid."

"I'm not threatening him. Not at all. I'm just telling him, *and you*, that I'm not spending one more second in this goddamn frozen hell than I have to." He taps the gun grip lightly. "Right Matt?"

"Yeah…yeah, sure," he stammers. "Take the snowmobile. No problem."

Ben smiles at Morgan. "See. No Problem."

44

While his son was discussing travel arrangements with Ben Treager, Big Dwayne is leaned over the controls of the Sno-Cat, navigating the tracked machine through deep drifts of snow. Beyond the windshield, the snowfall is getting heavier by the minute. Dwayne is also getting more worried by the minute. He hasn't seen a trace of his older boy in quite some time now. It isn't unusual for Matt to ride ahead of the slower moving Cat. Sometimes he was out of sight for periods of time. But never this long. And certainly not with a storm brewing in the angry sky. The boy knows better.

"I still don't see him, daddy," Danny says from the seat next to him. His younger son is gazing into the white forest through a portal window in the side of the cab. Though he is only eight years old, he knows perfectly well that his father is beginning to worry. This time Matt is really going to pay for being such a boner.

"He'll turn up," Dwayne says, careful to keep his tone even. "Your brother knows these woods as good as I do. He can take care of himself."

"Yeah, but it's been a long time," Danny reminds him unnecessarily. "He's not s'pose to go so far."

"No," his father agrees. "He's not. And that's something he'll have to answer for. But right now, I don't need you carrying on about it. Just keep quiet and let me concentrate."

"But what if he's lost?"

"I told you he ain't lost," Dwayne barks. "He knows perfectly fine where he is. He's probably avoiding us 'cause he's smart enough to know there's a deep load of doo-doo waiting when I get my hands on him."

"You gonna give him the strap?" Danny asks, a mischievous tone in his voice.

Dwayne glances at the boy. In reality, he has never actually taken *the strap* to either of his sons. Now, despite the circumstances, he can't help but find it mildly humorous how eager Danny is for this particular form of punishment to become more than just a threat, at least when it involves his old brother. "Don't you worry about what's gonna happen to Matty," he says, using a considerable amount of willpower not to smile. "You should be more concerned about what's gonna happin' to you if…"

"Daddy," Danny cries out suddenly, pointing towards the windshield. "What's that?"

Big Dwayne wrenches his head around, slamming his foot down on the brake peddle before he even knows what he is trying to avoid. The tracks of the Sno-Cat dip forward into the deep snow as the machine jerks to a halt.

"Dammit boy," Dwayne roars. "What are you shoutin…" Then he sees what has startled his son. Something is laying in the snow about twenty yards ahead of where the Cat has stopped.

Dwayne leans forward, straining his eyes against the falling snow, trying to make out what is there. He can see tufts of brownish fur poking up, surrounded by what can only be blood. A lot of blood. Obviously, they have stumbled across some predators killing ground. The sound of the approaching Sno-Cat must have scared the animal, forcing it to abandon its prey. So, whatever kind of animal has done the killing is most likely still very close.

"What is it, daddy?" Danny asks curiously, but with a hint of fear in his voice as well.

"Something dead," Big Dwayne tells him.

This is nothing new. Often in their journeys out to clear the roads and trails of new season snow, they would come across scenes like this. Normally he would just steer the Cat around and continue on his way, leaving nature to take its course.

But there is something about this that feels different. Perhaps it is the size of the carcass, or the color of the fur, or even the amount of blood. Any of these things, or something else that Dwayne can't quite put his finger on. Whatever, he decides it deserves a closer look.

He twists around as much as his large body will allow and pulls his 30-30 Remington rifle from its slot behind the seat. "You stay here," he says to Danny. "I'll be right back."

"But daddy," the boy complains. "Where are you going? What about Matt?"

"I'm checking this out." He pushes the Cats door open. Instantly a gust of freezing wind invades the cab, sucking out what little warmth there is in the small space. "I'll only be a minute. It'll give Matt a chance to rethink his situation and get his ass back here." He swings his legs out and climbs down from the vehicle. Then he turns and looks in at the boy. "Just do as I say and stay here."

"But I wanna come," Danny cries. "I wanna check it out too. Please daddy."

Dwayne says, "No. Stay here. Be a good boy." And slams the door before his son can say another word.

45

A white world stretches out before his eyes. Yet in his mind, where color normally has little meaning, everything is veiled in a haze of red. A deep, crimson red. The color of blood. Painting the snow and the trees. The whole forest. Even clouds in the sky seem to be shedding bloody flakes down, covering the earth.

This is the color of his rage. A rage that now, as he lays hidden in the snow, is the dominating force that drives him. Everything else has ceased to matter. Territory, mating, family; all the instincts that had once made him a Siberian Tiger, are gone. Drowned in the red ocean of his rage.

It is because of Man. Man has done this to him. It has killed his family. It has chased him across the land that was his home. It has caged him, tormented him, put him in a box.

Man has changed him.

And now Man is all that matters. He will punish Man. Kill it and devour it until none remain in this world. Erased. Maybe then, and only then, will he find what has been lost. All these things that have been stolen from him. Maybe he can be a tiger once again.

Yet, with all he has lost, there is still one instinct that remains. One that has, in fact, been heightened by his insatiable rage. Growing in unity with his massive size. An instinct that is now the only thing keeping the rage at bay, allowing him to be patient. To wait for the exact instant when his ravenous need for revenge is guaranteed to be satisfied. Even if only for a few moments.

His hunting instinct. Abilities that were taught to him by his mother, then sharpened further by years of survival in the mountains of Russia, and now enhanced by his time within Mother's Womb. Instincts of patience and cunning. Sight and sound and smell. Silence and speed. All coming together in flawless unison to create the perfect killing machine.

It had been effortless for him to stock and kill the animal that now lies in the snow ahead of where he is crouched. But unlike Man, he had not felt the burning need to kill this animal. He was not hungry. It had not harmed him in any way. He could have just left it to live out its life. And yet, deep inside his mind, he somehow understood that the carcass of this animal—this specific animal— *would attract Man. Man's desire for blood and carnage would draw it to this spot.*

He had been right.

The huge metal machine has stopped. Now the largest Man that he has ever seen is lumbering through to snow. It is just as his instincts had foreseen; Man is incapable of ignoring death.

His mouth begins to salivate as he watches Man, his need to destroy grows stronger with each second. But his hunting instinct forces him to remain still. Only his tail moves, swishing back and forth across the snow. This Man has the strange stick, *like the one used to kill Tiger's mother. So, he will be patient. Waiting until just the right moment. Sooner or later it will come.*

The time to attack and destroy.

46

In all his years living on Deadman, Dwayne has spent countless hours exploring the forest. He has thoroughly mapped an area of twenty square kilometers around the lake, making note of every rise in the land, every valley, every body of water. He knows the trees and the hunting paths. Every trail and road, even when they are buried under two feet of snow. He has been everywhere and seen everything.

Up until this moment.

Standing here now, with his feet freezing in the snow and his rifle leaned over his right shoulder, Dwayne stares down at something he has never seen before.

"A mountain lion," he murmurs. "Goddamn if that ain't a mountain lion."

Seeing a dead mountain lion is definitely not anything new or strange. Dwayne has seen plenty. To be truthful, he and his 30-30 have been the cause of many. In fact, there is a large male specimen in the lobby of the Lodge, frozen forever in a crouching attack position thanks to the magic of taxidermy.

The mountain lion that lies before him now, circled by an ever-widening stain of blood, is bigger than that one standing in the Lodge's lobby. Of course, the cat's size is also not what's unusual. There are large males like this one roaming all over these mountains. What is strange, however, is the way the animal has been killed. No hunter's bullet, or arrow, or even the up close and personal bowie knife has ended this creature's life. There is no doubt in Dwayne's mind that whatever has brought about this big cat's demise is not a man.

Something has torn its throat out.

Dwayne raises the rifle off his shoulder and grips it with both hands, his eyes darting from side to side, searching the woods around him. In his mind he begins to run through the list of creatures that are powerful enough to have done this. It does not take long. It is a short list.

Grizzly bear would be the most obvious. But grizzlies, or any type of bear for that matter, will be hibernating right now, not out stalking the woods looking for cougars to kill. So grizzly is out. A wolf? Not likely. There has not been a wolf sighting in this area for over fifty years. A coyote? No again. Way too small. Even a pack would not have the balls to attack a mountain lion. Then maybe another mountain lion? Also very unlikely. This is a large male, probably the dominant male in the area. There would not be another cat close to this one's size for twenty kilometers. And even if there is, these animals tended to avoid one another rather than attack. Any confrontations are just quick scuffles, ending in the weaker one slinking off with its tail between its legs. Dwayne has never heard of an incidence where one lion killed another.

So, what then? There is no other animal in these woods skilled enough to catch a mountain lion off guard, or powerful enough to hold it down and rip its throat out. What the hell could have...

Tracks.

As the word pops into his mind, Dwayne shakes his head, feeling stupid that he hadn't thought of it sooner. Everything leaves tracks. It doesn't matter if it is man or animal or machine, if it travels through the snow, it leaves tracks in the snow.

On the opposite side of the carcass from where Dwayne stands, all the snow is disrupted and pounded flat. Blood is splashed across this flattened area in a widening fan. Strangely, there is only a single path leading away, disappearing into the trees about thirty feet from the carcass.

Dwayne frowns, taking his hand off the gun long enough to brush fresh snow from his forehead. It is snowing quite hard now, dusting the whole area in new powder.

Only one path? The mountain lion, the attacker, and the retreat. But only one path. Whatever had killed this cat is indeed cunning. Following in the same tracks as the prey, reducing noise as it approached. Then, leaving the same way. Branch away once it's in the cover of trees. This makes it substantially harder for someone to track.

Someone? Like who? Who would it think is following?

And, even a better question, what goddamn animal *thinks* at all?

Clutching his gun again, Dwayne pushes his way around the carcass and steps into the area where the snow has been trampled down. There are tracks all around, pressed into the flattened snow. It is easy for Dwayne to identify most. They belonged to the mountain lion. But there are others. Larger ones.

Much larger, Dwayne thinks. He kneels, wincing as his straining knees pop. Studying the track, he is surprised to see that it looks quite similar in detail and shape to the cougar print, but is at least double the size.

"Shit," Dwayne breathes. "What the hell are you?" He brings his gloved hand down and lays it in the track. It fits easily, with an inch of empty space all the way around.

If this was another mountain lion, it would have to be weighing in at five or six hundred pounds. Maybe more. As far as Dwayne knew, there was no documented case of a cat getting that big. Not even close.

So not a mountain lion. *Then what?*

"Daddy! Daddy, where are you?"

Dwayne's head jerks up as these words float across the air. He stands up quickly, overbalances and almost topples onto his huge ass. Barely regaining his footing, he spins, looking towards the Sno-Cat.

Through a haze of falling snow, he can see Danny waving at him. The boy is halfway between the machine and the cougar carcass, standing thigh deep in the snow-trench his father's massive body has dug.

"Daddy," he calls again, smiling now. "Whatcha find? Can I see?"

Why do none of my children listen to what I say, Dwayne thinks miserably. "Dammit, Dan," he hollers back. "I told you to stay in the Cat!"

"But it's boring," Danny replies, starting to move towards him again. "And I wanna see whatcha found. Please daddy. Just a quick look."

Dwayne takes his hand off the gun and raises his arm, signaling the boy to stop. "No," he roars. "Just stop right there and go back to the Cat. There's nothing here—"

Then boy does stop, dead in his tracks, his eyes widening in sudden horror. Any color that was in his cheeks vanishes as quickly as water down a drain. Both his arms fly up, one hand to his terrified face, the other to point. "Daddy!" he screams. "Daddy behind you!"

As the words leave his son's mouth, Dwayne feels it. Part is a rumbling in the ground, like standing on a gym floor while a fat guy does jumping jacks right behind you. The other feeling—more of a sensation really—is less defined. The displacement of air. Something large moving forward; perhaps a train, roaring through a black tunnel, speeding closer and closer to where you stand, riveted to the tracks. It bears down on you, its white light piercing through your retinas and straight into your brain like a crossbow bolt.

With this strange image in his mind, Dwayne grunts, turning his large body around as fast as nature will allow. In the crucial split second between his eyes registering what he is seeing—*My God, is that a tiger?*—and the tiger hitting him, Dwayne completely forgets about the rifle in his hand.

The animal does not launch itself, as would be its regular nature, but instead comes in low, like the freight train of Dwayne's thoughts, driving its open jaws into the man's thick midsection. Dwayne is shoved backward, losing the forgotten gun from his grip, until his calves plow into the deeper snow. He grapples with the animal's huge, twisting head. Sinking his fingers into its coarse yellow and black fur, he is somehow able to keep his footing—*for the moment*. The tiger comes in again, snapping and shaking its head from side to side.

Dwayne feels another sensation then. It is odd, yet easy to define. The release of pressure. All the pressure that has been building up under his skin for years. Increasing more and more with every pound he gained. Stretching his body like a balloon stretches when it's filled with helium at some snotty kid's birthday. Suddenly, all this pressure is letting go in one giant whoosh. Water rushing through a broken dam and splashing onto the ground in a giant flood.

Oh my God, Dwayne's spinning mind thinks. *I'm being ripped open by a tiger in the woods of BC. Who will ever believe this shit?*

As if to confirm, the tiger suddenly jerks backward several steps, dragging out a mass of Dwayne's insides. They drop into the snow like coils of misshapen, gray eels.

"Ahhh, mother fucker!" Dwayne bellows as pain explodes in his midsection. He starts grabbing at the ropes of intestine, trying desperately to shove them back into the ragged hole the tiger has torn into his gut. But they are too slippery, and his hands are too numb and they keep sliding through his fingers, splattering blood down the front of his pants.

The tiger leaps at Dwayne again. It comes in higher this time, slamming all of its eight-hundred pounds into his chest. With no chance of saving himself a second time, Dwayne stumbles and goes down, landing on his back under the tiger. A large, whooping belch escapes him as the last of his breath is shoved out of his lungs.

For a moment the animal remains still, straddling him, staring down into his swollen, purplish face, each panting breath wafting with the smell of carnage. In its bright yellow eyes, Dwayne can see something burning there. The soul, driving force dictating its every move.

Hatred.

In those last seconds—before the tiger's lips peel back from its blood-stained teeth—Dwayne realizes he can still hear Danny. His son is screaming and screaming. He wishes the boy would stop. He needs him to stop. Stop screaming and run away as fast as he can. It will be the only way he can escape. Because, inside Dwayne's quickly fading conscience he knows one thing without any doubt—*when the beast is finished with the father, it will be going after the son.*

Then the tiger's jaws close around his head and with one quick snap, it peels off Dwayne's face.

47

Matt Trapper is angry. Furious in fact. Written in some of the fancy stories he is forced to read in English class, it might have said his anger is *'Red Hot'*. This description would have been exactly right, except he is actually freezing cold.

He is standing in the snow, his arms curled around his shivering body, *being angry*—at the whole world and everyone in it. He is angry at that dumb plane for crashing into *his* woods and causing all these problems in the first place. And with those two stupid girls—*even though Sidney is hot*—for getting in his way and forcing him to get involved with this whole stupid thing. He is furious with his father for not being exactly where he needs him when he needs him to be there. And his brother for…well for being such a whiney, poop face, shit head booger eater. But most of all, he is angry at Morgan—*who is even hotter than Sidney*—for acting so nice and sticking her tits out and tricking him into giving her his jacket, but then being a bitch and letting that asshole Ben—*who thinks he's so tough just cause he's got a stupid gun in his pants*—steal his snowmobile and leave him stranded out here in the woods and not even offer to give him his jacket back so he wouldn't freeze to death!

After he watched Morgan and Ben ride off on *his* snowmobile, Matt had started towards the wrecked tail section of the airplane. But he had quickly changed his mind when he saw all the blood splattered everywhere. He is not as keen on the idea of seeing dead bodies now that *he* is the one stranded. *No Thank-you!*

Now, after a lot of time spent just standing, contemplating the situation, he is headed north, plowing his way through the deep drifts. The snow has begun to fall harder, making it difficult for him to see much more than fifteen feet through the trees. But this isn't much of a worry to him. Matt has a great sense of direction and, even though they don't normally head west first run of the season, he has traveled Loggers Pass with Big Dwayne many times so he has a pretty good idea of where his father will be by this point.

That is, as long as he hasn't changed course to look for me.

This thought chills the boy even deeper than the cold. Just the idea of how angry his dad is going to be, instantly dulls Matt's own anger, leaving him feeling only weary and frightened. He is now wondering which fate would be easier; finding the Sno-Cat and facing the wrath of Big Dwayne, or freezing to death. He has heard that freezing to death is actually quite a pleasant way to go. First you're cold, then you're warm, then you're sleepy and then… *lights out.* That doesn't sound so bad. He is already cold and that has to be the worst part. Anything will be better than the holy hell he is in for at the hands of Big Dwayne.

Of course, in reality there really is no question. He would never choose death over punishment, even if it meant being grounded for two weeks with no snowmobile privileges. So he trudges on, his head down, eyelids lowered against the whipping snow—*the asshole had even taken his goggles.* He thinks about calling out. Maybe his dad is close enough to hear him. But he is in the middle of the forest. What if he calls out and something else comes for him instead of Big Dwayne. Like a cougar. Or even a bear. Matt has no way of defending himself against anything that might decide to take after him.

No. Calling out is a bad idea. Better to just keep moving. Maybe if he can't find the Sno-Cat, he might find a hollowed-out tree or something. A place he can hold up until the storm passes. An abandoned cabin would be good, though he has never seen one before. He supposes there could be one, hidden out here somewhere that he hasn't noticed. It's a far-fetched idea, but still poss—

Matt stops suddenly, his head popping up. He can hear something. In the distance and quite faint, but definitely…

something. He begins moving again, hurrying towards the sound as fast as the snow will allow. Getting louder. The sound…is it… screaming? Yes. Screaming. Floating out of the snow blanketed forest are the screams of…*his brother*!

Matt stops again, cocking his head, listening. The screams continue. There is no doubt now, it is Danny. Screaming and screaming. Crying out in horror. Something very bad is happening to his brother.

"Danny!" Matt calls. "Where are you? I'm coming Danny! Hold on, I'm coming!"

Frantically he starts forward, bending low, shoving with his legs and dragging with his arms. "Hold on Danny, I'm coming!"

There is one finally piercing shriek, then the screaming stops. But Matt doesn't notice. He is pulling, dragging, kicking himself through the snow, his eyes wide with terror, calling out to his brother.

48

As Danny Trapper watches the tiger ravage his father, he does feel fear. But it is not the dominant emotion coursing through his body. It is also not fear that is causing him to scream. What he feels more than anything else is horrorstruck wonder. He has never before experienced a nightmare that is so vivid or seems so real. He can feel the chill of cold air and the falling snow tapping against his cheeks, as well as a warm dampness spreading out from his crotch and down his legs because his bladder has let go.

All around him is the rustle of the building wind as it laments through the winter-dressed branches. And ahead of him, there are the wet tearing sounds as the huge animal dismembers Big Dwayne's body. All his senses are firing, picking up every nuance of the moment with intense clarity. *All so real.*

But shock has folded over his young mind like a protective shroud, and for this moment it will not allow him to believe that what is happening is anything more than a nightmare. Just like the monsters creeping under his bed or hiding in his closet do not exist outside of dreams, neither does this tiger. Tigers do not live in the woods around Deadman. The boy is only eight, but he knows this is a fact. Tigers live in faraway places. Other parts of the world, like *Brazil* or the *Congo*. Some places that are so distant he doesn't even know their names. Tigers live there. They can exist in all the lands with strange names, but not here. *Not in Deadman.*

So, this must be a nightmare. But with each second, it is becoming worse. Danny does not like the sounds of his father being torn apart. They make him feel sick. As well, his fear is growing, turning into terror. He wants the dream to end. He needs to wake up now.

This is the reason he is screaming. If he can scream loud enough in the dream, maybe he can wake himself up in the real world. If he screams and screams, maybe he can even wake up daddy. He'll come bursting into the room, hollering, "What kind of nonsense is going on in here!" Or his brother will wake totally pissed off, he'll jump out of bed and give Danny a good hard noogie. That would be okay. A noogie would be better than this dream. Even getting the strap from his daddy would be better. Anything that will end this horrible nightmare.

Danny screams until the tiger's head comes up. It turns and looks at him. A final shriek dies in the boy's throat, though his mouth remains frozen in a perplexed 'O'. Even at the distance of thirty or forty feet, through swirls of heavy snow, Danny can see the tiger's eyes. They are shining from inside its fiery face. Tiny orbs of yellow that finally pierce through the shroud of shock and drill the truth into Danny's mind. It is a truth more terrifying than anything he has felt before.

This is not a dream.

This is really happening. The tiger is real. Somehow it has gotten into these woods, and now his daddy is dead. It has killed him. Ripped him apart like he was made of paper mache.

Oh daddy! How can this happen, daddy? How?

The tiger steps over Big Dwayne's corpse, its eyes never leaving Danny's face. It begins a slow saunter towards the boy, pushing its massive body through the deep snow with ease. Its tail is raised high, twitching from side to side like a dancing cobra.

Danny watches it, transfixed. Trapped in the cat's yellow gaze. It is coming for him now, and yet he cannot move. His body is as frozen as a snowman.

Then, behind him, from deep inside the forest, Danny hears someone call his name. It is only once, and so distant that the word is almost inaudible. But it is enough to break the cat's hold over him. He spins and runs for the Sno-Cat. He is still in the trench plowed out by his father, so moving is easy and quick. Once at the machine, he leaps onto the track, not allowing himself even the quickest glance over his shoulder. He grabs the door handle and pulls.

The door won't open.

Danny begins to cry. He clutches the handle with both hands, twisting at it as hard as he can. It creaks and moves slightly. He tightened his grip, pulling down with all his weight. He wants so badly to look back. See where the tiger is. But he won't. Not until he is inside the Sno-cat. Tears are streaming down his cheeks as he pulls. The handle creaks some more, but still doesn't move.

"Please," Danny cries, frantic, nearing hysterics now. "Please! Please!" He yanks again, shoving his whole body against it.

There is another creak, then a cracking sound as the thin bead of ice that was jamming the handle breaks apart. Danny pulls the door open and jumps inside the cab.

He looks out the portal window in the door, his searching eyes terrified and wet. There is the tiger. Surprisingly it is still twenty feet from the Sno-Cat. It is just standing there, snow up to its belly, staring at the machine.

No. Not at the machine. It is staring at Danny. Its eyes cutting through the fog of swirling flakes as easily as the moon through a black sky. For just a few seconds the two are perfectly still. The tiger and the boy. Lives that should have been worlds apart, only coming together in the dark hauntings of a nightmare.

Then the tiger's ear twitches and it lifts its head, sniffing at the air with its scarred nose. A moment later, without looking back at the boy, it turns and, with two giant leaps, vanishes into the trees.

After it is gone, Danny lets his eyes wander back to where the tiger has left his father. Through the heavily falling snow, he can see no more than a discolored hump against the white forest floor.

"Daddy," he murmurs and begins to cry again. At this instant he wants to jump out of the Sno-Cat and run to him. Save him. But with the same clarity he now understands that this is not a dream, he also knows Big Dwayne cannot be saved. All the time the boy has spent sitting on his father's knee, laughing at the large man's funny stories—*always enhanced with plenty of gross sound effects*—or helping him make pancakes on Saturday mornings, or popcorn on movie night or riding with him on countless journeys in the Sno-Cat. All these happy times are gone. *His father is gone.*

So, instead he drags his eyes away from the meaningless hump in the snow and looks down at the control panel of the Sno-Cat. On a few occasions, when Big Dwayne—*oh God, my daddy is dead*—was in a particularly good mood, he would let Danny sit in his lap and steer the machine. That, plus the hours he has spent sitting in the cab watching his father drive, Danny thinks he can probably...

Without any more thought, he reaches out a trembling hand and pushes the ignition button. The engine roars, coughs twice, and dies. He pushes it again. The engine roars, coughs, and then smooths out to the constant rumble Danny knows so well. He grips the stirring wheel with one hand and grabs the gear shift with the other. In the footwell, the pedals are at least six inches below where his feet are dangling. Still holding the wheel tightly, he shimmies his bottom forward on the seat until he is almost slipping off the edge. Ignoring the clutch, he stretches out his foot and jams it down on the gas pedal. The engine howls frighteningly. Danny screams and pulls his foot back. He is crying harder now, tears spilling out of his eye and down his cheeks in tiny rivers. Visions of his father—*who he will never see again because he's dead*—swirl about in his mind like a funneling tornado. He stomps his foot on the gas again. This time he pays no attention to the screaming engine and shoves the shifter ahead with his right hand. With a loud growl of protest, the transmission clunks into gear and the Sno-Cat lurches forward suddenly, snow spitting out from beneath its heavy tracks. It plows through the snow quickly, heading straight for his father. Danny shrieks again and pulls the steering wheel hard to the left. The cat turns slowly, barely missing Big Dwayne's body, coming around in a wide arc. The mirror on the passenger side smacks against a tree and shatters into dust. Another tree clips the back of the machine, tearing off a taillight. Danny straightens out the wheel, then screams and jerks it to the right, shaving the bark off a large pine tree. He grapples with the steering wheel, having to stretch his neck as high as he can just to see over the dashboard. Beyond the windshield the snow whips and whirls like static on the television when daddy—*Oh daddy, my poor daddy*—falls asleep watching the news. Still sitting in first gear, but now traveling at just under thirty kilometers an hour, the Cat's engine howls angrily as the RPM gauge climbs closer and closer to the redline. Danny finally has the machine going straight, but his visibility is near zero. He can barely make out the trees as they whip past on either side of him. If one comes up in his path, there is a very good chance he won't see it in time to steer around it. This, however, does not matter to the boy. All that matters is that his father is dead, and he needs to find Matty. A tiger has killed Big Dwayne. A tiger that is still out there, lurking somewhere in the woods. But if he can find Matty, then it will be okay. He won't let the tiger kill Matty like it did his daddy.

So he ignores the screaming engine, and he ignores the whipping snow and the tree flashing by, and he keeps his foot pinned on the gas. He will get to his brother in time. No matter—

When Matt suddenly runs out of the tree line directly in front of the Sno-Cat, Danny doesn't even have time to scream. With only a split second of panicked thought, he jerks his foot off the gas and yanks the steering wheel to the right almost simultaneously. If he had turned the wheel to the left, he would have come to a stop between two trees. But because he went right, the cat pitches over the edge of an embankment, rolling and bouncing down a steep hill for thirty feet before slamming into a two-hundred-year-old evergreen tree.

The impact lifts Danny's light body up and forward. His midsection collides with the lower edge of the steering wheel, shattering his pelvis, but doing little to slow his forward motion. He hurtles head-first through the safety glass of the windshield and strikes the tree, his body folding around the thick trunk like a raggedy Ann doll. He hangs there for a second, snow landing on his broken face, mixing with his blood and running across his cheeks in ragged lines. Then he slides slowly down the trunk and flops into the snow beside the Cat. Miraculously, the machine's engine is still idling; a low, rumbling sound, similar to the purr of a large cat—*or perhaps a tiger.*

49

After watching the Sno-Cat go over the edge of the embankment, Matt stands where he is for a moment, staring through the falling snow at the spot it had disappeared. He had gotten only a split-second glimpse inside the cab before the machine veered right to miss him, but it was enough to see that Big Dwayne was not the one driving. It had appeared that there was nobody behind the wheel at all. Of course, this was impossible. Someone had to turn the Cat at that last second.

As his mind is beginning to process what he has just seen, a loud crash echoes up from depths of the embankment. It is the horrific sound of twisting metal and shattering glass. A scream rises in Matt's throat, but he forces it back, allowing only a small gasp to pass his lips. Then he is moving, kicking his way through the snow. In this slight clearing before the ground drops off, the drifts are deeper, piling almost to the boy's hips. It takes him two or three minutes of fighting before he is able to peer into the shallow gully. The Sno-Cat is there; its front end crushed against a large tree. A curl of diesel fumes still rises from its tailpipe, mixing with the swirling snow into a thick, blackish fog. Just ahead of the Cat, lying next to the trunk of the evergreen, is…something else. Matt strains forward, trying to see what is there. He can just make it out. Something…blue and green. Yes. Blue and green, slowly vanishing beneath a blanket of new white flakes.

Danny's parka is blue and green! Oh man, is that Danny down there? Could it be? He had been screaming, and now…could that be him?

"Danny!" Matt calls. He steps over the edge of the embankment and starts pushing his way down the slope. "Danny, are you okay? Danny! Answer me!"

The incline gets steeper very quickly. Soon it is only the deep drifts that are keeping Matt from pitching forward and rolling the rest of the way down. Instead of fighting against the snow, now he is leaning back into it, grabbing it, using it to keep his balance.

Drawing closer to the wreckage, he can now hear the steading, muffled rumbling of the Cat's engine. He can also see more of Danny. There is no doubt now. It is him, Matt's brother. The blue and green of his parka stands out in stark contrast to white snow. But there is something else. Deep crimson, leeching into the snow, fanning out in a large circle around his head.

"No...Danny," Matt moans. He stops beside the boy, staring down at him with unbelieving horror. Danny is laying on his back, his upper body twisted at an odd angle from the waist. One of his legs has been broken at the thigh and is sticking straight up in the air. His face is virtually unrecognizable under a shroud of dark blood.

Crying now, Matt kneels and takes the boy by the shoulders, pulling him gently into his lap. He cradles his brother's head, tears spilling from his eyes. They dripped down onto Danny's face, rinsing away some of the blood from his cheek.

"Danny, you stupid booger eater," Matt whispers. "What were you doing? Why were you driving the Cat? Where's Big Dwayne?"

Danny's chest hitches once, then rises as he takes a small, gasping breath. His lids flutter and open. Eyes, two tiny ponds in a field of red, roll from side to side and up and down, finally locking on Matt's face. His mouth begins to twitch as he stares up at his brother, but only a faint gurgling sound passes his lips.

"Danny," Matt cries. "I....I thought you were...you know..."

Danny coughs, spraying bits of red spittle onto Matt's sweater. "Ti...ti..." he murmurs, spilling more blood out from the corner of his mouth and down his chin. "Ti....Ti..."

"Where's dad?" Matt asks again. "Why were you driving the Cat? Big Dwayne would never let you drive the Cat by yourself. Where is he?"

"Got him..." Danny croaks. "Got him...ti...ti..."

"What do you mean got him? What got him?"

"Ti...Tiger." Danny shoves the word out as though it is poison. "Tiger ki...kill daddy..."

Kill daddy. The two words hit Matt, punching into his mind, and for a moment everything starts to go blurry. He suddenly feels on the verge of passing out. Which probably would be the best thing. He can pass out and when he wakes up again, he will see that all this craziness is just a dream. Everything. He did *not* discover the wrecked airplane, his snowmobile was *not* stolen, leaving him stranded in the frozen woods. And his brother—*who is almost certainly dying because his body is twisted in weird ways and anyone who coughs up blood always dies*—was not laying in his arms telling him a tiger had killed Big Dwayne.

But, instead of passing out, he shakes his head hard. Taking a deep breath, he forces himself to stop crying. He needs to be calm now. It is the only way he can help Danny, and Big Dwayne too if it comes to that. "What do you mean, Danny?" he says at last. "How could there be a tiger? They don't live here. You know that, right?"

"Tiger," Danny repeats. "Tiger killed...daddy. Have to run... Matty. Ti...tiger..."

"But that can't be. Dad can't be dead. He's stronger than anybody else. He can't be dead."

Tears well in Danny's eyes. "I Don't feel....anything. Can't move. Am I dyin' Matty?"

"No," Matt says firmly. "You're not dyin' and daddy's not dead. There's no tiger, and nothing has killed daddy. You're wrong! I don't know why you were drivin' the Cat, but you're wrong about dad. He's not dead!"

"You gotta…run…Deadman…hide," Danny says, his voice so low now that his brother has to lean closer to hear him. "Run… tigers coming…" Danny's eyes close. "Can't feel…Matty. Can't…" Then the boy falls silent.

"Danny," Matt says, and gives his brother a gentle shake. "Danny. Wake up." No movement. No breath. Matt shakes him again. "Wake up you booger eater. Wake up or I'll give you the hardest noogie you ever felt." Matt hugs him; the tears he'd fought back now fill his eyes. "Please Danny. Please wake up. If you wake up, I'll double you on my snowmobile. Whenever you want. We can go…wherever…"

Matt's words are lost in his sobs then, so he just sits, weeping and rocking his dead brother in his arms.

50

The view from the kitchen window of Eli and Barb Foley's cabin on Deadman Lake was one of majestic brilliance. No matter what direction the eye turned, the horizon drew a jagged line of glacier capped mountain ranges. Dense forests skirted these mountains, with lush old growth Evergreens and pines reaching high into the deep blue sky. The lake itself stretched out from the cabin's dock, its crystal waters alive with the shimmery sparkle of lazy afternoon sunshine. The occasional rainbow trout would jump, snapping hungrily at mosquitoes that hovered just above the glassy surface of the water. It was a scene forged by the creative genius of Mother Nature, still virgin and uncorrupted by the touch of man.

It is also a scene owned exclusively by the summer months. Now unfortunately, as Saul sits at Eli's kitchen table staring out the same window, summer is no more than a fond memory. The true scene beyond the pane of glass is much different. A gray world exists here, as blank to the eye as a sheet of paper; its lonely, bleakness broken only by frenzied swirls of wind-driven snow. The dock and the lake and the forest that spreads out around them are lost. Buried under winters white anger. Even the mountains—a domineering presence as everlasting as the sky—are hidden behind the shroud of the storm.

Saul sighs, drawing his eyes away from the window and back to the people gathered around the table. To his left, Eli is seated beside his wife, a mug of coffee half drained and forgotten in front of him. Across the table, Sidney is just finishing up the details of what the two girls have found. Chloe is next to her, silent except to nod her agreement on certain points. The story his daughter is telling was one Saul has already heard. Sidney and Chloe had come to him first; cold and excited and prattling on about crashed planes and tracks in the snow. It had taken him close to half an hour, and two cups of hot chocolate, to get them calmed down enough to tell what had happened in a manner he could comprehend. Afterward, feeling stunned by such an unimaginable situation, Saul was forced to admit he had no idea how to proceed.

Therefore, he had made the only decision that made sense. They should talk to Eli.

The walk between the Jenkins place and Eli's cabin took ten minutes—in the summer months. In the deep snow and building storm however, it takes at least twice that. Saul had suggested the girls take the snowmobile, but they declined. Chloe felt the snowfall was too heavy for her to navigate the trail safely and both girls, still quite shaken and weary, thought the walk would do them good. So, thirty minutes later when Eli opened his front door to them, they were all shivering and exhausted.

Now, remedied by more hot chocolate and an extra log in the stove, Sidney finishes her story and falls silent. All eyes at the table turn towards Eli, who is staring down at his coffee mug with a strange intensity.

Barb rubs her forehead. She has a throbbing headache, and her nerves are on fire. Her husband's apparent lack of interest in the situation annoys her immediately. "Well," she snaps at him.

Eli looks up. "Well what?"

"What are you going to do?" she replies sharply.

Eli's brow creases. "Do about what?"

"Were you not listening to the girl? A plane crashed in the woods. There could be survivors."

"I heard her plain as day," Eli says. "But I'm still wondering what you think it is I should be doing?"

"Maybe we could put together a search party," Sidney offers hesitantly. She knows it isn't much of an idea, but at least it is something. She really doesn't like the way Mrs. Foley is looking at her Husband. She has daggers in her eyes.

Eli looks at her and smiles. "If we gathered together every able-bodied person in a five-mile radius around Deadman, we'd have a grand total of six people. That doesn't amount to much of a search party. Toss in the fact we got two feet of snow on the ground and a storm brewin' that's likely to drop another foot or so by midnight, I'd say there's no chance of finding anything in those woods but a whole lotta trouble."

"But we need to do something," Saul says. "If there are survivors, they'll freeze to death out there."

"Any survivors got just as much chance finding us as we do finding them. Besides, the girls saw Matt out that way, so maybe Big Dwayne's already found them. Seems a bit odd, though. Dwayne usually heads east up Granger Trail first run of the season, but any man can be unpredictable on occasion I guess. For all we know, he could have them warming in front of a fireplace right now."

"But what if he didn't find them?" Sidney asks.

"Then there's a decent possibility they're already froze," Eli states bluntly. "I'm a compassionate man. Maybe not as much as some, but enough I don't lay awake at night feeling guilty. But I also got responsibilities." He nods towards Barb. "Keeping this lady safe is one of them. Keeping you all safe as well, I guess. Everyone on this lake kinda counts on me to do the right thing by them. Heading out into the woods in the middle of a snowstorm, looking for people that may or may not be alive? Well that ain't the right thing as far as I'm concerned. Not by a long shot."

Barb sighs. The ache behind her temples rages on, but now she can see her husband's point. Finding anybody in the coming storm will be next to impossible. But, true or not, there has to be something they can do. "So, what then," she asks. "We just sit here and do nothing?"

Eli shakes his head. "That's not what I'm getting at. There is plenty we can do. Start by taking a wander over to the Lodge. See if Big Dwayne's back. Maybe he's picked up these survivors, maybe he ain't. Either way, it'd be good to get his take on the situation. Plus, he's got the satellite phone. We could try getting someone on that. Planes that drop out of the sky don't go unnoticed. I guarantee there are plenty of folks that know this thing went down. Doubt they'd be doing a whole lotta searching yet, because of the storm. But I'm sure they ain't just sitting idle either. They'll be planning something."

"What about after the storm," Sidney asks. "Could we go searching after the storm. Like tomorrow."

Saul looks at his daughter. Sometimes she is too brave for her own good. "I don't think…"

But Eli is already nodding. "Could do. Wayne's probably got most of the snowmobiles torn apart right now, doing maintenance before the season starts, but I'm sure he's got a couple he could gas up for himself and Saul. Plus I got mine. And Dwayne in the Sno-Cat. Not a great search party, but it's a start. Plus I'm sure the city folk will be throwing in their two-cents as soon as things clear up."

"And me," Chloe pipes in. "Me and Sidney."

"Maybe," Eli says, glancing at Saul. "But maybe not. Snow will be real deep by then. Tough riding."

"I can ride as good as anyone," Chloe says.

"That is not in doubt here, little lady. But it's something we'll have to wait and see about. For now, you just need to stay put. No taking any more joy rides without letting folks know, right?"

Chloe huffs stubbornly and crosses her arms.

Eli chuckles. "Guess I'll have to take that as an affirmative."

"Don't worry," Sidney says, nudging her friend with her elbow. "We won't be going anywhere,"

"Good girls."

Suddenly Barb leans across the table and touches Chloe's arm. "I saw it too," she says softly. "Last night. I saw the plane."

"You did?" the girl breathes.

Barb nods. "I saw it through the window in the sitting room. A bright light streaking across the sky. Same as you, I had no idea what it was. I thought it was a falling star, or maybe a meteorite. I never dreamed it could be a plane. Those poor people. Maybe if I'd said something earlier. Maybe…"

"Let's stop that right now," Eli barks. "Whatever idiot let that plane fly through a storm is the only one to blame. With sonar and radar and all that other crap, they should have known better. Someone fucked up and that's all there is to it."

"Eli," Barb gasps.

Eli looks around the table. Everyone is staring at him with humorously surprised expressions. He smiles, clears his throat and adds, "Pardon my French."

"French indeed," Barb says while both girls giggle behind their hands.

"Anyway," Eli continues. "That being said, just because someone…*made an error in judgment*…it don't take away from us doing what we can to ease the situation. So, I say we finish up our coffees, then myself and Saul here will take a scoot over to the Lodge before this storm really starts whuppin'. From there we can assess the lay of the land."

"What about us?" Chloe questions, her tone once again edged with stubborn defiance.

"Only got the one snowmobile. On foot, here to the lodge? That'd be quite a jaunt. S'pose we could get Chloe's machine over at Saul's place, but I think that's a bad idea. With this storm buildin', it's gonna be a tough ride, even sticking to the road. Better you girls just stay put. Besides, Mrs. Foley's feeling a bit peckish. I'd appreciate it if you two stayed and helped her out with supper."

"Eli, I'm fine," Barb states.

Eli holds up his hand. "Sure, sure. But that don't mean you couldn't use the help." He looks back at the girls. "What do you say? Hang tight here and when Saul and I get back we'll all sit down to a good meal."

The girls glance at each other, then nod, though Chloe's comes more reluctantly than her friend's.

"Good. That's settled." He picks up his mug and slurps down the last of the cold coffee.

"Your snowmobile is big enough for both of us?" Saul asks, sounding slightly less than confident.

"You ain't a large fella," Eli says, going to the sink with his empty cup. "Can't see it being a problem."

"It's been a few years since I've been on one."

Eli turns and grins at him. "That's precisely why I'll be doing the driving."

51

When Betty Abernathy hears the high-pitched howl of Matty Trapper's snowmobile approaching her cabin, her first thought is: *Is Big Dwayne really fool enough to let his boy go out riding with another storm just getting started?* She puts her cup of English Breakfast tea down on the table beside her rocking chair and stands up, her old knees creaking like rusty box springs. Howard, a half-breed Irish Wolf Hound, Great Dane, also clambers to his feet. The massive dog—his shoulder coming to just above the old woman's waist—is well seasoned to life in the woods and generally does not show much interest in sounds outside the cabin walls. He also seldom barks; a trait that makes him an excellent guard dog. When Howard approaches, there is no warning.

But in this case, if Betty is interested in a noise coming from outside, then so is Howard. He follows her to the window and gazes out when she pulls back the heavy wool curtain.

Even at close to three in the afternoon, Betty is still recovering from the nasty hangover brought on by the previous evening's festivities. She usually gets bad headaches and stomach pains when she overdoes it with alcohol, and this time has been no different. It seems funny—at least to her—that everyone living around Deadman Lake thinks she is some kind of crazy alcoholic who is pickling her brain with gin tonics and whisky sours, when the truth is alcohol has never agreed with her and she seldom partakes in its consumption. The only time she does tip more than one or two is when she is feeling extremely anxious about something. And almost all of these bouts of anxiety are brought on by one of two things: large gatherings of people, or her *Living Dreams*. Thankfully, both of these are rare. In a year there are only two or three gatherings she feels obligated to attend—one of them being the annual fall Funeral—and she typically used booze to get through them. The living Dreams—which is the name she had given them when she was eight years old—are a bit more common, but still rare. Most are no more than vivid dreams and she is usually able to convince herself they are no more than that. Occasionally, however, these dreams are so utterly real and overwhelming, she has no choice but to admit what they really are: *Visions*. Sent to her by spirits that live in the forest, these visions are warning of things to come. Some are only about her own life, while some are about another's life, or, in the case of her latest dream, about the fate of all those around her. Alcohol again is the only way she can cope with these threads of knowledge she should not have. After she'd dreamt about the terrible fate awaiting Kenny Ferguson, she had known she needed to warn him. It was her duty to do whatever she could to save him from being crushed by that tree. But the only way she'd been able to do what was right was by sitting at the kitchen table and gulping down four large glasses of orange juice spiked with vodka. In the end, it had proven worth it because Kenny is still alive today.

    Unfortunately, the funeral yesterday afternoon had been a full-on double whammy. Not only was she anxious about being at the celebration, but the very night before she'd had one of the most powerful—and by far darkest—Living Dreams of her life. A premonition of black doom from the sky. So she had drank. And drank and drank, trying to flush the terror from her mind. Then Wayne Trapper had come along and...well, things had gotten heated, and she had spouted a lot of things she had not intended.

So, with the damage already done, there is not a thing she can do about it. People will think what they want—*as they always do*—and say what they want—*as they always do*—and hopefully she will be wrong about all of it, and everyone's lives will continue along their meaningless paths.

Now, with her headache still fierce inside her skull, Betty's brow creases as she looks through the window and into the chaotic haze of afternoon daylight. She sees right away that she had been correct in her original thought; there is no mistaking the snowmobile that has stopped in front of her porch. It belongs to Matt Trapper. But neither of the two riders sitting on its seat bore the slightest resemblance to Big Dwayne's son. Even with swirls of angry snow obstructing Betty's view, it is easy to see the driver is a woman. Her Reddish hair is billowing back and forth in the gusting wind. The passenger, perched behind her with his backside almost sliding off the short seat, is a man. By the way he is hunched over and leaning awkwardly to one side, Betty thinks he must be injured.

"What strangeness has the storm blown into our yard, Howie," Betty murmurs.

The dog whines softly in response.

She begins to turn, meaning to go into the bedroom for her parka. She thinks she might also wake Earl from his afternoon nap. Let him know there are strangers on the porch. Not that he'd be much help; when it came to anything not involving pork rinds or hoagie buns, Earl is about as useless as a trap door in a canoe.

But before she has made it more than one step towards the bedroom, she remembers her dream again and stops dead in her tracks.

A Judgment. Sent down by the spirits to reap the debt owed by every man, woman and child. The cost of our sin.

Her headache forgotten, Betty brings a trembling hand up to her mouth as she turns slowly back to the window. Her eyes are round and filled with dread.

Outside, the woman has climbed off the snowmobile and was now helping the passenger as he struggled to dismount. Fat flakes of snow swirled all around them, making them look hazy and out of focus.

Like Ghosts, Betty thinks. *Come down with the snow to pass their judgment.*

Beside her, Howard suddenly begins to bark.

Betty jumps, screaming and twisting away from the sight of the two riders in the storm.

"What's that?" Earl calls. A moment later he lumbers out of the bedroom, fighting with the zipper of his pants and babbling groggily. "What is it? What's happened? What's Howie barking at? What the heck is going on?"

Betty looks at him, her wrinkled face etched with fear. "Get the shotgun, Earl," she says. "Think we might have to shoot ourselves a couple of ghosts."

52

When the front door of the cabin is pulled open and Morgan finds herself staring down the twin barrels of a shotgun, her first thought is, *will this misery ever end?* Ben is beside her, his arm draped across her shoulder. He is shivering very badly and each breath that puffs silver into the air is ragged and short. His right hand is swollen to the size of a baseball glove, its deep purple hue now leaching past his wrist and up his arm in jagged, thin lines. They had been forced to stop several times on the journey to Deadman because Ben could not hold on any longer. And even though they were sharing Matt Trapper's parka, switching it back and forth every twenty minutes or so, it has done little to help the uncontrollable tremble that is racking Ben's body. He needs warmth and medical attention soon, or his time is going to run out.

Unfortunately, at this first cabin they have come across, it appears unlikely they will be finding either.

"What are you two doin' on my porch in this weather?" The old woman in the doorway asks. She has the stock of the shotgun jammed into her shoulder like she is preparing to fire at a grizzly bear. Directly behind her is a bald man holding onto the collar of a dog that is almost as big as a grizzly bear. The man's expression is concerned and nervous, while the large animal appears to be no more than mildly interested in the two people standing in the snow.

"We've had an accident," Morgan says, her voice raised to be heard over the wind that howls unsympathetically around them. "He's badly hurt. Please can you help us?"

"What kind of accident? Only a fool be out in this weather at all."

"Our plane crashed," Morgan tells her. "In the woods. About ten kilometers from here."

"A plane…" the woman murmurs, her gaze shifting up towards the furious white sky. *Out of the sky, the judgment would come. Just as the snow falls, covering the ground.*

"Please," Morgan says again. "Won't you help us? We're freezing."

The woman looks back down at Morgan. Her expression is still suspicious, but now there is also a nervous glint in her eyes. "How is it you're riding the Trapper boy's machine?"

"We…he came across us in the woods. He gave us his snowmobile so we could get out."

"And his parka too I see," she says, pointing the barrel of the shotgun at Ben and the coat wrapped around his shoulders. "Never known Matty to be so generous."

"Yes," Morgan begins. "He was very…"

But Ben interrupts her. "Look lady," he says, grimacing as he forces himself to stand up straight, facing the old woman eye to eye. "You're either going to let us in or you're going to shoot us. Leaving us out here is not an option. I would sooner take a slug in the chest than freeze to death in this hell hole." He takes a step towards her. "We will gladly tell you everything you need to know once we're inside, but right now you have a decision to make. Pull the trigger or move aside."

"Darn it Betty," the bald man says. "Just let them in. He's hurt and what's the worst…"

"You shut your mouth, Earl," Betty snaps. The shotgun barrel—now only a foot from Ben's chest—does not waver an inch. "This is my goddamn house and only I decide who comes in."

"Then decide," Ben growls.

Betty sizes him up, her eyes narrow and distrusting. "Not just the gun you need to worry about. That dog rip you to shreds just as soon look at you. You understand that?"

Ben nods. "Great. I love dogs."

Betty stares at him a moment longer, then shifts her gaze to Morgan. "You promise what he's saying is true? I let you in, no shenanigans?"

"We just need to get warm," Morgan pleads. "That's all."

"Fine," The old woman says at last and lowers the gun. "Come on in then."

53

"Sounds to me like this pilot of yours ain't much of a loss," Betty Abernathy says. "Only an iggit would try flying through a BC snowstorm"

They are in the kitchen of Betty's cabin, three of them sitting at the table. The shotgun is leaning against the back of the old woman's chair and Howard is sleeping at her feet. Ben, who is too sore to sit, is standing by the wood stove warming his good hand over the hot iron. His bad arm is in a sling—the bed sheet Betty has supplied him is managing the job much better than the strip of leather from the plane—and his ribs are now wrapped in a Tensor Bandage. The old women had also supplied the bandage. She brought it out of the bathroom and handed it to Morgan, telling her, *"I got this 'cause it helps my varicose veins. Far as medical supplies go, it's all you'll get from me. And the only medicine I got is tea or whiskey."*

So, she gives them both a healthy dose of Jim Beam in their tea and after hesitating for just a moment, an even healthier dose in her own. Her stomach is getting worse now, as it always does in the company of others, so what the hell. *Goddamn black judgment is on the way anyhow. What's a little nip gonna hurt?*

It is over these steaming brews that Morgan tells Betty of the events leading to them arriving at her cabin on Matt Trapper's snowmobile. Ben remains quiet through most of it, using only his eyes to let Morgan know when she has gone far enough with the details. There is no mention of Mother's Womb or blood-soaked snow or the tiger that is now lurking somewhere in the woods surrounding them.

"I guess he used poor judgment," Morgan says in response to the old woman's observation. "He…he seemed like a good pilot though."

Betty raises her eyebrows cynically and swallows the last of her spiked tea. "Don't really matter much I guess," she says, clunking the mug down on the tabletop. "Cause the end result is the same. Now you've become my problem."

"If you can supply us with a phone or radio, we'll be out of your hair in a flash," Ben says. "I've got people I can call that will have this all cleaned up in an instant." So far, the gun has remained hidden in the back of his pants. He has not felt the need to introduce it to Betty Abernathy yet. But the time for chit-chat is quickly drawing to a close.

The old woman chuckles. "S'pose you ain't much brighter than the pilot. Do I look like a person that's got a satellite phone just lying around? There's no one in this world's much worth calling, that's what I think."

"Okay," Ben sighs, choosing to ignore her insult. "I get that. But somebody around here must have one. For emergencies."

"Big Dwayne's got his down at the Lodge," Earl says. "Won't do you much good though. Not till the storm breaks. Not even a satellite phone's gonna cut through this cloud cover."

"I'm willing to take my chances," Ben says. "Where is this *Lodge*?"

"Other end of the lake," Earl tells him. "Head south about five klicks, that'd get you there."

Ben frowns. "Why go around? The lake is frozen. Couldn't we just go straight across?"

Betty barks out laughter again. "Sure. If you're in the mood to take a very cold swim."

"Darn right," Earl agrees. "This weather we got now is what you might call a *freak of nature*. Normally we wouldn't be seeing snow for another two or three weeks. First it gets real cold for maybe a month. Freezes the lake up good and solid. Then the snow comes. This year though, the storm came early. The ice on the lake is still thin. Barely hold the weight of a coyote, never mind a man on a snowmobile. Bust through in the first thirty yards and sink right to the bottom, that'd be my guess."

"I don't think you'll make it another five kilometers, Ben," Morgan says. "You can barely hold on."

"I'll make it," Ben says.

"Doesn't matter to me one way or the other," Betty says. "But you ain't staying here. I got me a nervous stomach. Really gets actin' up when I'm around other people too long. And right now it's already brewing like a witch's cauldron. You two will need to be on your way right soon."

"But Betty," Earl begins to say. "You can't…"

"Shut your trap, Earl," Betty snaps. "Or you'll be heading out with them. This is my house and I'll do as I see fit." She turns her angry eyes towards Ben. "Don't know if the story your spinnin' is all bullshit, or only part bullshit, but I definitely smell shit one way or other. I've been living on this lake a lot of years. Know the people here pretty good, too. I don't for one second believe that Matt Trapper just stood there in the snow and watched you ride off with his snowmobile and his jacket. Not out of the kindness of his heart anyway."

"He said his father was nearby," Morgan tells her desperately. She can see the situation turning bad very quickly, and with Ben being injured and tired, she has no idea what he might be capable of if this woman keeps pushing him.

"I heard what you said deary," Betty continues. "But that don't make it the truth. Now, I've done all I can for you and it's time you pushed on. I'll give you a last bit of advice, though. Forget what Earl said. Without knowin' the way, you won't make five kilometers in the dark. Not in this weather. Go north about a klick from here you'll come across Eli Foley's cabin. He's the old sheriff of Terravale. Go peddle your story to him and see what he thinks. If he's more accepting of bullshit than I am, maybe he'll help you out. I think he's got a radio linked to the Lodge. He might be able to call down to Big Dwayne, though with this storm, it's hard to say. He's also got better snow machines. Strike out for the Lodge in the morning, once it's light and this storm lets up a bit."

"Maybe I could get the Imp running" Earl offers hesitantly. "Be a little better..."

"Goddamit Earl," Betty growls. "I told you to shut your trap."

"But we should try..."

"Shut it!" Betty screams again and starts to turn, reaching around for the shotgun.

But before she has a hand on it, Ben takes one big step away from the stove and plucks the gun out from her grasp.

"You give that back," Betty yells, her wrinkled face twisting with rage. "I'll sic my dog on you."

At her feet, Howard's head comes up. The animal looks at Betty, then at Ben. After studying him for a moment, he looks back at the old woman again, his head tilting inquisitively.

Cradling the rifle with his bad arm, Ben reaches around and brings out the Beretta. For the moment however, he keeps it pointed towards the ground. "When I said I liked dogs," he says calmly. "I wasn't lying. I think they're great. But if you make any effort to turn that animal on me, then I'll be forced to put a bullet in it. I don't want to, but believe me, I will."

"Betty, please," Earl says.

But she whirls on him. "Please what, you coward! Just sit there and shut up like the useless pussy-ass coward you are!"

Morgan gets to her feet and hurries across to Ben. "We don't have to do this, Ben," she pleads, though she already knows it is too late for anything to change. Ben will now do whatever he feels is necessary.

Howard, who seems completely unimpressed by the situation, has put his head back onto his paws. His breathing is deep and sleepy.

Betty glares at the dog with disgust. "Useless man, useless dog. Story of my life."

"We're not doing anything, Morgan," Ben says. "I'm just sticking up for the rights of my fellow man." He turns his attention to Earl. "So, don't you listen to her, Earl. I want you to go ahead and tell me about the Imp. What exactly is that?"

Earl glances at Betty nervously, but her eyes are now focused on the Beretta, and she pays him no attention. "Well…" he says, rubbing his lips. "I got a 1975 Thiokol Imp."

Ben stays quiet, waiting for him to continue. After a couple of seconds, realizing Earl has no intentions of elaborating, he sighs. "You may think I know what that is, and I probably should. But with all the excitement of the day, I'm coming up blank. So, you're going to have to tell me, Earl. What is a *1975 Thiokol Imp?*"

"It's a snow crawler. Like a Sno-Cat, only…different."

"Ahh," Ben exclaims happily. "Now Sno-Cat I know. Sno-Cat is much better than any junky old snowmobile. So where is it… this Imp?"

"In the shed," Earl says, tilting his head towards the back door. "Out back. But it ain't been started in….jeez, two years I guess. Betty don't like riding in it cause it's too claustrophobic. Probably take a bit to get it runnin'."

Ben hands the shotgun to Morgan, who stares at it apprehensively before finally taking it with obvious hesitation. Then he says to Earl, "But you *can* get it going, right?"

"I expect. Might have to charge the battery is all. Maybe prime the cylinder, but that ain't much of a problem."

"Excellent. Now we've got a plan. You go back to the shed and get the Imp running, while we three wait here in this nice warm kitchen. I'd also like you to take Howard with you just in case Betty gets the mind to *sic* him on us again."

Earl looks confused. "You…you mean now?"

"No time like the present."

"But it's darn cold out. We should wait till the storm breaks, that'd probably be best."

"I disagree, Earl. And I'm sure Betty does as well. She's got that nervous stomach and all. The quicker we get out of here, the happier everyone will be." Ben smiles at Betty. "Isn't that right old girl?"

Betty snarls back at him. "Just go get the damn thing running, Earl. Least then you won't be totally useless."

"Young love," Ben says to Morgan as he sticks the pistol into the band of his pants. "Doesn't it just melt your heart?"

54

The Tiger steps into a cleared area of ground and stops. Above his head, a shelter extends out from the man dwelling, protecting this small patch of dirt and grass from the relentless fall of snow. He shakes his large body, puffing up a billow of icy flakes. The cloud hangs over him for a moment, swirling in the air like a tiny tornado, before being whisked away into the storm by a gust of angry wind.

The animal lowers his scarred nose and sniffs at the ground. It stinks with the same odor that has drawn him here. A sour, cloying smell. One created no more by nature than the strange thunder sticks man carries. It is the smell of their machines.

It is so strong that he has been able to follow it easily, despite the quick moving wind of the storm. It belches out from exhaust pipes, filling the air with a poisonous, black fog. There were even times as he tracked the machines when the stench grew too powerful and it would begin to make him feel sick. He had to stop and drop his head to cool his nose in the snow.

But, in the same way his instincts told him killing the cougar would draw man to him, he also understands that this stink will lead him to man. They need their machines. They are nothing *without them. Naked and defenseless. A deer can run, and a boar can gouge with his tusks, yet man can do none of these things. They are slow and weak. It is only their machines that give them speed or strength.*

Inside this man shelter, there is a machine. If there is a machine, there will also be man. Now The Tiger raises his head again and sniffs at the large door. The wood is old and smells rotten. It will be weakened. Easy to crash through and catch man. Soon he will destroy the machine and devour man.

But for now, he waits. He will know when it is time. His instincts will tell him.

55

"Christ on a cracker," Earl groans, fumbling with the padlock on the shed door. His fingers are already so cold he can barely hold the key. Snow flurries around his head, getting in his eyes and stinging his red cheeks.

Howard is beside him, whining and scratching at the door frantically with his large front paws. His dark gray fur is quickly becoming white.

"Hold on Howie," Earl says. "Just about got it." The key jiggles back and forth in his trembling fingers, but finally slides into the slot. Laughing in triumph, he pulls the lock out of the latch and shoves the door open.

They both scrambled into the shed and Earl slams the door, sliding a dead bolt into place so the wind won't blow it open again. "That's got it," he says to the dog and pats its head.

The interior of the shed is gloomy and dim. Shadows fill every corner, stretching dark fingers into the crevasses of the vaulted roof. The musty smell of damp wood and gasoline hang in the chilled air.

Earl turns and flicks a light switch by the door. Nothing happens. He clicks it down and back up again. Still nothing changes. "Shit." He turns the switch off, waits a few seconds, then flicks it up hard. A bare light bulb on the wall flickers once and comes on. It is powered by six car batteries, which are wired in unison and themselves charged by a solar panel on the roof of the shed. Not the brightest light, only forty watts on its best day, but it is still better than nothing.

The Imp sits in the middle of the floor. It is a red, two-seater, double tracked vehicle. Not as versatile or powerful as Big Dwayne's four track Tucker Sno-Cat, but still quite agile in moderately deep snow. There is a short, four-foot plywood flat deck behind the cab. One headlamp is missing and there is a dent in the right front corner, giving the small machine the same look as a beat-up prize fighter.

Earl steps up to the Imp and touches the front panel. It is ice cold.

What'd you expect, he thinks, shaking his head. *It's darn near as cold in here as it is outside.*

He looks at Howard, and Howard stares back at him expectantly. Reading the animal's inquisitive green eyes, Earl sighs and says, "Sorry boy. You may as well get comfortable. Think we're gonna be here for a while."

The dog whines softly and slumps down to the dirt floor.

"I hear yah Howie," Earl groans. "I really do." He saunters past the Imp to a large Craftsman toolbox sitting against the wall and begins opening drawers, rummaging through a multitude of wrenches and screwdrivers.

Twenty minutes later Howard is asleep on his side, his long legs stretching out across the ground. Beside him, Earl has the cab of the machine tilted up and he is leaning over the engine compartment using a wire brush to clean rust off the battery terminals. A small propane heater by the toolbox hums softly, warming the shed just enough that Earl's fingers are no longer numb. He is whistling 'On top of Old Smokey' and feeling not too bad. At the best of times, it is always nice to get away from Betty for a while and tinker in the workshop. Of course, this is not the best of times, but it still feels pretty darn good. She can be a difficult woman to live with. Hard, opinionated and sometimes even downright crazy. Especially when it comes to her *Living Dreams,* as she calls them. Earl himself knows—as do most other folks around Deadman—that these *Living Dreams* are nothing more than plain old regular dreams. Sure, there may have been a few instances when some of the facts seem to come true—like Kenny Ferguson and his hunting tree, though that one was before Earl even knew Betty Abernathy. But, in Earl's opinion, it doesn't change nothing. As far as he is concerned, any person who goes around yelling and fussing about every darn dream that pops into their head is bound to have one or two of them come true eventually. It is the law of averages. Like trying to guess cards in a deck. If you guessed at just one, chances were you'd be wrong, but if you guessed every card, flipping them over one at a time, eventually you would get one right.

Yet, despite her shortcomings, and his own—which according to Betty, are many—he still loves her. She cooks for him, cleans his clothes, and welcomes him into her home and bed. If it wasn't for Betty, he'd probably be living in the Imp right now. Or even worse, huddling under a cardboard box, freezing his nuts off. He happily accepts that this fact gives her the right to treat him poorly from time to time. In the end, it is all just a part of life.

Right now he needs to concentrate on getting the Imp running so the two strangers can be on their way. Their presence is upsetting Betty. The longer they stay, the more upset she will be. Which means the more he will suffer. At this point, Earl expects two or three days of misery before she will begin to calm down again. Given the way that Ben fellow is pushing her, it may be even longer. There is also a chance, if she gets upset enough, she might stand by her word and send him packing right along with them. Geez. He needs them gone.

Finished cleaning the second terminal, Earl pops the battery cable back on and begins tightening the bolt. If he is lucky, this will be just what the doctor ordered, and the Imp will fire up first turn. If he isn't—which the law of averages seems to suggest—then he will have to spend the next two hours charging the battery. That would be bad. For Betty...and even worse for himself.

Thump! Something bangs against the bay door of the shed.

Startled, Earl jerks his head up. The back of his skull connects hard with the lower edge of the cab chasey. "Oww, shit," he groans, putting his hand to his injured scalp. There is dampness, and when he looks at his fingers, they are painted red with his blood. He can feel more blood trickling through his thin hair and down his neck.

"Shit," he says again. Now he will have to go into the house and tend to his head. That is not going to make Betty happ—

Thump! Louder. This time it is Howard who is startled. He yelps like a puppy and scrambles to his feet, swinging his head around, trying to look in all directions.

Earl chuckles. "Great watchdog you are. Afraid of your own—"

WHUMP!

The impact rattles the old wooden door on its hinges. Howard barks once and darts past Earl to the front of the shed. He puts his nose down, sniffing at the bottom crack between the lip of the door and the ground. A low growl begins deep in the dog's throat.

"Don't worry, old boy," Earl says, stepping up beside the dog. The door is two panels, hinged on each side and chained with a bicycle lock on the outside. He puts his hand on the left panel and his eye to the slim space between them. All he can see is the shifting gray movement of the storm. "Probably just the Trapper kids fartin' around," he continues, though his tone is slightly hesitant. "You know how they like to aggravate Bet—"

Something big crashes against the outside of the door, flexing the boards inward, almost to the point of breaking. Several of the weaker boards splinter and cracked.

"Damn!" Earl cries, stumbling backward. His lower thighs strike the edge of the Imps flat deck, shooting pain up his legs and into his back.

Howard also jerks several steps away from the door and begins to bark savagely. Thick strings of saliva fly from his mouth, splashing the ground and the side of the Imp. The animal's frightened roars are deafening inside the confines of the shed.

Earl claps his hands over his ears. "Darn it, Howie!" he shouts. "You gotta stop! It's too goddamn loud! Com'on boy! Stop barking! Stop…"

Suddenly he does. The last bark echoes through the space for a second, then there is nothing. The deep snow that surrounds the small building acts as a natural insulator, so even the sounds of the forest outside are nonexistent. The silence is total.

Earl turns his head—the creak of his neck sounding unusually loud in his ears—and looks at Howard. The dog is standing stiff legged, his head down, his eyes pinned on the splintered door. The hair on his haunches and back stands straight up, like the quills of a porcupine. He is trembling noticeably.

Earl looks back at the door. Tiny chunks of wood littered the ground and several of the boards in the left panel are now bowed inward.

Jeez, he thinks. *Whatever hit it almost come right through. Once more and—*

The door explodes. Wooden boards shoot every direction like crazed missiles. One large chunk crashes right through the back window of the Imp and smashes out the windshield. Another flies past Howard's head, taking a chunk out of the animal's left ear. Earl—who is a firm believer in the law of averages—is not so lucky. A two-foot splinter of wood impales him through the neck. He falls back onto the flat deck of the Imp. Not a second later, before he has even registered what is happening, something is on him. Something big.

Maybe it's Howard, his mind rambles. *Good dog. Good Howie. Come to save me.*

Then the tiger's lips peeled back from its crimson fangs and Earl understands. As hot breath washes over his face, he knows that this is not Howard. This thing grinning down at him now is exactly what Betty has foreseen. It is judgment. Come down to bring punishment to the sinners.

Sorry I doubted you old girl, he thinks and opens his mouth to scream. All that passes his lips is a gush of blood.

56

Inside Betty Abernathy's cabin, the thirty minutes between Earl leaving to repair the Imp and Howard starting to bark have been quiet ones. Betty's time has been spent productively, sitting at the kitchen table drinking Jim Bean from her coffee cup. Ben and Morgan are standing closer to the stove, the shotgun lying on the countertop beside them, watching her drink. Once, when Ben suggested she slow down a bit, the old woman had stopped in mid pour and glared at him with angry discontent. "Just 'cause you got that gun don't mean you get to tell me what to do in my own house. I'll slow down when this bottle is empty, or you and your lady friend are gone. Not before then."

Ben smiled at this and made no further comment.

The bandage wrapped around his chest has begun to help a little. Breathing still hurts like a bastard, but at least each breath doesn't feel like it could be his last. His wrist, however, is getting progressively worse. His entire forearm is swollen to the size of a presto-log, and the purplish color in his hand and wrist has now darkened to almost black. It is obvious that something very bad is going on under his skin. It has been about sixteen hours since the crash, which Ben thinks is not enough time for gangrene to set in, but he also knows if he doesn't get medical attention soon, it will, and that could mean losing his arm.

Looking on, Morgan can recognize the pain drawn in his face, and once she had asked him if he was okay. He had only looked at her without making a response. There is nothing to say. He is not okay, and they both know it.

Unlike Ben, Morgan is feeling quite a bit better. She is wearing an old moth-eaten wool coat that Earl had retrieved from a trunk in the parlor. It stinks of stale leaves, but it is warm. She has also been able to wash up, finally cleaning the dried blood off her face. She was relieved to see that the cut on her forehead was not a bad one and had already begun to scab over. Of course, she has not had any sleep in a long time, so fatigue is becoming a factor, but compared to the tribulations Ben is facing, this is a minor issue. She would gladly stay awake for days if it meant they could get out of this alive.

Betty is reaching for the whiskey again when the volley of savage barks echoes out of the storm. Her hand jerks and hits the near empty bottle, knocking it off the table. It strikes the wooden plank floor and shatters with a muffled *'pop'*.

Morgan, who is startled more by the sound of the breaking glass than the barking dog, cries out and clutches at Ben's bad arm.

He grimaces, pain shooting up to his shoulder, and pushes her away. "Jesus, Morgan," he roars. "It's only the goddamn dog!" But his good hand has already found the grip of the Beretta. He pulls the gun out and turns to the old woman. She is staring at the backdoor, her thin fingers still holding the empty cup.

"What is it?" Ben asks. "Why is the dog barking?"

"How should I know?" Betty says. "But Howie ain't normally much of a barker. Last time I heard him go off like that was a bear had got into the wood-shed."

Ben crosses the kitchen to the back door and gazes out the window. The beginnings of early evening are setting in now, making the already bad visibility even worse. He is just able to make out the dark silhouette of the shed about ten yards from the cabin. There is a thin bead of light near the ground in the back wall of the building; light from inside the shed, shining through the lower crack of the door. The front of the shed, where the bay doors would be, is hidden from view. Nothing that Ben can see through the swirling clots of storm seems unusual. So, except for the barking, all else is…

The barking suddenly stops.

Morgan comes up beside Ben and peers out the window. "It stopped," she says.

"Yes," Ben agrees.

"Maybe he was barking at a rat or something," she offers.

From behind them, Betty chuckles. "My Howie wouldn't get excited by no rat. He'd just as soon eat it as bark at it. I told yah he ain't no barking dog."

"Well, he was barking at something," Ben says. He looks at Morgan and can see the fear etched into her face. He understands it well because now, he is also afraid. He is afraid of what he *knows* is out there.

"I think we should go," Morgan tells him in a frightened whisper.

As Ben is just beginning to nod his head in agreement, a huge crash echoes out of the frenzied twilight, loud enough to vibrate the cabin door on its hinges.

"Gods above!" Betty cries out. "What the hell was that?"

Morgan is groping at him again, but Ben ignores her, straining his eyes against the haze of funneling snow. The front of the shed is still beyond his line of sight, but now he can see light spilling out from there—a dirty yellow glow in the deepening darkness. Within this light, shadows move. Featureless specters dancing and twisting, sometimes coming together as one, yet moments later independent of each other. Distinctive. The swishing tail of the animal; a thick, black snake against the white snow. Its arched back and haunches, like the gray shadow of a mountain range. And its head, rising and falling. Its jaws opening and closing, tearing at something. Something that had once cast the shadow of a man but is now only a lump. The cat is ripping chunks out of it, flicking them from side to side. One flies out the front of the shed and lands. It looks like a large red exclamation mark in the snow.

"Oh Ben," Morgan groans, staring at the shadowy scene with horrified disgust. "Is it...is it eating him? God...it is. It's eating him. I can hear it. Tearing..."

Ben can hear it too. Even through the door and the billowing storm, he can hear it. The wet sound of ripping flesh. "We need to go right now," he says, whirling around suddenly.

Betty is still behind them, but now she is standing at the counter. She has the shotgun up, socketed into her shoulder, the twin barrels glaring at Ben like hollowed-out black eyes.

"Betty," Ben murmurs, keeping the Beretta at his side for the moment. "What are you doing old girl?"

"Why have you done this to us?" Betty wails. "Why have you brought down this black demon?"

Ben takes a slow step forward, keeping Morgan behind him. "You got it wrong, Betty," he says calmly. "We didn't bring anything down. Just ourselves when our plane crashed. No demons. Not at all."

"You're a lying devil. You brought the beast down so it can lay its judgment on us. Judge us of our sin and cast us into the darkness."

Ben shakes his head. "No. That doesn't sound good. I don't want any of that. What I do want is to get out of this cabin. And that's what you want too, isn't it? So just lower the gun and we'll be on our way."

"But you will be judged as well," Betty cries. The barrel of the gun remains unwavering. "The beast will recognize your sins, and you will be punished, just as we shall be."

They are halfway across the kitchen now, Ben in front of Morgan. Each step is no more than a shuffle. Ben feels confident that if he can get near enough to the old woman, he will be able to grab the gun away from her. Just a few more careful steps and—

The back door flies open, slamming against the wall. The window explodes inward, sending shards of glass careening through the room in a silvery cloud. Howard bolts through the opening, blood pouring from his torn ear. He skids and stumbles, his large rump knocking into the table as he races through the kitchen and disappears into the parlor. There is another crash as he bangs open the door into the bedroom.

At the exact moment that Betty is distracted, swinging the barrel of the shotgun towards the backdoor, Ben raises the Beretta. They both fired at the same time.

The shotgun blast tears a ragged hole into the wall just to the left of the doorway. The nine-millimeter slug tears a hole into Betty Abernathy's chest just to the right of her heart. As she falls back against the countertop, the gun slips out of her grip. It hits the wooden floor and discharges the second round of number ten buckshot point blank into the iron stove. Pellets rebound off the metal in all directions, several of these burying themselves into the hard muscle of Ben's left calf.

Ben Shrieks and starts to fall, but Morgan is able to grab him under the arms in time to keep him up. He screams again, this time the pain slashing up his arm and through his chest.

He stumbles away from her. "Take the gun," he moans, holding out the Beretta. It felt like something had taken a bite out of his calf. "Now before I fall on my ass."

She takes the gun.

Ben drags a chair over and sits down, careful not to jar his arm. The leg is bad, but Christ, the arm is still much worse. He reaches down with his good hand and feels the back of his leg. His pants are already soaked with blood. "Shit. She got me good."

"You…You shot her…".

Ben looks at Morgan. She is staring at the old woman sprawled on the floor. Her once beautiful face is now pale and drawn. Dark circles color the underside of her eyes, and her lips are dry and cracked. She looks twenty years older than she had only two days earlier.

For just a second, as he watches her, Ben feels sorry. He has caused this. All the death and carnage and pain that surrounds them now is his doing. He can try to blame others, like Pete the pilot, or even Collique, but in the end the truth is the truth. Everything that has happened is because of his greed. Not a greed for money this time, but for power over other living things. He knows it. And Morgan knows it too. At this moment, he wishes he was able to cut the crap and finally come clean. Tell her how sorry he is. How much he loves her.

But then the pain in his arm flares up again, sending lightning rods of venal reality into his brain.

Fuck it, he thinks grimly. *When we get out of this, she can sue me. Everyone can sue me for all I care.*

To Morgan, he says, "She was going to shoot us. What was I supposed to do?"

"I think she's dead."

"Look around you Morgan," Ben snaps, forcing himself to his feet. He grabs her by the arm and twists her around "Look at this dump. She was already dead."

"No," Morgan says tonelessly. "She wasn't. Not until you shot her."

"Christ, Morgan. It was her or…"

A thump from outside, resonating through the open doorway. Then a creaking sound, snapping boards, the crunch of snow… and something else. A faint noise, still quite distant, and yet totally recognizable.

It is the rumbling purr of the tiger

"We need to get out of here," Ben says, pulling Morgan out of the kitchen. He is limping badly, his leg throbbing with each step. But he takes this pain and thrusts it into the same cold, dark hole he has used to hide the pity he felt only moments before. There it will have to stay until he can get them out of this nightmare.

57

Betty Abernathy does not hear as Ben and Morgan open the front door of her cabin and escape into the storm. Everything in her slowly dying world is silent. The shotgun blast right next to her head has ruptured her eardrum, leaving her almost completely deaf. So now she cannot hear the tick-tock of the grandfather clock in the parlor; the one her father had made years before she was born. Nor can she hear the drip of the kitchen faucet that Earl still has not found time to fix. Or the strange gurgling sound as she draws in each shallow breath. She does not hear the crunch of broken glass as something comes in through the back door and pads across the kitchen floor. Or the gravelly rumble from inside its chest as it stands over her.

It is not a sound that finally causes her to open her eyes and stare into the blood smeared face of the tiger. It is the rank smell of decaying flesh, drifting over its teeth and out of its parted jaws, surrounding her in a pungent death shroud.

Though her eyes see the tiger, its face hovering only inches above her own, her mind refuses to acknowledge what she is seeing. It is not a tiger, but a black demon pretending to be a tiger. Using the form of a deadly animal in an attempt to frighten her. Trick her into admitting her sins. Then it will snatch her soul and whisk it down into the darkness of purgatory where it will remain for all eternity.

But she knows of its tricks. She will not give in to its attempts. She will keep her soul and float with it all the way to heaven. She looks into its thoughtless, yellow eyes and grins.

"Take...your...judgment," she croaks, blood trickling down her chin. "And peddle it...somewhere else. Cause I ain't buyin' you son of a bitch."

58

The Tiger tilts his head inquisitively. Like many times before, he hears the sounds coming out of man's mouth, but he does not understand them. They are meaningless grunts and squawks to his ears. The air around this female has a sour smell. Not as cloying as the stink of its machines, but still unpleasant. Most smells that surround man are unpleasant. Except for its blood. There is nothing else in The Tiger's world that pleases him more than the smell of man's blood.

He can already smell the blood of this female. It is leaking from a hole in its chest. He wonders briefly what has injured it. There is a thunder stick laying near it, so it can protect itself. Yet it is still injured. Strange. Perhaps he will find out as his hunt continues.

It makes some more noises, coughing and grunting, blood coming out of its ears. Then its body begins to shake violently. Bouncing up and down like a deer battling for its life. When it finally becomes still again, its eyes are shiny and blank. The foul air pulsing from its mouth stops. It is no longer injured. Now it is dead.

The Tiger sniffs its face, then sniffs the bloody wound in its chest. His urge to tear and rip dulls. He has not killed this one, and he feels no need to kill it further.

He lifts his head and sniffs the air. He can smell the dog, the one that had been with man and its machine. It is somewhere hiding; he can hear its soft whimpering. He could hunt and kill it. But this idea also comes with no urge.

Instead he will find new prey. Better prey. Man prey. This is a good thought. It brings the urge. Hunting is almost as good as the kill. He will hunt now. And then kill. And hunt. And kill...

He turns his large body around and leaves the kitchen. Moments later he has vanished into the storm.

59

Wayne Trapper takes a hard pull off his cigarette, filling his lungs with the sweet nicotine that his body craves unrelentingly. When he speaks, only a hint of remaining smoke curls up from his mouth. "If there's anyone up there, Dwayne'll find them. No worry there."

Wayne, Saul and Eli are standing in the workshop of Deadman Rentals. Outside, the storm rages on as early evening darkness is beginning to take its foothold over the land. The journey from Foley's cabin to the rental shop had been a hard one. Eli had found himself forced into the painful realization that he was not as young, or strong, as he used to be. With the deep snow and the storm, as well as the added weight of Saul, navigating the snowmobile along the narrow pathway through the trees had proven much more of a fight than Eli had anticipated. Only halfway into the trip and already overwhelmed by exhaustion, he had no choice but to stop and let Saul take over the controls. After a few minutes of helpful instruction, Saul demonstrated excellent ability as a rider, and they arrived at the rental shop with no further incident.

That was twenty minutes earlier. Now, with the story of the girl's discovery told, Eli is confused by Wayne's initial statement. "The girls did cross paths with Matty, which is an oddity in its self. Doesn't Dwayne usually head east up Granger Trail? The wreckage is west, towards…"

"John Oliver," Wayne finishes for him, tapping ash onto the floor. "Pretty sure that's the direction he headed."

Eli shakes his head. "Obviously, but why would he do that? Never heard of him going west first run of the season. It don't make no sense."

"Because I asked him to," Wayne comments mildly. "Seen that same light myself, last night. Thought it could be something, so I asked him to check it out. Simple as that."

"And he agreed? That doesn't sound much like the Big Dwayne I know."

Wayne shrugs. "Maybe, maybe not. He decided without much fuss, though. Guess he was curious himself."

From behind them, Wayne's fifteen-year-old son's head pops up from the engine compartment of the Skidoo he is working on. "They still ain't back, Pa," Greg Trapper comments. "Him and Matty both."

"Course I know that," Wayne barks at the boy. "Just mind your business before you screw up that carburetor."

"But aren't yah worried," Greg asked. "With the storm building and all. Don't you think they ought to be back?"

Wayne turns and looks at the boy. He is a heavy-set lad with dark hair and almost the spitting image of his Uncle Dwayne. "I said mind your business," he snaps. "Dwayne can take care of himself fine enough without you fussing on about it."

Greg sighs. For a moment he considers saying more; it is a very interesting conversation they are having, and he badly wants to be involved. But he quickly decides this would not be a wise decision. Though his father is generally a soft spoken and mildly tempered man, there were occasions when he would get a darkness in his eyes that meant *watch out*. And right now, even from across the width of the workshop, he can see it there as plain as day. So, instead of commenting further, he leans back into the compartment and continues with the carb rebuild.

Wayne watches him briefly before turning his attention back to Eli and Saul. "Boy's a decent mechanic, but not much of a listener," he says.

"I think he's got a good point," Eli says. "Dwayne's always been smart enough to respect the power of a storm. He knows better than to get caught in one, especially with Matty in tow."

Wayne takes a drag from his cigarette and shrugs again. "He also ain't afraid of them. He knows these woods better than anyone, storm or no storm."

"What about Matt," Saul asks. He is also surprised by Wayne's apathetic attitude. Given the circumstances, he would have expected the man to be at least mildly concerned about his brother and nephew. He is finding his indifference rude and annoying. "He's just a boy."

"Wouldn't worry about him any more than Dwayne. He's a good boy. Lot brighter than this one." Wayne cocks his head towards Greg. "Besides, it's you two going on about survivors and all. Right now, they're probably busy sorting whatever kind of mess is going on out there. That'd be my guess."

"That could be true," Eli agrees. "Not a lot of room in the Sno-Cat for folks other than Big Dwayne and the young one. Guess they'd be riding the flat deck or doubling behind Matty. Be mighty cold."

"Better than dying I expect," Wayne offers.

Eli nods. "True. Smarter idea, though, would be to set them up some shelter and warmth, then come back here for extra help. Once the storm breaks, it'll be a lot easier getting them to safety." He pauses, pulls his hat off and rubs his head thoughtfully, then adds, "Chances are good the calvary from Terravale or somewhere is already putting together a search party. Maybe even a helicopter. Might be better to just leave them to wait it out. Safer than trying to load folks onto the flat deck in this storm I'd say."

"Dwayne's no fool," Wayne says. "He'll do whatever's best."

"Course. Still wouldn't hurt to have a couple more snowmobiles gassed up and ready to go if needed. Dwayne probably be getting back shortly. If he did find survivors out there, and thought it best to go back for them after the storm, chances are he'll want to head out first light. He'll be right pleased you had the foresight to prep the machines. And if by chance he doesn't get back, guess you'd be wanting to go on and look for him a-sap. Either way, best to be prepared."

Wayne snuffs his cigarette into an empty Diet-Pepsi can. "Appreciate the advice," he says, pulling a fresh smoke from the pack. "But I got two machines good to go already, and a third ready by tonight. That *foresight* enough for yah?"

"Now don't be that way, Wayne," Eli says and pats the skinny man on the shoulder. "You know I mean nothing by it. Just my cop instinct to be thorough is all. Guess you also thought to try calling Dwayne on the two-way?"

Wayne scoffs. "You know that thing ain't worth spit in this weather. Two cans and a string would work better."

Eli nods, knowing this was the truth.

"The satellite phone," Saul offers. "Couldn't we try calling someone on that?"

"Locked up in Dwayne's office across the way," Wayne says. "Besides, with the clouds so heavy, it wouldn't work any better than the two-way."

For a moment, silence falls over the three men, the only sound in the workshop being the soft clank of tools as Greg works. Each is waiting for the other to say something. Voice another suggestion. But it seems there are no more to be made.

Finally, Eli sighs. "Okay then. It's time Saul and I got going. I want to get back to those ladies before dark. You and your boy keep up the good work, Wayne. Hopefully, Big Dwayne and his boys will show up shortly. But, either way, we will be back here in the morning. The storm is supposed to ease off sometime tonight so we can head out early AM if needed. If this damn cloud cover breaks, we can also give the satellite phone a try. How does that sound? We all agreed?"

Saul and Wayne glance at one another briefly, each finding distaste in the other's eyes. Then Wayne nods and Saul also agrees, "Sounds okay."

"Good," Eli says, picking up his gloves and pulling them over his liver-spotted hands. "Hate to ask, Saul, but would you mind handling the driving again? Afraid I'm still feeling a bit worn out.

"Of course," Saul says.

Eli smiles at him. "Getting old ain't the problem. It's what getting old does to the body is the real bugger." Then he turns to Wayne. "Take care of yourself and that boy. We'll be back early tomorrow."

"Don't need to worry," Wayne says, the freshly lit cigarette bouncing in the corner of his mouth. "Not about me or Big Dwayne neither. He's the king of these woods."

"Don't I know it," Eli agrees, though Saul can now see worry showing in the old man's eyes.

60

When Matty Trapper's snowmobile runs out of fuel, they are about two hundred yards from The Foley's cabin. Immediately Morgan begins to swear under her breath and thumb the starter button over and over. Looking over her shoulder, Ben is just able to make out the log building's bulky shadow through the trees. With the growing darkness closing in around it, one window glows the yellow, flickering light of a lantern. A thick curl of smoke drifts out of the chimney to be torn apart in the snow-ravaged sky. To their right, the flawless expanse of the lake stretches out like an endless white field.

With a final shout of distressed anger, Morgan slams her hands against the handlebar. "Now what?" she wails.

"Guess we walk," Ben says, his voice raised enough to battle the unyielding wind.

Morgan swings her leg around and climbs off the snowmobile. The deep snow swallows her to mid-thigh. "How?" she asks, tears beginning to swell in her eyes. "You've been shot. You can't walk."

Ben looks down at his leg. He had been able to make a tourniquet with one of the ties from Morgan's makeshift jacket. It does help to slow down the flow, but the bleeding has not stopped it completely. The lower leg of his pants is soaked in blood, and a thin trail of red follows the tracks of the snowmobile from the direction they'd come. His head is also beginning to spin sightly. He knows this is a common effect of blood loss that will only get worse if he doesn't find a way to bandage the wound properly. So, at this point, he has no other choice. If they don't walk, he will die. Either from blood loss or...

His tiger.

Even now, with his mind swirling and full of pain, he can still sense it is out there. Watching them from inside the trees. Stalking them. Waiting for the right time.

"Just help me off this thing," he says to Morgan. "We need to keep moving."

"But how?" she asks again, taking the arm he has stretched out to her. "You'll bleed faster if you don't stay still? You could die."

"I'll die if we stay here," he says, grimacing as he struggles off the seat. His leg throbs, his arm throbs, his chest throbs. He hurts in more places than he ever dreamed possible. And somewhere inside, he knows that death could bring glorious relief. The end of his suffering. His agony gone, disappearing into the darkness.

Yet, he will never give in to it. The black hooded skeleton is not going to have him. He is Benjamin Treager. A fighter. He will fight on and on until he has won. No matter how long it takes, or how many more have to die, he *will* win. If it means sacrificing everyone in this shit hole called Deadman, then that's what he is willing to do. And in the end, he will be victorious.

Once off the snowmobile, he tries putting more weight onto the leg. It screams agony, shooting pain up his thigh and into his spine like burrowing termites. Groaning deeply, he forces himself to straighten up. His leg cries out again, clawing and threatening to put him on his ass. Then finally it quiets slightly, and he is able to stand.

"Are you okay?" Morgan asks, gazing at him fearfully. "Will you make it?"

"I'll make it," he says and takes his first step forward. "Just try to keep up."

61

"Do you think they will be back soon?" Sidney asks. She is standing at the sink, peeling carrots, and gazing into the darkening storm. "They've been gone quite a while."

"Not that long," Chloe disagrees. She is beside her friend at the counter, cutting potatoes to go into the stew that Barb is directing them how to make. A pot of broth bubbles gently on the stove. "It is a long ride to The Lodge and back. And all this snow will slow them down too."

"I'm sure they'll be back shortly," Barb says from the table. Her attempts to tear up fresh herbs are proving futile. Her fingers ached so badly she can barely pick up the tiny plants, never mind rip them into pieces. The headache she has been battling from before Eli and Saul had left is still plaguing her. Now, however, it has successfully crept into her shoulders, so each movement of her arms feels like sandpaper grinding away the sensitive nerve endings in her joints.

But despite this discomfort, which has now become as much a part of her life as hunger or thirst, Barb is content. Having the girls with her is a joy. Just listening to them joke and giggle together as they prepare the stew gives her enough strength to push the pain down, forcing it to relent some of the hold over her. She cannot truthfully use the word *gone,* but for the first time in a long time, *manageable* would not be a lie.

"It's snowing so hard," Sidney adds, her voice high and worried. "And it's starting to get really dark."

"Try not to worry, dear," Barb says. "Eli has made the run down to the Lodge countless times. I'm sure he could do it blindfolded. But he is also a cautious man. Safety is always his top priority, so he'll be taking his time."

Sidney nods her head, though the worry does not leave her face.

"And besides," Chloe says, grinning playfully. "You've got me here to protect you from *the big, bad snowstorm.*"

"Oh great," Sidney groans and pokes her in the ribs with a carrot. A moment later they were both laughing and poking at each other with vegetables.

Barb smiles. She feels happy for them both. To find someone to bond with in such an isolated place is rare enough, but to find someone to love? This is almost unheard of. It had not taken her long to recognize what was developing between the two. She saw it for certain in Chloe; the way she would look at Sidney sometimes, from the corner of her eye, guarding herself from possible hurt and yet with such open, unhindered love it was impossible not to see. Obviously, she has not yet expressed her true feelings to the other girl, so it is difficult for Barb to sense Sidney's feelings, though it is still obvious she feels something towards her. Love as friends, or love as more than friends, it is hard to know.

And it is also none of my business, she scolds herself suddenly, turning her eyes back to the task of tearing herbs. *Just leave them to their own discoveries and quit being such a nosey old woman.*

There is a thud from outside the backdoor, muffled but loud enough to be heard. All three ladies look that way expectantly. Another thump…and another. Eli had cleared most of the snow from the back steps and porch before he and Saul left. Now this is the sound of someone laboring up those steps, each footfall slow and distinct.

"They're back," Sidney squeals, dropping carrots into the sink. She turns and starts towards the door.

"Wait," Barb says, holding up her hand. She feels a strange unease. There had been no sound of an approaching snowmobile. Also, despite the lack of deep snow on the stairs, the footsteps seemed heavy, as if someone is not walking but lurching up the steps.

"It's dad," she says, either not hearing or choosing to ignore Barb. She rushes past her to the backdoor and yanks it open excitedly. "Daddy, thank God. I was really starting to get…"

62

As they approach the back stairs of the cabin, Morgan suddenly stops. Ben has his good arm around her neck and is leaning on her heavily. The jerky halt sends pain shooting across his chest and into his bad arm. "Christ," he moans. "What are you…"

"Before we go into this house," she says, turning her head to look at him. "We need to agree on something."

Ben can see the Malo stubbornness in her stare. Whatever she is about to say, trying to debate it will be a futile effort. Which doesn't matter because he is too weak to debate with her anyway. "What," he asks reluctantly.

"We need to tell these people the truth," she replies. "They are in danger, and they deserve to know why."

Ben chuckles. "What truth? That there's an eight-hundred-pound tiger killing people. That'll be great. We may as well tell them it's being ridden by little green aliens from Mars. They won't believe it either way."

"They'll have to. We'll make them. We both know that thing is out there, and probably on its way here. Our only chance is to keep running. All of us."

"Fine," Ben says. "tell them what you want. But if I sense it going bad, like it did with Betty, I'll have to react. I promise you that."

"I'll make sure it doesn't. So just keep your gun in your pants, okay."

"One more thing," Ben adds. "When you're telling your tale, keep in mind that what we have done is very illegal. I can still get all of this cleaned up, but not if you start spilling too much truth. I have no intentions of making it out of here just to end up in prison. So, say what you want, but watch what you say."

Morgan glares at him. "You can be a real asshole."

"Just think where you'd be if I wasn't," Ben says, smiling.

"At home, in bed."

"And how unexciting is that?" Ben quips, stepping onto the first stair riser. He stands there for a moment, with Morgan beside him, testing the pain level in his leg. It is high, but not unmanageable. He nods. "Okay." They take the next step, and then the third. By the fourth, he can feel a fresh run of warm blood trickling down his leg.

As they step onto the fifth and last stair, the back door comes open suddenly and a blond girl rushes out, her face lit up with smiles and excitement. "Daddy, thank God. I was really starting to get…" She stops dead, all the happiness vanishing from her expression. She takes a quick step back towards the doorway, fear darkening her blue eyes. "Oh, I thought…who are you?"

"My name is Morgan," she says, helping Ben onto the porch. "Our plane crashed in the woods. Please, we need help."

63

The snowmobile sticks out of the snow like the misshapen bulk of a fallen elk. The Tiger approaches it slowly, his head low. His purring has stopped for now. He isn't afraid—he has not felt true fear since man killed his mother and sister—but the stench of man's machine is strong, stinging his nose and eyes. These things are fowl and loud, ceaseless in their destructive capability. He hates the machines almost as much as he hates man. Yet he also understands that without man controlling them—guiding them along whatever caustic path they chose—these machines are no more than unmoving carcasses. Dead without having to be killed.

He steps up to the machine, close enough to sniff at the snow cover seat. The stink of fuel and exhaust is strong, but even stronger is the scent of man. He cuffs, excitement swelling inside his huge body. And with his excitement comes the sound of his purr, erupting out of him like the starting of a diesel engine.

This is not the smell of any man. This man he has smelled several times; before he had woken in this forest and begun his vengeful quest. It had been there when he was in the cage, tormented by a different man with the lightning stick. That man The Tiger was able to destroy, but not this man. It had later shot him with the stinging dart that made him sleep. And after, in the bright room that reeked of poison, it had been there also. It had put him inside the invisible cage. Oh yes, he knows this man well. It is his capture. The man responsible for everything.

The Tiger raises his head, drawing in the air around him. In one direction, where a yellow light glows through the trees, he can smell the man. Immediately, the urge flares inside him, burning hot and red. He sees himself bounding over the snow towards the light and pouncing on the man that has caused his rage. He would bite it, and rip it, tear it to pieces until there was nothing left. And he would also destroy any that were with it. All man who dared walk on two legs or ride atop machines would fall.

Then he shifts his nose, pointing it in another direction. Here, past the light and deeper into the trees, he can smell something else. An offensive odor, not as enticing as the smell of man. But it does work to dull his urge momentarily, allowing his instincts to assume control. This is a smell he also knows very well. It has led him to this point, lingering all around him like a black cloud. Man's machines.

His nostrils flare open, pulling in the pungent aroma. His senses tell him that here, in this direction, there are many more machines. All collected together like a herd of wildebeests. If he goes this way, following his instincts instead of his urge, he may be able to eliminate all of man's machines. Without them, man will be weak and slow. Helpless against his attacks.

If these were thoughts being processed by a human mind, filled to the point of overflowing with emotions and doubt, this would have seemed the wiser choice. But in Tiger's mind, where urge and instinct ruled together, overshadowed only slightly by the animal's enhanced cunning, the distinction between these two ideas is not as simple. One moves his urge to kill, while the other moves his instinct to hunt. Both are equal in their intensity and sharpened by his intellect. Neither is more correct than the other.

So, for now he will wait. Eventually, something will push him one way or the other. Until then, patience is the only choice.

64

Chloe's father is Dr. Burt Cooper. In his past life, the one before Deadman, he had run a thriving medical practice in Vancouver. This had kept him away from home roughly sixty hours a week. As well, along with his wife, they were respected members of the community, often working with several different charities at once. Planning fundraisers, attending events and, in his last year before his life turned upside down, he was nominated chairman of the Mountain Pleasant community center. He was known as a man who would continuously, and without argument, put other people's needs ahead of his own.

When he was forty-two he suffered a massive heart attack. Triple bypass surgery and a long recovery changed a lot of Burt's views on what was important in life. He had spent so much of his time giving to others that he had neglected the one person that meant the most to him: his daughter. Over the past ten years, he had become so distant from Chloe, he barely knew who she was anymore. So, one rainy afternoon as he lay in his hospital bed, he made a vow that this would change.

Within six months of his return to health, Burt had sold his practice and moved his family to Deadman Lake. He took a small salary as the doctor in residence for the community, and between himself and Chloe's mother Colleen, they home schooled their daughter through the last years of high school. When she said she wanted to take one year off before attending college, maybe spending some time helping her father with his few patients, they supported the decision wholeheartedly. Nothing would make them happier than to have her around for another year.

This was how Burt Cooper ended up becoming Doc B., the soul medical practitioner for Deadman Lake. There was of course Dr. Dean Travis down in Terravale, but it was rare that his services were required outside of town, a fact that Doc B. was mighty proud of. And now, his daughter was learning first aid practices and talking happily about medical school. Something else he was mighty proud of.

On the stormy evening that the two strangers showed up on Barb Foley's back porch, Doc B. was stuck in Vancouver with his wife and therefore was unable to bandage Ben Treager's bloody leg. If he had been there, he would have immediately recognized the wound for what it was; shotgun pellets. But instead, it is his daughter Chloe that tends to the leg, and shotgun never crosses her mind. She simply assumes it is an injury from the brutal plane crash. It is bandaged up and no questions are asked. This is a fact that makes Ben very happy.

"I think that should keep the bleeding under control," Chloe says, peeling latex gloves off her small hands. "At least for now. There's not much I can do about that wrist though. He should get to a real doctor as soon as possible."

"Thank you," Morgan says. She is sitting beside Ben on the couch. His bad leg, now clean and bandaged, is propped up on a chair from the kitchen.

Barb is standing in the kitchen doorway, her hands balled together under her breasts. "Thank God we keep that first-aid kit. Running a B and B, you can never be too careful. But who would have ever thought…and on the very night Doc B. is away? It's all just so…" Her eyes shift from Morgan to Ben for a moment, then back to Morgan. "Unbelievable." She finishes and smiles.

"Well I sure appreciate the help," Ben says genuinely. "Don't know where we'd be if we hadn't stumbled across your place."

"And thank you so much for the food," Morgan adds, motioning towards the crumb littered plates on the coffee table. "You really did save us."

"Oh posh," Barb says. "Just a couple of ham sandwiches. There'll be more food in an hour or so. Once the stew is done. You're welcome to a bowl. Homemade bread as well."

Morgan looks at Ben, her eyes questioning. Ben stares back at her. Finally, he sighs, shifts his bad arm, and nods.

"Thank you so much," Morgan says again. She gazes around the room, from Barb, to Sidney, to Chloe. "All of you. But I'm afraid we can't stay."

Barb Frowns. "Can't stay? That's nonsense. Where do you think you'll be going on a night like this?"

"We need to keep moving," Morgan says. "It's…it's not safe here. For any of us."

Barb takes a slow step into the room. "Dear, I understand you've been through quite an ordeal. A trauma that I couldn't even imagine. But you're perfectly safe now. This cabin has stood through many a storm and this one is bound to pass soon."

"It's not the storm," Morgan states, shaking her head. "It's what's in the storm that I'm afraid of. Out there right now. It could already be too late."

"Now let's just calm down," Barb says. "There's no need to frighten the girls. What is it you think is out there?"

Morgan was about to say more, but then Ben put his hand on her leg and squeezes gently. She closes her mouth.

Ben says, "If we could just get to a phone, everything can be taken care of. I understand there's a satellite phone at the lodge. If that's true, then that's where we need to go."

"The Lodge," Barb breathes. "No one could walk to the Lodge through this storm. And in your condition? It's impossible."

"Of course," Ben agrees calmly. "I can barely walk to the bathroom on my own. We would need machines. Snowmobiles. In a place like this there's got to be a skidoo or two laying around."

"Mines at Sidney's place," Chloe says, sounding strangely excited by the idea of danger. "Two more at my cabin, but I guess they'd be no good. My Dad hasn't got the tracks back on them yet."

"Chloe," Barb snaps. "You hush. No one is going anywhere." She looks at Morgan, her brow a straight cut over her eyes. "What is this about? Tell me what you're afraid of."

Morgan glanced at Ben again. He meets her gaze, his eyes telling her to tread lightly. She sighs. Of course she will tread lightly. She doesn't want to go to prison any more than he does. But something has to be said. Something has to get these people moving before the tiger gets here. She can feel it out there. Waiting for them. Its yellow eyes watching, tail twitching in the air like a dancing eel. Ready to pounce. Devour…

"When the plane crashed," she says, turning her head away from Ben. "There was something with us. Something dangerous. I…we think it survived."

"Like a virus," Chloe offers excitedly. "My dad's always talking about these man-made viruses that the Government makes. They can be used as weapons. Doomsday stuff. Killing millions in like a week."

"Chloe, will you please…"

"No," Ben laughs suddenly, interrupting Barb. "Not a virus or a doomsday weapon. Nothing like that. It's an animal. And we're not even sure if it did survive. There's no proof one way or the other."

"Ben," Morgan says, but again he stops her.

"But…It's better to be safe than sorry. Morgan is right about that. We should keep moving. If it is still out there, it's in our best interest to not stay still long. If we can find ourselves a Skidoo and get to that phone, I can call in the calvary and everything will be a-okay. But it is true, the sooner we move, the better."

"What is it?"" Sidney asks. She can't believe she is the only one asking this obvious question. She also can't believe how Chloe is acting towards the whole thing, like she is excited by it. Just some game they are playing, with no real consequences. But Sidney can see the truth in Morgan's face. The woman is terrified of whatever is hiding in the storm. Any consequences they could be facing are very real. "What was in the plane with you?"

Morgan looks at Sidney. "A tiger," she tells her. "It is a Siberian tiger."

65

Twenty minutes later, and after a good amount of discussion, Barb is still unsure if she believes what the two strangers are saying. *A tiger loose in the woods, stalking people, possibly even killing...* It all just seems so fantastic that it is difficult to be taken as reality. She has no doubt that they are not *lying*. They seem to truly believe what they are saying, but a lot can happen to the human mind after such a trauma. It is possible they are confused, imagining the whole thing.

And yet, despite these doubts swimming in her mind, when Barb emerges from the bedroom with her husband's Browning .308 lever rifle cradled in her arms, it seems she has made the decision to trust them.

She approaches Morgan with the weapon. "I know your friend has a gun tucked into the back of his pants, but I think it's best that you take this as well. I'm trusting you with the welfare of these two lovely ladies, so some extra firepower can't hurt."

Morgan stares at the gun for a moment, trying to remember the last time she has used any sort of firearm. Nothing coming directly to mind, she accepts the weapon anyway, careful to keep the muzzle pointed at the floor. "Thank you," she says. "I wish you would come with us. It really isn't safe here."

"I agree," Sidney says from behind her. The two girls are back into their parkas, hands gloved, and woolen caps on their heads. Barb has, with much fuss and argument, convinced them both it was for the best if they accompanied Ben and Morgan to the Jenkins cabin, while she remains here, waiting for Eli and Saul to return.

"You should be coming with us," Chloe adds.

"Nonsense," Barb says. "The boys will be back anytime now. Someone needs to be here to let them know what's happening."

"We could leave a note," Sidney offers.

Barb shakes her head. "No. I can't do that to Eli. Plus…I'm not up to the journey. I would slow you down."

"We can help you," Morgan insists. "We should all be going."

"You'll already be dragging along one invalid," Barb says, looking at Ben. "You don't need another. And besides, I've still got the shotgun, and Eli has his service revolver. Though I doubt…" her words faded off as her eyes meet Morgan's.

"You don't believe us." Morgan states. "You think we're lying."

"No. If I thought you were lying then those girls would be staying put. It's just that…this all seems so…" she pauses, trying to choose the correct word. "Impossible."

"This is a big world," Ben says. He lifts his leg off the table and struggles to his feet. "A lot of things that were impossible twenty-five years ago are considered normal today."

"A tiger stalking the woods around Deadman Lake is not normal," Barb challenges. "Not twenty-five years ago or today."

"No," Ben agrees. "But removing an endangered species from the hands of poachers and relocating it to a secure environment, guaranteeing its chances of survival. That is a perfectly normal action by today's standards."

"In a snowstorm," Barb counters.

"My pilot had bad judgment. And now he's paid the ultimate price for his mistake."

To this, Barb has no reply. Death is indeed a price that cannot be argued.

Ben moves carefully around the couch towards the front door. "I do understand your doubts," he says to Barb. "This is a crazy story. I wouldn't believe it myself. But obviously there is some part of you that knows it is at least possible. Or, as you said, these girls would be staying put. If there is even the slightest possibility that what we're saying is true, if there really is a tiger out there, then the walls of this cabin are not going to stop it when it decides to come in. Keep moving, all of us, that's the right decision. Our only hope is to stay ahead of it. Get to the Lodge, use the satellite phone, and end this."

"Then go to the Jenkins' cabin," Barb says. "Get the snowmobile. I'm not arguing that fact. But I am staying here. When the boys get back, I'll send Saul after you. I know Eli will insist on staying with me. He'll protect me, and this cabin, from anything that tries to *come through the walls.*"

Ben nods. "I hope you're right." Then he turns to the girls. "It's time to go."

Sidney and Chloe both rush over to Barb and wrap their arms around her. Neither of them notices the pain in her face as they squeezed her. "We should stay with you," Sidney says. "We can all wait for my dad."

"No," Barb says, hugging them as hard as her fatigued muscles will allow. "I will not put you two in danger just because I'm stubborn." Then she lowers her voice so only they can hear. "Morgan is not pretending. She seems rational and alert, and very afraid. She is terrified of something. I can see it in her face. I don't know if it's a tiger, but she truly believes there is something out there, and I think Ben does too. So, no more fuss. You two need to go with them. Get to the Lodge. It will be the safest place for you. I will send your father along as soon as he arrives."

"But we're not finished the stew," Chloe complains glumly.

"It's a hearty dish. It'll still be waiting when all this silliness is behind us." She draws away from them. "Now you two pull those hats down over your ears. And stay together. The cabin isn't far, but in this weather, it can feel like miles. Stay close to Morgan. She'll protect you if…well…" She glances at Morgan. "If anything happens."

Morgan nods. "I'll keep them safe."

"*We'll* keep them safe," Ben adds. "I'm not totally useless." He takes another awkward step forward. Pain shoots up his leg and he stumbles, barely catching the back of the couch to keep from falling. Grimacing, he straightens up and looks over at Morgan. "Okay, maybe a little help here, Darling."

66

As Saul and Eli approach a half kilometer from the Foley's cabin, the snowmobile suddenly begins to cough and sputter.

The engine's power drops instantly, slowing the forward motion of the sled and causing the heavy machine to bog down into the deep powder. A second later, the left side ski snags a root that is hidden under the snow, and the sled jerks to an abrupt stop, almost sending Saul headfirst over the handlebars. The engine coughs once and stalls.

"Well shit," Eli shouts from behind Saul. Around them the wind screams through the trees, whipping the falling snow into a frenzy. Night has not quite taken the forest, but its black grip is tightening, slowly strangling any remaining color from the sky.

Saul twists around on the seat. "What happened?"

"The exhaust hood must have been torn away," Eli tells him. "Sucked snow into the pipe."

"Can we fix it?"

"I expect so. Hope we didn't bust a ski, though. Then we'd really be up shit creek without a paddle."

"We could walk," Saul offers.

Eli looks at him, his brow arched under his cap. "Could, but don't sound like much fun to me. Let's check things out before we start getting all panicked and talking crazy."

"Of course," Saul says. "I just meant in a worst case scenario, you know?"

Eli swings his leg across the seat and climbs off the sled. "Well, thankfully we ain't quite there yet." He pushes his way through the snow to the back of the machine. He kneels down, disappearing from Saul's sight.

"Ah yeah," he calls out a few moments later. "Just like I thought. Hoods gone. Goddamn pipe is as plugged up as my colon. Son of a whore!"

"But you can fix it?" Saul asks, glancing around nervously. The trees creak and sway like overworked soldiers. Dark shadows dance between them.

"Reach into the duffle bag on your left," Eli says. "Fetch out my hunting knife. Should be able to dig the snow out with that. Then we'll check the ski."

"Sure." The bag is slung over the seat behind him. He reaches down and begins fumbling with the latch, but quickly discovers it is impossible to get a hold of it with his gloves on. He straightens up and pulls off his left glove. He is just beginning to tug at his other glove when something catches his eye. Some movement inside the trees. He squints his eyes, studying the forest, trying to spot the source of his distraction. Snow swirls and trees lean in the wind, but he can see nothing else. It had been something, though. He is sure of it. Something had moved…

There it is again. A shadow moves in between two trees, then disappears behind another. A second later it reappears, still moving, vanishing behind one tree, reappearing on the other side. Traveling forward. Heading directly towards them.

"Eli," Saul shouts over the wind. "There's something in the trees."

"What?" Eli replies without looking up.

"There's something in the trees," Saul repeats. "And it's coming this way."

"Something," Eli grumbles. He straightens up, his back creaking almost as loud as the trees. "What the hell is a *Something*?"

Saul Points. "There. About twenty yards out. Coming this way."

Eli's eyes followed his finger. Even through the deepening darkness, it takes him only a second to spot what Saul is pointing at. A distinctive shape, making its way out from the thicker forest. It is still too far away to recognize exactly what it is, but Eli does notice one thing. Its stride is strangely smooth. Like every other creature that walks the forest floor, this…*something*…is fighting its way through almost three feet of snow, yet its movements seem effortless. Almost graceful.

"What is it? I can't tell."

"Neither can I," Eli answers as his hand moves to the gun holstered on his hip. "But not to worry. We'll be finding out in another second or two."

It continues moving, drawing out of the shadows. Seeming to materialize from the storm itself.

Saul's eyes widened as it comes into view. "Jesus, Is that…"

"I do believe it is," Eli says, now choosing to leave the gun where it is.

Matt Trapper steps out of the trees and stops ten feet away from them. He has earmuffs pulled down over his ears, but his cheeks are glowing red and beginning to chafe. His nose is an even deeper red, almost the color of a ripe tomato. He is wearing no jacket, only a gray and black woven blanket wrapped tightly around his shoulders. There are snowshoes strapped to his feet, which is how his movement through the snow had seemed so fluent.

"Matt," Eli says, stunned confusion aging his voice. "Matt Trapper? What in God's name are you doing out here?"

Matt is staring at them, his eyes blank. Silvery tracks of frozen tears run down his face.

"They took my parka," he says listlessly. "And my skidoo. But I found this blanket in the Sno-Cat. After Danny crashed, I got inside and found it. Snowshoes too."

Eli can barely hear his garbled words over the storm. He takes a step closer to the boy. "What? I don't understand. Danny crashed the Sno-Cat?"

Matt nods his head. "Yeah. It's my fault though. He swerved so he wouldn't run me over. Went over an embankment and hit a tree."

"Jesus," Saul breathes.

What Matt is saying makes no sense to Eli. He thinks the boy must be delirious, probably brought on by hypothermia. "Matty, what are you saying? Why was Danny driving the Sno-Cat. Where's Big Dwayne."

"He's dead," Matt says, fresh tears swelling in his eyes. "Danny said it was a tiger that killed him. But I couldn't look. I could see him layin' there, but there was all that blood. I just couldn't look."

Now Eli steps up to Matt and puts his hands on his shoulders. The boy jerks, as though he has only just noticed the old man at that very moment. "Big Dwayne is dead?"

Matty nods again; a movement so slight it is almost unnoticeable. "Him and Danny both. Tiger got dad, tree got Danny."

"Tiger? A tiger killed your dad?"

"Yeah. Danny seen it, I guess. He told me before…" Matt reached up and mopped his eyes with the back of his gloved hand.

"There are no tigers here, Matt," Eli pushes. "Only mountain lions. Is that what he meant? A mountain lion got Big Dwayne."

"Tiger!" Matt shouts and pulls out of Eli's grasp. He stumbles and falls backward, landing on his butt. His snowshoes are now sticking straight up from the snow like gravestones. "Tiger, tiger, tiger…" he continues, his voice getting quieter and quieter, then after a moment the words fade to nothing and stop. His eyes glaze over, find his hands, and stay there.

"Matt," Eli persists, shaking the boy lightly. "Matt. How could it have been a tiger, Matt? This ain't India. There ain't no tigers here. Matt?"

"He's in shock," Saul says.

"He ain't right in his mind," Eli counters. He looks at Saul. "What he's saying can't be true."

"No," Saul agrees. "Shock can do strange things. Play games with the mind. We need to get him back to the cabin. Warm and calm is what he needs. Then maybe we can find out what's really happened."

"Can't see Big Dwayne being mauled by no mountain lion," Eli continues, his eyes drifting back to the boy. "Not as big as he is. Any lion in these parts would shy away from a man his size. A grizzly maybe, but that don't make no sense neither."

"Eli," Saul shouts. "We need to get Matt out of this weather."

Eli jerks, snapping out of his thoughts. "Yeah, yeah. Right." He steps around Saul to the snowmobile and bends over the duffle bag. "Get the pipe cleaned out and we'll be on our way. Long as the ski's okay, that is."

Saul watches him for a moment, then goes over to Matt and kneels beside him. "We're gonna get you out of here, Matt," he says as gently as the weather will allow. "Get you warm and dry, then we can figure this out, okay."

Matt shifts slightly but does not reply. For now, it seems his hands are all that matter.

67

Barb stands in the open doorway, her checkered apron billowing in the frozen wind like a red and white flag, and watches as Ben, Morgan and the two girls set out on their journey to the Jenkins cabin. She waits until every trace of them is swallowed up by the stormy darkness, then steps back into the kitchen and closes the door. She begins to turn away, but as an afterthought, reaches up and throws the deadbolt. Tiger or no tiger, it is better safe than sorry.

Sure, she thinks as she makes her way to the icebox, *because everyone knows tigers can open doors.* Just as Ben said, if an animal of that size decides it wants in, no walls—*or deadbolts*—are going to stop it.

She takes a bottle of Aquafina from the icebox and sits down at the table. She can feel the weight of her pills in the front pocket of her apron. For a while, as she was dealing with the two survivors, she had been able to defuse the pain. Almost forget about it. But now, in the silence of the empty cabin, it has woken up and is back with a vengeance. Throbbing, in her legs and arms, running up her spine into her neck. Each beat of her heart is a rhythmic pulse of agony in her mind.

Barb reaches into the pocket and brings out the bottle. OxyContin 15mg is printed on the side of the small white container. She opens the lid and shakes two pills into her palm. She swallows them with a sip of water. When she picks up the bottle again, she means to put the cap back on and return it to her apron. Instead, she holds it for a moment, staring at the label. Then she dumps out two more pills and swallows them as well.

She sits back, her hands balled under her breasts, and takes a deep breath. Her feet twitch and move under the table. In a little while, after the Oxycodone has dissolved in her stomach and found its way into her blood stream, her feet will stop shaking. Then the pain will subside to tolerable levels, and she will be able to think more clearly. For now, her thoughts are swirling masses in her mind, confused and jumbled together like ten TVs playing different shows at the same time.

Had sending Sidney and Chloe away been the right choice. What if everything Ben and Morgan had said is a lie. What if they are actually escaped prisoners or mental patients? Is it possible I have just turned the girls over to murderers? Of course it is. But it is also impossible, isn't it? Morgan is too lovely and sweet to be a murderer. Also Ben is badly injured. He can barely walk, much less hurt anyone. Then there's the story they had told. A plane transporting an endangered species crashes into the woods. Now there's a tiger hiding in the trees. Maybe killing people. It makes no sense. Why would anyone come up with a lie that is so unbelievable? So ridiculous. Unless it is the truth. Then it isn't ridiculous at all. Then it is terrifying. God, I need Eli. I need him so badly. Why are they not back yet? Did they have an accident? Are they hurt? Or worse yet, what if the tiger has gotten them. What if Eli's dead? What will I do then? How could I go on? I suppose I will just give up because that's all that will be left. Wash down the rest of the pills with a bottle of vodka and be done with it all. *Maybe that would be for the best anyway. Even if Eli isn't dead, the fact that I am slowly killing him doesn't change. Each day he's with me, sharing my moment-by-moment misery, is surely driving him closer to an early grave himself. Is my worry that he could not survive without me just an excuse to continue tormenting him? Maybe he'd be better off without me. Maybe he would be happy—*

Suddenly both of Barb's arms shoot straight out. "No," she screams and slams her fists onto the table. An instant bolt of pain tears up her forearms and explodes in her elbows. She squeezes her eyes shut, enduring the agony. This is pain she deserves. Payment for her selfish thoughts. She will not betray Eli that way. Taking her own life—or even thinking about it—is an unforgivable sin. It is God who decides when her pain will end, and until that time she has to remain strong. For Eli. For Saul and the two girls. Even for Morgan and Ben. Anyone who may need her.

Barb opens her eyes. The pain in her arms is subsiding. As is the pain in the rest of her body. Also, her feet are no longer shaking. The Oxy is beginning to work its narcotic magic. Soon she will be able to stand up, go to the stove, and finish the stew. She will get everything ready for when Eli comes home. A nice hot meal is the least he deserves after such a hard journey.

Then, as if in response to her thoughts, there is the creak of straining wood as someone mounts the back steps.

Barb smiles. "Oh Eli, thank God," she breathes and gets to her feet. The room swoons, spinning before her eyes. She grips the back of the chair and puts her hand to her forehead. Dizziness is an unfortunate side effect of the pills. But, like the pain, it is something she has learned to live with. If the room spins, then dammit, she will spin right along with it. All that matters now is that Eli has finally come home.

She rounds the table, holding the edge as the room waxes and wanes. Then she crosses to the door and pulls back the bolt. "Eli, I've been so worried," she says, dragging open the door. "So much has happened since you—"

68

When the door comes open The Tiger shrinks back, dropping his body close to the wooden deck. All his muscles tighten at once, coiling up, ready for the explosion of power that will hurtle his massive body forward with the same destructive force of a tank. His lips peel back and an excited cuffing sound pushes past his fangs. The hunt is over. Now he will destroy.

This one is another female, like the one where the dog had been. Yet it is different. It looks thin. Sickly. Like a deer in its fifth winter. An easy kill.

But there is something else. Something in its face causes The Tiger to hesitate. When the door first came open, when it had been making those high-pitched man noises, the urge had been strong. And the hatred was also there, shrouding everything in blood red. But now, staring into its wide eyes, something is different. He can smell its fear of course. A sour odor that permeates from its skin, like the pong rising off a stagnant body of water. And he can see it as well, in its eyes and smeared across its face. Its frail body is trembling all over. But below the fear, beneath its skin, deep in its muscles and organs, there is…

hurt. Not the same kind of hurt as the other female; there is no hole in its chest that leaks blood. This female's hurt is different. Foul. It courses all through its body like a poisoned river, reeking of fester and sickness. For a moment, his urge is drowned in the stench of this female's pain, leaving him with only confusion in its place. Suddenly he wants to turn and run away from it. Leave it here to die on its own.

Then, as he watches the female begin to slowly back away, he feels a new emotion rise up inside his body. One that is not instinct or urge. It is an alien emotion, like nothing he has felt before. It fills his heart, pumping through his veins with each beat. It flows into his mind, dictating what his next actions will be. He *does* need to kill this sickly one. But not in the same way he kills the others. Not because of urge, or even hate. He needs to kill it because of pity. It is the only way to put an end to its hurt.

69

The first thing Barb thinks when she sees the tiger crouching on her back porch is that she is hallucinating. Tricks of the mind—*and the eyes*—are another known side effect of OxyContin, though she has never experienced anything like this before. But, when the animal's lips peel back from its teeth and it begins making a strange coughing sound, she suddenly knows this is not a trick of the mind. Hallucinations, no matter how real they may seem to the eyes, do not smell. The breath coming out of this huge beast is rank.

Fear tightens in her chest, squeezing against her heart like a vise. Her hands rise impulsively and ball together under her breasts.

Thoughts run rampant through her mind. Images and memories, dropping in for a mere second before being pushed out again by the next idea. Her life flashing before her eyes. One of these memories was a vacation she and her husband had taken. It had been a long time ago, when they were still living in Vancouver and Eli was working as a security guard. They had just learned that Barb could not have children, a devastating blow to any young couple. But instead of wallowing in self-pity, as Barb would have done, Eli suggested they do something different. Something a family would do. "We may only be two, but we're still a family," he had said. So, they had taken a trip to Disney World in Orlando, Florida. And while they were there, they made sure to do it all. They went on all the rides, even the ones for the little kiddies. They had their picture taken with Mickey Mouse and Goofy. They didn't eat a single vegetable the entire trip. Only fun food, like hamburgers and hotdogs, popcorn and cotton candy. Barb had diarrhea for two days after they got home, but it didn't matter. They had fun. Real *family* fun. On the third day of their visit, they had rented a car and done the two-hour drive to the Central Florida Zoo and Botanical Gardens. The sun rode high in the sky that day, and by noon it was thirty-seven degrees. After only two hours of walking around in the blistering heat, Barb was ready to call it a day. But Eli would not have it. He had been uncharacteristically stubborn. There was still one thing left he needed to see. So, he took Barb by the hand and dragged her halfway across the compound, promising her the whole way that it would be worth it.

Normally there were five animals inside the large tiger complex, but on this particularly hot day, only two tigers had ventured out of the much cooler brick paddock. At the moment Eli and Barb had stepped up to the fence, these two were invested in a very serious game of *Tag, You're It*. To the delight of everyone watching, one tiger would give chase, leaping over logs and rocks in pursuit of the other. When it caught up with its playmate, it would swat it playfully in the hindquarters. Then the tables would instantly turn. The pursuer becomes the pursued. The chase would be on again. But instead of it ending in harmless swat, this time the *It* tiger had sprung into the air and tackled the other animal in mid gallop. They rolled around on the ground, batting at each other with their front paws, yowling and hissing. This lasted for only a few seconds, then they were off again, one chasing the other across the compound. It had gone on this way for several minutes, back and forth, *It* and *Tag*. When it did end, it had been in a perfectly timed mutual agreement. Both animals suddenly stopped and flopped onto the ground, panting and gazing at the onlookers with little interest.

"Usually tigers are solitary creatures," Eli told her as they walked back to the car. "Those two playing together like that? They must have been related. Maybe brother and sister."

Barb had spent the rest of the ride back to the hotel thinking about the two tigers. How happy they were. Carefree, needing nothing but open space to run. She remembered promising herself that she would make Eli and her own life just like that. Even if they would never have children, she would still work hard every day to make Eli as happy and carefree as those tigers.

God how badly she had failed.

This memory, along with so many others, flashes through her mind in a matter of seconds as she stands in the doorway, locked in the tiger's yellow stare. Wind rushes between them, pulling at the animal's fur, but doing little to break its hold on her. She can see her reflection in its eyes. Even through the shifting darkness of the storm, her face is shining brightly in their glassy surface. An old woman gazing out at her.

Barb takes a slow step back, needing to get away from this image of herself as much as from the tiger. It has stopped making the strange coughing sounds, but its lips are still peeled back from its teeth. It watches her, grinning, making no move to follow. She takes another step, never allowing her gaze to leave its. She vaguely remembers this may have been something she read in one of the survival books Eli was always leaving around. If you come across a bear in the woods, look into its eyes and don't look away. Or... could it have been *don't look into its eyes?* God, now she wasn't sure. Her mind was swirling. The Oxy was fully dissolved into her system, and the extra pills she has taken are adding to its potency. This is probably the only reason she had not suffered an instant heart attack the moment she opened the door. *Ahh, but it's still on its way, isn't it?* She could feel her heart hammering in her chest like a snare drum.

She takes a third step back. She is inside the cabin now. One more step and she will be able to close the door. Maybe then it will just...

The tiger comes out of its crouch, straightening up to its full height.

A moaning sound pushes out of Barb's throat as her eyes follow the animal's rise. At five foot five, Barb is an average height woman. The crest of the tiger's shoulder is now level with the bridge of her nose. Its head is the size of a beachball. The tigers she remembers chasing each other at the Florida Zoo would have looked like bob-cats compared to this creature.

Its head remains low, its scared nose almost touching the gathering snow, but its huge yellow eyes never leave Barb's face. It is studying her. Daring her to move again. She stays where she is, her entire body vibrating. Fear is still tightening its grip on her heart, squeezing mercilessly. But it is not only the fear that stops her from moving. A strange fascination rises inside her, and suddenly she feels drawn to the animal. Fascinated by it. For all her failings, the weakness and frailty of her body, her anguished suffering and dependency on painkillers, this tiger is the opposite. Powerful and strong. A thing pure of nature, without influence by worldly things. Unpolluted and true. She almost…envied it.

The tiger takes a step towards her. The wooden planks of the porch moan under its immense weight. Now its fire striped face is only five feet from her own. Its breath is hot and sour. Barb also takes another step back. She should be able to close the door now, but she cannot get her hand to move. No matter how hard she tries, it remains frozen where it is, balled inside her other hand.

Again, the tiger moves forward, its paws crunching in the snow. Barb matches it with a backward step. Her breath is no more than quick gulps of air, and her heart is racing inside her chest. God, why hadn't she been able to close the door? At least then there would have been wood between her and the animal's hypnotic stare. Now, as the cat takes another step, moving through the doorway and into the kitchen, the chance is past. The small room makes the beast look even larger. It is an odd illusion that triggers another memory in Barb's mind. When she was a child, no more than eight or nine, her parents had given her a kitten for Christmas. It had been the cutest little thing, and so full of energy it was hard for Barb to keep up with it. It just ran here and there and all over, never seeming to tire itself out. Finally, Barb was called to the table for the holiday feast, so she'd left the tiny furball to fend for itself. After a wonderful Christmas meal, Barb went looking for the kitten, but couldn't find it. As children tend to do, she panicked almost immediately. She cried to her mother, begging for her to find the lost kitten. They looked around the house frantically for about five minutes before her mother called to her, giggling softly under her breath. She looked where her mother was pointing and immediately began to giggle herself. Another gift Barb received from Santa that year was a completely furnished, 1/12 scale dollhouse. It seemed the kitten had found itself a cozy spot to fall asleep. Inside the miniature kitchen, right between the tiny fridge and the sink. Now the kitten was a giant, mutant cat that had invaded some poor innocents' home

This is how the tiger looked, standing between the icebox and the sink. Except this is a regular sized kitchen, and the animal is no mutant kitten.

It takes another step, its tail sticking straight up, swishing back and forth. The tip is only inches away from brushing across the ceiling.

Barb steps back, one of her hands now feeling around behind her for the doorway that will lead into the sitting room. The other hand is at her chest, pressing down against her hammering heart. The pain has begun to creep across her chest into her left shoulder.

The tiger moves forward. Its top lip has dropped down, hiding its monstrous fangs. Its face appears calm now; almost majestic, its eyes sparkling madly in the dim glow of the flickering lantern. In some enigmatic way it resembles an Egyptian artifact come to life.

Then it starts to purr.

Even within the suffocating confines of her fear and Oxy rattled mind, Barb finds this odd. She has always thought tigers incapable of this particular cat talent. In fact, she is quite sure she has heard this fact in at least one or two documentaries. Yet this animal is suddenly rumbling like a chain saw. Very unusual…

The tiger lurches ahead now. Barb yelps and jerks away from it, floundering back two steps. She is able to grab the door and save herself a fall onto her backside. Another massive bolt of pain shoots down her left arm. She moans, clutching at her chest, and staggers backward. She is standing on the old throw rug in the sitting room now. To her left is the stone fireplace, still cold and dark; waiting for an evening fire that will probably never come. To her right, the tattered woolen sofa where Eli takes his afternoon naps, and directly behind her will be the rocking chair. Barb has spent many hours sitting in this chair, knitting scarves and mittens and other things she gave away to neighbors and friends.

The tiger is still for a moment, its head tilted slightly to one side, watching her with mild curiosity. The purring continues; an uneven, choppy sound that would have seemed more natural coming from the engine compartment of a tractor than from a giant cat's chest.

When it finally begins to move again, its forward motion is smooth, slow and deliberate. Each step forces Barb to retreat deeper into the sitting room. Her eyes remain locked with its. Unwavering. No glancing from side to side, no seeking a way out. She knows there is no way out. This game—*the tiger's game*—has only one inevitable ending and she is destined to play it to that end.

The back of her knees hit the rocking chair, and she allows herself to fold into it. The pain in her chest and left side is growing with each beat of her heart. It is no mystery pain. She understands exactly what is happening. She is having a heart attack.

The tiger stops with a mere three feet separating them. Its head is low, its nose inches above the carpet. But its eyes are turned up, looking into Barb's face. It is like staring into twin mirrors, affording her the chance to watch as the last few moments of her life slip away.

Another dagger of pain in Barb's chest explodes as the final throbs of her failing heart pump jagged shards of agony into her left shoulder and down her arm. She moans again and squeezes her hand tighter against her chest. It is a pain like nothing she could have imagined, and in the last few years she has learned to imagine a lot. A bulldozer parked on her breasts would not have been worse. Each beat of her heart was excruciating, as if the life sustaining muscle itself is charlie-horsing inside her chest.

But, through it all, her eyes never leave the tigers.

It does not move. Its massive head hanging in the air only inches from her face. Motionless. Like a multicolor apparition. Even its strange purring has ceased.

For the last few seconds, as her vision begins to swim and fade, she thinks she can see more in the creature's eyes than just her reflection. There is a curiosity in them. A thoughtful interest. As if the animal is trying to understand what is happening to her. Its nose twitches, sniffing the air around them, taking in the odors of her diminishing life. The smell of her pain.

Something else is there as well. In its yellow stare. Hidden behind the curiosity, yet still readable. A strangely human emotion in the eyes of a beast. *Empathy*

Then its head does move. It draws in closer to her. Its nose is now an inch from her cheek. Barb closes her eyes, at last inviting the darkness to surround her. She feels her fear dissolving into the darkness. Evaporating like the mist that rises off Deadman Lake on a warm summer morning. She thinks of Eli. Is he already waiting for her? She hopes not. He still has so much life to live. It will be better if she waits for him. She is patient. She can wait. She will at last be in a place with no pain. She will happily wait there as long as it takes…

70

The Tiger listens. Even with the wind howling just beyond the walls of the cabin, he can hear the female's heart beating. Before, as he forced it into this larger room, the beats had been fast. Fluttering and sporadic, like a fleeing deer. Now it is slowing. The silences between each thump are longer. He sniffs the skin of its face. It still smells foul.

Sick. But like its heartbeat, this smell is also fading. Soon it will be gone, and then The Tiger will leave.

He could bite it. Lay its throat open with one jerk of his head. That would end its sick quicker. Just the thought of blood, sweet man blood, brings the urge back. He could bathe in its blood. Spread it around this man place. A warning to all the others who enter here. He could do this. He wants to do it.

But inside his mind, buried under his instinct and urge, something else is fighting to be recognized. Something that, like his purr, has never existed in another tiger. His rage towards man is prominent. Dominating most of his thoughts. Yet, beyond his anger, there are tiny sparks of something else. There is no way for his brain to describe what he is feeling, language and words mean nothing to him. But it momentarily dulls his rage. For reasons beyond his understanding, he senses this female is not his to kill. Its death is already imminent. Any attempt to kill it more will be pointless. Also—though this new sensation is alien inside his animal mind, it still comes with enough power to be recognized—it would be wrong to hurt it anymore.

So instead of biting, The Tiger leans in and kisses the female, dragging his spiny tongue up its cheek. A soft moan creeps out of its throat as the hundreds of tiny barbs on the surface of his tongue cut through its paper-thin skin. Immediately blood begins to well up in these shallow slices, running down its face and dripping off the edge of its jaw.

When The Tiger draws away, the unpleasant taste of its dying blood coating his tongue, he looks down into its face again. Its eyes are closed, but its chest still rises and falls with labored breath. Its heart has slowed even more, each slight beat separated by long silences.

Knowing it will soon be dead, The Tiger begins to turn away.

A sudden, thunderous boom echoes through the dwelling, and the wall just to the right of his head erupts into a cloud of wood chips and dust. The Tiger jerks to his left, and in one fluid motion that should have been impossible for an animal his size, drops his body close to the ground and twists around. His enormous back leg strikes a small end table. It, and the oil lamp that sits on it, fly across the room, and explode against the far wall.

Now The Tiger is facing the doorway that leads back into the kitchen. Another man stands there. Its knees are slightly bent and both arms are stretched out towards him. Clutched in its hands is a black object. The Tiger has not seen one this small before, but his instincts tell him exactly what it was. Rage courses through his body, shoving all the alien emotions he has been feeling back into the darkness of his mind. All that matters is killing this man. Or, if he cannot kill him now, he will escape from this place so he can kill him another time. Whichever way it happens; he will bring savage death to the man… and then all the others.

The Tiger hisses at the man, spittle and blood flying out of his mouth. He bats at the air with his front paw.

The small thunder stick in man's hands booms again…and pain erupts inside The Tiger…

71

Before Eli Foley was offered the job as deputy in the Terravale Sheriff's Department, he had been working as a security guard for Oakridge Mall in Vancouver. Like most entry level security jobs, he was afforded a billy-club as his sole form of defense. Of course, with the largest criminal concern generally being kids smoking dope in one of the many inset doorways, the lack of a gun at his hip had been no issue. Eli—who had never been a hunter and had, in fact not pulled a trigger ever—was perfectly fine doing the job with only a club. He had always been a true believer that a gun in the hand was the fastest way to escalate a minor confrontation into a major one.

When his good friend Joe Williams—who at the time was the sheriff of Terravale—came to him with the deputy job, Eli's first instinct was to turn it down. A deputy, even in a town as small as Terravale, was required to carry a firearm. This went against Eli's moral beliefs, and also made him very nervous.

But two things changed his mind. The first was Joe. He did this by promising his friend that the only shooting going on in *his* town was by the hunters in the woods. People who visited Terravale to snowmobile or hunt, or camp in the summer months, were so happy to be away from their mundane city lives that violence, or any criminal activity for that matter, was very rare. And the townspeople—those privileged enough to live in this paradise of trees all year round—were equally as content, receiving all visitors with open arms and joy. On the few occasions that a situation did turn violent—usually because of alcohol and ignorance—it was the local detachment of RCMP that stepped in to deal with it. In his five years as sheriff, Joe had been forced to pull and fire his revolver only three times in the line of duty. Once was to scare off a small group of coyotes that had surrounded a young boy and his Beagle. The other two times both involved grizzly bears that had wandered too close to town. The truth was a gun on the hip was like a badge over the heart. A symbol of authority. In Terravale it had little other use. So little in fact, Joe went so far as to tell Eli he would not be forced to even wear a pistol if he chose not to.

The second thing that had helped change his mind had been his wife. Eli was beginning to worry about her happiness. Normally a vibrant, active woman, Barb had recently begun showing signs of discontent. She was unhappy with her job, and the hustle and bustle of the city had been wearing on her nerves. Because he had sensed this in her for some time, he wanted to get her away from the smoggy, hectic life they had in Vancouver. What better escape could there be than the clean air and beauty of Northern British Columbia? It would be the best thing for her…and him.

So, making the biggest decision of his life, he moved himself and his wife to a small town that neither of them had ever heard of. And true to Joe's word, in Eli's three years as deputy and ten years as sheriff, he had never strapped a gun belt around his waist.

In many ways, this fact makes the horror of what is happening even worse. Nine years after trading in his badge for the quiet responsibilities of a bed and breakfast on Deadman Lake, it is only now that he holds a gun in his trembling hands.

He had known something was wrong from the moment he stepped onto the porch of his cabin and saw the door gaping open. Behind him, Saul is still helping Matty up the stairs. Suddenly the boy jerks out of his grasp and stumbles back down, falling into the deep snow at the bottom. Saul looks down at him from the stairs, confusion on his face. "What is it…"

That is when Eli notices the tracks. Animal tracks. Made by a very large animal. The boy has also seen them. He is staring at them with terror in his eyes, his mouth working, opening and closing like a fish, but only silent breath passing his lips.

"Tracks," Eli says to Saul, pointing at the imprints in the snow.

Saul's gaze follows his finger. At first his expression remains confused, not sure what he is looking at. Then realization comes, and his eyes fill with horror. "Jesus," he moans, looking back to Eli and the opened door of the cabin. "The girls…"

"Stay here with Matt," Eli says. He pulls his gun from the holster on his hip. Though he had never carried one during his years as sheriff, he has developed the habit of wearing a weapon when he ventures away from the cabin. The loud bang of a gun would scare away just about any critter he was bound to come across, regardless of its size.

"Eli," Saul says. "We should go together…"

"No," Eli replies, twisting around to face him. His mind is swirling with thoughts of cougars and bears…and tigers. "You stay here with the boy. I'll check inside and make sure it's safe. Then I'll call you. But for now, stay put."

"My daughter is in there, dammit!" Saul shouts.

"I Know. And so is my wife. But if there's something else in there with them, I can't have you stepping on my heels. Please, Saul, stay with Matt."

Saul's eyes blazed, but he says no more, and when Eli turns away and steps through the open doorway into the cabin, he makes no move to follow.

72

The first shot had been a critical mistake. When Eli enter the sitting room and saw the tiger standing over Barb, he was so utterly stunned that every muscle in his body had tightened at once, including the finger that was pushed through the trigger guard. The gun popped, firing the bullet wide. It punched a hole into the wall two feet to the right of the animal's head. It was a dumb, rookie mistake. One that would very possibly cost him and his wife their lives.

Now the cat moves with incredible speed. Before Eli can begin pulling the hammer back for a second shot, it has dropped low and come around. Its huge body collides with a table, shattering it into pieces. Its lips peeled back from its fangs as it begins to hiss savagely, swiping a massive front paw through the air.

Eli's eyes dart back and forth between his wife and the animal. Barb is slumped over in her chair. Her eyes are closed, and blood is running down her face in tiny rivulets. He thinks he can see her chest rising and falling, but it is very slight and could easily be a trick of the flickering lantern light.

God please... hang on Barb. Hang on!

Pulling back on the hammer of the gun, he looks back at the cat. He has seen tigers before, on TV and at the zoo in Florida, but nothing could have prepared him for what he is seeing now.

This animal is the size of a horse. Even crouched down its shoulder was easily three feet from the floor. It has to weigh eight-hundred pounds, probably more.

In the few seconds that the two lock eyes with one another, there is only one word Eli can think of to describe the beast crouching before him. *Abomination.*

The tiger swats at him again, hissing and spitting. Eli can see its muscles tensing and rippling under its thick fur. It is preparing to leap at him. He fires again before it can.

This time his aim is true. The bullet strikes the animal in the right shoulder, tearing through its dense fur and into its flesh. Blood spurts from the wound and splashes onto the carpet. The cat grunts, twisting its head towards the sudden explosion of pain. But it makes no other movement. No stagger, no hint of a retreat. When it turns back to face the old man again, Eli is momentarily stunned by what he sees in its yellow eyes. He knew most animals were capable of some degree of emotion, but not like this. The raw, burning hatred he is seeing now is so blatantly recognizable it borders on human. In its stare he can see himself being attacked by the tiger; it leaps at him, knocking him back and laying open his throat with one bloody bite. And in this short moment, Eli feels this to be just. It is what he deserves. Himself and all of mankind. Payback for centuries of ignorance.

But then he remembers Barb. Slumping in the chair. Possibly dead. She did not deserve this. She is kind and thoughtful. Giving and patient, and so full of suffering and pain that any debt she may have owed has already been paid back tenfold. The tiger has no right to bring any of its hatred to her. NO…

"RIGHT!" Eli shouts at the animal and pulls the trigger.

At the same instant the gun fires, the tiger leaps. But not towards Eli. Instead, it pulls its huge body backward and to the right, ducking down behind Barb. The bullet barely grazes the longer fur on the side of its head. It hits the large picture window that is directly behind Barb's chair, shattering the glass in a glittery CRASH! Shards spray through the room and out into the darkness of the storm.

"Bastard," Eli growls. His wife is now partially blocking his view of the animal. With a risk of hitting her, his aim will have to be much better this time. His lack of handling a gun—which had never been an issue during his cop days—has suddenly become a huge factor.

Shit! An ex-cop that can't aim worth a damn! Stupid ass...

The tiger shifts, turning its body sideways behind Barb. Now it is looking at Eli again, its yellow eyes crackling with rage, then its lips peel up again, baring its teeth, grinning at him.

Eli sights in on the animal's head. "That's right," he says, returning its grin with his own. His white teeth shimmered in the dancing lantern glow. "Smile for the camera you son of a whore..." He squeezes the trigger.

Nothing happens. "Shit." His attention flicks to the gun, searching for the problem. He spots it immediately. *The hammer.* He has forgotten to cock the hammer. *Damn single action piece of junk.* He pulls the hammer back, cursing himself for never having upgraded to a better weapon. Then he re-sights on the tiger and...

It is gone. In the few seconds Eli's attention was diverted, the tiger has again moved with uncanny agility and speed, bounding through the broken window with a single thrust of its back legs. Eli can hear the crunching of packed snow as the animal retreats into the stormy night. It fades quickly into nothing, leaving only the howl of frenzied wind.

A second critical mistake and now he has missed his chance. "Damn you, old fool," he curses, wanting to feel angry at himself for how useless and old he had become. But the anger will have to wait. There is no time. For now, only one thing matters. His sweet Barbara. He jams his gun back into the holster on his belt and rushes across the room to his wife's side.

He kneels next to her chair. "Barbara," he whispers, gently laying his hand onto her chest. At first, there is no movement at all. Then a slight, hitching draw of breath. "That's it, stay with me." Much of the skin on her right cheek has been peeled away. Blood seeps out from the exposed flesh and drips off her jaw, staining the collar of her terry-robe an angry crimson. Horror circles all around the room, like the storm circling beyond the shattered window. It is trying to sweep in and overtake Eli's mind, but he will not give it any foothold. He forces it away—*holstering* it just as he had his useless gun.

"Please Barb," he croons. "Come back to me."

She pulls in another ragged draw of air, exhaling breath that smells of stale tea leaves and Polydent.

Saul steps into the doorway of the sitting room and stops there. Matty comes up behind him, peering past his shoulder nervously. Saul's face is drawn with confusion and worry as he scans the room. The boy's eyes, however, are wide and filled with terror. They lock onto the broken window behind Eli and Barb and stay there, his entire body trembling like leaf in a breeze.

"Eli," Saul stammers. "What happened here?"

"Truth," Eli replies without his turning his head away from his wife's pale face. "The boy was tellin' the truth."

Saul throws a quick backward glance at Matty, then asks, "Truth about what?" though he already knows the answer. He has also seen the tracks in the snow.

"Tiger," Eli spits. "Goddamn tiger was in here. It…it was standing over Barb…like it was watching her." Now the old man does look up at Saul. His listless eyes shine behind a glaze of building tears. "Watching her die."

"My God," Saul breaths. He wants to go to Eli. Put his hand on his shoulder, Comfort him. But his legs will not move, as though he was standing knee-deep in quicksand. So instead he looks around the room again. "Where are the girls?"

Eli's brow creases. *The girls?* Had he seen the girls since entering the house? Hiding somewhere. Maybe in the bathroom? The bedroom? Maybe…But *no*. He has not seen either of them, and until the moment the four words left Saul's mouth, his shock was so deep he had not even remembered they were here at all. *You stupid old man.* To Saul, he says, "I don't…"

"Gone," Barb croaks. Her eyelids flutter, trying to stay open. She shifts in the chair, leaning closer to Eli. He leans over as well and takes her gently into his arms. Then her eyes do come open, peering around frantically. Finally, they touch on her husband and remain there. "G..gone," she repeats softly.

"Don't speak," Eli says. "You need to save your strength."

Barb takes a deep, rattling breath. "Hush," she says, her voice very quiet, yet still carrying the edge of scolding that Eli knows well. "Strength…doesn't matter. The girls…all that matters. They…are gone…"

"Gone where?" Saul asks. At last finding his legs, he comes across the room now and kneels in front of Barb. Matt makes no move to follow. He stays where he is, staring through the broken window into the darkness.

Barb's eyes close momentarily. When they open, she is looking at Saul. "Gone...to the Lodge. With Morg...Morgan."

"Morgan," Saul echoes, not sure he has heard her correctly.

She Nods. "Morgan and..."

"Ben," Matt says from behind him. When Saul and Eli both turn towards him, he has gone back to studying his hands. "They're the ones," he adds reluctantly. "The ones from the plane wreck. The ones that took my Skidoo."

"I don't understand," Saul says. "Why Barb? Why would the girls leave with two people they don't know? Why would you let them?"

Eli frowns. "Careful Saul..."

But Barb touches his hand softly, stopping him. "They said... an animal...a tiger was coming. Said to keep moving. Stay ahead... only way to...be safe. I sent the girls for safety. I stayed, waiting for you." She tries to smile at Eli, but only half her mouth will work, producing little more than a crooked sneer. "I knew you would... be along soon."

"The Lodge?" Saul questions, rubbing his forehead. His brain has suddenly begun to thump painfully in his skull. "That's at the other end of the lake. They couldn't walk. Not in the storm."

Barb shakes her head weakly. "Snowmobile. Chloe's snowmobile. At your cabin."

"Could all four of them fit on one snowmobile?" Saul asks Eli.

He does not appear to hear. He is leaning over his wife, stroking her hand in both of his.

"Eli," Saul says. "I'm sorry for what has happened here, but please, help me. My daughter is out there."

The old man looks at him. His eyes are two gray holes inside a sea of wrinkles. He seems to have aged ten years in the last half hour. "I…don't know," he says in a voice so hoarse it is hard to hear. He coughs and clears his throat. "I suppose, if she's got Doc B.'s 1200cc Bombardier. Might fit four. Be awful tight though, so maybe not…Shit, I don't know for sure."

"Okay." Saul touches Barb's leg softly. Her eyes have slipped closed again and the skin of her remaining cheek is the color of pale ash. Each short breath she takes is labored and raspy. "Hang in there, Barb," he says and stands up. Then, turning to Eli, he continues, "I need to take your snowmobile and go after them. Are you okay with that?"

"Of course," Eli replies. He reaches down and pulls the revolver from its holster. Holding it out to Saul, he says, "Take this. Remember to cock it. Go get your daughter."

Saul hesitates, eyeing the gun nervously. "You need that. What if…*it* comes back?"

"Take the gun. I have others."

Reluctantly Saul reaches out and takes the weapon. "Matt should stay with you."

Eli shakes his head. "No. You take the boy. We'll be fine."

"But Eli…"

"No," Eli repeats. He is hugging his wife close to him. "This woman has taken care of me for most of my life. Now it's time for me to take care of her. It's…It's something I gotta do on my own."

Saul watches him for another few seconds before finally nodding his head. "I wish I could do more…"

"Just go get them girls. That's the most you can do."

"Okay, I'll be back as soon as I can."

But Eli has begun whispering into Barb's ear and makes no reply.

73

As Saul is making his decision to take Matt and go after his daughter, his daughter is making a decision of her own. But unlike her father's, Sidney's decision is met with immediate disapproval.

The three girls are standing in the kitchen of the Jenkins' cabin. A few minutes early, with a flashlight in hand, Ben had hobbled outside to check on the fuel level and condition of Chloe's snowmobile while they lit a small fire in the stove, attempting to warm up as much as they can before the long, icy trek to Big Dwayne's lodge. It has been ten minutes since they heard the gunshots. The ceaseless howling of the storm had dulled the power of the shots, yet there was no doubt in anyone's mind what the three, crisp popping sounds had been. It had been these unmistakable sounds that had fueled Sidney's sudden announcement.

"I'm going back," she says, pulling her gloves on. She had been warming her hands over the stove, her mind churning with grisly thoughts of what could be happening back at the Foley's cabin. They had abandoned Mrs. Foley, and now God only knows what terrible things are going on.

Chloe and Morgan are both staring at her with round, unbelieving eyes. "What," Chloe asks, sure that she has heard her friend wrong.

"I'm going back," Sidney repeats. "I...I have to make sure Mrs. Foley is okay."

"Are you out of your mind," Chloe says. "We all heard the gunshots, and that can mean only one thing. The tiger is out there."

"That's why I need to go back. We left Mrs. Foley there. She was defenseless."

Chloe is shaking her head. "She wasn't. She said there was a shotgun. That's probably what we heard."

"Come on Chloe," Sidney says. "You know she's sick. She probably couldn't even hold a shotgun, never mind aim one at a tiger and shoot it."

"I don't..."

But then Morgan lays her hand on Chloe's shoulder. "Wait," she says. "Let's think about this for a second."

Chloe twists around and looks at Morgan. Her brow is pinched angrily, but she remains quiet for the moment.

"Okay," Morgan continues. "I agree with Sidney..."

"No," Chloe snaps. "You can't..."

"Not about going back," Morgan pushes on, cutting off the younger girl's rant. "In fact, I think going back is a very bad idea. What I do agree with is that the woman did not look well. She looked frail and weak, and I don't think she could have fired a shotgun. Especially not three times. But that point is irrelevant because the shots we heard didn't come from a shotgun."

"How do you know that?" Chloe asks, folding her arms across her chest stubbornly.

"It's obvious. Shotguns go BOOM and handguns go POP. What we heard was a pop. A handgun. Barb didn't have a pistol, her husband did. He must have fired the shots. I'm sure Ben will tell you the same thing."

"Okay," Sidney agrees. "But I still think I should go back."

"Why?" Morgan breathes, frustration darkening her tone. "If Foley and your dad got to the cabin, which I'm sure they did, then what good could you do them by going back? They fired the shots either to kill something or scare it away. After that Barb would have told them what had happened and they're all probably on the way here. You going back is pointless."

Now Chloe is nodding her head fervently. "Pointless," she echoes triumphantly, as though the entire statement had been hers.

Sidney is quiet, tossing things around in her mind. She knows Morgan is probably right, but she still can't help feeling guilty for leaving Mrs. Foley. And she is worried about her dad. Saul is a city boy. Has been all his life. He is still getting used to being in the woods, and he certainly is not a hunter—as far as she knows he has never even held a gun. Now he is possibly facing off against a man-eating tiger. Sure, Eli Foley is with him, and Eli had been a policeman. But he is old now. His hands shake and he coughs a lot. Would he be much better against a tiger than her dad? *God, she is so confused and scared.* Two days ago she was living a simple, happy life. Now everything is crashing down around her.

Finally, she gives in. "Fine. I won't go back. But I'm not going to the Lodge either. Not without my dad."

"What?" Chloe asks. "What does that mean?"

"It means I'm waiting here." She looks at Morgan. "If what you say is true, then my dad and the Foley's should be on their way here. Probably with the other snowmobile. I'll wait for them."

"I don't think that's a good idea, Sidney," Morgan says. "We should keep moving. Everyone else will catch up to us at the Lodge."

"You and Ben go. And take Chloe too. But I'm staying here. When my dad is here, then maybe we'll come. It'll be up to him."

"I'm not leaving you," Chloe says. She goes to her friend and hugs her. "If you stay, I'm staying too."

"You shouldn't," Sidney says, embracing Chloe. "I want you to go. It'll be safer."

"Not a chance. Not without you. You're my best friend and I…" She hesitates, then pulls away and looks into Sidney's eyes. "I…I won't leave you," she finishes at last and hugs her again.

Morgan watches them quietly for a moment, understanding that this has just become an argument she cannot win. These two…friends are an alliance. With Sidney's need to be with her father, and Chloe's single-minded stubbornness, there will be no changing their minds, despite how bad—*and Morgan thinks it is very bad*—the idea is.

Just as the girls are drawing apart, each smiling at the other as if they have just shared some special secret, the kitchen door pushes open with a blast of snow and frigid air. Ben sidestepped through the opening, then has to use his whole body to force the door closed against the power of the pounding wind. He shakes his head, sending a cloud of silvery flakes through the warming kitchen. He grimaces, clutching his bad arm against his chest. His leg throbs as well but is still merely an inconvenience compared to the relentless agony his arm and shoulder are causing him. Again, he has begun to think about a life without his right arm. At first, it had been only a fleeting thought. A worst-case scenario. But now, as each hour goes by, it is becoming more and more like a reality he may have to face.

But that will have to be dealt with later. Right now, he needs to push these thoughts aside and focus on the tasks at hand. The first—and obviously most important—of which is staying alive. The second is getting to the satellite phone as quickly as possible so he can stop this unimaginable situation from spiraling any farther out of control. He still feels confident he can clean up the messes that have been made. A few phone calls, a clean-up team, and a lot of dollars in the right hands should make all this go away like a child's nightmare when the sun comes up. But time is running short, and the tiger is getting closer by the minute. If the gunshots he'd heard had not brought the animal to its demise—and Ben feels strongly that they had *not*—then it could be showing up on this doorstep at any moment. They need to get moving right now.

But there is still one problem…

"Okay," Ben says, moving closer to the stove to warm himself. "I have some good news and some bad news."

"Please Ben," Morgan says, exasperation in her tone. "Don't play games. Just tell us what's going on."

Ben looks at her. Again, he feels amazed by how much she has aged. "Okay. Have it your way. The machine has just over half a tank of fuel, which I would think is enough to get us to the lodge. Also, it seems to be in good shape, not like that P-O-S our boy Matty was riding."

"Of course, it is," Chloe says. "My dad takes care of his things."

Ben smiles. "Right. Except for his daughter during a blizzard."

Chloe's brow furls above her eyes. They blaze hot needles at him.

Morgan steps in front of the angered girl before anything else can be said. "For Christ's sake, Ben" She demands. "Just tells us what's wrong."

Ben chuckles. "Sorry kid. I was just trying to lighten the moment. No harm meant." He directs his attention back to the stove, and continues speaking with his back to them "So, the problem is, the snowmobile is not…"

"I'm not going," Sidney announces suddenly.

Ben's mouth clamps shut.

"And neither am I," Chloe adds, her tone thick with contempt.

Morgan sighs. She walks over to Ben and in a lowered voice says, "They want to stay here and wait for her dad and the old woman. Help me. Tell them it's a bad idea. Tell them they have to come with us."

But Ben's smile returns. "On the contrary," he says, turning to face the girls again. "I think that would be for the best. The storm is really kicking up shit out there. You two staying put would be the safest thing. Plus, someone needs to be here when your old man shows up. Give him the low down on what's happened. Just in case the old woman didn't feel up to it."

Morgan is staring at him, flabbergasted. "What are you talking about? You said we had to keep moving. Stay ahead of it."

Ben shrugs. "For all we know, the tiger could be dead. We all heard the gunshots. But, if it's not, if it's still out there, chances are it'll follow the sound of the snowmobile. We'll lead him away from the cabin. Once we get to the lodge, we'll have the phone. Then it will all be over."

"Just like that? It'll all be over?" Morgan asks, sounding doubtful and ready to stand her ground.

Ben eyes her, impatient anger beginning to etch his expression. "Just...like...that," he repeats. "This is our only play here, Morgan. We need to go."

"I won't leave them," Morgan insists.

"Christ," Ben bellows. "They're not little children. They made their own decision. They want to stay, they stay. That's the goddamn end of it!"

Sidney approaches Morgan and puts her hand on her shoulder. When she turns to look at her, tears are swelling the young girl's eyes. "It's okay," Sidney says. "He's right. This is my choice. My dad is all the family I have left. I can't leave him."

"It's *our* choice," Chloe adds. "And besides, there isn't enough room on the snowmobile for all of us anyways. The seat is too small, and it would bog down in snow this deep."

Morgan frowns and glares at Ben.

"Well, yeah," Ben agrees sheepishly. "There's that too."

"You're a selfish son of a bitch," Morgan hisses.

"I'm rich. It's my nature."

"What if I stay too? How would that fair your *nature?*"

"That's not happening, and you know it. So let's just cut the crap and get going."

"I'm not a child," Morgan says. "Isn't that what you said? Not a child. So, I can make my own decision. And maybe I've decided to stay."

"If you're not a fucking child, then why are you acting like one? We are going, even if I have to drag you out of here by your curlies."

"Tell the truth," Morgan shouts, fire burning in her green eyes. "You only want me along because you can't drive the snowmobile on your own!"

Suddenly, as Ben looks at her, she is young again. All the age that has crept into her face over the past two days is peeled away by her rage. She is voracious and perfect. Sexy. God, she is the sexiest thing he has ever seen. Has she ever looked this erogenous? This ravenous? This…*alive?*

"Okay," he says, forcing his voice lower, calming his face. It is time to bring her back to the home team. "You're right. I do need you to drive the snowmobile. But I know you can't believe that's all it is? All our time together? All the things we've done? You have always been the most important part of my life. The chaos would have eaten me alive a long time ago if it wasn't for you. Saving me from myself time after time. More times than I would ever want to remember. Always by my side. What we have cannot be called love. It can't be called devotion. It is so beyond either of those things that it is beyond any sort of description. So, if you stay, then I'll stay too. I won't have any choice. Because I can't ride the snowmobile alone, but also because I can't face this life alone. That's all there is."

Ben sees Morgan is continuing to study his face for some time, probably weighing the truthfulness of his words. But it doesn't matter. Looking into her eyes, he can recognize that it has been enough. In a few seconds, she will give in, and he will win.

Finally—*and just as he knew she would*—she sighs, and a little smirk touches her lips. "You are so full of shit it's almost painful," she whispers, then stretches her head up and kisses him. "But God you're cute."

"Can we go now?" He asks, his tone submissive.

She nods. "But we're leaving them the rifle," she says. She goes to the counter across from the stove and picks up Eli's .308. Then she turns to the girls. "Have either of you ever fired a rifle before?"

"Sure," Chloe says confidently. "I've done a lot of target shooting with my dad."

"Okay," Morgan says and hands her the gun. "Keep this ready. Use it if you have to but use it carefully. Give it to Sidney's dad when he gets here." She hugs them, pulling them both close and whispers, "I'm going with him to make sure he does right by all of you. That satellite phone is going to be used to get help up here as fast as we can. Nothing else. I promise."

"Thank you," Sidney says.

"Thanks," Chloe says.

Morgan smiles at them. Then she zips up her jacket and walks to the door.

Ben hesitates a moment, holding his bad arm against his chest. To the girls, he says, "Stay focused. That's the key. If you can stay focused, you can survive anything. This will all be over soon."

With a nasty sneer from Chloe as their only response, Ben turns and follows Morgan into the dark storm.

74

Emotion. Fundamentally defined as a mental state associated with the nervous system. Chemical changes in the brain that are being constantly manipulated by internal and external stimuli. Degrees of pleasure and displeasure, often extreme in circumstances beyond one's control. Capable of overlapping into a confused jumble that can leave one unsure of how to react, proceed to the next moment, or even go on with their lives at all.

This is the state of Eli's emotions as he sits, cradling the woman he had married thirty-five years ago in his arms. It has been fifteen minutes since Saul and Matt left for the Jenkins' cabin, and five minutes since Barb's chest rose and fell with her last labored breath. In those ten minutes between—the final minutes Eli would spend with his beloved wife—her eyes had not come open again. No other words had passed her lips. She had ended her life just as selflessly as she had lived it, using her final moments of consciousness to help Saul find his child.

Now Eli is alone, with only his swirling thoughts left to guide him. The heavy sadness he feels—as dominating in his mind as the gray sky looming above Deadman—cast a colorless shroud over his very spirit. Yet this grief is not the only emotion coursing through his body. He also feels a mild, almost numbing sense of alleviation. Barb's battle is finally done. No more suffering.

No more pain. There is a joy in his heart for her. She has always believed that there is more beyond this life. Not necessarily God or heaven or the Holy Savior depicted in the words of the bible, but something. A second chance in an old world, or a fresh beginning in a new world. A different body, a different species. Perhaps even a different lifeform. It was these beliefs that carried her through the pain. On days when it got so bad she wanted to give up, she would remind herself that this life was bestowed to her merely as a steppingstone. By making the best of each moment, good or bad, stone after stone, the spirit would be rewarded.

Now she has jumped off this stone and onto a new one. So even with his deep sorrow, Eli is glad for her. If it means she may not be waiting for him when he finally makes his own leap from this old rock, he is still happy. Wherever she has gone to, he is confident it is exactly where she wants to be.

So many emotions, swirling in his mind, bumping into one another, and yet none of them, no matter how strong or numerous, are enough to transport Eli beyond this point and into his next move. Grief stricken, but also strangely at ease, he is content just to sit here, holding his sweet Barbara and doing nothing more. Let the events beyond the walls of this cabin play out as they will, moving towards their inevitable end without any further involvement from him.

That would be the easy thing to do. Yet there is another feeling lurching below all the others. It has been quiet for a time, allowing itself to be forced down, trampled upon. But now it is what Eli turns to. He pulls it up from the depths and drapes it over his shoulders like a mystical cape. *His anger*, deep and powerful. His anger, finally giving him the strength to do what his grief could not: he gently shifts his wife's body and rests her head against the chair, then stands and walks stiff-legged to the couch. Lying across its back is a blue and yellow quilt Barb had knitted before her hands got too bad. He takes it back and covers her body with it. Now, with such a simple action, the woman that has shared his bed for the last forty years has been turned into nothing more than a multi-colored shape lurking within this dimly lit room.

His anger boils up again, bubbling and growing inside his brain, drowning all other emotions in its wake.

The tiger. The tiger has taken his wife from him.

Eli knows this is the ultimate truth; the tiger has caused his wife's death. But, is blaming the animal alone not the same as putting a gun on trial for murder. It is a mindless beast, with actions that are not calculated or planned, but instinctual. Electro-impulses in the brain dictated its every move on a fundamental level. Hunger, survival, procreate. Nothing is personal.

The real ones at fault—as is almost always the case—are *humans.* The ones making all the decisions an animal is incapable of. It is human beings who chose to take an endangered species from its home, stick it in an airplane, and fly it through one of the worst Fall snowstorms in BC history. The ones who had stolen a boy's jacket and snowmobile and left him in the frozen woods all alone. Now they, *this Ben and Morgan,* have somehow convinced two young girls that their safest move is to run with them, leaving an old, defenseless woman alone in the process.

No animal was to blame for this nightmare. In many ways, the tiger is as much a victim in all of this as anyone else.

But this truth does not change the fact that it is dangerous and needs to be put down. Eli will take his anger and use it to track down the tiger and kill it. There will be no mistakes this time. Then, once it is done, once everyone is safe, he will find the real culprits and make sure they pay for all the horror and death that has been brought done upon the undeserving people of Deadman.

Eli spares another moment to look down at his wife. He reaches out and touches the roundness of her head. "I'm sorry this happened my sweet," he says. "Be at peace and I'll see yah soon."

Then he turns and goes into the bedroom for his shotgun.

75

As The Tiger bounds through the deep snow, following the smell of man's machines, he is filled with a rage so powerful that calling it anything less than true emotion would be an error. As well, given the fact that this rage is in a small part directed at himself, it is also an emotion that teeters on the edge of cognition.

He understands that he has made a mistake. He has allowed his urge to move him in a direction that goes against his instincts. He should not have entered the man shelter. He should not have shown mercy to the old dying one. He had been fooled, letting it draw his attention just enough that the other man could slip in behind him. Injure him. He had taken several minutes to lick the wound and now the bleeding has stopped, but the pain will remain as a throbbing reminder of his mistake.

He will not make another. His rage and his instincts are all that drives him now. Pushing him through the thick black of night. Through the swirling columns of snow and the howling wind. His *destination is clear. He will find man's machines and destroy them all. Then, without its pieces of metal and roaring engines, man will be defenseless, like a newborn fawn unable to walk. The Tiger will feed on its blood. No more mercy. The shimmer of empathy he had felt has been extinguished within his rage. He will not allow it to return. He will continue to kill them, and kill them and kill them until none remain. All man shall die. By The Tiger's tooth and his claw, their carcasses will be spread red across the white snow...*

76

"Dad, I'm hungry," Greg says, his words echoing through the stagnant silence of the garage.

Wayne Trapper is leaning over a Bombardier snow sled, pouring gasoline from an old metal jerry-can into the machine's tank. There is a cigarette in the corner of his mouth, curling smoke up his face and across his smooth head. At the unexpected sound of his son's voice, his hands jump. The can jiggles, slopping gas across the seat of the snowmobile and splashing onto the cement floor.

"Christ, boy!" Wayne shouts. "What the heck you yelling for?" He turns and slams the can down on the workbench behind him. "Now I got a mess to contend with,"

"I didn't yell. You're handling the yelling just fine on your own."

Wayne glares at him. "You sassing me? If I say you were yelling then goddamit, you were yelling. Don't need no smart mouth from you about it."

Greg brings his hand up, hiding the huge grin that is stretching across his face. He loves goading his old man, as long as he is careful to not take it too far—*into the dangerous region of no turning back*. Watching Wayne get all heated and red in the face is a fun way to pass the time. His Uncle Dwayne, on the other hand, is an entirely different situation. There is no goading Big Dwayne at all, unless you relish a swift whack to the back of the head, which Greg definitely did not.

"Sorry," Greg says. Then, hoping his old man will get the hint, he adds, "I can mop up and shut everything down if you want to head in."

Wayne eyes his son for a moment longer, then plucks the butt from his mouth and pinches it out over a coffee can on the bench. "Never mind," he says, fishing in his pocket for a new smoke. "Just get back to work on that carburetor."

Greg sighs. "But I'm hungry."

"Then you should have eaten all your dinner."

"We haven't had dinner," the boy points out. "Just breakfast."

Wayne lights his smoke. "Well, make sure you eat all of it when we have it."

"Come on Wayne," Greg moans. "We been at this all damn day. Can't we take a break?"

"Watch the cussin'," Wayne barks. "And don't call me Wayne. It's goddamn disrespectful."

Not as disrespectful as asshole, Greg thinks and grins again. "Sorry...*dad*. But can't we take a break? We're gonna run out of propane for the shop heaters if we keep goin' much longer."

Wayne throws his son another annoyed scowl. "You see that cage back there," he says, pointing over his shoulder with his thumb. "You know just as well as I do that it's loaded with six more tanks of propane. Plus, two drums of kerosene and three of gas. We could heat this garage straight through to next winter if it comes to it. So cut the yammering. We still got a lot to do. Especially if we got to head out tomorrow and look for that downed plane."

Ah, here it is. This is the very topic Greg has been waiting for. He jumps on it immediately. "You think it's true, what Eli Foley says?"

"Can't see any reason he'd lie. He's always seemed an honest enough fellow."

"Maybe those girls were lying to him. Chloe and that new one. Maybe they made the whole thing up."

Wayne frowns. "Now why would they do that? What good would a lie like that bring to anyone?"

Greg thinks about it for a moment but finds he can come up with no logical reason. "I don't know," he admits. "But it sure seems like a crazy story."

"I guess," Wayne says, shrugging and puffing on his cigarette. "But crazy things do happen."

"Are you worried, Dad?"

Wayne looks at his son. "Worried 'bout what?"

"About Uncle Dwayne," he answers sheepishly. "And Matty and Danny. They should'a've been back by now. Long time ago in fact. What if—"

"Time spent worrying about Dwayne is wasted time," Wayne says. "Dwayne knows these woods better than anyone. If he ain't back, then it's for a good reason. Maybe the storm got ahead of him, and he held up somewhere with his boys. Ride it out till morning. Or maybe he did find those plane crash survivors. Helping them out would slow him down plenty. There's lots of things could have slowed him up. And not one is worth worrying over. You just need to stop thinking about things that don't matter and start concentrating on what you're doing. Only worry on your mind should be getting that carb cleaned up."

"But how do you know?" Greg pushes. He knows he is edging closer to *no turning back* territory, but he isn't ready to let it go just yet. "There's plenty of bad that could happen too. It's impossible to know for sure."

"Goddamit, Boy!" Wayne bellows. "You're starting to give me a headache with all this yapping." Then, to the surprise of his son, he reaches into his pocket and pulls out a two-dollar coin. "You want to take a darn break so bad, then take one." He flicks the coin to Greg. "Go out to the vending machines and get a bag of chips or something. Eat them, take a piss. Do what you gotta do. But I want you back to work in fifteen minutes. And without another word about plane crashes or your Uncle Dwayne. Got it?"

Greg is staring at the coin in his palm with amazement. This is a sudden turn of events that he was not expecting. As much as he enjoys goading Wayne, he is on uncertain ground now. Best to not push it. "Sure, Wayne…er, *dad,*" he says, sticking the two-dollars into his pocket. "Fifteen minutes and not another word. You got it."

Wayne watches as the boy hurries his way through a maze of toolboxes and snowmobiles. Then, with a last quick glance back at his father, Greg pushes through the large double doors that lead into the main office and the vending machines.

Feeling exasperated and tired, Wayne leans against his workbench and takes a long drag from the cigarette. He grimaces as pain pinches the left side of his chest. It is nothing new, and in fact not the worst it's ever been, so he just shrugs it off and takes another puff.

He can hear Greg whistling inside the main office, probably as he scrutinizes the various treats and snacks within the vending machines, determining the wisest way to spend his unexpected windfall. Wayne isn't sure why he had given the boy the money. Perhaps it had been to shut him up. His son has a way of testing him. Seeing just how far he can push before Wayne will push back. This evening, for whatever reason, he has been pushing really hard. Maybe this was the reason he'd given him the money. Get him out of the garage before an inevitable confrontation arose.

Though this seems reasonable enough, Wayne also knows it isn't the truth. Whether he is willing to admit it to himself or not, he does know the real reason he'd given his son the money. There were occasions—perhaps too many—that Wayne would joke about his son being dumb when actually, it is quite the opposite. Greg is too smart for his own good. Observant and very intelligent. If Wayne had allowed the questions regarding Big Dwayne to continue, eventually the boy would have gotten to the truth.

Wayne is worried about his brother. Very worried.

Big Dwayne and Wayne Trapper have been running the rental shop and lodge on Deadman Lake for a better part of ten years. In that time, and with all the multitudes of trail runs and clearing runs and mapping runs he has done, Dwayne has never failed to return to the Lodge before dark. He has never been caught behind a storm, or slowed up with a breakdown, or stopped by a snow.

Not once, ever. Even Big Dwayne himself would say that if he didn't return from a run by dark, it can mean only one thing: *he was dead*. Of course, he said it with a laugh of good humor. But now, standing alone in the garage, with gas fumes and the smell of grease and cigarette smoke sitting in the stagnant air, Wayne finds no humor in his brother's mock prediction. Far too many predictions had been floating around lately and frankly, Wayne is tired of it.

Betty Abernathy's dark prophecy pops into his mind again. He just couldn't seem to shake the old woman's words from his thoughts. Now with the plane crash and Dwayne missing, it was seeming all the more real…

In the office, Greg's whistling stops. There is silence for a moment, then Greg calls out from behind the heavy, double doors. "Hey Dad."

"I said no more," Wayne shouts back. "Just eat your darn chips, boy."

"I… I think there's something outside," the boy says.

Something, Wayne thinks. His son is vague if nothing else. "You mean besides two feet of darn snow?"

"There's something," Greg calls out again, his voice sounding suddenly nervous. "Moving around. Something big. Maybe a bear."

Or maybe Dwayne. Wayne feels an overwhelming relief course through his body. "It must be Dwayne," he says, stepping away from the workbench. "I told you all that worrying was worthless."

"It ain't Dwayne," Greg says, his words more muffled now, like he has moved farther away from the doors, closer to the office windows, probably trying to get a better look. "It's real big. Bigger than Dwayne."

Bigger than Dwayne? Nothing is bigger than Dwayne Trapper. "Dammit, boy," he growls, starting towards the double doors. "If you're still trying to push me…"

"I…OH GOD—" And then Greg shrieks.

Wayne stops dead in his tracks and…

A booming crash shakes the entire building. Like a wrecking ball had just plowed through the front office.

Wayne jerks backward, trips over a small toolbox and slams his back into the workbench. The jerry can of gas tips sideways and falls onto the floor. Gasoline belches out of the opened spout and pools around the tracks of the snowmobile he'd been working on.

But Wayne notices none of this. He is slumped back against the bench, one arm stretched out across its top, a forgotten cigarette still dangling from his mouth, listening to the screams. They had begun after that first shriek and the boom of the wrecking ball. Screams, like none he has ever heard before. He is frozen where he is, terror filling his eyes as he listens, wider and wider until they are the size of the two-dollar coin he had given his son.

His son…is…screaming. Deep, guttural sounds. Bouncing and moving. Like some poor creature caught in a giant blender.

Oh God…my son…my son…God, what is happening to my son?

It goes on and on, each second tearing into Wayne's sanity. Yet he still cannot move. He can only listen…listen to the destruction of his boy.

Something slams against the double doors, and for a moment the screaming seems to stop.

Oh thank God, thank God, please let it be over…

Another *thump* from behind the doors, flexing them inward. And a different sound. A wet, crunching sound. Like a turtle in a vise. Then the screaming again, even louder than before. Frenzied and unnatural. Almost...non-human in their monstrous depth. This isn't his son he is hearing. Not his boy. Greg could never make sounds like this...This *horrific*.

Please let it stop...please let it stop...please—

Suddenly it does. Mid-scream it stops...*No*. Not just *stopped*. *Cut off*. As instant as cutting the power to a blaring radio.

Wayne waits, staring at the double doors with his wide eyes. The cigarette trembles in the corner of his mouth, sending loops of gray smoke across his face. The silence stretches out, quickly became a presence. Looming. As thick in the air as the stink of gasoline. It is trying to fool him. Calm him into thinking it is over. But he knows better. He would not be fooled. Whatever is happening...whatever has happened—*to my boy, oh God my poor boy*—is not over. Those gruesome screams will start again, and they will keep going, tearing away the last shreds of his sanity like tissue paper. Until nothing...is...

Unless this is all a joke...a sick, horrible joke...

Wayne straightens up suddenly, the fragile remains of his rational thought grabbing onto the idea with desperate need. *All a joke*. Yes. That has to be it. Greg has been pushing his buttons all evening. Trying to get under his skin. But Wayne had not given in. He'd stayed strong. In control. There is work to be done and... dammit it is gonna get done.

Now the boy has taken the push a step farther. Planning this elaborate hoax. Probably with the help of Big Dwayne. *Of course*, that is it. Everything makes sense now. Dwayne has gotten back after all. In fact, he must have been here the whole time. Still pissed off about this morning when he almost fell on his fat ass. So, he is helping the boy. Scheming with him. They set this entire goddamn thing up together. Now they are having a big laugh…a great, big goddamn laugh.

"Boy," Wayne calls out. *Ugh*, his tone is high, like a girlie voice. He plucks the cigarette out of his mouth and clears his throat. "If this is some kind of game you're playing, you'll be regretting it in a quick hurry."

No reply. Silence continues to fill the garage. Wayne takes a long pull off the cigarette. He wishes he had a coffee. Coffee and smokes go hand in hand. Like peanut butter and jam. There is a pot of relatively fresh brew in the office. All he has to do is march in there and get himself a cup.

He takes one hesitant step away from the bench. "You hear me, boy!" he shouts. "I'm done playing with you. Get your ass out here before I decide to take my belt to it!"

There is movement behind the doors, followed by a strange smacking sound, like a wet towel being dropped on a concrete floor. Then…another sound. A deep, rumbling noise. As if someone has started an old lawnmower. An old, sick lawnmower. In desperate need of oil or lubricating. It sputtered and hick-upped. All broken up…like…*the purr of a cat.*

One big goddamn cat.

But it doesn't matter. This noise is the same as the rest of it. All part of the joke. Nothing more. Just a big, funny, *let's dick with Wayne* joke. He is done playing along.

He takes another drag from his cigarette, relishing the numbing effect of the nicotine, and starts towards the office.

"Now I'm comin' for you boy," he says in a low voice. "Big Dwayne ain't gonna help you outta…"

Before he has made it three steps away from his workbench, both doors burst open with a screech of twisting hinges. They whip all the way around, slamming against the cinder block walls with a crash that echoes through the garage. A second later, something flies out of the open doorway, bounces off another workbench, and smacks onto the floor in front of where Wayne is standing. Locked in mid-step and stunned even beyond the ability to scream, he stares down at the thing that has landed there. His jaw begins to work, opening and closing, trying to make a sound. Any sound. But none will come. Only the tick, tick, tick as his teeth come together.

At first, his tired mind doesn't recognize what he is looking at. It is only a thing. About a foot long, bloody ribbons on one end, five independent protrusions on the other. Nothing important. Nothing to get upset about.

Then he notices the watch. A Timex Ironman. The exact same watch he had given Greg this past Christmas. He remembers how happy the boy had been. To receive such a fancy, expensive watch. He had hugged his father—*a very rare thing on its own*—and told him how careful he would be. How he would never take it off. Not even to shower, which was okay because it was waterproof to 300 feet. To this day, as far as Wayne knows, Greg has kept his promise. The watch never left his wrist.

But now, strangely, here it is. His son's treasured watch. Laying on the floor of the garage, attached to a tattered, bloody…

If Wayne had looked up at that moment, he would have seen something else come hurtling out of the darkness beyond the open double doors. Something very big. But, because it is impossible for him to tear his horrified eyes away from the sight of his son's severed left arm, his death comes quickly and with no questions.

77

The Tiger leaps, propelling his huge body into the air with graceful ease. An eight-hundred-pound avalanche of muscle and bone comes down on the man, crushing him into the greasy concrete floor. A half-smoked cigarette pops out from between the man's fingers and lands on the floor by a workbench. As the grisly sounds of tearing flesh and breaking bone begin to echo through the garage, the cigarette is consumed by a spreading puddle of gasoline.

WHUMP!

This strange sound is loud enough to draw The Tiger's attention away from his kill. He looks up just in time to see the first flicking orange flames jump up from the toppled jerry can. A moment later, more fire races across the floor, devouring a trail of fuel with voracious hunger. The legs of man's workbench, saturated with years of grease and oil, burst into dancing flame. The Tiger steps back as another streak of fire finds its way to one of man's machines. Soon, this too is engulfed, throwing billowing clouds of black smoke into the air.

He continues to watch all of this with mild interest. He has had very few experiences with the fire in his life. Once he witnessed a tree struck by the fire that came down from the sky. It had burned until there was nothing left but a pile of ashes. And again, after man had captured him and put him in a cage, there was one man there that could make the fire with a stick. A cracking, thin fire. The man had tried to frighten him with the fire. But The Tiger had not been afraid and later punished this man when it ventured too close to the bars. He still remembers the taste of its blood.

Now, as he watches the flames grow, he can feel the heat building. It moves through his fur like a warm breeze, but he feels no fear. He understands that the fire can hurt him, even kill him. Yet, it is also his ally. It will do to man's machines what it had done to the tree. Turn them all into ash. Then man will be nothing.

But, fear or no fear, The Tiger's instincts are now telling him to flee. Soon this place that stinks of fuel and smoke will be consumed by the fire. If he does not get out now, it will consume him as well. He is not ready to be consumed. His urge is not yet satisfied.

The Tiger turns, blood still dripping from his jowls, and walks back towards the double doors.

At that same moment, the snowmobile explodes.

78

Thanks to a couple of tiny pills Barb had given him before they left the Foley's cabin, Ben is drifting inside a peaceful oxycodone stupor when Morgan brings the snowmobile to an unexpected stop. He snaps awake in an instant panic, trying to look every direction at the same time. Not only an impossible endeavor but a pointless one, as complete darkness surrounds them on every side except forward. A pair of halogen headlamps mounted on the machine's motor cowling are managing to cut a good-sized hole of light through the trees ahead of them, but night owns everything else.

"What are you doing," Ben asks. The pain in his leg is almost gone—*again thanks to Foley's Pharmacy and Gift shop*—but the arm is still screaming bloody murder. If someone even remotely skilled with a hatchet were to come along right now, Ben would happily let them take the whole damn thing as a souvenir. "Why are we stopped?"

"I'm tired," Morgan says, swinging her leg around the seat. She looks at him. Tiny icicles are hanging from her eyelashes. "And I have to pee."

"Christ," Ben groans. "You're a big girl. Hold it. We'll be to the Lodge soon."

"Really," Morgan says skeptically. "How do you know? You've never been there before."

"The old woman told me where it is," Ben counters. "And I'm an excellent judge of distance." This, of course, is a lie. He isn't even sure how long it has been since they left the two girls at the cabin. But, looking into the glow cast by the headlamps, he can see that the snow is finally slowing. This is a good thing.

"I'm so tired." Morgan moans. "I'm barely able to keep my eyes open. We're going to end up smashing into a tree."

Ben begins to rub her back with his good hand. "No way. I trust you completely. Just watch the trail, and we'll be there in an instant. I promise."

"But it's been so long. Maybe we passed it."

Ben sighs. Sometimes she seems more like a child than a grown woman. "I told you, I know exactly where—"

An explosion roars out from the trees, loud enough to vibrate heavy clumps of snow free from the branches. One thumps to the ground just behind the snowmobile.

"Ohh," Morgan screams, throwing her gloved hands to her mouth. Her eyes are wide and frightened. "What was that!"

Ben is staring straight ahead, trying to see anything beyond the beam of the headlamps. "It was an explosion," he says. "I'm not sure how far away, but it did—"

Another boom, this one much louder than the first. The sound reminds Ben of the destruction of the Death Star near the end of the original Star Wars film. So powerful he can feel the ground beneath the snowmobile rumble. In the distance, a massive ball of orange light erupts inside the forest, fanning out through the trees and up into the black sky.

Morgan's hands have moved from her mouth to her ears, and she is screaming. Not over and over. Not with short breaks to catch her breath. Just one, long, continuous scream. Her eyes are locked on the flickering glow in the sky.

Ben shakes her. "Morgan," he shouts. "Stop. You're going to hyperventilate. Come on. Snap out of it." He takes her chin in his hand and forces her head around, so she is looking at him. "Snap out of it, goddammit! Now!"

Finally, the scream begins to quiet, turning into a sob; the sob into a hitching sniffle. "Wh…what was it Ben?" she asks, her round, terrified eyes staring into his. "It sounded like a nuclear bomb went off."

Ben shakes his head. "No, not a nuclear bomb. But something big just went up. My guess would be the lodge, or another building around it. Maybe a fuel hut, something like that."

In the sky above them, the moving orange glow is already beginning to fade. "All this snow seems to be snuffing the fire pretty quick, though," Ben adds, watching as the light gets dimmer and dimmer. "Don't think we're in too much danger of a forest fire."

"It was so loud," Morgan moans. "My ears are ringing. How could something just explode like that?"

"It wasn't just like that. Something caused it. But I don't know what, and I'm sure not in the mood to start guessing. So, let's just get moving."

"Where? Back to the cabin?"

Ben stares at her, stunned. "Back to the cabin? Why would we go back to the cabin? Has something changed that I don't know about?" His expression twists into anger. "Fuck, Morgan! Think about it. There was nothing at the cabin before, and there's nothing at the cabin now. We need to go forward, not backward. We need that goddamn satellite phone. And the satellite phone is at the Lodge. The Lodge is that way." He points into the lit-up trees ahead of them.

"That's fine." Morgan says, wiping frozen tears from her cheeks. "But you said that explosion could have been the Lodge. What good is a burnt-out building going to do us? At least we know the cabin is still there."

"I said it *could* have been. But it probably wasn't. We can't give up on that satellite phone until we know for sure."

"Even if we get to the Lodge and find the phone, we don't know it's going to work. The old woman said it might not in this weather."

"The weather is clearing," Ben shouts. "Why are you fighting me on this. You know this our only chance."

"*Our only chance!*" Morgan echoes, her voice now thick with her own guilt-ridden rage. "And what about everyone else? What about those two girls we abandoned? Or Barb Foley? Or the old woman you shot? What chance have they got? When the tiger we brought into this forest, *into their home*, shows up on their doorstep, what chance have they got then?"

For a moment Ben doesn't know how to reply. Up until now, he had thought he had her, *hook, line, and sinker*. But this? This sudden guilt trip? It has caught him totally off guard. Now, he will have to tread very lightly. Because the fact is, if she decides to take the snowmobile and go back to the cabin, there isn't much he could do to stop it—short of pulling his gun on her. This is something he does not want to do. He *will*, if she leaves him absolutely no other choice, but he doesn't want to. So, he needs to reason with her. Talk her down. Win her back to the side of the good guys. He has done it enough times before, there is no reason for him to think he can't do it now. After all, she does love him.

"Come on, Morgan," He begins, keeping his tone level. "You know what I meant. I need that phone to get this contained. All of it. Including the goddamn tiger. My guys know this animal better than anyone else. They've been studying it since day one."

"Like Bronson Collique?" Morgan snaps.

"Better. Collique was a big game hunter. Nothing more. But the team I assembled to deal with the tiger at the compound? They know the animal. How it thinks. They can predict its next move before it makes it."

"How can they do that? It's impossible."

"This is an animal, Morgan," Ben says. "Driven by instinct. And instincts are predictable. Right now, the only thing on that cat's mind is self-preservation…"

"That sounds familiar," Morgan quips, eyeing him distrustfully.

"It's probably held up somewhere," Ben continues, choosing to ignore the obvious jab. "Waiting until it feels safe. Then it will try to run, and my guys will be waiting for it, whatever direction it goes."

"So, you don't think the tiger had anything to do with those explosions?"

"Of course not," Ben replies confidently. "Shit like that happens in these back-woods places all the time. Someone's distillery probably went up." He knows this is not the truth, but a little levity to lighten the mood. Could be just what this situation is screaming for.

It doesn't work. "God, you really are a pompous ass. All this shit that's happened is our fault. Yet, you still find a way to make these people look like the dummies." She stands-up on the rail of the snowmobile. "Talk about being predictable."

"What are you doing?"

"I think I need to be away from you for a minute," Morgan tells him. "Is that okay—"

The tiger erupts from the darkness of the forest and hits Morgan in the side, just above the waist. Its massive weight propels her up into the air, over the handlebars of the snowmobile and far out into the deep snow. She lands with an UFFF! as all the air is driven from her lungs. But despite her lack of breath, she starts fighting instantly; kicking with her feet and flailing her arms, trying desperately to fend off the animal's attack...

Except there is no animal. Morgan is alone in the snow. She sits up, grimacing as pain bolts across her midsection. Ben is still on the snowmobile. He is shouting something at her and struggling to get the gun out. She cannot hear what he is saying. The night seems to be gone. Everything is too bright and shimmery. She turns her head slowly. The tiger is there, laying on its side next to her, its rib cage rising and falling as its panting breath puffs silver clouds into the air. There is a wide, flat piece of metal sticking out from between two of its ribs. Blood is running down its side, darkening the white snow beneath.

Ben is still yelling at her. She looks back at him. He has the gun in his hand and is pointing it at her, shouting at her. Over and over again, "...of the way! Get out of the way! Goddammit Morgan, get out of the fucking way!"

With the blinding haze of the snowmobile's headlamps filling her eyes, Morgan finally understands. She drops backward into the snow and starts rolling towards the machine.

Ben levels off the gun, sighting in on the tiger's head, takes a deep breath, and pulls back the trigger.

Another lump of snow breaks free from a branch directly above him. It hit his outstretched arm just as the gun pops, forcing it and the bullet down. The slug tears through the motor cowling of the snowmobile, into the aluminum engine block, and out the front grill, punching a hole into the snow only inches from Morgan's thigh.

A split second later, as Ben is cursing his bad luck and pulling his arm free from the hard pack of snow, the tiger is back on its feet. It springs at him. With a desperate cry, Ben jerks the gun up and fires again.

This bullet finds its target. It rips into the right side of the animal's face, blowing out its cheek in an explosion of blood and teeth.

But the impact does little to slow the tiger's forward motion. It slams into Ben with the same force as a Mack truck, hurtling him backward into the dark. He flies fifteen yards through the air, bounces off one tree and collides with a second, the weight of his body driving the broken remains of a branch into the meaty flesh just above his waist. Ben screams, searing agony tearing up his side and into his brain.

Still, somewhere in the darkness, he can hear the tiger purring.

"No," Ben screams. "No, you son of a bitch! You're dead! I blew your fucking face off!" He raises his arm. Somehow the gun was still in his hand. He fires it into the dark. "Die you bastard!" He fires again. "Die!" And again. And again. He keeps firing until the slide locks back. Then he throws the gun. The motion drives daggers of pain through his side. He begins to weep. "Die...you..."

"Ben!" The word floats out of the black forest.

Ben forces his head around, looking towards the sound. In the distance, he can see the glowing light of the snowmobile's headlamps. Morgan is standing on the back rail, a flashlight gripped in her hand. Its long, yellow finger of light cuts through the dark to his right.

"No, the other way!" He calls out, tears still pouring from his eyes. "Here! I'm Here!"

The beam moves. Searching. "Where?" Morgan cries. "Where are you, Ben?"

"Here," He shouts again. Each time he calls out, a pain of red fire rips through his body. "Please, Morgan, I'm here."

The light moves again, circling around until, at last it finds his face and stops.

"Oh my God, Ben!" Morgan wails. "What happened? Are you alright?"

"No... I'm..." He tries to look down at himself, but the slightest movement of his head feels like scalpels slicing into his flesh. Slowly he reaches up and touches his side, just to the right of his belly button. His fingers brushed across the wet and gnarled stump of a branch. It sticks out six inches from his flesh. "Jesus," Ben moans. "I'm impaled, Morgan. I'm impaled on this fucking tree!"

"Impaled?" Morgan replies, echoing the word with confusion. "What... are you all right? Can you move?"

"Of course, I can't fucking move!" Ben screams, as much in agony as in anger. "Didn't you hear me, I'm impaled! There's a fucking branch jammed through my side! You gotta help me!"

Morgan takes a hesitant step into the snow. "You were shooting everywhere. I think one hit the snowmobile. Is... Is the tiger dead?"

As if in answer, the tiger's rumbling purr starts again, drifting out of the dark directly to Ben's left. He twists that way, ignoring the throb in his side, and stares into the forest. But there is nothing to see. The deep blackness of night guards it all.

"Ben," Morgan calls again, taking another step forward. "What is it? Are you all right?"

"Wait," He shouts. "Stay there! The tiger...it's not dead! I...I think it's out here. Christ, I think it's right beside me!"

79

Right beside me. The words ring out in Morgan's mind with terrifying clarity. Their meaning, beyond the obvious intent, brings with them a strange sense of finality, like the end of an era. Yet, for the moment, they carry little else. Of course, she is afraid. Has been since the first big bump during the doomed airplane ride. But this fear, and the dark feeling of horror that comes with it, are not directed towards Ben's approaching fate. There is a very real possibility that Benjamin Treager Jr. is about to die. The man who had brought her into the fold of Treager Enterprises, mentored her, trusted her with secrets; ones he shared only with her. And in this same way, she has shared his bed. In the five years they have been lovers, she has let him do things to her she would never have allowed another man. Because she thought she loved him. Truthfully and eternally.

But now, at the moment of his inevitable destruction, she finds herself void of any feelings towards him at all. Not love or hate. Empathy or remorse. After all the atrocities he has committed, her only real urge is to shout out *I told you so! Goddamit, you son of bitch, I told you so.*

"Christ, Morgan," Ben calls out. There is a deep sound of terror in his voice. "Its moving. I can't tell which direction."

"What should I do?" Morgan asks. Even with the distance between them, she can see his face twisting in pain and fear. But still, her heart remains empty.

God, she thinks despondently. *I've become a monster. All the things we've done have turned me into an unfeeling monster.*

"Sh... shine the light that way," Ben tells her, signaling with his finger. "Try to see where the fucking thing is!"

Morgan moves the light off Ben, panning it across the dark trees. She can see nothing moving but the slight sway of branches in the diminishing snowfall. "I don't see it, Ben."

"Keep looking! I... fuck... I think it... it's behind me now. I can hear it purring! The goddamn purring is all around me! I can't tell where it's coming from. Christ, help me Morgan! Find it!"

Morgan takes two more steps towards Ben, kicking a path into the deep snow. She moves the yellow beam back to Ben, then to his right. Again, all the light reveals is winter choked forest. The fall of snow has almost stopped completely now. She searches the trees, straining her eyes to see any movement. "There's nothing Ben. I can't see it."

"Wait," Ben calls, his voice still panicked and full of pain, but with less fear. "I...think... Yes, it's stopped. The purring has stopped. It's gone now, Morgan! It's run off...or something! Please, come and help me! Help me off this fucking tree! I'm dying out here Morgan! You gotta help me!"

"I'm coming," Morgan cries out, shifting the light back to Ben. "I'm—"

The tiger is there, standing no more than a foot from Ben. Its huge body is turned sideways, and its tail is swinging back and forth, digging a trench into the snow. It is looking directly at Morgan. She gasps, reaching up to hold the light steady with both hands. The side of its face is a ruined crater. Blood and saliva dripped out in thick runs from the jagged hole where its cheek had been. Its tongue, swollen and purple, is pushing open its jaw into a permanent, wide mouthed grin. It is the twisted reincarnation of every evil clown from every child's nightmare.

But it isn't just the carnage left by Ben's bullet that has caused Morgan to gasp. It is also the tiger's eyes. Two blazing yellow holes punched into its face, glowing with a hatred so old and deep it seemed endless. She can feel it, cutting her as if the animal itself is dragging its claws across her middle. She shrinks away from it, trembling. The flashlight bounces in her shaking hands, moving the beam from the tiger to Ben and back again. In Morgan's eyes, it seems the light is connecting them. Making them one. *Just as they have always been.*

She knows that warning him now would be futile. But she has to do something. Does she not owe him at least that much? "Ben," she cries out. "It's there! Right…"

Without taking its eyes away from Morgan, the tiger's front leg shoots out suddenly. Its three-inch claws rake across the front of Ben's thighs, slashing four red trenches into the muscle. Ben shrieks, his body hyper-flexing forward violently. The involuntary movement forces the piece of broken branch down, tearing deeper into his back. He shrieks a second time, his tortured voice stabbing between the trees.

Morgan watches, a stunned horror preventing her from looking away, as the tiger lashes out again. Its claws slice through Ben's hip and into his groin. Thick ribbons of blood splash over the snow.

"Run Morgan," Ben begins to scream. His entire body is convulsing now, grinding against the trunk of the tree. Puffs of blood and dried bark are flying into the air around him like colored confetti. "Run! Run! Run…"

"Ben…" Morgan wails again, but this is all she can manage. The cat's massive paw hits him a third time, shredding through Matt Trapper's parka and into the soft flesh of his midsection. Morgan screams and jerks the light away just as Ben's insides spill out over his belt.

What little food there is in her stomach tries to come up, but she fights against it, choking it back down. Then, she does the only thing left that she can do; following Ben's instruction for the final time, Morgan runs.

80

The Tiger watches as the bouncing beam of light disappears into the trees. When the great pain in his side caused him to fall, this one had evaded his ambush. Now it is running away, like an injured doe. For a moment he is tempted to give chase. Even with the pain in his side and his mouth, he is still faster and stronger than man. Without its machines, it will be slow and clumsy. It would not escape him again.

Then the one pinned to the tree groans, drawing The Tiger's attention away from the fleeing doe. He will let it go, for now. Its time of punishment will come soon. This man, *broken and bleeding and nearing* The Death, *is not finished being punished.* This man.

It was there in the beginning when The Tiger was captured and caged and tormented. This man. *It took him from his home. Dropped him in a strange world. It changed him. Filled his mind with confusing images. All the rage. The burning hatred. The pain. Everything was because of* this man.

He takes a step closer to it, stretches out his neck and sniffs, wanting to smell its blood. But he can't. All his brain registers now is the sickening redolence of his own blood. So this too, his sense of smell, has been stolen from him. By this man.

The rage is there again, boiling up inside The Tiger like a volcano of molten lava. Burning away everything. Consuming his mind. Oh, how badly he wants to bite the man. Tear away its throat. Pull out its heart and swallow it whole. Steal its face, just as it has stolen everything from The Tiger.

But the injury to his mouth is very bad. It is stopping him from biting the man. The bullet has shattered the lower, right side of his jaw. His saliva, a natural antiseptic as powerful as most soaps, has cleaned the wound, and the clotting of platelets inside the damaged tissue has already slowed his blood loss substantially. So, the injury, though severe, is not life threatening. The loss of movement in his jaw, however, is cataclysmic. With the simple act of opening and closing his mouth being impossible, his ability to hunt and eat has also been lost. The Tiger will die of starvation within a month.

This, of course, has no meaning to him. The complexities of his mortality mean nothing inside his animal mind. Even his physical pain has no meaning. Like the trees or the mountains or the snow, it is simply there. A part of his being. His instincts and his need to bring destruction to all man will continue to push him. Ignoring his pain, his hunger, his thirst; he will keep moving forward. Bringing his punishment. He will not stop until the black grip of The Death locks its fingers around him and drives his body back into the earth.

One thing man has not stolen from him is his eye-sight. Keen and sharp, The Tiger sees through utter darkness better than man can see in a dimly lit room. Now he looks at the broken man. Its face is twisted and shines with sweat, but it is alive. It still pushes shallow, ragged breaths into the air. Its eyes are open and it is staring at The Tiger.

Its lips begin to move, making the man sounds, "Go ahead... you son of a bitch. Finish the job. Morgan is gone and... I've finished you. One way... or the other... you'll be dead in a week. So, go ahead..."

Raspy and quiet, the sounds also have no meaning to The Tiger, and yet they anger him. Amplifying his hatred even more. This one is strong. This man. It is bleeding, its insides lay at its feet, and still it lives. Pinned to a tree, unable to flee, it looks at The Tiger as though it is not afraid; making its man sounds. Mere squeaks and squawks in his ears, yet somehow, they mock him. Enrage him. His huge body is shaking with the power of his rage. His heart is racing.

The Tiger strikes out at the man, pulling his claws through its chest. It screams. A good sound. Not squeaks and squawks, but a loud, agonizing sound. He hits it again, in the face this time. Its cheeks and nose are shredded away. There are small popping noises as both of its eyes burst inside its skull. Again and again The Tiger attacks. Each time the man screams. Even with no lips, it still screams. It doesn't stop until its throat is torn open, splashing a jet of dark blood across the tree trunk it is pinned to. But its silence is not enough. The Tiger continues to attack. Hit after hit. Slicing and tearing until his claws drag against bark.

When he finally stops, his vision is swimming. The forest spins around him, circling and moving like it is alive. He stumbles and falls sideways, landing in the blood-soaked snow. He lies there for a time, staring into the shadowy trees. Once again, something beyond his understanding has happened. During the volley of frenzied attacks, the piece of metal from the exploding snowmobile has been forced deeper into The Tiger's side. It has now punctured his lung. He can breathe, pulling in large gulps of air over his swollen tongue, and yet the oxygen levels in his blood are diminished substantially, causing dizziness and loss of motor function.

After a while, as his heartbeat slows and his vision begins to clear, The Tiger gets to his feet again. He looks around, confused for a moment. Then he sees the carnage spread over the snow and remembers. This one is finished. His urge is satisfied. But the one that escaped, the fleeing doe. It is out there in the forest. It may even think it has gotten away. Oh, how wrong it is. There will be no escape this time. The Tiger knows exactly where it is going. He will be waiting.

81

In the depths of complete darkness, time moves differently. It still passes of course, each minute ticking by as it should. But without any visual stimulation to draw on, seconds could have been minutes, and minutes could have been hours. It is jumbled together in the dark, moment after moment, becoming no more distinctive than a single flake of snow on the side of a glacier. Time has become... insignificant.

This is exactly how Morgan feels as she forces her exhausted body forward, trudging through the snow in the nothingness of night. *Insignificant.* Lost in a sea of black. More alone than she has ever felt in her life. Even the sounds, normally abundant in the forest, have abandoned her. The crickets, gone except for their eggs buried deep underground, are silent. Birds slumber quietly in the treetops, waiting for the sun to show its orange face again, if indeed it ever does. Morgan feels drearily certain it will not. It seems only the wind can survive in the icy dark. It whispers through the snow-laden branches like a moaning specter.

She is heading back to the cabin where they had left the girls. This had been the last argument between herself and Ben; the Lodge or the cabin. Ben would have surely gotten his way eventually, as he always did. But now he is gone, and his single-minded direction has gone with him. Morgan is choosing the cabin, but not simply to defy his last want. Following the tracks left by the snowmobile is easier, and it is the guaranteed choice. No speculation as to how far it is, or if it is still there at all. The cabin has not been destroyed in the explosion, the Lodge may have been. Satellite phone or not, her gut has told her this is the right direction.

But now, with every step forward a struggle, she is beginning to wonder if Ben may have been right. They had left the cabin on a snowmobile. The conditions were dark, and the snow was deep, forcing her to keep their speed at ten to fifteen kilometers per hour. After thirty minutes, fatigued to the point of almost complete collapse, she had stopped. Then the machine was damaged by a bullet—*and Ben was killed by the tiger, don't forget that important point*—leaving her no choice but to battle the return journey on foot. A distance of maybe five kilometers. No problem, right? Back in the real world—*so far away now it has become barely a memory*—Morgan jogs that distance three times a week. But throw almost three feet of snow on the ground inside a pitch-black forest with a man-eating tiger lurking somewhere in the darkness, the five kilometers may as well be one hundred.

She still has the flashlight clutched in her hand. For the time being, however, she is keeping it off. Not because she's afraid of the tiger tracking the light; she is educated enough about the animal to know they have excellent night vision. It has the ability to track her just as easily whether the flashlight is on or off. But the light had begun to flicker shortly after she fled from the tiger—*and left Ben to be torn to pieces… don't forget, don't ever forget*—and she was concerned the batteries might be failing. So, she had turned it off, conserving it for when she really needs it. Following the trench left by the snowmobile is easy enough, even in the complete darkness. Above her, the cloud cover must be breaking up. She has glimpsed the occasional star winking at her through the dark. She tries desperately to convince herself that this is a good thing. The storm is over, the sky is clearing and soon it will be morning. Then everything will be okay.

Lies. Morgan's mind is sleep-deprived and groggy, and yet she still understands this. Nothing will ever be okay again. If she survives this night, *nothing will be okay*. If she is rescued and the tiger is killed, *still nothing will be okay*. What has happened in the last two days is not a dream. The events cannot be changed or undone. They will alter her life forever, regardless of what happens next. Ben is dead and she is…

Morgan falls. Her legs simply give out from under her, pitching her forward. Her face smashes painfully into the hardpacked snow. There is an immediate warmth, pouring out of her nose and over her lip. Her mouth fills with the coppery taste of blood. She sits up, tears swelling in her eyes, and clicks on the flashlight. The bulb flickers several times and goes out.

"Come on, come on," she cries, banging the light on her palm. The tears are rolling down her cheeks now. "Please…"

The beam flickers again and finally comes on, filling the trench with yellow light. Morgan rubs her gloved hand under her nose. It comes away streaked with blood. More is dripping off her chin into the snow. "Dammit," she murmurs, fighting the sobs that so badly wanted to consume her. She digs a little hole in the snow and carefully perches the flashlight in it. Then she unbuttons her coat and tears off a small piece from the bottom of her blouse. She tilts her head back, holding the material against her nose. A steady trickle of blood runs down her throat into her empty stomach. It instantly makes her feel sick. Her vision doubles, leaving her with the feeling she is about to pass out. Her eyes slowly close.

When she opens them again, she is lying sideways in the snow, the swatch of bloody blouse is clenched in her hand. It is still dark, and the flashlight is on, but the beam of light it casts has dimmed noticeably. Groaning, Morgan sits up. There is a saucer-sized red stain in the snow where her head had fallen. She pulls off her glove and touches her nose again. She feels crusts of blood around her nostrils and on her upper lip, but the bleeding itself has stopped.

"Shit," She whispers, looking around. Her mind is swirling. How long has she been unconscious? Had she passed out or simply fallen asleep. She feels so utterly exhausted, it seems the latter is more likely. Even now she can barely keep her eyes open. When is the last time she has slept? She had been knocked unconscious when the plane crashed. That had been maybe twenty-four hours ago now. How long before that? Twelve hours? Eighteen? More? She has no idea. God, it would be so nice to lay her head down again, just for a moment. She would be asleep in seconds. A few minutes is all she needs. Just a little cat nap.

Cat nap.

She chuckles at this thought. "Cat nap indeed," she mutters, and turns her head to spit blood onto the snow.

She needs to rest. Even for just for a little while. If she doesn't, there is the risk she might pass out again, or fall. What if she really hurts herself the next time? Breaks her ankle. In snow this deep, hidden roots and branches everywhere, it wouldn't be hard to do.

Yes. Sleep is definitely required. But she won't do it here. She is too exposed. She needs some kind of shelter. A place where she will be protected from the cold and…

Morgan shakes her head, not allowing herself to finish the thought. She pulls her glove back on and grabs the flashlight. Standing up, she shines the beam of light into the trees. With the diminished batteries, the glow does not penetrate very far. She pans the light around. Humps and bumps everywhere. Strange shapes lurking between the trees, hiding in the shadows. Nothing but bushes and shrubs buried under the snow, but in this eerie darkness they seem alive; moving and mysterious.

She continues to search, ignoring these enigmatic shapes. Finally, ahead of her and to the right of the trench, she spots something interesting. This too is only a hump bulging up from the snow. But it is larger than the rest, and misshapen. All around it, long, jagged protrusions push into the air.

Cautiously, Morgan starts towards it, holding the flashlight steady with both hands. As she moves closer, she begins to see green spots showing through the white cover. Spiny green arms. Like branches. Evergreen branches.

She stops a few feet away, staring at it. A fallen tree, some kind of a large evergreen. Lying ten feet from the trail. She hadn't noticed it when they passed going the other way. Why would she? It had no meaning to her then. Now, however, it could mean everything. Shelter, protection, and sleep.

She hurries over to it, holding the flashlight in her armpit so she can dig through the snow with both arms, dragging herself along like a swimmer doing the breaststroke. In her mind she is pleading; *Please let it have fallen before the snow. Please, please.*

The thick branches are spread out over the ground like a natural lean-to. Others poke into the air as high as twenty feet. Morgan dives down between the fan of branches, shoveling out the snow frantically. She breaks through the outer crust and slips into the space between the branches and the ground. There is no snow here. The forest floor is knotty and cold and blanketed with a thick cover of pine needles, but it is also completely dry, protected from the snow by the fanned-out branches above. Morgan pushes her way farther inside the space, closer to the trunk. She has two feet of space all around her now and, though it is still far from cozy, it has to be at least two or three degrees warmer within the tree's protective branches.

Morgan rolls onto her side and pulls herself into a ball around the flashlight. A tiny bit of heat radiates from the bulb, warming her face slightly. She will keep the light on, batteries be damned. Soon the sun will rise and then she won't need it anymore.

The tree settles around her, groaning under the weight of the snow. As Morgan slips towards sleep, she wonders briefly what would happen if the branches collapsed. She supposes she would be trapped here. Buried beneath the snow. Suffocation or hyperthermia. One or the other. Neither seems that bad really. Compared to what is waiting for her in the forest, they seem not too bad at all.

Then, in the dying glow of the flashlight, Morgan sleeps.

82

As Morgan tumbles into her dreamless sleep, Sidney sits in the kitchen of the Jenkins' cabin, staring out the window. A propane lantern hisses on the table beside her half empty water glass, filling most of the room with bouncing yellow light. Outside the window however, night still owns the forest. Anything beyond the edge of the porch is lost in its black grip. The snowfall has completely stopped now, and the wind has diminished to barely a breath. In the sky, the moon is nowhere to be seen, but the odd star twinkles here and there like bits of shimmering glass in a sandbox.

Sidney has not noticed them. Since her father's return with young Matty Trapper in tow, she has been having a hard time noticing anything past the borders of her own fear. So many unbelievable things have happened that it is becoming more and more difficult for her to shake the feeling that it is all just a dream.

It has to be. Events like these, airplane crashes and savage wild animals, just don't happen in the real world. At least not in *her* real world, where sanity and structure rule all, and tigers don't roam the woods. People she knows and cares for are not being killed like so many sheep lined up for slaughter. These things are not supposed to exist in her real world.

Yet, here she sits, staring into the dark woods, watching for any signs of movement, and knowing in her soul that this is not a dream. This is *her* real world. The stories her father and Matty had told, as unbelievable as they seemed, completely confirm everything Ben and Morgan had already said. There is a tiger out there, and so far it has caused the death of at least two people, one being Matty's little brother who was only eight years old. It has hurt Barb, and possibly Eli as well. Now Sidney is terrified it will be coming for them next. Are windows and locked doors enough to stop it? Certainly not if it is as big as her father describes it. He admits he'd only seen it for a split second as it leaped through the Foley's front window, but from what he said, it sounds bigger than any tiger she has heard of before. Is a door strong enough to stop eight-hundred pounds of animal that has decided it really wants in? Sidney doesn't think so. They do have the two guns, the rifle they got from Barb and the pistol Eli has given her father, but is this enough? If it is, why does she still feel so unprotected? Was staying here like sitting ducks the right thing to do? Again, she isn't sure. Chloe seems to believe they are safe. The sounds of her sleep have been drifting out of Sidney's bedroom for several hours now.

Sidney does not understand how sleep is even possible. With so many images of death and horror floating around in her mind, the idea of closing her eyes is terrifying. Matt is also asleep, passed out on the couch in the family room. But his mindset must be similar to hers, the sounds of his slumber are disquieting and troubled. Moans, groans, and soft cries. The echoes of a nightmare. She had briefly considered waking him, but then did not. If anyone in this house needs—*or deserves*—sleep, it is Matty. What he has been through in the last twenty-four hours is… *unimaginable.*

The sound of a creaking floorboard pulls Sidney out of her thoughts. She twists around, eyes round and frightened, half expecting to see the tiger crouching directly behind her, ready to pounce. Of course, this is not what greets her. Instead, it is her father standing in the doorway.

He smiles apologetically. "Sorry. Didn't mean to startle you."

Sidney sighs. "That's okay, Dad. I think almost anything would startle me tonight."

Moving towards the refrigerator, Saul nods his agreement. "True enough." He takes out a carton of orange juice and sits down at the table beside her, groaning softly as he does it.

"No glass?" Sidney asks, mocking him with her eyes.

"Screw the glass," Saul replies and takes a long swallow directly from the carton.

His daughter giggles behind her hand. "Never thought I'd see the day."

He sets the juice down and shrugs. "After this night, I guess anything is possible."

"Agreed," Sidney says glumly.

Now Saul looks at her, his eyes showing worry. "You holding up okay?"

"I guess," she replies, staring into the darkness beyond the window. "Can't sleep, though. I'm afraid to close my eyes."

"I get that," Saul says. "Your friend doesn't seem to be having any trouble. I heard her snoring through the door."

"She's a heavy sleeper alright," Sidney agrees, smiling a little. "It's good. She needs her rest. So does Matty. He's… suffered a lot. I can't even imagine what he must be going through."

"Dealing with loss can be a heavy burden. I think we both understand that."

"Yeah," Sidney breathes. "I guess."

They are silent for a moment, both looking out the window, searching the night. The hiss of the lantern fills the space between them.

Finally, Sidney turns her head to look at Saul. Tears are beginning to shimmer in her eyes. "Dad, why did you agree to move here?"

Saul appears puzzled by the question. "Why? I thought you wanted to come here?"

"I did… I mean I do. I love it up here. But why did you come here? It kinda goes against who you are."

Saul's brow arched. "What do you mean? I've always considered myself a rough and rugged outdoorsman." He flexes his left arm. "Check these pipes. They were meant for this life. Rock hard, just like me."

"Get real, Dad," Sidney scoffs jokingly. "You're such a city slicker I had to teach you how to light a fire."

"Not true, not true," Saul balks. "You had to teach me how to light a fire without burning myself. There's a big difference."

Sidney rolls her eyes. "But seriously, Dad. Why did you agree to move up here?"

Saul thinks about this, rubbing the thin beard growth that speckles his chin. When he speaks, his tone is soft and thoughtful. "Your mother brought me up here for the first time just after we were married. Couple of years before you came along. It was the first time I'd ever been in the *real* woods... you know, besides Stanley Park." He chuckles lightly. "She loved it. Everything about it. The air, the trees, the water. All of it. I have to admit that I really didn't get it. To me, it all just seemed... dirty. But it made Penny happy, so I went along. After you were born, we stopped coming for a while. Life got busy. School and ballet and horseback riding. Trips to Disneyland and Palm Springs became more the norm. Then, when you were about ten, your mom suddenly got it in her head that we needed to start coming up here again. I'm not sure why. Just the whole *nature* thing I guess. She didn't want you missing out on it. I wasn't too keen on the idea, but like I said, it made her happy, so I went along."

"I'm glad," Sidney says. "I loved our trips up here."

Saul nods. "I know. Just like your mom. I tried to love it, like you two did. But... it was hard for me. With work and all the after-school stuff I was involved in, PTA and private counseling and all that, time was...short. It got to the point when I was up here, all I could do was think about the things I should have been doing at home. Penny knew that, and it was upsetting to her. She thought that I was pulling away."

"Were you?" Sidney asks.

Saul takes another drink from the carton before answering. "I don't think so," he says hesitantly. "That's not how it felt to me. I had responsibilities. That's all it was. Responsibilities. Then Penny got sick. Sick enough that we couldn't make the trip anymore.

I think that was one of the things that hurt her the most. She missed Deadman. You remember, near the end, how much she talked about it?"

Sidney nods, tears rolling down her cheeks. Memories of their camping trips to Deadman Lake were one of the few things that could make her mother happy once the pain got really bad.

"After she was gone," Saul continues. "There was this great big hole in my chest. Right where my heart used to be. I tried to fill it with my work, but that didn't work. There was no… fulfillment left in it anymore. Then you mentioned Deadman. Coming up here again, not just to camp, but to live. And I thought, God, how much your mom would have loved that. Living in this place that meant so much to her. So, I guess I came up here because this was the only place where I might find some of Penny. Not just the memory of her, but a little bit of her soul. *Here*. In the air, and the trees, and the water. Maybe that little bit of her could help fill the hole in my chest."

"Did it?" Sidney asks, touching his hand.

"No," he says, shaking his head. "In the end, there was only one thing capable of helping me find my heart again. It was you, Sidney. You fixed the hole in my chest."

Sidney leans over and hugs him. "I love you, Daddy."

"And I love you," he says. "With all my heart."

They embrace for some time, in the glow of the lantern. When they separate, Sidney wiping tears off her cheeks with the back of her hand, Saul asks, "So, what about you? Why did you want to come up here?"

"Because I knew this place could heal us both," she answers confidently.

"Well, I guess you were right."

"What about now," Sidney says. "With… all this happening. Do you regret coming here now?"

"None of what's happened has anything to do with this place. It's not the lake's fault. Or yours. Or mine. Someone made a mistake and caused this trouble. We can't blame Deadman any more than we can blame the sky or the air. So, no. I don't regret coming here."

"It's Ben's fault," Sidney says. "And Morgan's too, I guess."

"That could be. But I've never met them, so I won't judge them."

"Do you think they made it? To the Lodge I mean."

"I don't know," Saul admits. They had all heard the explosion, but it had sounded quite far away. On a lake that is over six kilometers long, it was impossible for anyone to tell exactly where it came from. For now, however, in the interest of *hope*, Saul is choosing to believe it was *not* the Lodge. "I hope so. That would mean they have called for help."

"How long will it take for help to get here."

Saul looks at her. Her face is tired and worried. He wants to comfort her. Tell her everything will be alright. That's what fathers are supposed to do, right? But he finds himself incapable of lying to her. "I don't know. If the weather clears, maybe not too long. But I really don't know."

"Do you think Barb and Eli are okay?"

God, are there any questions she can ask that have a positive answer, Saul wonders grimly. "I don't know, Sidney. Eli is a good man. He'll do everything he can."

"We should have gone to help them," Sidney says. It is not the first time she has voiced this opinion.

And to it, Saul replies as he had all the previous times. "Not in the dark. It's too dangerous. When the sun comes up, we'll consider it. But for now, we stay put."

Sidney groans, just as she had all the other times. "I feel so… useless, just sitting here."

"And that's fine," Saul says, lifting the juice to his mouth. He takes a sip and sets it back down. "You go right on ahead and feel that way. But it doesn't change my decision. We wait until light."

Sidney crosses her arms and stares out the window. She knows he is right, of course. In darkness this thick, just finding the Foley's cabin would be hard enough. And while they are stumbling around blind, the tiger could be watching them, hunting them. Attack without being seen until it's too late.

Another silence stretches through the room. It isn't a comfortable one, but for the moment, it is a necessary one. They both sit quietly, looking into the night, wondering who will speak next.

At last, feeling finished with the game, Saul groans and stretches his arms above his head. "Well, maybe we should both—"

"Can I ask you something, Dad?" Sidney says, her voice soft but very serious. "Something…important?"

Saul lowers his arms slowly. "Of course," he says, frowning slightly as he studies her face.

She continues staring out the window, her eyes unblinking and thoughtful. "If I was… different, would it change how you feel about me?"

"Different?" Saul echoes. "Different how?"

"Just different. Not what most people think I should be."

"I'm not sure what you're trying to say, Sidney, but I promise you, nothing could ever change the love I have for you. *Nothing.*"

Now Sidney does turn her head. She gazes at her father, her blue eyes shimmering in the flicker of lantern light. Then she smiles. "I… I think I'm falling in love."

"In love," Saul says, puzzled. *How does falling in love make her different? She is a lovely young woman, smart and independent. He has no dissolutions that she will be his little girl forever. He wants her to find love, and everything that comes with it. Fall in love, get married, have kids. With the right…*

His thought pauses there for a moment. *The right… what?* Then, suddenly he understands. Really, he has suspected for some time now. He had seen the way they were together. Friends and companions, but also… more.

"With Chloe," Saul adds, returning her smile.

Sidney's eyes widen with surprise. "How did you know that?"

"I'm your dad," he says. "Dad's notice things. Even the ones that have a shot of rum in their coffee."

Now it is Sidney who looks puzzled. "How long have you known?"

"For sure? Not until this moment," he replies. "But I think I've had some suspicions for a while."

"And… you aren't disappointed if I'm…you know…gay?"

"Of course not, Sidney," Saul says, putting his arm around her shoulder. "Even if there were things you could do to disappoint me—*which there are not*—who you choose to fall in love with would not be one of them. I love you unconditionally. Whether it's a woman or a man who is lucky enough to share your life, your happiness is all that matters to me. Nothing will ever change that."

Sidney hugs him again, tighter this time. "How did I get so lucky to have a dad like you," She whispers. "I love you so much."

"Wow," Saul says. "This is the most bonding we've had in quite a while. We should stay up all night more often."

"It's too tiring though," Sidney says, still hugging him. "If we could do…"

Saul suddenly jerks, his entire body stiffening in her arms. Sidney pulls back and looks at him. "What…" she begins, then closes her mouth with a snap. His handsome face has become stiff, like a stone carving. The fear that she sees there is etched, as if it has been cut into his features with a hammer and chisel. His eyes are locked on the window, staring into the dark forest.

"Dad, what is it?" she asks, turning her head and gazing through the window herself, trying to see what has startled him so badly. "What did you see?"

"Something moved," He replies. "Back in the trees. Too dark to see exactly what it was, but it was big."

"I don't see anything," Sidney says, narrowing her eyes as she scanned the forest's edge.

"It's…gone now. But it was there. We shouldn't have this lantern on. It's too bright." He reaches out and twists a nob on the side of the light. The glow immediately dims to almost nothing, only a soft shimmer of the cooling filament remaining. Saul stands up in the darkness. "And we shouldn't be sitting by this window. We're too exposed here." He takes Sidney's hand and pulls her up.

"What did you see, dad?" Sidney asks again, scrambling to her feet. "Was it the tiger? Is it here?"

"I don't know what I saw," Saul says. He starts towards the doorway to the sitting room.

Sidney follows close behind him, almost stepping on his heels. "Could it have been Eli? Or someone else. Maybe Big Dway—" She clamps down on the name, remembering that it could not be him. The tiger has seen to it that it will never be him again.

"I don't know. I… think it was too big to be a man. It was only a shadow, but I think it was too big."

They walk into the sitting room and stop. Both of them stare down at the shadowy lump that is the couch. Even in the gloom of the room, where darkness rests in the corners, they can see the blanket thrown back. The couch is empty, Matty Trapper is gone.

83

Morgan's eyes spring open. She stares down at the dead flashlight clutched in her hands. She is still curled up around it, just as she had been when she went to sleep. That had been… how long ago? Minutes? Hours? She has no idea. Shadows are thick here, inside the natural lean-to, but there are also slivers of light now, shining in through tiny chinks between the branches. Morgan turns her head. Her neck muscles creak and groan in protest. An instant thump settles inside her skull; each beat of her heart sending cords of pain across her scalp. She groans and tries shifting her body. Her back and legs feel no better than her neck. Crawling out from under the tree is fated to be a difficult endeavor. She can barely straighten her legs. Even her arms feel heavy, like lumps…

Something moves outside the lean-to. Morgan freezes, eyes wide, listening. More crunching sounds. Hard snow being disturb. Just beyond the fan of branches. Could this have been what woke her so suddenly? It must have been. God, it is right outside!

Then new sounds; scraping and snapping twigs. Digging sounds. It is digging its way in, just as Morgan had done. It will have her in mere seconds. She tries to scramble away, but sharp branches are tearing at her back and thighs, there is nowhere for her to go. Her eyes lock on the growing circle of light. It is breaking through now, reaching for her. Morgan screams. She thrashes her legs, ignoring the agony of muscle cramps. Kicking and screaming, beating at it with her feet, but she isn't strong enough, it is still coming. It grabs her ankle, pulling her towards the opening. She shrieks, kicking out at it even harder.

"Damn, girl," it shouts suddenly. "Quit your darn kicking. One of them boots is liable to bloody my nose."

Morgan stops. There is an old man peering in at her, morning light circling his head like a halo. He is still holding her ankle but releases the moment she stops kicking.

"There we go," he says. "Now, I ain't gonna hurt you, so you can come on outta there if you like. Sun's just coming up."

"Who… Who are you," Morgan stammers, her heart and head pounding in speedy rhythm. "How did you know I was in here?"

"I found a snowmobile not too far away. All shot to hell. And there was a whole lotta blood. Seen your tracks leading away. I decided to follow them. Ain't much of a tracker mind you, but this deep snow makes it a damn sight easier. My name's Eli Foley. I got a place on this lake."

Morgan stares at him, stunned. "Foley…Like Barb?"

"She'd be my wife," he says. "Now, come on outta there. I can't stay crouched down like this much longer."

Morgan lets him help her out, and just as she suspected, the endeavor is an agonizing one. But once outside the branches, with the cool air washing over her face, the ache in her head begins to subside almost immediately. Looking up, she is relieved to see the storm clouds have all drifted away, leaving the sky a crisp, pale blue. Above a jagged horizon of white treetops, the hazy orange glow of the sun is just beginning to materialize. This is a morning destined to become a beautiful winter day, despite the fact it is still autumn.

Eli stands close by, giving Morgan time to brush the snow off her clothes. Beside him, poking up from the crust of snow, is a set of snowshoes. The barrel of a shotgun strapped to his back rises just above the fur-lined cap that is pulled down over his ears. He smiles at her as she straightens up. His eyes, as pale blue as the sky, give no indication of what he might be thinking.

"Thank you," Morgan says, returning his smile.

"None required," Eli replies. "But, you know my name. Now, how about I take a stab at yours? Morgan, right?"

She nods. "Yes."

"Good. It's always nice to know who you're conversing with." Then the smile fades from his face. "I suspect the blood back there was your friend. Ben?"

"Yes." Morgan says. "The tiger…"

Eli raises his hand, stopping her. "I understand," he says.

"But, what about your wife, Barb? And the two girls. Are they okay?"

"Ain't seen the girls for a bit. I'm sure they're fine though. Saul's watching over them. Barb…" Now, he rubs the back of his gloved hand across his lips. "Afraid she's moved on from this place."

"Oh my God," Morgan moans, her face drawn with shock. "She... died?"

Eli nods reluctantly.

"But..." She was about to ask *how*, then stops herself. It is a question she already knows the answer to. "It was the tiger, wasn't it?"

Eli shrugs. "In a 'round about sort of way, I guess. Her heart gave out before it could have a real go at her. I got a shot off. Hit the thing in the shoulder. I don't think it even felt the bullet though. Got out through the window and run off into the woods. I took after it of course. I'm not much of a tracker, but like I said, with this snow cover, it ain't too hard. Followed it for some time. Then the explosion..."

"You heard it too," Morgan breathes, horrified by what she is hearing.

"Course," Eli continues. "I guess folks all the way down in Terravale would have heard it if they'd been listening. It was Wayne's rental shop. Went up like the world's biggest cherry bomb. I pray him and his boy were well away when it blew. Did always warn him about keeping all that goddamn fuel inside, but Wayne's never been one to take advise, sound or otherwise."

"Rental shop? So, the Lodge? The Lodge is still okay?"

"Yup. Enough space between the two buildings it barely got singed."

"Then the satellite phone is still there? Can we go get it?"

Eli shakes his head. "Ain't there no more," he says. "Cause it's right here." He unzips his parka and pulls out the phone. "With all that's happened, I took it upon myself to kick in the door of Dwayne's office. I already made the call, too. Got a direct line to Sheriff Porter down in Terravale. Woke the poor son of a bitch out of his sleep. But we had a fine conversation, regardless. He's callin' in the Calvary. Should be on the way right quick I would expect."

"Thank God," Morgan exclaims. She jumps through the snow to Eli and hugs him. "Thank you, Eli. Thank you."

"Now, now," Eli grumbles, taking her by the shoulders and moving her away. "As I said, there ain't no need for that." He looks at her, his face firm, a picture of unmoving calm. But now his eyes have changed. She can see sadness in them. Grief so deep it pains her heart.

It is my fault. I have brought tragedy down on this poor old man.

"I'm… sorry," she whispers, tears swelling up in her eyes. "I'm sorry for it all."

"Ain't no more need to be sorry," he says, still holding her shoulders. "then there is to be thankful."

The tears slipped over her eyelids and streak down her cheeks in tiny rivulets. "It's all my fault. Everything… that has happened. We… caused it. Ben and I."

"Now, that's not altogether true," Eli says. "You two made some mistakes. Some real doozies in fact, but that don't mean this is all your fault. You didn't bring on the storm. You didn't crash the plane. And you sure as heck didn't kill anybody."

"We brought…it here. The tiger…it's here because of us."

"God I wish you hadn't," Eli says, drawing his hands away. "And I was plenty mad, I'm not gonna lie to you about that. But after I seen what happened to your friend, I realized there's a lot more suffering going on here than just my own. What's done is done. All the anger in the world ain't gonna change that. Pointing fingers. Laying blame. None of that's going to help anyone right now. Guess it'll all come about later, but for now, what we gotta do is get moving. It's a good three kilometers back to Saul's cabin. They could be needing our help."

"I still don't understand," Morgan cries. "Why would you want to help me. Your wife…is gone because of me…"

"My wife is gone because it was her time," Eli tells her, his tone still smooth and calm. "The Lord decided her fate, not you. And sure as hell not some goddamn animal. She went because she wanted to go. As sad as I am that I don't have her with me anymore, I'm also happy her pain has finally ended. So, let's just stop all this nonsense and get moving."

Morgan passes her hand over her face, wiping away tears. "I really liked Barb," she says. "In the short time I got to meet her. She was kind and generous."

Eli nods, reaching around to retrieve the snowshoes. "Yes, she was." he agrees and hands her one of the shoes. "Use this to dig snow out from in front of you. It might make the going a little easier. I'll stay right behind you. Keep mindful of the tree line and shout if you see anything."

"It's hurt," Morgan tells him. "Ben shot it in the face. And there's a piece of metal or something sticking out of its side."

"Good. Maybe we'll get lucky, and the fucking thing is already dead." He pauses. "Excuse my French."

"That's okay, I don't speak French," she says, then turns and begins to plow through the snow.

84

"Can I ask you a question?"

Morgan stops. Frosty clouds of her labored breath plume into the air around her face as she turns to look at Eli. "If… it means we can take a break for a minute… you can ask me anything you like," she says.

They have been walking—for lack of a better word, though hardly a fitting description of their grueling forward battle—for close to an hour. The sun, completely free of the mountains now, is smiling warm light down from the sky. The snow-covered surface of Deadman Lake shimmers in its brilliant glow like a field of diamonds stretching out across the valley.

Sweat glistens on Morgan's forehead, despite the false-winter cold that still grips the forest. Her legs and back are burning, and her lips are so dry she is surprised they haven't cracked right off her face. Even if she felt like smiling, which she definitely does not, it would have been a painful expression indeed.

Eli pulls a thermos out of his parka and offers it to her. "Tea," he says. "Not sure how warm it will be. It was the last of a pot Barb had made."

The sadness creeps into his eyes again. Morgan supposes it will be a long time before he can say her name without that pain being there. She accepts the thermos. "Thanks."

He watches as she drinks, then takes it back and has a swallow himself.

"So," Morgan says as he stuffs the tube back into his jacket. "What's your question?"

Eli looks at her for a moment, then picks up his snowshoe again. "Maybe we should just keep going."

"Go ahead and ask," Morgan insists. She already has a good idea of what is on his mind. "You are rescuing me, Eli. After everything we've done, you're still rescuing me. The least I can do is be truthful with you. So, ask."

"Alright," Eli begins. "As I said, this really doesn't matter now. What's done is done. It could even wait till we get where we're headed I suppose. Hell, I got a feeling you'll be telling the exact same tale over and over in the next little while. But I'm an old man and my curiosity is killing me. I been trying to wrap my head around this the whole time we been walking, but I just can't seem to piece it together. What was it you two were doing?"

"Doing?"

"Doing," Eli repeats. "With the tiger? The plane? All of it. I know it's got to do with money. There's little that goes on these days that don't. But what I can't figure out is how? How is flying that animal over BC in a snowstorm gonna benefit anyone? Financial or otherwise."

"Obviously we weren't expecting the snowstorm," Morgan says, though her tone is unconvincing.

"Naw," Eli says, frowning. "Anyone with half a brain can look at a weather report. Between you and that fella Ben, I'm betting there's a hell of a lot more than half a brain. I think you were hurrying. And I also think nobody knew you were even there. No right-minded airport official would let a plane fly into weather like that. I got a pretty good hunch you two were cruising under the radar. But why? Where were you taking that cat?"

Morgan thinks about this for a moment. Finally, she says, "You want the long version or the short version."

"Well, it's damn cold and we still got a way to the cabin, but I'm also curious as hell. So, how about the in-between version."

Morgan nods. "Okay. The man I was with, Ben—his full name is Benjamin Treager Jr. He is the CEO of Treager Enterprises. Have you heard of it?"

"Sure," Eli replies. "Big financial gobble monster in the states somewhere. Think I read something about it in some business magazine once."

Morgan smiles. "*Gobble monster?* I guess that describes it as good as anything else. It's based out of Seattle. Basically, we loan money to other businesses in return for shares in their futures. If they pay off, we benefit in the royalties, if they don't pay off, we foreclose. Pretty much a win-win. But that's just the tip of what Ben is involved in…" she falters, glancing back the way they had come. "*Was* involved in…"

She talks for fifteen minutes, giving Eli express accounts of the prison in Russia, the hotel conference in Kamloops, and finally their tragic experiences over and around Deadman. Other than a brief coughing fit, Eli remains silent and contemplative for the entire story. When she finishes, he is gazing across the iridescent surface of the lake.

"Well," Morgan asks, though not exactly sure if she wants him to reply at all.

"Well," Eli says, rubbing a gloved hand over his chin. "That is quite a tale, alright. Seems to me you're as much a pawn in all this as the rest of us. And the tiger also. God Almighty, what a mess."

"I should have stopped it," Morgan states. "Right from the beginning, I should have stopped it."

Eli looks at her, his brow arched. "You seem to be a very strong woman, Miss, and under all that frost and grime it's plain to see you're about as lovely as they come. That being said, I hope you won't take no offense when I say I don't believe he would have stopped for you or anyone else. I've met a few fellas like him over the years. A special breed. Sitting up in their tall buildings, looking down on us small folk. They always think they know better and think they know best. Most would sooner stick a loaded gun in their mouth than take a word of advice from anyone. And unfortunately, they don't tend to learn from their mistakes until it's too late. Just like your friend. Now he's paid the ultimate price for his ignorance, and took some innocent people with him in the process. I'm afraid he's also left you with a whole lot to answer for."

"It's what I deserve," Morgan says, fighting back tears. She doesn't want to cry again. She has cried enough in the past two days to last her a lifetime.

"I don't believe that," Eli says. "Course, I'm just an old man and my opinions don't tally much authority. Heads are gonna roll, that's for certain. There are people going to pay for what's gone on. But I will do what I can for you. I don't think it'd be right if you alone end up shouldering the weight of Treager's Fuck up... Pardon my French."

Morgan smiles, but her eyes remained morose. "I can't understand why you're being so kind to me. But…I thank you. You truly are a good man Eli."

"Ahh," Eli groans. "Wish I gave my Barb more reason to feel that way. Thankfully she was a patient woman though, God bless her beautiful soul."

He turns his head and gazes out at the lake again. Morgan stays quiet, watching him and wishing she had never met the man named Ben Treager.

"She loved skating on the lake in the winters," Eli says after a moment, his voice mild and thoughtful. "It was one of her favorite things before her joints got bad. She would just skate around, doing spirals and spins and figure eights. For hours she'd be out there, and when the sunshine hit her silver hair just the right way, she looked like an angel dancing in the clouds." He pauses, smiling softly.

After another minute passes, Morgan reaches out and puts her hand on his shoulder. "Eli."

"Not this year, though," he says suddenly, clearing his throat and turning back to Morgan. Mild embarrassment is pulling at his expression. "Storm came before the lake had a chance to freeze up solid. Thin ice is hiding under all that snow. Anyone trying to skate out there now had better be a good swimmer." He straightens up, stretches his back, and grabs his snowshoe, all in one quick, rather jerky motion. "Well, we best get on the move. If our luck holds and that damn cat leaves us be, we should make Saul's cabin before the coffee pot is empty."

"Okay," Morgan says, pulling her own snowshoe out of the snow. "Onward and forward."

"Slowly but surely," Eli adds, and they both laugh.

85

The Tiger raises his head. He has been in a half stupor, half sleep for some time now, and it is the sound of man's laughter that brings him out of it. For a moment, as he peers through the white forest, he thinks he is home. The laughter he hears comes from the ones that have killed his mother and his sister. The urge for vengeance flairs up in his thoughts like wildfire, and in that split second, he almost charges down the hill to attack them.

Then, as his body begins to tremble with anticipation, the pain from his destroyed jaw wakes suddenly. It races into his brain, flooding his mind with memories and images of all that has happened. He is not home. Home is far away. It is a time before the pain in his mouth and side. Before the simple act of breathing had become a labor. Home is gone and these things are a part of his life now, just like this strange new world. He accepts them without question.

The ones that laugh now; they are not the ones that killed his mother and his sister. What they have done is far worse. They have robbed him of home. Soon he will rob them of life.

Remaining low, he stretches his neck higher, watching them over the drifts. There are two, digging through the deep snow. The fleeing doe is ahead. The old one that has hurt him is following. A thunder stick is strapped to its back. It is good The Tiger had not rushed down the hill. He is far away and the old one may have had time to point the stick at him. If this had happened, The Death *may have come for him. Though he understands little about* The Death, *he does know he will not give in to it until he has finished these two. He will catch them and punish them for all that has been taken from him. And after this happens, perhaps the urge that burns inside him will at last be satisfied. Then he can close his eyes and rest. Let* The Death *cover him like the snow covers the ground.*

His ability to bite is gone, as is most of his sense of smell. But his eyesight and hearing are strong, and his hunting instinct is still a powerful force. It guides him now. Moves him slowly through the snow as he follows them. Patiently and quietly. Staying down, hidden by the drifts. With each step, he creeps closer and closer. He will not strike until he knows the time is right. It takes time, but he does not allow himself to hurry. Soon enough it will all be over.

86

"We want to go with you," Sidney says, her tone thick with exasperation. She can not understand why he is treating her this way. After all the honesty they had shared early that morning, now he is speaking to her as though she were a child. She is eighteen years old. Maybe that isn't old enough to buy a drink in a bar, but it is plenty old enough to make decisions without needing her father's approval.

But Saul obviously does not understand this. He is still shaking his head and says, "No. You and Chloe will be safer right here."

"But you'll be safer if we go," she states angrily. "More eyes watching. More ears listening."

"And more people in danger," Saul replies. "I won't allow it. I need you to stay here. Besides, what if Eli shows up? Or someone else? I need you here to tell them what's happened."

"Then we can leave Chloe."

Chloe, who has so far remained outside of the argument, looks at her friend, stunned. "No way! I'm not staying here by myself! No way!"

"No," Saul says as he pulls on his gloves. "You're not going to be by yourself because Sidney is staying with you. I'm not arguing about this anymore. I'm going to find Matt. You two are staying here. End of discussion."

"But Dad—"

"No!" Saul roars suddenly. Sidney jerks away from him a step; her eyes wide with shocked surprise.

Saul immediately feels guilty for shouting. Before he speaks again, he closes his eyes and takes a deep breath. "I'm sorry," he says calmly. "I shouldn't have yelled. I know you're not a child, Sidney. And I understand that you want to help Matty. But I can't risk losing you. We've already lost your mother, and I won't take a chance of anything happening to you. Either of you. You're all I have. So please, Sidney, stay here. I won't be gone long. I'll follow his tracks and find him and bring him back. That's it."

"What about the Foleys?" Sidney continues stubbornly. "You said we would all go to their cabin when it is light out. Now you're changing your mind."

"Yes, I am. And I'll keep changing it until I know that tiger is dead. I'm not letting either of you leave this cabin."

"But I'm worried, dad. About Barb and Eli. And about you. What if something happens to you?"

"I've got the rifle," Saul reminds her, picking the .308. "I'll be fine."

"You've never shot a gun in your life," Sidney comments.

"That's not true," he says and slings the weapon over his shoulder. "I had a .22 when I was a kid. It'll all come back to me, just like riding a bike."

Understanding there is no way she can win this argument, Sidney finally gives in. She goes to her dad and hugs him. "Please be careful," she says. "Because I don't know what I'd do without you."

Saul returns the hug gratefully. "I'll be alright, Sidney. Out and back. You won't even miss me." He looks across her shoulder at Chloe. "You take care of her."

"No problem," she says and touches the revolver sitting on the table in front of her. "We've got this if anything happens."

"Only if it's absolutely necessary," Saul warns. "That gun is just as dangerous as a tiger."

Chloe nods. "I know."

He turns away from them and pulls open the door. "Lock this behind me."

"I don't think tigers can open doors, Dad," Sidney says.

Saul pauses, glancing back at her. "This one can."

Sidney watches him march across the porch. Once he has disappeared down the stairs, she closes and locks the door.

Chloe steps up behind her. "You okay?" she asks.

"I'm so scared," she replies. She turns around, tears welling up in her eyes. "I've never been this scared."

"I'll protect you," Chloe says, putting her arm around Sidney's shoulders.

"I know. But now who's protecting Dad? Or Barb and Eli? Matty? Everyone else on this lake? I just feel so useless and afraid."

"I'm afraid too," Chloe says. "But we're not useless. There's a reason we're here. I'm not sure what it is yet, but there is definitely a reason. You'll see."

Sidney looks at her, tears on her cheeks. She smiles softly. "Thanks," she whispers. "I…I think I might love you."

"I *know* I love you," Chloe replies and kisses her cheek. "But we'll talk about that later. Right now, we need to be ready. Something's gonna happen. I can feel it."

87

Morgan looks up into the pale blue sky. The sun sits in the center of it, shining yellow brilliance across the treetops. Morgan doesn't know for sure, but from the sun's position, she thinks it must be closing in on mid-day. She is tired and hungry and, thanks to the tea Eli had given her, now she has to pee.

"Do you think it's much farther," she calls out to Eli, hoping they are close enough she can stave off a cold squat in the snow.

Eli stops, drives his snowshoe into a drift, and leans against it. His breath is coming out long and labored, and his cheeks are glowing as red as apple skin. "Not far," he says. "Over…this…rise and the trail…will widen out…some. Then…we should be…able to see Saul's place."

Morgan stares at him with concern. "Are you okay," she asks. "Your face is really red."

"No problem," he pants. "Tickers working overtime is all. Guess I shouldn't have given up my jogging regiment all them years ago."

"Should we rest?"

He waves his hand in the air. "Naw, I'm right as rain. Let my lungs catch up to my breath for a sec, then we're off. Just as soon get back before our friend decides to show his stripy face."

"Maybe it's dead," Morgan says hopefully.

"Could be. Ain't seen hide nor hair of it since I let its tracks go at the snowmobile. If Treager did manage to shoot it in the face, I guess there's a damn fine chance it's bled out somewhere."

"I think it's dead," she repeats. "I'm… sure of it."

"Well, sure or not, let's get a move on." Eli straightens up. "Unless you need a couple more minutes?" he asks over his shoulder.

She thinks about it for a moment, and finally admits the truth. "Maybe I better squat behind a tree before we go," she says, unbuttoning her jeans. "No peeking. And don't leave without me."

Eli chuckles. "No worries, my dear. When nature calls, it don't stand to be ignored."

88

As Eli had predicted, they crest a slowly rising hill, and the trees begin to spread out. The slope drops on the other side for a hundred yards and then levels off at the edge of Deadman Lake. The space between the trees continues to widen until they are walking in a narrow field that cuts between the forest and the shoreline. About three hundred yards in the distance, where the curve of the lake begins to turn west, the Jenkins cabin is little more than a lump in the snow. Behind it and on its far side, the trees close in again, surrounding it like giant white soldiers standing their post. A curl of gray smoke rises from the chimney and breaks apart in the soft breeze that is whispering across the lake's frozen surface.

"There it is," Eli says, pointing with his snowshoe. "Right where we left it."

"Thank God," Morgan sighs. In her exhausted mind, she cannot imagine anything looking more beautiful. "How far away is it? I can't tell."

"It can be tough to measure distance by sight when everything looks the same," Eli tells her. "It's about three hundred yards. Normally a five-minute walk. Probably half an hour at the snail's pace we're moving."

She feels a massive wave of relief. A half-hour and they will be at the cabin. Then they can barricade themselves inside and wait it out until the police, or rangers, or whoever it is Eli called comes to the rescue. Soon this nightmare will be over…

And a new one will begin.

But she will not let herself think about that now. All that unpleasantness can be dealt with later. Now she will only think of pleasant things. A warm fire. The smell of coffee brewing in the pot, or bacon frying in the pan. A soft chair to sit on, a cozy bed to sleep in. And a hot bath with bubbles and ivory soap. Then a comfy terry robe and slippers to slide into. All these things she had once taken for granted. But not anymore. Now she will cherish each one as if they are to be the last pleasant experiences of her life.

"We should start moving," Eli says, dragging her out of her thoughts and back into the real world of ice and snow. "Unless you have to…"

"I don't," Morgan snips at him.

He smiles. "Just checkin'." Then he turns and starts moving again.

89

In the open area of the field, unprotected by nature's umbrella of tree branches, the snow has piled to over three feet. It is also no longer light and powdery. Warming in the glow of autumn sunshine, it has become thick and heavy, making each step forward grueling, like pushing a wheelbarrow through wet concrete. This makes progress much slower than Eli had predicted, and after fifteen minutes, when he comes to a sudden stop, they have barely made it a hundred yards.

Morgan stops behind him. "Let me… guess," she says through panting gulps of breath. "Now you have to go."

Eli is staring at the cabin, shading his eyes against the bright sunlight. "The girls," he says, his tone curious. "They've come out onto the porch. I think they're waving at us."

Morgan brings her hand up to her brow, shielding her eyes, and follows Eli's gaze to the cabin. The girls are indeed there, only an inch tall in the distance, standing at the railing of the porch. It does appear they are waving at them. It is very difficult to see them past the glare radiating up from the snow, but to Morgan, it did not look like a pleasant, single hand, *hey welcome back* wave. Their arms are both up, flailing around in frantic gestures. They are also shouting something that is impossible to hear over the wind.

"What are they doing," Morgan asks Eli.

He has stuck his snowshoe into the snow and now has both hands arched above his eyes. "Not sure," he replies hesitantly. "Almost looks like they're dancing."

"They're shouting something," she adds.

"Yeah," Eli agrees. "Can't hear it, though."

One of them—Morgan thinks it is Sidney—has now begun gesturing. She narrows her eyes, desperately trying to see the girl better. No, not gesturing, it is more specific. She is pointing—pointing towards the tree line. "I think she's pointing at something."

Eli nods his head. "Yeah, but wh—" At the same moment he suddenly understands that the girls are not waving, but trying to warn them of approaching danger, he hears a crunching sound to his right. He bellows, swinging his body that way and reaching for the shotgun on his back. The tiger is there of course, crouching and tense in the snow. It leaps just as he pulls the gun strap free from his shoulder, hitting him high in the chest, driving him backward. The rifle flies out of his grip, flipping end over end, and vanishes beneath the snow. A second later Eli is down with all of the animal's weight on top of him, snapping several of his ribs like popsicle sticks. A strange *whooping* sound erupts from his mouth as an incredibly large push of air vacates his lungs all at once. His vision begins to swirl and fade. But just before unconsciousness takes him, he chomps down hard on his tongue and everything pops back, if only for the moment.

The tiger is above him, its gnarled face only inches from his own. Blood and slobber drip down from its mangled mouth, splashing against Eli's cheeks. Grunting with what little air is left in his lungs, he tries to move, but can't. The cat has him held tight; both of its huge front paws planted on his shoulders, shoving down on him. He can feel his collar bones twisting and buckling under its weight.

It has begun to purr now; a gravelly rumble coming from far down in its chest. Then, by simply flexing the strong muscles in its paws, all eight of its claws sink into Eli's flesh like stiletto daggers. His eyes bulge above his open mouth. He is trying to scream, but there was no air left to make a sound. Silence and blood are all that pass his parted lips.

90

It happens in the blink of an eye. One second Eli is next to her, and then he is gone, buried under eight-hundred pounds of tiger. For a moment, as her brain scrambles to process what is happening, all Morgan can do is stand there, staring at the horrific scene with stunned fascination. Her first coherent thought is to run. Get the hell away from here and try to make it to the cabin before the animal can catch up with her.

But, even as the thought is filling her mind, she knows it is impossible. Running is no longer an option. This needs to end, right here and right now. She will not allow anyone else to be hurt.

She glances around desperately, looking for... *she has no idea.* Anything. Anything that might stop the tiger from killing Eli... then she remembers the snowshoe Eli had given her. She still has it clutched in her hand. Without giving herself time to contemplate the intelligence of what she is about to do, Morgan raises the shoe above her head and brings it down on the animal's back with all her strength.

The tiger's head snaps up, and with amazing fluidity and speed, it turns on her. She stumbles away, barely keeping her footing. It strikes out at her, slashing its claws through the cold air only five feet from her face. Morgan backs up another step, gripping the snowshoe in both hands. Matching her retreat, the cat advances a pace. Its swollen tongue flops out the side of its face like a dead, purple eel. But above this carnage, its yellow eyes blaze in the bright sunshine. She can see the intelligence in them as it watches her. It is studying her, processing her actions. The fucking thing is trying to anticipate her next move.

So, Morgan does the one thing it may not be expecting. She shrieks and lunges at it, swinging the snowshoe around like a baseball bat. The tiger jerks back, but not far enough. The front edge of the aluminum shoe slices into the already savaged flesh of its face. Fresh blood splatters against the snowbank. The cat makes a sound like a guttural howl and staggers sideways into the deeper snow. Morgan swings again, hitting it in the shoulder this time, just below the wound made by Eli's bullet. The tiger hisses at her, spraying a pink mist of blood and saliva into the air. It leaps forward, striking out again with its front leg. Morgan screams, pulling away at the last second and swinging the snowshoe wildly. One of the animal's long claws catches the lacing strap of the shoe, tearing it out of her hands. It flies thirty feet across the snow, glinting and glistening as it spins through the brilliant blue sky.

Morgan turns and dives into the snow, kicking and dragging herself along, frantic, expecting to feel the tiger's claws slice into her back at any second. She throws a desperate glance over her shoulder, sure she will see the animal right behind her, reaching out with its long legs to grab her. What she does see, however, causes her to stop in her tracks. She turns, staring back with stunned surprise. The tiger is there, but it is thirty feet away, lying on its side in the trench.

With silver shoots of light cutting slants across the snow, Morgan waits and watches. She wants to go back and help Eli, but the distance and the glaring sunshine are making it impossible to tell if the tiger is still breathing. It had passed out like this when it attacked her in the dark, and minutes later it killed Ben. Was this the same? Was it only momentarily unconscious? Or could it really be dead this time? Her mind is trying to tell her it is and, *oh God* does she want to believe it, but with all that has happened, she just can't. She is even beginning to wonder if it will ever die. Is it possible that whatever they had done to it inside Mother's Womb has somehow made it immune to death? Given it the ability to keep going, walking the earth, erasing every person it comes across until there is no one left. *Is it possible?*

As if in answer, the tiger's leg twitches. Once. Twice. And then, amazingly it raises its head and looks at her.

"No," Morgan cries as she watches the animal lumber slowly to its feet. "God Please, no!"

But to this, she will get no answer. The chainsaw rumble of the tiger's purr is the only response. It is completely up now, its huge body wavering back and forth like a drunkard after a night at his favorite watering hole. It stays where it is for the moment, its head low, staring at Morgan with hatred burning deep in its eyes. Blood drips down from its mouth in globs, splattering the white snow like paint on a canvas.

Morgan's heart races in her chest as she watches it. Her expression is stunned disbelief, and yet in her mind, she is not surprised. She understands now. The tiger is destined to destroy her. It doesn't matter how hard she fights or how far she runs, in the end it will punish her like it had Ben. Her fate had been sealed long ago; from the moment she laid eyes on it in that filthy Russian prison. They have become connected in life, Morgan and this animal, and now it is only death that will separate them. Hers…

Or the tigers.

"What are you waiting for," she calls to it. "You son of a bitch. Let's get this over with!"

The tiger does not move. The ragged purring sound continues to resonate from somewhere inside its chest. Its eyes stay riveted on hers as if it is trying to stare into her soul so it can destroy her from the inside out.

Morgan scoops up a handful of snow. "Bastard," she screams and throws the snowball. It lands at the animal's feet with a faint thump. Still, the tiger remains motionless.

She bends and digs up more snow, packing it into a tight ball in her gloved hands. Having no real idea of what she is expecting to accomplish, she flings it at the animal anyway. It smacks home, hitting the tiger in the forehead directly between its eyes. If it had been a round from Eli's rifle instead of a snowball, the white ground behind the animal would now be carpeted with cat brains.

"Ha," Morgan exclaims triumphantly. "How do you like that, fucking cat! I got lots more where that came from." She reaches down, gathering up more ammunition.

The tiger shakes its head. A pinkish cloud of blood and snow puffs into the air. Then, as the cloud settles to the ground around it, the animal takes a step towards Morgan.

Still bent with her fingers buried in the snow, Morgan's breath catches in her chest. She freezes, watching the animal closely. It takes another slow step forward, then another. It is not rushing towards her or pouncing or leaping, or any of the things a tiger should do. It is…sauntering, as if in no hurry at all. A stroll in the park on a sunny spring day.

But, as meandering as its movements are, the tiger does have long legs. In just three steps, it has cut the distance between itself and Morgan by almost ten feet.

"Shit," Morgan breathes. She turns and starts pushing her way through the snow again. In the jumble of her mind, she remains unsure of what she is doing. *Is this what she had wanted? For it to take after her? Of course she had known it would react in some way. Isn't that why she had antagonized it? But what had she expected it to do? Leap across the snow and attack her? Kill her? Is that what she expected? Or… is that what she wanted? Is it? And if so, why is she running from it now? Why not stop?*

Because there are others involved than just herself. Eli lying injured in the snow. The girls at the cabin. Matt. Anyone else unlucky enough to be on Deadman Lake this day. She needs to try…*anything*. Even if she has no idea what the *anything* is.

She looks over her shoulder. The tiger is there, following her, matching each of her steps with one of its own. But she is struggling, fighting against the snow. Its forward motion is easier, its steps longer. It is slowly gaining on her.

Then give up, her mind offers again stubbornly. *Stop now and let it be over. Because really, what good is this doing anyone? Running. The tiger will never stop pursuing her. And, even if she can stay ahead of it, what will she do then? Keep on following the trench made by the snowmobile, after all, third time is the charm, right? Eventually she will pass the fallen tree she had slept under. Then the shot-up snowmobile, and the blood-soaked snow that had once been her lover. Then... what? The Lodge? Keep going? What was after that? The other side of the lake. Old Abernathy's cabin again. How long can she run? How far...*

Then something else rises up in her mind. A memory. Vague at first, but somehow very important. Something about the old woman, Betty Abernathy. It was something she had said before Ben shot her in the chest. Something about... *a very cold swim.*

Yes. That's it. Ben had asked the old woman why they couldn't cross over the frozen lake. She had said the ice was too thin. Because of the early snowfall, the ice was too thin to support the weight of a snowmobile.

Also, hadn't Eli said something like that as well? When he was reminiscing about Barb skating on Deadman. *But not this year,* he'd told her. *Storm came early, before the lake could freeze. Thin ice is hiding under all that snow.*

With her heart hammering in her ears, she spares another glance over her shoulder. The tiger is still following, about fifteen feet back now, gaining a little bit more with each step. She doesn't have much time.

Morgan turns to the right, lunging out of the trench into the deeper snow. Here it is almost to her hips. The bitter cold immediately oozes through her jeans like an invading virus, numbing her legs all the way up to her waist. She groans behind chattering teeth. The top inch of the snow, melted slightly by the bright sun, has now re-frozen into a hard crust. Beneath this crust however, it remains powdery and soft. For a moment, Morgan is afraid she will not be able to walk in this depth of snow at all. But she quickly discovers that by breaking through the top layer with her hands, then using her legs and arms to thrust her body forward, moving through this deeper powder is actually easier than the packed snow in the trench.

She does not need to look back to know the tiger is still following her. She can hear its massive body breaking through the crust of hard snow. It sounds close. So close that if she did take a moment to turn back, it would surely be waiting directly behind her, ready to snatch out her throat with its claw armored paw. Terror induced adrenaline swells up inside her, forcing a desperate cry past her lips. She begins to dive forward, not breaking the crust with her hands anymore, but slamming through it with her upper thighs. Each lunge ahead feels like glass breaking against the muscles in her legs, but she is moving faster. She can see the edge of the Deadman Lake now, distinctive because the wind-blown surface of the water has substantially less snow-pack than what she is fighting through on solid ground. She jumps forward, dragging her body along, ignoring the burning agony it is causing her legs. Now she can hear *and feel* the animal behind her. Each time the weight of its footfall comes down, the ground beneath her feet rumbles.

God, she is trying to outrun a freight train on four legs. At any time it could be on her, driving her body down, shattering her spine under its monstrous weight. Then it will simply tear her to shreds like it had Ben. A befitting end to anyone arrogant enough to think they can steal from nature for the entertainment of man.

But she still needs to try. This isn't just for herself. It is for everyone that has suffered because of what she and Ben have done. It needs to be finished, one way or the other.

At last, she breaks through the thicker cover of snow on the ground and steps out onto the surface of Deadman. On the lake the snow is barely a foot deep, making walking easier than it has been since they ventured out from the destroyed fuselage the previous morning. But Morgan also understands this *ease of foot* is a cruel deception. Here, close to the shore, the ice is more stable, but farther out, as the water gets deeper, the ice will also get thinner. She just hopes it will stay strong enough to support the tiger, at least until it is far enough from the beach to drown if it falls through.

As quickly as she dares, Morgan ventures another twenty feet out, treating each footstep as though it could be her last. Then she finally allows herself to stop and look back. The tiger is behind her. But it has stopped as well, with only its front paws past the threshold of the frozen water. It is staring at her, its yellow eyes smoldering golden in the glaring light.

Morgan's rapid breath billows from her mouth in silver clouds. With her heart a galloping race horse inside her chest, she raises her hand and smears away a skim of sweat from her brow. Out here, where the ice is thinner, she can now hear the water of the lake bubbling and shifting under her feet. It is a foreboding sound that chills her as much as the cold.

After a few more seconds catching her breath and the tiger still not moving, Morgan calls out, "Come on, you son of a bitch! Don't give up now!"

91

The Tiger hears the noises coming from the female, but as before they mean nothing to him. In his brain, the urge for vengeance is awake and screaming. Leap at it, break it, tear it and rip it, bath in its blood. This will take the Great Pain *away. It will fix all that is broken.*

But for now, he ignores the urge. Not just because his instincts are telling him to—though some instinctive impulses set deep in his subconscious mind are definitely warning him to proceed very carefully—but also because he is so tired. His vision has become blurry, turning everything around him into something alive and moving. Each breath he draws is labored and painful, as if his lungs have been filled with shards of gravel. His face hurts and his shoulder hurts and though he accepts the Great Pain *as part of his existence now, it continues to grow with each passing minute. Soon it will overpower even his instinctive thought, and then there will be nothing left. The darkness of* The Death *will have him.*

This does not frighten him. The Tiger is incapable of fear. When The Death *comes for him, he will accept it just as he has accepted the* Great Pain. *But he does sense a feeling of ill - ease. His need for vengeance has not been fulfilled. There is still one more that must be destroyed before he can rest. It is this one,* the fleeing doe. *So close he* can smell its stink even over his own blood. So close that if he leaped right now he would crush it under his body. Yet he resists. Somehow he understands that if he leaps, or runs or exerts himself in any way, he may fall into darkness again. This one has proven clever. It has escaped numerous times because he has fallen into the darkness. He will not allow it to escape again. He will continue to hunt it, chasing it to the end of the world if necessary. When it tires, he will still chase it. When it slows, he will be there. And when it finally stops, he will have it. This one's blood will quench the thirst of his urge. Satisfy the hunger of his vengeance. Then he can at last be at ease.

More noises start coming out of the female. Louder now. It is flailing its limbs and wailing. The sounds are high pitch and agitating. He wants them to stop. He needs them to stop.

The time has finally come. The Tiger takes a step towards the fleeing doe.

92

As Morgan attempts to entice the tiger onto the ice, for a moment she wonders if it has suddenly been struck blind and deaf. Despite all of the yelling and wild waving of her arms—she feels like a chicken trying to fly—the animal does not move. It just stands where it is, staring at her with little more showing in its eyes than blank interest. Even the ever-present rage seems to have diminished. The left side of its face is a gnarled horror of blood and torn flesh. If Morgan had even the slightest interest in comic books—which she did not—she would have been reminded of Two-face from the Batman series.

She is about to resort to the snowballs again when it finally moves, taking a step forward with unmistakable care. A second step, again with a smooth fluidity that is obvious caution. A third and a fourth, each with slow precision.

Morgan feels bemused. How can it know? It is only a goddamn animal, with no more cognitive thought than a dog or a cat, and yet somehow it is aware she is leading it into danger. It isn't possible, is it?

But what about Mother's Womb, she reminds herself. There's no way of knowing what was going on inside that box. Not even Ben knew all the different drugs or chemicals or whatever were being pumped into its system. Into its brain. It has managed to comprehend enough to stay alive all this time, so why should it be impossible to believe it senses the danger she is dragging it into now.

Yet it *is* taking the bait. It is following her onto the ice. What does that mean? Does it want to die…

Suddenly she realizes that not only is it following her onto the ice, but it has gotten to within five feet of where she is standing. Staring into its eyes as she watched it walk, it has somehow drawn her into a strange, incoherent trance. Now it is almost on her. It slashes at her with its front paw. She yelps, scrambling backward. Blood-stained claws whistled through the air only inches from her face. She back steps two more panicked paces, not taking her eyes off the tiger. It matches her steps and swings at her again. At the same moment, her feet tangle in each other and she falls, landing hard on her behind. The tiger's leg passes above her, close enough she feels the sting as several hairs are caught and yanked free from the top of her head. A millimeter closer and she would have been scalped. There is a dull crunching sound under her body, and then freezing water is gurgling up around her. She screams again, flinging herself back, struggling with her feet and hands in the snow. The tiger also lunges forward, coming down only inches from Morgan's kicking feet. There is another loud *crack* like breaking glass as the animal's immense weight smashes through the already weakened ice. Both of its hind legs disappear into the ice-cold water. Its chest crashes down against the more solid ice and it grapples with its front legs, digging its claws into the frozen crust. With its back legs continuing to kick uselessly, it slowly begins to drag itself forward.

Morgan crab walks several more paces away from the struggling animal, then staggers to her feet. This far onto the lake the ice has become much thinner. She can feel it flexing under her feet. All around her muffled cracking sounds and moans of fatigue whisper up from beneath the cover of snow. She stands statue-still, suddenly afraid to make even the slightest movement.

Fifteen feet away, the tiger's battle for purchase continues. It has managed to bring one of its back legs up and has hooked its claws over the edge of the ice. At the same time kicking out with its hind leg, it drags itself ahead with its front legs. Its hindquarters slip out of the water and back onto the ice. The animal rises slowly to its feet again. Then, like Morgan, it stays where it is, moving only to lower its head and sniff at the frozen surface of the lake. Under the tiger's eight hundred pounds, the ice groans and pops.

"Just you and me now," Morgan calls out. "Come on over, big guy. I'm right here."

The tiger raises its head and looks at her. The hatred is in its eyes again, burning there like yellow fire. It is not purring anymore. There are no sounds coming from it now except a ragged draw of breath.

"Come on," Morgan yells at it. "Tell you what, just to show I mean well, I'll meet you half-way." With that, she takes a slow, very pensive step towards the animal. The ice creaks dangerously below her feet. "See, no problem."

The tiger watches her with blazing fury in its eyes, but still makes no move.

Morgan sighs. "Okay. One more." She lifts her foot, pulling it out of a foot of snow, swings it forward and brings it down again. She waits, holding her breath. The ice groans, but holds. She carries her other foot over to join its mate. "See, no—" The ice shatters under her. With no chance to scream, she flays her arms out, folding backward at the knee as her legs plunge into the frigid water. Again her butt comes down into the snow, slowing her forward motion. She drops onto her back, spreading her arms like she is about to make a snow angel.

93

Recognizing his chance, The Tiger tenses, lowering his body as he prepares to attack. But before he can spring at the female, the ice below his front legs gives out, pitching him headfirst into the lake. Immediately the sudden cold devours more of his deteriorating energy. Desperate, his tail dancing in the air like a demented snake, he kicks and claws with his hind legs, trying to pull his front half back onto the ice. But each time he pulls back with his powerful legs, more of the ice breaks away from under him, until finally his entire body drops into freezing water.

Now, paddling frantically with his front legs, The Tiger drags his head above the surface. He swims to the edge of the hole and begins clawing at the ice, trying to get a strong enough hold to haul himself out. But again, his weight is his enemy. Every time he gets his claws to sink into the ice, it breaks apart as he fights to pull his massive body out. A constant stream of icy lake water pours in through the hole in his face and down his throat. It is filling his stomach, weighing him down more and more. With each attempt to pull himself out, The Tiger's heartbeat grows faster, and his breath becomes shorter. Finally, his struggles begin to slow. His head slips under the water for a moment, but surfaces again. He pulls in another shallow gulp of air through his nose. The darkness is coming now. It flows in like a gray fog, erasing the mountains and the sky, the snow and the cold chill of the water. But it also floods his mind with new images. Different from the ones that have dominated his thinking for most of his life. These images are not filled with hate and blood. They do not feed his need for vengeance. They are visions of calm. Warm and joyful thoughts. Of home. He is home. His mother and his sister are there, drinking cool water from the river. He runs to them and drinks his fill. And here, under the bright sky, where there are no thoughts of man, he and his sister will play forever, running across endless snow-covered hills.

94

Morgan sits on the ice, her legs pulled up to her chest, shivering. In front of her, the hole that had almost swallowed her alive gaped open like a giant blind eye. Ten feet beyond this, in another larger hole through the ice, the tiger's head has just disappeared below the water for the second time. Morgan is quite sure it will not come up again.

She had watched the animal's struggle with a surreal curiosity that bordered on hypothermic shock. Despite the severity of its injuries, the tiger's fight for life had been long and gallant. There was even a moment, just before its head went under that first time, when she thought it might drag itself out. But the thin ice had jilted it again and in the end, Deadman Lake claimed its prize.

As the sun passes its highest crest in the sky and begins a slow descent towards the mountains, Morgan is a little surprised to find she has feelings of pity for the animal. It sits heavy in her heart and threatens to bring more tears to her eyes. She does understand the truth, as many others will as well—*the tiger was a beast*. What it has done in such a short amount of time; the terror and death it has brought—some deserving and some not— is nothing short of mindless evil. As the story surfaces, becomes global, this is all most will see. The devil itself brought up from hell to wreak havoc on the innocent. But this truth, though undeniable, is only a small piece in the puzzle of reality. The tiger has indeed committed all of these heinous acts, and yet can it be held accountable for any of them? It is an animal, stolen from its land and thrust into a situation completely out of its control. No more to blame than the atomic bomb that killed over one hundred thousand people in Japan on that fateful August day in 1945. The minds of human beings had created the bomb, and their vengeful hatred had pushed the button that released it. Just as it was human beings—*man*—who are the true culprits now. It was man that had taken the tiger from its home, forced it into a cage and turned it into a monster. It was also man that had released this monster upon the land, once again causing the death of far more innocents than guilty.

It will be man that answers for these crimes. Morgan will see to it. If, that is, she lives to do it.

The tiger's struggle may be over, but hers is far from it. She slowly pulls her eyes away from the animal's watery grave and looks past it, towards the shore. Like before, it is difficult for her to estimate the distance. If, however, she was forced to guess—and at this point she has little choice—she would think it to be about sixty feet. In a normal situation, this would not seem far at all; one-sixth the length of a football field. Yet, with a lake of snow-covered thin ice separating herself and solid salvation, the distance may as well be six football fields. Beyond the shore, the Jenkin's cabin looks very small, nestled under its blanket of white. She cannot see the girls anymore. They have left the porch, probably gone the help Eli.

Morgan is afraid to move. Even just shifting her weight slightly causes the ice to creak threateningly beneath her. Her legs and feet are soaking wet and freezing. Cramps are developing in her calves, and her butt is so cold it has gone completely numb. A frigid breeze cuts across the ice, tossing powdered snow into the air. It seems to hang there, churning and moving, just above the surface of the lake, an iridescent, silver fog in the brilliant sunlight. Bellow this fog, the unstable ice continues to groan ominously.

Morgan takes a moment to run through her options. It doesn't take long because there are not many. She can stay here, sitting in the snow with her butt freezing and hyperthermia slowly setting in, waiting for the ice to thicken enough to support her weight. That would take…oh, maybe a week. No problem—if she had a fridge full of food and a nice blazing fire to warm her tootsies. So, that idea was out. She can scream for help. Hope that one of the girls or Sidney's dad or anyone else within earshot will hear her and come rushing to her rescue. Rational thought maybe, but also out. What good would it do to draw someone else onto the ice just to have them break through and drown? It is best to leave those on the shore alone to help the ones that can be helped.

That left…*what?*

Morgan knows exactly *what*. She has to move. There is no other option. She is terrified by the idea, but also it makes sense, in a logical sort of way. She had gotten herself out here so, presumably, she should be able to make it back. If she moves slowly, avoiding old footprints where the ice may have been weakened, testing each step before putting any weight down.

Possible? Yes. Enjoyable? Hell no. But again, there was no other choice.

"You can do it," she murmurs. "Just take it slow." After several deep breaths, she begins shifting her weight forward, readying herself to stand up. The ice immediately creaks and moans under her, flexing noticeable...

"I wouldn't do that."

The voice comes from behind, startling her. She twists around, her eyes searching. Beneath her weight, the ice cracks with alarming clarity.

"Careful," Matt Trapper says. "Don't move again or you'll be swimming."

Morgan freezes, staring up at the boy. He has a black woolen cap on his head, a bright red parka zipped all the way up, and a long stick in one of his gloved hands. Somehow he has been able to creep up behind her and is now standing only five feet away, the tiniest hint of a smile playing at the corners of his mouth. "How..." Morgan stammers. "How did...you get here?"

Matty frowns. "I walked. How else?"

"But...the ice. It...It's too thin."

The smile returns, but now pulls farther into a grin. He lifts one of his legs. There is a wide snowshoe strapped to his boot. "It's all about weight distribution," he says, lowering his foot again. "My dad taught me that. Spread your weight across more surface area, the less likely you are to break through the ice. Snowshoes work good."

Morgan continues to stare at him with disbelief, her mind playing with the idea that he is only a figment of her imagination. At any second he will turn into a puff of powdery snow and drift away. "Where did you come from?"

"Over there," he says, pointing towards the shore to the east. "The trees are taller there. They protect that part of the lake from the sun, so the ice is stronger. If you'd led the tiger that way, he probably would have got you."

Morgan is silent for a moment, gazing towards the shoreline. "Eli," she says suddenly. "What about Eli? The tiger surprised us. It attacked him. We need…"

"Sidney's dad is with him," Matty says. "He's hurt bad, but he's still alive. Probably a chopper will have to fly him out of here, I guess. Be kinda neat to see a chopper."

Morgan sighs softly. "He's still alive…Thank God."

"We need to go," Matty says, stepping towards her. He holds out his hand. "Your nose is starting to look frostbit."

Morgan shakes her head "I can't. I'll break through the ice if I move."

"Naw," Matty says. "You can trust me. I know all the right places to step. If you stay on your knees, and we go nice and slow, I can get us back. Just, take my hand."

Morgan looks at his outstretched hand doubtfully. "Are…Are you sure?"

"I told you I would be your hero," Matty says, an edge of sadness marring his tone. "I couldn't save my dad or my brother, but I'm gonna save you. I promise."

Morgan hesitates, looking into his eyes. "Thank you," she says finally, then reaches out and grips his hand.

Matty smiles. "Heroes don't need to be thanked."

At that same moment, high in the crystal blue sky, a helicopter appears over the glacier capped-mountains.

Deadman- After

One beautiful June day, almost twenty months after Matt Trapper had guided Morgan Malo off the frozen crust of Deadman Lake, she once again strolls up to its rolling shoreline. A soft, late spring breeze passes over the water, creating tiny ripples that gurgle and burp as they lap against the rocky beach. In the sky, the glowing face of the sun smiles down, warming her cheeks and shimmering diamonds across the rolling surface of the lake.

Morgan isn't surprised by the beauty of the place; she has imagined it time and time again over the past year and a half as her life was being dissected. But to see it at last, like this, unshrouded by the white, monotone hand of winter, in its true, color-infused splendor. It is almost enough to take her breath away. She smiles, drawing in the fragrant air, enjoying the heat of the sun against her face.

She is wearing blue jeans and a plain white blouse. Her hair is shorter now, cut into a bob that falls just to her shoulders. She wears no makeup on her face and there are dull swatches of purple under her eyes, the sign of many sleepless nights. And yet, somehow, she is even prettier now than she had been. Fresh and clean. Hopeful. She is a woman ready to put the past where it belongs and charge headlong into an unknown future. No more interrogations. Endless questions that she had already answered a hundred times before. No more courtrooms, where the staring eyes of her peers have judged and condemned her before even a single word passes her lawyer's lips. No more feelings of guilt as she lies awake in her bed, so heavy against her heart that at times she wished it had been her the tiger punished that night instead of Ben.

This is all behind her now. Over. Now, she has only her life, and wherever it decides to take her.

Which, for the moment, is back to Deadman Lake.

There is a crunch of gravel behind her, and a hand touches her shoulder. She turns, already smiling.

Eli Foley is there, a large grin set between his wrinkled cheeks. "Thought it was you," he says. "Changed your hair, though."

"Eli," Morgan exclaims and hugs him tightly. "It's so good to see you."

The old man grunts inside her embrace. "Careful now," he croaks. "Old bones and all that."

"Sorry," Morgan says, loosening her arms, but still not letting him go. "I'm just so happy to see you."

"And I'm happy to see you, darlin', but from here I can only see your backside." Eli chuckles, patting her on the back. "Not saying that's a bad thing mind you."

At last, Morgan releases him and draws away. "Still as naughty as ever," she says, giggling. "Guess some things will never change."

"Darn tootin'," he agrees. Stepping back, he regards her with curious eyes. "Well, you look just as lovely as ever, so it seems you are correct."

"I feel old," Morgan says.

"Baw. You don't know the meaning of the word. Come back in fifty years and we'll talk."

"I'm sure you'll still be here," Morgan laughs. "Just as naughty as always."

"So, how have you been?" Eli asks, still studying her with his eyes.

Morgan shrugs. "I'm okay. Just happy to have everything finally over."

He nods. "And they stuck to their word? No jail time?"

"No jail time. With my cooperation in the pending civil suit against Treager Enterprises, they even dropped the house arrest. Time served and two years' probation. And it's all because of you Eli. Thank you for everything you did. I'd be in prison right now if it wasn't for you."

"Baw," Eli growls again. "I didn't do much. As I said before, the word of an old man don't carry much authority. I sure am tickled that it all worked out though. You deserved a break."

"Well, you can go ahead and make little of it if you like, but if it wasn't for your testimony and the petition you started, things would have turned out a lot different." She takes his hand in both of hers. "But how about you? I've barely heard from you in the last two months."

"Just been busy is all," Eli says. "Got my cabin sold and I'm living up at the Lodge full time now. We're calling it Trappers Lodge. Matty and me should have it ready to receive clients by early July. Staffs all in place, kitchen is stocked. We'll even have the new rental shop finished in time for winter. Snowmobiles be in by first snow. All is looking good."

"Matty is..." she looks down at their joined hands. "Doing okay? Is he still dealing with... things."

"Afraid he'll never be done dealing with things, Darlin'. But he's doin' fine. With all that's happened, I guess it pushed him into manhood a bit quicker than most. He sure is loving bein' the boss, I tell yah. Even if it's me making the big decisions for now, it's still his name on the paperwork. Big Dwayne's will made sure there was no doubt about that."

Morgan smiles. "Good. I'm sure he'll make a fair and honest boss. And the girls? How are they?"

"Like two peas in a pod, I'd say. They've been living in the Jenkins cabin over the winter. A big help to me with…you know, getting Barbara's affairs settled and all that. Saul is back in the city teaching. But he'll be up soon enough for the summer stretch. Hear he's bringing a lady friend with him. Should be interesting. They'll all be heading out come the fall, though. Sidney and Chloe both got accepted into UBC for the new semester."

"That's great," Morgan says. "Those two are real troopers."

"That they are. Why don't we head on up to the Lodge? Matty's up there fartin' around in the kitchen. He'd love to see yah."

She nods, but makes no sign of moving. "I just want to stand here a minute longer. It's so beautiful."

"It is indeed," Eli agrees. "Lot different from when you seen it last, I guess."

"Yes." She falls quiet for a moment, looking out at the lake. "Have they… found anything yet?" she asks at last.

"No," Eli tells her. "It's a big lake. Take them years to drag the whole thing. After that first winter, the body could have drifted under the ice a long way before it got water down and sank. Could be anywhere, buried at the bottom under ten feet of silt and dead logs. Good chance that old cat will never be found. Wish that weren't the case, though, cause the whole area has become a goddamn touristy nightmare. Don't see that changing any time soon neither. Whether they're gold diggers or just the curious type, all these city folks been swarming around. Coming out to get a look at the lake that swallowed a man-eater. Heard a few people calling it Tiger Lake now. Good for business I guess, but old Dan Slowfoot would roll over in his grave if he heard that. Deadman itself ain't never gonna be the same, that'd be my guess."

"I'm sorry," Morgan says, a single tear tracing a line down her cheek. "For all of it."

"Darlin, your days of being sorry should be long behind you. It's time to stop being sorry and start living. You need to get on enjoying the life you've got before it's too late. Time has a way of sneaking up on yah right quick, you can take that as my word."

"But how? How can I ever enjoy anything again?"

"Start small," Eli says, grinning. "Like standing by a beautiful lake, sharing the view with a naughty old man." He squeezes her hand playfully.

"Somethings will never change," Morgan says again, and at this, they both start to laugh.

They stay there for a while longer, holding hands and sharing the view. Finally, as the sun begins its journey back down to the mountains, they turn and walk towards the Trappers Lodge, leaving Deadman Lake behind them.

Author's Note

Although the lake in this story is fictitious, it is based on two lakes that are quite real. The name Deadman comes from a small meteor lake in the Princeton area where I took my wife and two daughters camping. Its size and shape come from Gun Lake, located in the Bridge River district near the abandoned Bralorne gold mines. For the sake of the story, I did move it about seven-hundred kilometers north-east towards the town of Valemount (the real *Terravale*). My uncle had a cabin on Gun Lake when I was a kid, so growing up I spent quite a bit of time on its shores.

I feel very lucky to have many fond memories of both these lakes: Gun Lake when I was young, and Deadman when my kids were young. Thankfully, there are no tigers roaming around either.

CPSIA information can be obtained
at www.ICGtesting.com
Printed in the USA
LVHW040257230322
714166LV00019B/449/J